Still Here

The Memoirs of a Hollywood Legend

Acknowledgements

I am happy to finish a book because I fear I will end up with half of one stuck in a drawer. This one started after listening to Sondheim's *Still Here* when the lyrics stuck in my head. I wondered about the woman who could sing such a song and was reminded of someone. Thus, I discovered Babe. I wanted to tell a true history of Hollywood and had stories that were hearsay and couldn't be of use. Thus, a fictional actress who discussed actual events seemed the way to go. As Kirk Douglas once said, if you want to tell the truth, write a novel—if you want to lie, write an autobiography. I did both.

Part of my writing this book was to work on it with Marcia Lord who lived in Paris and with whom I spent Christmas Day every year. Today is Christmas, so I am thinking about her—she died before we could work on it together, but it's a story that I hope she would have liked and would have liked editing. It is my gift to her.

While clearly any work of cinema is a group effort, that is often true for the written word, too. I solicited opinions because I needed to know if others perceived what I had written in the way I had intended. Moreover, I don't want to make a fool of myself, which is often unavoidable when you put something out there for others to judge. My father is a legendary editor who has edited my work for a long time, including this book. He didn't like it, but this is not his kind of book. Susan Winter, my dear longtime friend who is a relationship expert and writes often about older women and younger men, encouraged me and carefully read my manuscript several times. My Yale buddy, Steve Skrovan, was wonderful in his suggestions. Allyn Delano Simmons inspired me by telling me stories of old Hollywood and her interactions with Elizabeth Taylor; I am sorry she is no longer with us to read it.

Some people I met are a part of this book, including John Kennedy, Jr., Gloria Swanson, Joe Gold and George Clooney. I went to Studio 54, where I met a few people who also ended up in this story. I used those interactions, changing them to fit the narrative.

There are friends to thank because I used anecdotes from them or about them—and several that I can't thank precisely because I used anecdotes from them or about them. Aurelie Zoetelief Tromp, Piper Sydney Brown, Anders Arjes, Jacqueline de Rochourchart, Claudio von Planta, Annette Insdorf, and Francoise George are a few that I can thank.

Many agents turned down this work: I wasn't famous and didn't have enough social media followers. I left the book in a file for several years and then decided to publish it. I liked Babe—she wasn't what I expected when I started, and then she became such a strong voice that she almost wrote herself. I liked her more and more as she emerged. She's not purely fictional, but she doesn't exist in reality, either. Parts of her are based on someone I loved and admired, but out of respect, they will remain unnamed. I wasn't sure if I could voice an inner woman and hope I succeeded. Yes, part of me is in Babe; but she is not me and, for sure, I am not her.

Please send corrections since there is a lot of data in the book. I will make them in the next edition. Thank you very much to those who took the time to read this.

Stephen Eliot, Paris—December 25, 2022

CONTENTS

FOREWORD

My mother is known to the world as Babe, two-time Academy Award winner. She wrote this manuscript 10 years ago as she prepared to do her one woman show on Broadway. She put it away because she was worried about what my brothers and I might think. She is a terrific woman but was less good with personal relationships with her husbands—she had six—and her children—she had three. Her career was always first and, as a Hollywood star, she got media coverage every time she turned around. We led a privileged life because of her, but sometimes we didn't want to get dragged into things, such as the endless media, as fallout.

On the other hand, when life with her was too much, we would go to her best friend for shelter and advice—Elizabeth Taylor. So, we really didn't have a great sense of reality, either. Bobby, her agent, and Lily, who handled her PR, are part of the family and we take care of them now as they are aging alongside my mother. What do we have to complain about? When we were young, we wanted to be ordinary. As Mom eventually points out, it takes time to understand that being different is a gift. However, my first marriage disintegrated because my wife couldn't take the pressure we grew up with.

My brother's granddaughter, also named Babe, will probably be the only other person in the family to go to Hollywood: she has already a press and Twitter following and is just 14. It may have something to do with the fact that she is the closest of all to her great grandmother-namesake; the two of them together in the media as Little Babe and Big Babe, whom Little Babe has called Grandma Monster all of her life.

Her children, now in our 50's and 70's with my adopted baby brother only 42, decided she should publish because my mother has nothing to be ashamed of. Yes, she embarrassed us. We have seen her breasts on screen far too often. But that shouldn't stop her from telling her story in her own words. We are proud of her. No one has a perfect childhood. We had a good one even if we didn't realize it at the time.

Mother is now 95 with her faculties intact. She walks and talks and shops—mostly on her own. She knows her time is limited and we want this book to come out while she is alive—so she can hear what people think. And she is looking forward to doing more talk shows.

She did go over the book to add a few things and, sadly, to include the deaths of several people who died after she put the manuscript into a drawer. She is open about how many that she knew are now gone and the fact she will one day join them. I think that is the main reason she agreed to let us publish. She wanted to tell her story.

I interject in italics at the end of a chapter, because she told me I should. "I wasn't always a good mother and didn't always understand the fallout of my decisions. So, tell your side. I told mine."

She doesn't discuss her early life or her parents until the end of the manuscript when she needs to do so for her show. I think it's fair to let her story unfold as she originally intended. What matters most is what we bring with us when we enter the room. That is really all people see and what they interact with. Her previous life affected her, but she made her own life. Even, her children didn't know a whole lot and she wanted it that way. She had a tough beginning and started working at 15 when she got discovered. To her, and to us, what matters most is what she did. Not what happened to her in her early life or its psychology.

We always knew how much she loved us. Yes, there were things to forgive, but on both sides. Three sons are not so easy, either.

Go meet Babe. And understand that she always had two sides as she points out—her business brand as a star of the screen—and yet also a private person who had to make her own way as a woman when women were not allowed to be equal citizens. Her struggle is what really makes her a star.

Anders

BROADWAY'S CALL

Nobody is deader in Hollywood than an aging blonde. If they wanted me on Broadway, I was finished. Too old to screw, and too old to be on screen except as a grandmother. In the early fifties, Betty Grable, the highest-paid star in Hollywood during the forties, warned me I might need to go to Broadway one day to restart my career, as she had. But she did Broadway when she was only twenty-three and, by the fifties, her stardom was over. She told me after a couple of drinks, "Babe, when the execs no longer try to jump you, you're kaput." How true.

My agent, Bobby, begged. Cajoled. And kept calling. I'd never done Broadway, and they kept ratcheting up the fee. After thinking it over (and over), I finally told him I would have one meeting with the lead producer. We showed up: Bobby, whom I trusted absolutely but found annoying on rare occasions like this one, and Lily, who ran much of my personal life although ostensibly her job was PR. She went to these meetings to take notes and act as a witness. Studios and producers lied and made promises they didn't intend to keep. Sitting there was not only the producer, but also the proposed director for the one-woman show I was scared to do. The show I didn't need or want but Bobby kept pushing for.

We didn't know the director—or that he was coming. Lily excused herself, got on the phone, and came back to whisper in my ear. The director had just finished a promising new action film, having gotten his claim to fame from a successful tampon commercial. He had a three-month gap in his schedule and wanted to do Broadway. I was already, God knew, in the news. How generous of him. Really, was I to go on stage with a guy who made tampon commercials? If we flopped, I could imagine the jokes.

The producer opened with how privileged he was to meet Babe and how he'd seen all my films and wanted to honor a legend. He did have the grace to get flustered when I pointed out I wasn't yet dead. Then, the director took over. He wanted an exciting show. Movement, lights, and good sets to keep things alive for the audience. He thought I should open with me in a wire harness, descending to the stage while belting out, "I'm still here!"

I said what popped into my mind, which was all I could think. "It's really great you want to keep things alive for the audience. It might be nice if you wanted to keep me alive, too, since I will have to descend sixty feet from the Belasco Theatre ceiling, and I'm sixty-two."

Now he was flustered, "We know how to keep you safe."

"But evidently not how to prevent me from being a cliché!"

The meeting didn't go very well. Bobby was beside himself since he knew I was deliberately pulling the plug in a way that would stop his phone calls. Besides, I was in two more films—yes, as character parts, but it was work, and it wasn't humiliating. I didn't need Broadway even if the money was good.

Worse, this was twenty-five years ago after my last messy divorce from No. 6. The usual headline—"*aging actress ditches young husband*"—was one of my favorites and much kinder than the others, as you may imagine. Elizabeth Taylor, who knew about ditching husbands and bad press, called up, laughing. While we had known each other forever as professional rivals, we had become much closer as my career grew in the early 1950's. Then, too, my longtime publicity assistant and confidant, Lily, had recommended Chen Sam, a so-called cousin, to handle

Elizabeth's PR issues and many private ones as well. Between those two chattering away and getting help from each other, Elizabeth and I were increasingly drawn into each other's orbits.

The media was relentless. Elizabeth called, cackling, to tell me she was relieved it wasn't her. "Usually, I'm out there all by myself. I get the stuff about my marriages, my husbands, my weight. Thank God they're picking on you. But don't worry. Get a face-lift, go on a diet, buy new jewels, and open Cannes. Then all they'll talk about is how great you look. The press has less memory than an Alzheimer's patient."

"Do I need a face-lift?"

"Babe, be serious. You're an Academy Award winner. Run! And lie. Tell them it's the first."

Of course, this was the same woman who asked, "Is anything still moving?" when I was worried about having had so much Botox that my face wouldn't move for a new role. When I said yes, her response was, "In that case, darling, you didn't get enough!"

My answer, "You would know," made her tone it down.

With this media, and Chen and Lily plotting with Pat Kingsley to keep me out of the press (I put money on Elizabeth's making phone calls to encourage it for her amusement), I was relaxing at home, having Sunday brunch with my adult children. Bobby called. He was a great agent but could only do what he could with aging goods in an arena that valued youth and firm breasts, plastic or not. In his low voice that rose in pitch when he was excited, which was most of the time, he said, "Babe, we got an offer to do a one-woman show on Broadway." I never knew if he meant *we* in the sense of him and me or the royal *we*, since he worked at CAA. I

3

suspected the latter. "They're offering $50K base plus $10,000 a week for a guaranteed ten-week run plus 10 percent of the profits." Twenty-five years ago, this was a lot of money for Broadway. "Don't do it for the money. Do it for you."

"I don't sing, I don't dance, and I'm not much fun all by myself," I said. Still, when Bobby talked, I listened. He was right more than he was wrong, and he guarded me like no one else. My prior agent had tried to make me a glorified showgirl and would have kept me from any drama if he could. I was to be a cash cow, a pretty one, but one that he only wanted to say *moo*. Bobby was different. We were a team. In meetings, I took cues from him. With a slight nod, I would go into my tizzy act or grand dame performance, whichever was required. After my years in front of cameras, that part was easy. Harder was learning to listen to Bobby, whose judgment was better than mine over the long haul. He would tell me things no one else would, even when it was something I didn't want to hear.

"You tell the story of your life. You start from your divorce and work backward." Here it was, *aging actress goes on Broadway to talk about ditching young husband.*

"I don't think so," I said, imagining the details they wanted.

"It's not the money," Bobby repeated. "Go on stage and say what *you* want. Tell your story. Get revenge. You won't get an offer like this again."

"What *I* want? You go talk about *your* sex life." There was a long-ish pause. He was single, early fifties, always with a really hot male assistant, whom the rest of us imagined he'd met while at the top of a trapeze at a sex club. When he finally came out of the closet, which was a

4

shock only to himself, Elizabeth told me she hit him up for a $100,000 donation to amfAR to make up for all the years he pretended he wasn't interested. When Bobby protested, she told him, "More people have seen your dick than have seen the Statue of Liberty—write the fucking check." He did.

After the long pause. "Yes, they want juicy bits. No one will pay that kind of money for costume changes."

"How much do they want to know? When he ejaculated, he kept going. First shot over his head. Second shot over his head. Third shot over his head. First, you think this is hot. By the sixth, all you can think is get a damn umbrella already. Enough detail for you?" This was mean of me, since I knew Bobby on the other end of the phone was thinking too bad No. 6 wasn't gay. Bobby wouldn't have wanted an umbrella. Longish pause again. I continued, "And then do I tell them even a sexual freak with a small brain is just a sexual freak after a while? Does he sue again for even more money?" The really tragic part was me: I had said "I do."

Another pause. "Well, I'm not sure Broadway is ready, but West Hollywood might be."

"I don't need the money. And I'm not doing a show so ribald that only gay fans will buy tickets. The producers certainly won't pay for that, so there goes your commission." That got his attention. He was, after all, an agent.

Later the same night, I remember attending a small dinner, seated next to an early computer pioneer. At least ten years younger, he'd had a distinguished career in chip production and then turned his focus to something called software. At that time, 1990, the first personal computers were being sold. I never imagined how they would change the world, but I liked being able to type and correct what I wrote using software that has long disappeared. I knew nothing about software or programming or the difference between them. Not a lot of people did then—how the world changed. This gentleman, named Sam, kindly explained what he did in a way I could understand. Then, he politely asked what I was doing. I told him about the one-woman show and how reluctant I was. I remember so clearly how he looked me directly in the eye and said, "Do it on your terms, or don't do it at all." I thought about those words a lot over the years and applied them to many things. I wondered if I would run into this man again, given we lived in different worlds. He was in the news since he was making a second fortune on the internet. He also said something else I remembered: "Mistakes are the price we pay for success." I wondered if the remark was directed at the one-woman show or my life in general. It was a good question.

What we should have done, while we were young enough, was a two-women show—*Elizabeth and Babe talk sex and husbands*. We laughed about it later as Elizabeth was dying. By then, she wore a turban wrapped around her head, or Jose Eber would come to the house to do her hair just so we could have tea. We had two teapots—one for me with Earl Grey, and I suspected the other was bourbon for her, which after her famous stints at Betty Ford was a no-no. Toward the end, when I would visit and sit on her bed, Elizabeth still resplendent in her jewels, which she always wore when receiving me, but her energy fading, it didn't really matter. Let her live as she liked while she could. I finally said, after a couple of visits, to just give me the good stuff. She smiled at being caught, and I sat on her bed, the two of us drinking bourbon out of teacups as we said our goodbyes. She remembered my one-woman show adventure, and we laughed about what it might have become if we had done it together. A bit snide, she commented, "Yes, something Debbie Reynolds might have done with us, but then she would have tried to steal the show." There was no point in reminding her it was she who was the greater thief, having stolen Debbie's husband years ago.

I miss Elizabeth terribly. Who else understood better what we had gone through to get where we were? She'd been there my entire adult life. We would talk pictures, family, press, and sometimes, business. I owe her my fortune. Not as great as hers, but nonetheless, I made a lot of money following her lead. For the last quarter of her life, she made her money from perfume. With an 8 percent royalty on sales, she made millions. It formed the bulk of her fortune, which they said was $1 billion when she died. It was a lot, but not that much, and what did the press know? Neither of us made real money at the height of our careers. We were contract players to the studios, who owned us, paid us, and controlled what we could do and how we could be seen while keeping the bulk of the profit. As one of the first to crack the studio system, Elizabeth was finally no longer under contract after her Academy Award for *Butterfield 8* in 1960 and then broke the $1 million barrier with *Cleopatra* in 1962. That film almost bankrupted Twentieth Century Fox, which scared them all. It took the rest of us until the seventies until we were truly free agents. Neither of us made fortunes from our pictures. Our heyday was the fifties. Yet Elizabeth was smart. Costume jewelry and fragrances paid royalties. She understood her fame better than anyone I have ever met. No one led such a privileged life except maybe Queen Elizabeth. She never used a pay phone, took a taxi, or looked for a public restroom. She seldom flew commercial, let alone sat in coach.

We were at PJ Clarke's, the burger joint, in New York for the Bicentennial. It was just four girls having a good time in the week of celebration. A woman came in, recognized us, and came over to the table. We thought she wanted an autograph, which would have been truly annoying, but all she wanted was to try on the Krupp diamond, which seemed less intrusive. After Elizabeth's death, the ring sold for $8 million. Surprisingly, Elizabeth took it off and handed it over. When the woman returned it with a thank you, the ring was passed around to the rest of us. I must say, for a thirty-three-carat rock, it didn't look bad on my finger. As Elizabeth told Princess Margaret when she tried it on, "It doesn't look so vulgar now!"

We told Elizabeth she was nuts to hand it over to a stranger who could have made a run for it.

"What could she possibly do?" Elizabeth asked, knowing every paper on earth would have the theft as its headline. She understood her position far better than the rest of us, even me, who has lived a similar life for so long.

Elizabeth was one of the first to monetize her celebrity, and she made hundreds of millions. I had previously followed Mae West's example by sinking my extra money into Los Angeles real estate. When Mae died in the mid-1970s, she had $60 million in LA real estate, worth ten times more now. I did well with small apartment buildings and shopping centers, but when I lent my name to a skin care line with sunscreens and lip balms, I became rich. I had wanted equity, but Elizabeth talked me out of it. She told me to let them use their money for marketing while I owned my own name, and they paid royalties. I didn't get 8 percent because I wasn't as famous, but 6 percent has paid very well on a line that does $250 million a year. I wouldn't have thought to do it, however, without Elizabeth's pushing. She made more. I made enough. While I don't have her jewels and never had as much notoriety, either, it sometimes seemed close enough.

Twenty-five years. Not as long as I thought. Not nearly long enough. And the one-woman show is back. Bobby, who was supposed to be retired, pushed out as CAA made another reorganization, returned. He made enough money to live well but not remain a power broker like he'd dreamed. He settled down with a succession of hot boys running through his Beverly Hills pool house, remained a wickedly good negotiator on contracts—and trotted out when they came back from the dead on this one-woman-show thing. As a joke, he brought matching umbrellas to our first meeting. I told him how I planned to use his umbrella if he said even one word. He just smiled.

Revisiting the one-woman show, I realized I would have to tell my story. I'm not book smart, but there is something to be said for the *University of Life.* In Hollywood, you either got your doctorate or disappeared into scandal, drugs, and bad films. I fought to be taken as an equal and learned to speak up. I refused to be just a pretty face. It got easier as I obtained success. Now I could say what I wanted without risking a future job. Very little worked after sixty to restart an aging blonde's career. I spoke up because I believe in fighting. Not only for me but also for others. An actress at her peak in the 1950s was not the same as an actress at her peak today. Women then didn't have the same opportunities they do today. For one, we got paid less. For another, we were owned by the studio.

As for critics who are going to savage me yet again: I make more money, I won a couple of Academy Awards, and I am a woman who succeeded in the 1950s. If they want to judge me, let them. Readers will judge, too. That's why I am going on stage. Don't think I won't judge my audience from up there, as well. I am always observing, evaluating, and judging. All actors do—it's how we inhabit our roles. I judge background, experience, wisdom, and humor (or lack thereof) fairly easily. Where the audience laughs, how they laugh, when they groan—it tells a lot. There are expected laugh lines. Then there are those that crack up the clever ones and those that crack up the dumb ones. Yes, I will be up there judging, too. It's life—everybody does it, although some pretend they are better than the rest of us.

Maybe Bobby was right when he said revenge was the reason to do Broadway. I hated being owned, particularly by the petty men who ran Hollywood—the studio execs, the agents, the lawyers, the accountants, not to mention established stars—who often looked at the female talent as a smorgasbord to be sampled for their pleasure. Yet that is too sexist— young hot guys also were considered part of the smorgasbord. Much of that story was hidden and lied about, so the few details that managed to rise to the surface were suspect. Nothing perfected the closet for gay stars and execs as well as Hollywood, which was a master of illusion on many levels, not just in the movies. Then, too, there were powerful straight women who had their boy toys. Some of those guys felt just as besmirched as we did. Others? Well, they just did it for sport and to move their careers along, laughing later about which of them had done the ugliest.

I learned early in my career not to let the studio guys triumph without a fight. I had to stand up for myself. No one else would.

There was another reason to consider the show. Just before my father died, he managed to shock me more deeply than anyone, which in Hollywood says a lot. He told me my good friend, Marilyn Monroe, had been my half-sister. Twenty years after her death, he decided to reveal this to me. The idea we had been blood relatives and never knew distressed me more than I can say. In front of the camera, she was better than I ever was. Yet I had the financial success and happiness she never did. I survived and, in the end, beat the system. Why, we'll never know. Einstein famously said that God doesn't play dice with the universe. However, he manages to do so with our lives.

I never told anyone of my blood connection to Marilyn. It was private and, if it got out, I doubted the press would believe me. It mattered only to me because by the time I learned, I was in my fifties, and it couldn't change my life. I thought my father, not to mention me, deserved what privacy I could manage. There wasn't much.

I wanted to acknowledge my sister. She wasn't as she seemed or was portrayed. She was a good friend, and I thought a lot about her over the years since my father's death. I thought about a lot of things as I approached my own.

I knew everyone who counted for seventy years. Kept my mouth shut. Now, for a Broadway show, they wanted me to sing like a canary, something I never did in any of my mob pictures. There are a lot of stories

I want to tell. A few I can't. My sons are old enough, so if they're shocked, there's not much I can do. My grandchildren won't know who I'm talking about. My really good friends, the great ones, are dead or doddering, so they won't care. Still, it's an affront I agreed to do the show. I ask myself why and still don't have a satisfactory answer. I suppose I could go to a shrink but found too many patronizing. I remember when Marilyn met Albert Einstein. She looked him up and down—you have to think he was doing the same thing—and asked in her breathless voice, "If you're so smart, how come I make more money?" I feel the same way about shrinks.

It's the Follies song, good times and bum times, but I'm still here, my dear. I just don't want to be "aren't you whoosis—whatever happened to her?" so I am dragging my ass out on stage. And I'm going to do it with a big glass of Scotch, because no one can tell me no.

When I go out on stage, I will shock everyone by what I say and, even more, by how I look. I used to be beautiful. Now it's hard to look in the mirror. I can still put myself together. Just putting on my face, however, takes forever. I see Joan Collins from time to time. She has the old Hollywood glamour—knowing exactly what hat to wear to keep her face in shadow and how to turn in the light at just the right moment so the photographers would get the best angle. While I would never call her a great actress, she's a real genius there. Good for her.

In the right light, I look okay, but I no longer see the same look of desire on men's faces. No one lusts after me, even if I pay them, as I clearly did with Husband No. 6. To reverse the aphorism, bad on paper, good in bed was certainly true in his case, but the bad on paper had a way of erasing everything else. Even with a good prenup, it was an expensive mistake that got me in the papers all over again. Today, it isn't just the papers, it's news, cable, internet, and tweets. It's what the young people remember me for, since most haven't seen my movies. Worse, that was twenty-five years ago—and they want me to start my show from there. The why-I-am-in-front-of-you-on-stage moment. They can go fuck themselves. But for a long time, I didn't know how to open—because I didn't know how to close. Until you know that, how can you write a show?

When a talent scout pulled me from oblivion, my hope was I would be able to survive as a working actress without having to wait tables all my life or be pulled into early motherhood and give up my career. I told God if he gave me that, I would never ask for anything else. He answered those prayers, and I went on to ask for a good many more things, which he also gave me. The things he didn't give me—the losses I suffered, the injustice at the hands of my fellow man, or just men—stayed with me far longer. Marilyn was not just a cautionary tale to me.

While I relish my successes and show them off like the Academy Awards on my bookshelf, I walked from one mistake to the next, each new one reminding me of the others. In my youth, I had hoped for more successes and fewer mistakes.

Most people live their lives on one path. It twists and turns, but there is a main road down the center following the (often bad) decisions we make. Some people, me included, change worlds. Our road suddenly changes—there is a gigantic interruption in the path, and the next part of the road, also paved with bad intentions, has very little to do with the prior, except the person walking it has memories and reactions learned in a previous life. To judge someone who has changed worlds, you have to know their prior one, because it colors everything. But you only see somebody's current world—prior ones are hidden or erased. Like immigrants who come to the new world whose children, to be more American, didn't learn German or French or Spanish. The rich ones reveled in multi-language sophistication, but they had no reason to forget.

An old friend of mine in Paris is a countess by birth and by marriage. When we first met, we sat in her elegant French apartment, and I admired her lineage—she could trace it back hundreds of years. She looked at me and said, "You know, Babe, every family has lineage, it's just poverty or persecution that makes people want to forget." It's true—those with good memories of past glory have something to hang on to. If you were raped by Cossacks, it wasn't a story to pass on to the grandkids.

The first time I changed worlds, I was too young to understand what it meant. I was a child, poor, my mother self-obsessed. My father left before I turned two. I blossomed by the time I was fifteen, when a talent scout put me into the MGM training school. I never looked back. I learned how to be a lady to the manor born, a character I have retained no matter what. Even when I played a whore or a gangster's moll, a great lady underpinned it all. It remains my greatest role—even when my makeup is off.

I never got to do exactly as I wanted as did Elizabeth Taylor or Marilyn. I was big, but they were huge. I had to remember that all this could vanish at any time. Thus, I played by the rules written by the men who ran Hollywood. My world didn't change again until I got a supporting role. First time out of the chorus, I was nominated for an Academy Award. After that, I was a leading lady. I skipped a lot of pain on the way up—

saving it for the way down. No one ever told me, as they did Judy Garland, you won't have to suck a dick to get a good role. Sex in Hollywood is a commodity. Rarely about love, almost always about attraction colored by material concern. If they like you or want you, do you get a better role or better camera angle? Or can you get the director fired or your costar in rehab? Do you get an enormous raise, or marry someone who can give you enough fuck-you money to tell off the studio? I must say that even I, who played the great lady, was guilty of all of the above, but I did it thinking I was Jackie Kennedy. And I stayed that way in the press.

I worry about how my children will perceive my telling of the past. It took us a long time to overcome my bad decisions and most of it took place in the media: husbands, sending my children away for safety, and my constant need to work. An actress works or disintegrates. But I had a lot of regrets and hoped that my children might one day forgive me. If I did the show, I was scared they wouldn't.

We might have been more upset about her book earlier in our lives, but even when my mother thought of doing the show originally so long ago, we were used to her being public property. I think I never understood why she was sexy—she was my mom, but so many years later, after I saw her movies, I understood. I didn't want to know about her marriages.

For a long time, I thought my life was normal. Everyone knew who my mother was and wanted to use me to meet her. My friends were in LA, New York and Paris, and I flew between them by myself, often in first class. The people in this book were famous and, as a child, I thought seeing them was normal.

Until I read her book, I had no idea about a lot of this stuff. It's true, I was angry at her for a long time. Somehow, we got past it, but it wasn't easy for me—and not for my brother Sebastian, either. He was there for me, but he didn't really have anyone there for him except Bobby and Lily. None of us can imagine her not being famous. While we understand she was once an unknown and had to start her career, to us, she was always famous. It's who she has always been.

Anders

HOORAY FOR HOLLYWOOD

I started out playing bit roles and got noticed. I had been trained how to walk and talk, what to wear, how to be seen, and had the full resources of MGM behind me, but without them, without work, I was nothing. I learned, as if genetically imprinted, to know my marks, the masking tape on the floor, because I wasn't important enough to have the cameraman and director follow me around. If I hit them, I was well lit and the camera set up with the right focus, which turned, even for a young girl, a good shot into a fantastic one. Six inches to the left made you less sexy or out of focus and, in those days, there wasn't much one could do in post-production. The other girls were sharks circling for a kill, too. I always hit my marks and figured out early on a way to keep the competition out of my light and out of focus. It was survival.

In the late forties, pictures were still mostly black and white. I understood how I looked in shadow was as important as how I looked in light. I played gangster's molls, showgirls, princesses, a mechanic during the war, a governess, and spoiled daughters. I tried to leave a dark side in even the brightest of roles because I thought it made them more interesting. Since I was small potatoes, the directors didn't bother to correct my underacting, which made my roles meatier amid the melodrama of my competitors.

I worked steadily, and my contract was picked up by MGM, who had put me through charm school. I was paid the lofty sum of $100 a week at a time when the average wage was $1000 a year. It was a fortune. My mother took all of it until I turned eighteen. When I escaped her legal grasp, I gave her $150 a month, more than a quarter of my salary.

However, nothing was ever enough.

Those early roles, where I was on screen for two minutes, and others when I had up to fifteen minutes, were my education. I read the scripts, looked up new words, listened to the directors, and hung out on set even when I wasn't on the schedule. I got coffee, made nice with the crew, and watched everything. I began to distinguish good direction from bad and good acting from great, recognize prima donnas, know how much difference a good crew made, and know who was sleeping with whom while pretending no one else could figure it out.

I knew my place, kept my mouth shut, and smiled a lot. I learned how to read a script so I could see the scene in my mind. In a couple of years, I was able to see variations on a theme because each scene could be played multiple ways—and I understood where the good directors wanted to go. When I couldn't figure out what objective they wanted while watching their direction, it was either because I was too green, or they were no good. I didn't stay green long.

While film buffs talk dolly shots, close-ups, fade outs, jump cuts, and steady cams, the technical terms used in screenplays, what mattered to me was the story and how an actor added to it. I wanted the camera to show what was in my mind by filming what I did with my body and my face. Yes, I needed to look good, which was my bread and butter in the early years. It took me longer to understand the editing process—what we did on set was to provide the editors with enough material to sculpt into a final product. I had good visual memory, so when I saw the editors at work and watched as the rough cuts turned into the final cut, I could see how it happened. I remembered the scenes we had shot and their variations. Not that I always agreed with the final choices, which were not just influenced by the editors, who reported to the director, who reported to the producer, who reported to the studio, who reported to its investors. At the end of the line, what mattered was money. I didn't have any, so I continued to keep my mouth shut, but from time to time, I realized some of these films could have been much better based on what we did in front of the camera. Some, much worse.

After two years, I got a raise to $150 a week, which was a huge achievement. I hired my first maid, who worked six days a week. I also purchased my first home, a modest house in the Hills, which I rented out when I moved up in the world.

I was also of eligible age, which meant I needed to be married off, lest the studio find itself with a young starlet sleeping around, which they didn't care about unless she got into the press for doing so. Pregnancy was less a concern. Studio doctors took care of that kind of thing, which took the rest of America another thirty years until *Roe v Wade*. Access wasn't unmitigated freedom, since many actresses were forced by the studios to have abortions because they were unmarried or about to star in a major role or needed to put off motherhood to protect a sex-star image.

Husband No. 1 came trotting along the path, and if he had been a horse, I might have kept him. A rich scion of a well-known family, he was good on paper, bad in bed. We looked perfect in the press, and I thought I was in love. What the hell, it was an arranged marriage, so I thought I had to be. He was attracted to me, because even with his looks and lineage, I was out of his league. I was on the way up (until I was on the way down, which was long after that marriage ended). He was where he was—

stationary, expecting to live out his life as a rich man from a good family and getting what he deserved. He got all three—his last wife made sure he got what he deserved. He is still getting over what she gave him in the press. His sexual abilities were extremely limited. He was too small to make anything move except himself. The papers had a field day with that tidbit. The divorce settled quietly the next day. No guy wants it known around the world that his dick is the size of a ten-year-old's.

I married him. The studio told me I had to. I was twenty, and what did I know about marriage or love, although I had figured out sex. I barely remember my wedding. I wore a long white dress, no surprise there. There were lovely flowers. I had been given a beautiful ring and earrings for the ceremony and reception, and the studio made sure I had a suitable trousseau. Nothing special sticks out in my mind about the first time I walked down the aisle, which should have been clue number one.

My first son, Sebastian, came along within fifteen months. I took four months off and then went back to work. It was almost a supporting role—I had fifteen minutes of screen time playing witness to a murder in a drama. Naturally, I was a "loose" woman with clothes to match. No one would say hooker on screen in those moral code days, but my tight costumes and cleavage would leave Middle America with no doubt of my lack of moral status. It was a miserable shoot. The director disliked me because I ignored most of his direction, yet my role was the only thing admired about the picture, and he took the credit. At an annoying awards dinner, I thanked him for providing me, an ingenue, with the guidance that made my performance. Since it was known all over town we hated each other and I had ignored his direction, it was an open joke in the industry but not to Middle America. A little man with a little agenda. However, I had to walk a very narrow road in my disapproval. I was still a nobody.

He wasn't the entire underlying problem: motherhood was. Motherhood wasn't hot. It was respectable. I was cast as the hot ingenue—pretty, sexy, and almost smart. The studio wanted cheesecake shots of me with as much cleavage as possible. Motherhood and apple pie applied only if I got into trouble. Even in those code days, it was sex that sold tickets. I needed to be sexy, but it was hard to do that with a toddler who needed his mommy in tow.

I couldn't appear in public with my son. *Life Magazine* did a carefully choreographed photo shoot at our house with the baby, where I was one of the budding actresses of Hollywood. Because the studio wanted me to be a sex symbol, I needed to leave him with a nanny.

My husband, who lived in my shadow, did not appreciate my work or career yet basked in its glory. I was a working woman whose earnings equaled my husband's trust income. We agreed that he paid for the house, our child, and our vacations, while I paid for my clothes and my maid and socked everything else into a real estate trust to provide income when my career fizzled. I had good lawyers, so I kept that trust during my divorce, although Husband No. 1 tried to take everything else and skipped out of child support because he knew I didn't want to end up in the press by suing him.

I wanted to be a good mother. I held my child in my arms and realized I had never loved anyone as much. I also realized this was not uncommon for a mother, so I wasn't unusual or amazing, although it felt that way.

What haunted me was my child's gaze. He looked at me with complete trust. He expected I would never let him down, catch him before he fell, be there when he needed me, and love him so he would develop complete self-confidence. I really tried but fear I failed him. I loved him, but I worked. I had my relationship with him, but like all celebrities, I was two people—the person I really was when interacting with real people, and the image I held in the press: how Middle America viewed me. There are scary people in Hollywood who care more about their image than real relationships. Then, there are the rest of us, who are human but need to make a living and protect our major product—ourselves.

Sebastian grew up with his nannies while I worked. I deliberately kept him out of the press to protect him. Yet years later, during an argument, when he threw in my face that it wasn't to protect him but rather to protect my image, he wasn't totally wrong.

How do you project sex, youth, and availability to people who buy tickets and lust after you or your life when you are a working mother cleaning spit-up off your dress? I didn't know any better. The studio told me to do things, and I thought they knew best. I sold out my firstborn thinking it was the right thing to do. I have no defense other than I was twenty-one. When I had my second son, Anders, I was thirty-seven and had grown up battered and bruised from life at the top of the Hollywood heap. I love my two sons and my adopted one, and I think they love me. The life I led provided neither the childhood they wanted nor the life they wished to remember in middle age. Getting drunk at sixteen with an aging Clark Gable seems cool to Sebastian now, but it did not amuse me at the time. That he knocked up one of the young maids made things worse. The studio intervened and took care of the maid while I packed him off to college. Between twenty and forty, my young adult life morphed into middle age. I had four husbands, two children, twenty-five movies, and one Academy Award. I also found myself waving a gun at Husband No. 1, who had threatened to knock me around if I didn't obey him rather than the studio.

I don't think I would have shot the father of my child, but I was tempted. I did not want to be physically threatened but should have found a better way to cope. Nothing shatters rose-colored glasses like brandishing a gun at your spouse. We filed for divorce that week. Oddly, after all our mediocre times together, we ended up almost friends when our kid became a teen, because we didn't want him playing us off against each other, which stopped when we started talking. Every year for my birthday, ex No. 1 sends me a diamond bangle bracelet. I never needed bracelets, but now I like the custom. In his own peculiar way, it's his way of showing I matter—and that matters. On the other hand, a diamond bangle is much cheaper than child support and years of private school tuition. Husband No. 1 got a good deal. I have sixty-seven diamond bangles, a few "lent" out, never to return.

My early career during my first marriage and its aftermath was rocky. Bobby wouldn't come into my life until the late 1950s. He was preceded as my agent by Victor Orsatti, who picked me up when it became clear I had a decent shot at a career following my well-received role as the witness-hooker. Before, I didn't make enough money. I'd had to hustle like everyone else considered unimportant. There were agents who took on young starlets in the hope they would be profitable, but their profit was more current casting couch than future cash. There was a lot of slime out there, petty little guys who acted as pimps rather than professional agents. I didn't have a middle-class background or connections to advise me, but I had enough common sense to avoid those types of arrangements. That kind of relationship was less about putting out than selling yourself into indentured servitude. Very few came up for air, and those that did left themselves open to blackmail for the rest of their lives. That I was married helped even if the marriage was already on the rocks.

My problem with Victor was his conventionality, but he repped a string of stars, put Judy Garland in *The Wizard of Oz*, and advised Betty Grable on her record-setting twelve consecutive years as a top-ten box-office champ. He was smart, knew the studio pressure points, and wasn't bad looking. I was never tempted to have an affair with him because I saw what had happened to those who did. Victor liked me but steered me to conventional roles, many of which I took, since he wanted to make me into a traditional 1940s blonde, following Betty's blueprint. If I could be another Betty, his fortune would have been assured since she earned over $3 million during her career, which today would be twenty times more. The problem was that the forties were rapidly fading, and the fifties were not the same.

By the fifties, roles had started to change. The tension of film noire and the dark side of life became suburban postwar living. People wanted to forget the tragedies of World War II. The wit and banter between Claudette Colbert and Clark Gable morphed into Doris Day and Cary Grant, but with dialogue neither as quick nor as smart. Both Claudette and Clark were impossible to duplicate. I couldn't duplicate anyone, because I was sexy enough to be a threat to other women yet not dumb enough to remain a dumb blonde. Marilyn and I had that in common. But she could sing and dance.

Betty was starring in the 1949 romantic musical, *The Beautiful Blonde from Bashful Bend*, directed by Preston Sturges in his first Technicolor film. Sadly, it was also his last American production and as bad as its title implied. Victor arranged for me to have a small role with Betty, who played a Wild West saloon singer. The film was a cliché, which Betty understood as she approached the end of her brilliant career. It was the usual Hollywood story, one star on the way down alongside another on the way up. She sang and danced, which I couldn't, but I was a good foil for this leading lady. She understood her role in life and told me, "I'm the dumb blonde that makes the money so the shits can make the Academy-Award-winning dramas." She resented being a workhorse only appreciated for her profits. "I used to be bigger than Humphrey Bogart and Clark Gable, and now all I get are perky roles playing idiots. I'd like just one time to kill somebody, even if I'm still dancing, but that would ruin my image. I'm stuck forever as the girl with the million-dollar legs." As she famously commented in the press, "I'm the kinda girl truck drivers like," which didn't amuse the studio.

In the end, she earned more in Hollywood from 1943 to 1951 than any other star. I remembered her comments as we laughed about my need to go to Broadway because the idea seemed so far away. I was just twenty-two. That I would need a comeback was a joke. I needed a career first. Besides, comedy surrounded us because of the inanities of the production. People couldn't stop laughing about the eventual marketing line for the movie: *She had the biggest six-shooters in the West.* The tagline wasn't so much up to the line as over it, which got the Hollywood censors concerned. Even Victor, who I never thought had much of a sense of humor, came over to Betty at a marketing event and asked, "Is that a gun in your pocket or an extra bra?" We laughed politely.

The film, unfortunately, was not a great success. I was paid, got exposure, but should have dodged this bullet. I couldn't because I was still too junior and had no power. My roles were decided by the studio and my agent. I could give my opinion on the films Victor would suggest for me, but it was ultimately out of my hands. I did what I was told. I had a contract, and they enforced it. If I didn't like it, I would be blacklisted or fired. Thus, I would remain a pawn for my agent and the studios for another ten years.

Betty openly bad-mouthed the movie. She had the stature and box-office pull to get away with it. While I wanted her success, I didn't want a career where I never moved to different roles. She played the same part over and over. Then, too, she had far more experience with the casting couch than she ever let on. It was how she got her start.

I remember her telling me one afternoon, "It's the new old era, just more of the same. You'll be cast in the profit-makers while serious actresses get better roles and are pushed for the Academy Awards. That will never change. You're just a blonde with nice tits."

She told me to take every nickel. In the end, money was what really talked in Hollywood, and if you had it and made it, you were invincible. Her dim view of studio executives was exceeded only by her dimmer view of agents. She didn't dislike Victor, but she felt he was content to promote her for only moneymaking romantic musical leads with nothing that would push her forward dramatically.

Betty did, however, change my life forever. Her other piece of advice, which I use every day, was to work out as often as I could. She didn't get her million-dollar legs by sitting around. She worked out every day—rehearsing, weightlifting, swimming, and climbing stairs. You look at the major dancers of the romantic comedies—Betty, Ginger Rogers, Cyd Charisse, and Ann Miller to name a few—and they worked out all of their professional lives. It was one thing to do what they did at twenty. But by thirty, it was already hard work, and by forty, superhuman.

Betty got me to watch everything I ate. I'd never focused on my diet since I was twenty-two but had never let myself gain a pound. After my first pregnancy, I went on a strict diet, riding my bike up and down the hills.

I didn't know much about working out until Betty taught me. "Look, darling," she would say, "your ass is your fortune. Take care of it!" She got me my first trainer and said if I didn't work out five times a week, I might as well retire. "You'll never make it 'til thirty in this business otherwise." I believed her, and I've kept at it. In time, Betty introduced me to Joe Gold, who was already a bodybuilding genius long before it caught on. Joe got his professional start working for Mae West in her touring revue, which I always thought looked like a drag queen surrounded by gay fans. Mae was smart and a talented businesswoman, including her eye for talent—discovering not only Joe Gold but also Cary Grant in the thirties.

After Joe toured with Mae, he founded Gold's Gym. He stupidly sold it to go back into the merchant marines, where he had started out before Mae discovered him. He returned from his second stint, missed the gym business, and opened World Gym, which he owned until he died in his eighties. He was as responsible for changing American culture as much as anyone, including Jane Fonda, who later made a fortune with her workout videos.

Joe Gold understood that women in Hollywood needed to stay fit but not look like bodybuilders. His advice was priceless. When Joe started his gyms, most of today's machines didn't exist. He invented them. Lifting wasn't the fad it became later. When gay men started flaunting their muscles and going shirtless at the clubs (and doing a lot of drugs, including steroids), it filtered through society. Mae West understood bodybuilding and the eventual effect of steroids, commenting on the muscle guys in her films, "All that meat and such small potatoes!"

I started going to what passed for gyms in the late forties at Betty's urging. She would initially take me and teach me what to do. I moved over to World when Joe finally opened in Venice twenty years later. He made a comfortable living but missed out on the big bucks because he was a gym rat, not a businessman.

I owe my figure to both Betty and Joe.

Betty was a good mentor. She held her head up as her career was going down. She lost one of the great roles in history, Lorelei Lee in *Gentlemen Prefer Blondes,* to Marilyn Monroe, which would become Marilyn's signature role. Marilyn in a bubblegum pink gown singing "Diamonds Are a Girl's Best Friend" became one of the most famous musical numbers in film history. Betty was bitter but proved herself a lady by never blaming Marilyn, only the studio.

Betty was originally slated to play Lorelei but was in the process of renegotiating her contract with Fox. Negotiations became bitter, and she went on strike, refusing to show up for another production. So, Fox replaced her with Marilyn—something they might have done anyway because it was already clear that Marilyn was becoming the bigger star. Betty's reign was over, and she pushed her luck one time too many by going on strike.

Later, Betty and Marilyn starred together in Marilyn's next film, *How to Marry a Millionaire*. While Betty had top billing and earned a lot more money, Marilyn was the lead in all advertising. It was Betty's last big role. She understood her time was up and wanted to go out with a bang. She knew she needed a hit and believed Marilyn would be her insurance, so she swallowed her pride and cashed her large check.

Betty never got her big dramatic role. Maybe she was fooling herself. Her brilliant career was romantic comedy—maybe asking to be Katharine Hepburn was not in her range. We'll never know because she never did. And she made far more money than Kate. The studio execs thought she was nuts—she made the most money in Hollywood, so what did she have to complain about? By the mid-1950s, her career was over. I would see her from time to time, but she was a faded star. Her career was a parable for life in Hollywood—highest-paid star in the forties, nothing in the fifties. Life is over when your breasts start to point south. We all lose our charms in the end.

I can't imagine my mother not working out. She always trained and often took us with her to the gym, sticking us on a Stairmaster while she did her workouts. Our whole family worked out and, in time, it became our business. My mother is too embarrassed to go to the gym now, since she worries what people will think when they see how much she has aged, but her trainer comes to her apartment every day.

She told me that the last time she went to the gym, she kept getting stares from everyone—including one younger guy. While he waited for her to finish on her machine, she told us that he looked like he was worried she might stroke out before he got his chance to work in. She smiled at him and said, keep this up for the next 60 years and you'll look like me. She commented to us, "I think he probably went home and killed himself!"

That's my mom.

Anders

FIRST NOMINATION

While my movie with Betty was a stinker, I had a good part that got me some notice. I became attached to a film directed by Billy Wilder, and that changed my life. It was a true supporting role with my name just below the title. A leading role got your name in the credits above it, something the studios controlled unless you were a huge star—since they had everyone under contract, they could mostly dictate how we were billed. I got lucky when my name was prominently shown.

In time, billing became a whole section of a star's contract, and not only stars but also directors, producers, writers, casting directors, and studios. Greed was exceeded only by ego in Hollywood, and how big your name was, where it was placed, and its lettering led to long negotiations, fights, legal battles, and general bad behavior. One producer learned only when his film was released that while he had contracted to have his name placed where he wanted it in the same typeface and height as the others, he neglected to have width detailed in his contract, so his name was in a narrower width lettering and took up less screen real estate. While he never made the mistake again and wasn't surprised when others took advantage of his ignorance, he told me he felt a bit slimy being in an industry where so many took delight in taking advantage wherever they could. On the other hand, he fought long and hard ever after for his credits and his points. Money and ego again.

One of Hollywood's greatest directors, Billy was no longer concerned about fighting for credits, having won that game much earlier. He went on to do *Some Like It Hot* and *Sunset Boulevard*, giving Marilyn Monroe and Gloria Swanson their greatest roles. Little old me in one of his movies? I was beyond thrilled. I played a gangster's moll who slowly figures out that what she lives on comes from blackmailing widows and orphans. It was a comedy—certainly not a role as juicy and brilliant as Judy Holliday's in *Born Yesterday*, directed by George Cukor, but a great turn, nonetheless. George Cukor—who was well known for being gay, although not to the public—was famous for coaxing brilliant performances from his female stars but from the other direction of Billy.

In a twist of fate, Judy Holliday's performance as the dumb blonde in *Born Yesterday* won her the 1950 Best Actress Academy Award, over both Gloria Swanson in *Sunset Boulevard* and Bette Davis in *All About Eve,* which, with fourteen nominations, set a new record over *Gone with the Wind's* previous thirteen nominations, remaining as the most nominations for one film until *Titanic* in 1997 and *La La Land* in 2016. While I loved *Born Yesterday*, to think that Judy beat both Gloria and Bette makes you wonder about the voting habits of the Academy. Especially since the same year, *Sunset Boulevard*, an acknowledged masterpiece, had eleven nominations, including every acting category, but didn't win a single award. God laughing at us again, or merely not-so-bright academy voters? If I had been involved with either film, I would have been proud but angry. On the other hand, George Cukor, director of *Born Yesterday,* was forever thrilled.

All About Eve was Marilyn's first major picture, where she had a bit role with important actors. It led to her being a presenter at the Academy Awards and a major studio contract with 20th Century Fox. Filmed before we became friends, *All About Eve* was a discussion between us both because it was Marilyn's big break and because Bette Davis was a legendary bitch with a foul mouth rivaling any producer's. But she was a smart bitch who worked continuously on stage and screen except when she sued Warner Bros. in 1936 to get out of her contract because she felt they were putting her in mediocre films. Her complaint, filed in Britain because she found work there, stated that her life was controlled by the studio—she had to play any part given her whether she liked it or not or be suspended without pay. She was told what to support politically, and the studio owned her image and could use it in any manner they wished. It was more of the same. Old Jack Warner testified against her—and won. It took Olivia de Havilland to sue the studio in 1943 for the same reasons and win to begin loosening the studio's shackles.

Not to be forgotten, Bette was good friends with Hattie McDaniel, the first black to win an Academy Award (not incidentally for playing Mammy, the maid, in *Gone with the Wind*), and she was the only white to appear with Hattie when she performed for black servicemen in World War II. It is sad that she is largely remembered for playing an old lady in the campy horror films *Whatever Happened to Baby Jane* and *Hush, Hush Sweet Charlotte* rather than for being a great actress with numerous awards, including two Oscars and five consecutive years of Oscar nominations.

Bette was tough, and when she didn't feel she was given her due, she let everyone know. "Ooh," Marilyn cooed, talking about Bette losing the Oscar for *All About Eve*, "Bette was about to eat the presenter when Judy Holliday won!" She chomped down with her teeth and smiled. "Whenever there is confrontation on set, I ask, 'What would Bette do?' Everyone who worked with her does the same!" Following that chat, whenever I had a really difficult moment on a set, it was met with a 'what would Bette do' when I talked to Marilyn.

Bette Davis hated Joan Crawford, the pretty girl of the thirties, who started out as a dancer and chorus girl, Hollywood's usual route. Bette, on the other hand, was never a beauty but was known for her acting skills. There were numerous stories of their battles, not all untrue. Crawford was well known for her sexual appetite. As Bette once commented, "She has slept with every male star at MGM except Lassie." It was a far more sophisticated dig than immediately apparent. Lassie the dog was female in the movies but was always played by male collies because they shed less than females, because the shedding would cause continuity problems when filming. With her phrasing, Bette alluded to all the women Crawford carried on with as well, one of whom was Marilyn. Everyone at MGM understood the deeper insult.

I owed Cukor big time. He suggested Billy use Gloria Swanson as the star of *Sunset Boulevard*, and it was one of the greatest casting tips in the history of film. His other suggestion to Billy was to use me as a comedienne. I was forever grateful, and it turned out much better for me than for the history of cinema. It was a break in character, and I was thrilled to do something other than display cleavage. I showed that, too—it was why they paid me—but I got to show I could be funny as well. I was in heaven, but Billy was tough and made me do take after take to get the timing right for my laugh lines. The results were wonderful, but it was hard work.

I knew how to position myself, understood direction, and could improvise variations on the director's theme, putting all my past five years of work into this role. Billy was a master, and I was ready. He directed me to my first Academy Award nomination, which was the beginning of my career. I was twenty-two and still an ingenue, but a known one. My life as a star began then and, from that point forward, I changed paths. I joined the list of women stars created and launched by George Cukor and Billy Wilder. The list was formidable, and I would never have amounted to what I became if I had not been on it. I had no idea at the time that the film I was working on would change my life. I just trusted Billy knew what he was doing and saw things few others did when he was behind the camera.

After my first Academy Award nomination, I began to be someone who counted in the Hollywood hierarchy. I remember the excitement, the media attention, and, most of all, the fear. I understood while it might be an amazing beginning, it could also be the high point of my life, with the rest of it spent looking back to this moment and wondering what went wrong. There is a scene in the play *Pygmalion,* which became Cukor's amazing film *My Fair Lady,* after Professor Higgins has turned the flower girl Eliza Doolittle into a seemingly high-born lady, where she laments, "What am I fit for? What have you left me fit for? Where am I to go? What am I to do? What's to become of me?" Exactly how I felt. As a flower girl, Eliza Doolittle knew what to expect and how to fend for herself. As a lady, she needed to be protected. Without resources, she was without the skills that had previously provided her with a living as a flower girl.

I wasn't educated, couldn't hold a professional job, and came from nothing. My family background made me ineligible for a good match, but I would have to continue to marry well unless I made it as an actress because there was nothing else I could do. I understood that in 1949, I existed at the whim of the men who ran the studios, the male directors who made the films, and the male talent agents who profited from my paycheck. I led an exalted life on someone else's dime; despite my salary, I had very little of my own, not even my name, which had been changed. With that nomination, my life was transformed. I was out of the chorus forever, and what that meant was if I didn't make it as a leading lady, I would disappear into the unwritten history of Hollywood with thousands of other beautiful girls who showed up in Hollywood demonstrating potential brilliant futures but never achieving them.

My life was equivalent to those films about an heiress who loses her fortune, leaving her with only the clothes on her back and no job skills— which in Hollywood ends up as 1950s *Tea for Two*. Other than its star, Doris Day, there wasn't much demand for knowing how to walk gracefully, talk beautifully, and dress elegantly under all circumstances unless you were a courtesan. In Hollywood, those girls were always in demand.

There was no job security in pictures. Bright promise doesn't pay the rent or help you at the automat, as Marilyn sang in *Diamonds Are a Girl's Best Friend*. I was determined not to blow my big chance but was scared for a long time it would vanish as it had for so many others with greater talent. Why, we would never know. If ever there were cases of fickle luck, it was those who made it in our business. Those whom the camera favored, whom the public loved, who got the right role at the right time, and who had the skill to capitalize on the moment. That first nomination, before I was anything, was a wakeup call I understood. Yet, I knew little of the world and would have to learn as I went, which was not easy when you're living in the public eye under the increasing presence of the press with no one to teach you, no middle-class connections where your parents' friends were doctors, lawyers, and bankers, and no one to trust. My world consisted of those who fed off people who made it and those who destroyed them. Finding people you could trust and who understood how to protect you was rarer still.

This was no Cinderella story. No one found me and turned me into a princess with a glass slipper. While I would marry—and did so often—any hope I may have had that a man might come to my rescue never happened. I had to rescue myself. From the outside, I looked like I was a successful actress who had it all, but on the inside, I kept waiting to turn back into the wretch who cleaned the chimney, my Mercedes turning into a Chevy, and my ball gown into faded jeans.

The late forties were a confusing time in America. We had won the war, were benefiting from a growing economy, and were watching the growing power of the House Un-American Activities Committee and McCarthy hearings. The Hollywood blacklist destroyed lives and severed long-term friendships. It was a dark period, and I was initially too naive to understand the implications.

As the forties gave way to the fifties, studios were at the height of their power. While studio execs started off vowing they would never participate in any witch hunts, they doubled down later when they got scared and refocused on protecting profits at all costs.

I didn't really pay attention until friends started getting blacklisted and appearing before the House Un-American Activities Committee. It's difficult now to imagine the level of fear generated by this witch hunt.

People such as Leonard Bernstein, Dorothy Parker, Lena Horne, Orson Welles, and even Charlie Chaplin were blacklisted and couldn't work or enter the United States as in Chaplin's case. Yet, we danced on. It was easier to make musicals than risk controversy.

While we were shooting my yet-to-be-nominated role, Billy Wilder took time one evening to explain the underpinnings of the communist hearings. He was able to describe the controversy in a way that hit me. He told me there have always been forces of darkness who believe the end is justified by the means. He said Dostoevsky's *Crime and Punishment* detailed this brilliantly. My problem then was that I had no idea who Dostoevsky was but was too embarrassed to ask. He explained how some anti-communists were scared, some were opportunists, and some just weren't very smart. Freedom always has a price. "Pretending that freedom is free without sacrifice is delusional," he added.

He saw McCarthy and the ensuing struggle as a fight for freedom. That theme began emerging in his later films. His ideas were complicated and dark and involved unhappy endings. Obvious to me now, but not then, *Sunset Boulevard* was a reaction to McCarthyism and showed Hollywood in a particularly bad light. The film is about power and murder, debuting at the height of the fear over communists lurking within our midst. Its darkness correlates with the discussions Billy had with me on our shoot just before he made Gloria Swanson a star one more time.

Billy warned me to keep my head down. "You can't help the idiots or protect the heroes. Save your ammunition for when you'll need it!" It was a great line, and I'm embarrassed to admit I have wondered ever since from which script he stole it. He advised me to shut up politically and not do anything spectacularly stupid. I would have liked that warning before a few of my marriages.

Why would anyone listen to me anyway? I was just a Hollywood blonde nattering on. My image was a pretty young thing who couldn't possibly understand anything important. It was why I had loved my role with Billy—the dumb blonde slowly wakes up and finds out she's not so dumb, after all.

I wanted that to happen in real life. During the height of my career, it never did. For once, my being put down by the guys running things was an asset because it kept me out of the anti-communist hearings.

Billy was immune, too. Not only was he a big name, but he also filmed movies with a decidedly anti-communist bent, so his work stood as his protection. He had escaped Hitler and was loud in his antipathy against totalitarianism as well as its distant left cousin, communism. He wasn't completely untouchable—no one was at the height of the craze—but he was a known product and protected a lot of people, hiring as many as he could. He deserved a lot of credit for that, quite apart from his film genius.

Bogey and Bacall formed a committee to fight the blacklist. I knew them from when I'd been in the chorus of an early Bacall film, after she became a star in *To Have and Have Not*. I admired Bacall. She was a new breed. Tough, intelligent, articulate as well as beautiful. She wasn't window dressing—she was the center. She was a rarity, and I was envious of her toughness. I wanted those roles, too, where I was equal to men or smarter. By now, I was a star, but what I was known for was not my brains. Besides flashing my cleavage, which was much better than Bacall's, I wanted to play smart.

At a dinner one night, I told Bogie I was impressed with their efforts. His response, "You want to be a freedom fighter, do you?" made me feel like I had stepped into *Casablanca*. I tried to get into French resistance mode as I said, "You don't say, Rick?" which made him laugh. He was getting very drunk, and Bacall had to help him home before we could finish the conversation. I am struck that, even married to such a strong woman as Bacall, Bogie was amused by my presumption. I had hoped that separately from my public image, my private thoughts counted. I was wrong.

I thought a lot about Bogart in *Casablanca*. Not his best work, but certainly his most famous. The film was a complete accident. The script was written and rewritten even as it filmed. The ending changed multiple times, the cast was unsure of their lines until the last minute, and the film's success was uncertain. When you are working on a film like *Casablanca,* if you don't know whether it's any good or not, how can you know anything in this business? Clearly, no one does.

Casablanca premiered on November 26, 1942 in New York and went on to win the Academy Award for Best Picture. Only half the script was written when filming began. The censors removed a lot of the sex and innuendo. Goes to show what you can do without it. Not everyone liked it, and later critics as famous as Pauline Kael and Umberto Eco declared it mediocre, but I wish more films were like it. You can't take your eyes off the main characters, even Ingrid Bergman, who overacts every minute she is on screen to Bogart's understatement. Every time I go to the movies, I hope the film might be as good, but they rarely are.

That *Casablanca* was an accident tells a lot about this industry. No one knows anything. As far as the witch hunt went, we didn't either. We were scared, hoped we were right but feared we weren't. People smarter than me believed in a communist conspiracy. Was I to know better? Yet, this whole mania seemed based on a movie script, with the lead character looking for glory. That, at least, I understood.

I kept in touch with Bacall. We were reacquainted years later when she moved to New York, where she kept an apartment in the Dakota on New York's Upper West Side. Her son, Sam Robards, and mine got into trouble for lobbing eggs off the roof of her building, which was also inhabited by Leonard Bernstein, who had been on the blacklist. Lily managed to keep the egg toss out of the press, but for years, every time I saw an Easter egg, I was tempted to call Bacall for a drink. The things twelve-year-olds think up. Unquestionably, the issues of McCarthy might have been more forgivable if the thinkers were twelve.

What finally stopped McCarthy was Edward R. Murrow, the famed journalist who broadcast from London during the war. He had interviewed me when I was a fresh face in Hollywood, and I would occasionally see him at dinners, but we were from different worlds. I was entertainment, and he was a journalist at a time when journalism was serious. I will allow he had a gleam in his eye whenever he saw me, and I always found him very attractive—attractive with the added aphrodisiac of power. However, he was married with a child and gave up a fling with Pamela Harriman, later appointed by Clinton to be our ambassador to France and who had flings with a lot of men of power, when he became a father. Murrow and I were attracted to each other, but nothing ever came of it, so that was one mistake I didn't make. It might have come to nothing, but if it had come to something, he would have had to divorce. Either way, it would have risked a major scandal.

When Murrow finally attacked Senator McCarthy in 1954 as dishonest, self-serving, and abusive, it began McCarthy's downfall. He stood up at a time when no one was safe and risked his career in doing so. The head of CBS, William Paley, would eventually tire of having someone like Murrow go after the powerful, which brought an end to Murrow's CBS career. George Clooney detailed this in his wonderful movie, *Good Night and Good Luck*, which brought back memories and won six Academy Award nominations, including a best director nod for George. Although the film lost in all categories, Georgie Porgie, as he was nicknamed for his serial dating, has been nominated in six different categories over his career—equaled only by Walt Disney, whose Hollywood touch changed popular culture around the world. I couldn't imagine two more different peas in a pod than Walt and George. It implies a lot about Hollywood popular culture that the two of them remain in their own category together via the breadth of their respective visions. George has won two Academy Awards so far for supporting actor and best picture. If he were a woman, I'd hate him—far too much competition. How could you compete? Even his buddies, Matt Damon, Ben Affleck, and Brad Pitt—the new rat pack and, I must say, an improved version over the original—haven't reached his depth. Am I biased? Maybe, but if so, I'm not alone. George, while directing, didn't take the Murrow role but gave it to David Strathairn, who received a best actor nomination for his performance.

Before filming, George came over to ask about my memories of the era and learn what private details I remembered about Murrow. George was charming and smart. His edge has always been his intelligence although he kept that *secret* early in his career. I always thought it odd a man had to hide behind his looks, which was something I associated with starlets like me. Yes, he is good-looking in the vein of Cary Grant, but it is his wit that separates him as much as his looks. What a great combination.

I was pleased he wanted to talk as I was gratified to see how he had grown and made wise career decisions after his start as a too-cool-for-school heartthrob. I knew him as a kid, before he first shot to fame on *ER*, when he would show up at parties with his aunt, the famous singer Rosemarie Clooney. Later, I guest-appeared a few times on the television show *Sisters*, shot on the Warner Bros.'s lot in the early 1990s. Clooney played the cop love interest of Sela Ward, who was famous for doing take after take so consistently it garnered a crowd to watch her hit her marks with the same intonations, same reactions, same gestures in the same sequence—steady and consistent. George, on the other hand, gave more variation, which while less consistent, gave the editors more room to work. When he would leave the set, he rode off on his motorcycle, dressed head to toe in black leather, sometimes with a sleeveless black zip-up motorcycle jacket. I never thought he would amount to much, quite frankly, because he appeared to have gone Hollywood native, which was never a good sign. Fortunately, I was wrong. His two Academy Awards equal mine, but he has a shot of winning more and beating me. Although I hope I'm not out of the game just yet. Who knows?

Murrow was portrayed in Clooney's film as a strong, sexy hero, which was absolutely accurate. Murrow held his point of view even if others disagreed, and this strength in adversity made him even more attractive. I went to the premiere of *Good Luck and Good Night* at George's invitation since he remembered those who had helped him on the project. We ended up having a short chat at the premiere.

"How'd I do?" he started off.

"No black leather, no bike, short haircut, and now director. You did good." I laughed. He blushed. Was I flirting? I don't think so. I was almost seventy-seven then, but if I had been forty years younger, he wouldn't have known what hit him.

"I grew up," he responded. "We talked about your memories of Murrow, the feeling of the era. Did the film ring true for you?" he asked again, ever the inquiring director.

"You caught the tension, his bravery, his idealism. You were brave to shoot in black and white. I'm surprised you got financing. Murrow was sexy in his own way, so I'm sorry you didn't play his part." That comment got me a big hug.

"I should have listened!" he said with a laugh. "I couldn't both direct and take the best role," he said. He wasn't one to garner all the glory. He didn't feel the need and was just like Murrow in that way.

I told George something more. "What I detested most about McCarthy was the bullying. I always hated bullies. I was bullied my entire career but finally learned to fight back. Your film is how you stand up to a bully, and I love you for it."

Oh my God, what a wonderful look of appreciation I received. How I wished I could take him home with me. I didn't care about being a dirty old lady, but I did care about being turned down. I just smiled and was sad the next day when there were neither pictures of our hug in the press nor rude headlines. I had gotten too old for George Clooney, and certainly, too old for the press.

Given my other marriages, I sometimes wondered what might have happened if I had added one more? Was Murrow the "one" who got away? On the other hand, he died at such a young age, so maybe I was spared losing someone I loved once more.

I asked George Clooney about my mother recently and got the strangest look. He said, "You're her kid and I'm in my sixties, but whatever it is she had, she still has. She's a sexy beast!" It wasn't what I expected or wanted to hear—on the other hand, when I told my now 95 year old mother, she purred for hours.

When my brothers and I talked to the children of other stars, we had similar experiences. We were mortals related to immortals who aged in real time but stayed sexy and young forever onscreen.

I understood that she was reduced often by men and had to learn to stand up for herself. It's now a long time from the 1950s. When she talks about Betty Grable, she talks about herself. She could have ended up with nothing after she hit 40 and yet that's when most of her career happened. She was a single mom who made it.

THE BLONDES

We were the great blondes of the fifties—me, Marilyn Monroe, Kim Novak, Grace Kelly, Betty Grable, Doris Day, Debbie Reynolds, and Lana Turner, who was involved in a bigger scandal than the rest of us put together when her daughter murdered her lover, Johnnie Stampanato, a junior mobster, claiming he was beating up her mother. The daughter got off on justifiable homicide. I've had tough press, but nothing like that. And just when you thought it was all over, Johnnie's family sued Lana for millions.

Next on scandal row was Debbie Reynolds, whose most brilliant performance took place at age nineteen in *Singing in the Rain,* leaving her looking back the rest of her life. Despite having the role of a lifetime in one of the greatest musicals ever filmed, she remained jealous of Marilyn Monroe. Debbie understood that while she could dance and sing, no one glowed brighter on screen than Marilyn, which made her singing of "Diamonds Are a Girl's Best Friend" everything Debbie could do—except sexier.

Debbie started out all-American apple pie but ended up tarnished when her husband, Eddie Fisher, ran off with Elizabeth Taylor after her husband Mike Todd was killed in a plane crash. I stayed out of that one, given how vulnerable Elizabeth was after Mike died and how stupid Eddie turned out to be. I saw less of Elizabeth during her Eddie period. I didn't like him. Elizabeth and Debbie had been teenage friends from MGM charm school but didn't speak for years. It was the marital scandal of the

1950s. Debbie had been matron of honor at Elizabeth's wedding to Mike while Eddie was best man. She and Eddie named their second child, Todd, after Mike. Their eldest, Carrie Fisher, who died far too young only to be followed by her mother the next day, described Eddie in her memoir, *Wishful Drinking*:

> *Naturally, my father flew to Elizabeth's side, gradually making his way slowly to her front. He first dried her eyes with his handkerchief, then he consoled her with flowers, and he ultimately consoled her with his penis.*

Eddie left Debbie to raise two children on her own, not paying a cent, lowering his already low reputation. Frank Sinatra told me he'd warned her not to marry Eddie—that singers made bad husbands, something he would know—but she was young, in love, and not oblivious to the fact that the marriage made her part of a Hollywood power couple. In the end, Debbie appreciated Elizabeth's taking Eddie off her hands. While she finally made up with Elizabeth and later starred with her in Elizabeth's last film, *These Old Broads*, written by Carrie Fisher as a gift both to her mother and former stepmother, she remained estranged from Eddie. She savaged him in the media, although not as badly as his daughter, for being a bad father who didn't even bother to send Christmas or birthday cards.

I, along with millions, was crushed to hear about Carrie's sudden death followed by her mother's. Carrie was a great Hollywood wit who cleverly played off her Princess Leia role for the rest of her life. She also did copious amounts of drugs, in part to drive her mother crazy, and finally came back down to earth when she went on medication for being bipolar.

She managed for much of her life to be a constant source of pain and pleasure for her mother, and the two ended up living in houses next door to each other.

I never bonded with Debbie. At first because I was Elizabeth's friend, but later because life works out that way, and you can't be close to everyone. There was something else. I didn't appreciate how she played the nice one, the wholesome one, while being a complete diva. *Postcards from the Edge*, Carrie's novel that she turned into the great movie directed by Mike Nichols starring Shirley MacLaine and Meryl Streep, detailed just how much of a diva and gay icon. Now, I have no problem with divas. Elizabeth was one, and so am I, but we don't pretend. If you're going to be a diva, do it balls to the wall, so to speak. How many gay icons aren't divas? We all are. Too, Debbie talked about Marilyn Monroe's death, claiming she was murdered and how Debbie had warned her about her relationships with the Kennedys. More posing. She just wanted the media contrast between Marilyn's notoriety and her own goodness. There was just too much bullshit mixed with saccharine for me.

Nonetheless, I admired her. I felt sad at her death and the deep despair she must have felt losing her daughter. She'd already been slowly forced to stop performing due to failing health—that alone was killing her because she lived to be onstage. Carrie's death at age sixty finished her off, and she died one day later. Debbie also left a son and a granddaughter behind, but they were not enough for her to live. The biggest relationship in her life was Carrie—the two of them forming a symbiosis of sorts—two stars from age nineteen, the mother constantly worrying about her daughter's health, psychiatric condition, and drug use while the daughter took on the care of her aging parent. The death of a child is crushing, and for one in failing health, it is something clearly impossible to survive. I don't know what I would do.

I went to the funeral to stand in for Elizabeth. Debbie and Elizabeth remained close most of their lives. Debbie first forgave Elizabeth, a superhuman feat. When she could finally see Eddie for what he was, she became grateful to Elizabeth for breaking up her marriage. Because of bad investments and worse husbands, Debbie worked her entire life because she needed the money. She was a true survivor—another star who earned the right to sing "I'm Still Here." And it must be said, diva to the end, she managed to upstage her own daughter's death.

Another creature of scandal on the list was Jayne Mansfield, whose grisly death by near decapitation in an auto accident ended her storied life at age thirty-four. I can't say she was an actress. Or one of us. She was a personality. One of the first of *Playboy*'s playmates, she used her incredible figure to her advantage, but no matter how hot she looked, her films were not of note, and her acting showed little ability. She got lucky in a few roles. In and of itself, lack of talent never stopped anyone in Hollywood from making a name for themself. Jayne was famous because she knew how to grab attention. But she chipped away at her celebrity in the years before her death through a string of bad roles and a tawdry personal life whose sexual details were not well-hidden. We don't know how she might have turned out—thirty-four is an early death. Nonetheless, all signs pointed to a dismal end to her career.

Doris Day was the last of my world of 1950s blondes. Doris was a box-office champ, too. She sang, she danced, she was wholesome and perky—quite frankly, too much so. When movie tastes changed to less perky, her career began to decline. She was a huge singing star who crossed over into film, where she also became a huge star. Her roles were cute—she kept your eye on the screen, and she made money, which was what counted. Although she was one of the biggest film stars of the fifties and sixties, her original stature came from radio and recordings in the pre-television forties. As a film star, her enormous success in romantic comedy disappeared by the seventies. One can say that film tastes changed, but never far from reality was how a beautiful blonde aged out of popularity, both with the public and studio execs. We know she faded from view, but I'm not sure we'll ever understand exactly why. Growing old as a blonde seemed to savage any career.

The blondes ran into each other, competed for roles and sometimes men, compared notes, and understood each other in a way few others could. It would be hard to imagine a more bizarre life. We were concubines to the studios and had to be sexy and sell tickets. If we didn't make money, we were out. We were commodities—highly valued and very rare, but commodities, nonetheless. When a commodity lost value, it was like owning stock—it can make you a billionaire, but in bankruptcy, you're still just a bum.

Marilyn had the most enduring fame. Never has there been so much talent, insecurity, and self-destruction wrapped up in such a fabulous package. When she was on screen, no one could take their eyes off her. In the history of cinema, there have been greats and greater greats, but even Meryl Streep next to Marilyn on camera would be ignored. On the other hand, Meryl would show up for work the next morning.

I got to know Marilyn when she was filming *Gentlemen Prefer Blondes* since it was on the next soundstage. I had met her originally through Betty and lived through the drama when Marilyn beat her out for the lead role. This was the studio—younger was better. Jane Russell, her costar, who became increasingly unhappy with Marilyn's perpetual tardiness, finally warmed to her. She also got paid a lot more—$200,000 to Marilyn's $1500 a week studio contract. Yet Marilyn stole the show, and she stole it in a way even Betty understood she could never do. Marilyn illuminated the screen like no one ever has.

While on different shoots—I was doing a drama with Gregory Peck on the stage next door—Marilyn and I would get together in our dressing rooms when we had a few minutes off together to laugh and recharge. We'd become friends at a lunch at the commissary one day. I always felt a connection with her, and she told me she felt the same. We never had any idea we were related. Discovering we were sisters seemed such a convoluted plot—no one would ever believe it even if written in a 1950s musical. We had girl talk, career talk, and understood we were cogs in the studio production line. We'd never be people. We were just broads. Marilyn confided to me that her first agent, Johnny Hyde, had made her get her nose and jaw fixed. It was good plastic surgery at a time when the skill was just being developed. Maybe the surgery explained why, other than our blonde hair and breasts, we didn't look related. I didn't do any plastic work until I needed to look younger.

She also had an affair with Johnny during that time. "What else could I do?" she asked in her breathless voice. "I was alone, needed work, and had to make sure I got it." Johnny eventually left his wife for Marilyn and repeatedly asked her to marry him. Wisely, Marilyn refused. She said, "I loved him but wasn't in love with him. It would never have worked."

On the *Gentlemen Prefer Blondes* set, Marilyn was convinced Jane was a greater talent. She was terrified of being shown up. I arrived on set one day to find her hiding in my dressing room. I had a long dramatic scene that morning, one of the most important in our film. Sure enough, that was the day Marilyn decided to show up in a panic. I called my medication expert, Judy Garland, who had also been repped by Victor, to ask what I should give her, but she warned me MM was on enough stuff already. It was very telling that Judy thought MM was taking too many pills. That was really scary, so I had to use psychology, of which I was woefully ignorant.

That's another reason I hate shrinks: what they did to Marilyn. We had them at the studio, and they thought it was fine to give us pills to get up and work and then pills to sleep and get our beauty rest. MM wasn't out making cocaine deals at 3 a.m. on Santa Monica Boulevard. She was prescribed everything. She never knew anything else. Her shrinks prescribed her stuff as did her doctor, her gynecologist, and everyone else with a pen. When she died, they did an inventory of her house. Judy was right.

I needed to get her out of my dressing room. She was vulnerable. Her voice, less breathless off screen, was so sad, "I don't want them to find out I'm a fraud." She had it so wrong, because there has never been less of a fraud on screen who ever lived. She scribbled in girlish handwriting in her notebooks, some of which have been published long after her death. Her mind proved to be a most sophisticated one. Her judgments were telling and sharp. At first, she understood her persona, Marilyn Monroe, was not her. Yet it was whom she longed to be. Norma Jeane had so much baggage. Her line in *Gentlemen Prefer Blondes*, "I can be smart when it's important, but most men don't like it," was Norma Jeane's own addition. The line didn't apply just to the movie. Another famous comment, "Women who seek to be equal with men lack ambition," came from Marilyn Monroe. To understand her, one had to know she existed in a constant tug of war between Norma Jeane and Marilyn.

Norma Jeane started with enormous insecurities and a genetic predisposition to insanity inherited from her mother. As the image of the actress "Marilyn Monroe" evolved from Norma Jeane's work and press, MM became her own presence. Such enormous fame would have changed anyone, but for someone as insecure as Norma Jeane, Marilyn's larger-than-life image became a dangerous refuge. In the beginning, she could manage the differences between the professional persona and the real one. Later, they blurred, and she essentially became a split personality. Both were real, had their own personalities, and existed in the same body, and together, they drove her toward insanity. She told me in 1960, "It gets harder to step in and out of Marilyn Monroe's image when I spend all my time perfecting it." She lived to be Marilyn Monroe. It would have tempted anyone.

At the height of her career, Marilyn predominated. At the end, Norma Jeane did. Marilyn told me several times she understood she wasn't her image. "I wish I was Marilyn Monroe. Now that's a broad!" she told me over champagne one night. There was also her famous quote, "My problem with men is that they all want to go to bed with Marilyn, but they wake up with Norma Jeane." The relentless media presence, the demands of stardom, and her need to be loved all worked together to make her rely more and more on Marilyn's persona.

They filmed *My Week with Marilyn*, taking place when she was at the height of her fame married to Arthur Miller, when I knew her. Michelle Williams, who plays Marilyn, did a great job and received an Academy Award nomination. I had a hard time with the movie. As good as Michelle Williams was, you missed Marilyn. It was an imitation, a copy. Hamburger for steak. The character was interesting, and you understood Michelle Williams's skill, but there was never a moment when you didn't know you were watching a performance. What you wanted was the real MM because she was ten times more riveting on screen in a way that couldn't be duplicated. Michelle was brave to take on the role, because to compare yourself to Marilyn was pointless. There was no way to come close. The camera has never loved anyone more.

Bert Stern, the famous photographer for *Life Magazine*, who photographed us all at one time or another for *Life* and other publications, including our publicity stills for the studios, used to say the difference between photographing Marilyn and Elizabeth Taylor was that to capture Marilyn, you had to capture her movement, or it became a flat shot. With Elizabeth, it didn't matter. All you needed to do was point the camera because she was so beautiful you couldn't take a bad one.

Marilyn personified movement. She practiced all the time, moving her body, her facial muscles in the mirror, walking, sitting—everything she could do to make her body work better under her control. She understood movement and was a genius in comedy because she figured out how to manage her stunts exactly as she wanted them to appear inside the camera. She had a sixth sense. She asked for take after take, not only because of immense insecurity but also because she knew how she wanted to look and wouldn't settle until that look was in the can. Marilyn started with an acting coach and always had one with her, much to the annoyance of almost everyone. Her first was the German, Natasha Lytess, the head acting coach at Columbia Pictures who famously was followed by Paula Strasberg. Marilyn's critics always disparaged her because she wouldn't do a thing without her coaches. Her directors hated them because she looked to them for approval, not the directors.

As someone obsessed with movement, Marilyn understood the only thing that counted was how she looked on the screen. Her coaches were there to guide her performance while Marilyn focused on how she looked inside the camera. She worried about her acting ability and trusted her coaches to let her know when she was good. She alone knew how she appeared inside the lens. It was her particular genius. We discussed it a few times. I was struck when she told me, "Whenever the camera is on, I make myself exist in only two dimensions. I can't be a person. I have to be a character flat like a cartoon. How I'm seen on screen is all that matters, and I need to understand that image. Paula worries about my acting." She smiled. "Even the great Marilyn Monroe can't do everything at once." She winked.

Watching her as Lorelei Lee, or later in *Some Like it Hot*, is mesmerizing. Every straight man I know got a hard-on seeing her in her sheer dress for *Some Like it Hot*. Those were real breasts! She did indeed figure out how she appeared on screen in those days without real-time computer monitors. She waited until she was sure the perfect footage had been obtained. Insecure, yes. Ignorant, no. Impossible for the rest of the crew? Of course.

While I understand the Tony Curtis complaint that kissing her was like kissing Hitler because he was furious at her chronic tardiness, her vulnerable little girl act, and the constant retakes, it was a remark only a stupid, straight, white middle-aged man could say. As a guy, what did he have to complain about? It was, after all, Marilyn Monroe he was kissing. If he'd had to suck the dicks young actresses did to get parts or to advance their careers, well, good luck to him! Kissing is easy. Guys, ugly guys, guys using power, guys who think they are hot because they have a dick— how annoying.

In fairness to Tony, Marilyn told me that just to embarrass him in front of the crew, she deliberately aroused him during their romantic scene on the boat. She is "teaching" him how to kiss, wearing a skintight dress with her breasts barely covered, in full Marilyn Monroe aura. Tony tried to hide his erection, which just made it funnier for the crew and annoyed him even more that he could be such putty in Marilyn's hands, so to speak, because she had power over any straight man to make them do pretty much anything, and certainly after a long kissing scene such as this. It was doubly embarrassing for him since he succumbed to the woman who had enraged him while she made him wait for hours throughout the shoot, often while he and Jack Lemmon were dressed in a wig, dress, and painful high heels. He made his distaste obvious to everyone on the crew. Just as obviously, Marilyn made it clear to the crew that she had the ultimate power and, since they were all guys, none felt sorry for Tony.

In the end, Marilyn's dramatic as well as comedic talent shone. Her comic timing was evident from the beginning, but when you watch her last completed film, *The Misfits*, which was also Clark Gable's last, you see her as a senior lady of drama. She had found a way to know both how she looked inside the camera and how to act flawlessly at the same time. The great Marilyn Monroe could do it all at once.

I got MM out of my dressing room that day by telling her I was terrified of my scene with Gregory Peck, one of our greatest actors, and needed her help because I didn't want to make a fool of myself. She couldn't refuse. Together, we went to my scene, which was to be an all-day event of reshoots. I had told Lily to call her hair and makeup people to come over to do Marilyn while she watched and supported me. The first three takes were good enough that the director had what he wanted. The rest of the day was taken up with reaction shots and different angles for the editors or to match color stock.

After those first three takes, I snuck Marilyn back to her set on the soundstage next door. She was already made up and went to work happy, and instead of needing help, she was able to provide it. Evidently, it was good day, as reported back by Jane Russell.

But those notebooks! She showed them to me several times over the years. She could think. Odd to realize Arthur Miller was considered the intellectual while Marilyn a bimbo. You talked to her for five minutes and realized her IQ was higher than yours. She positioned herself flawlessly. For media interviews, she just turned it on and gave them what they wanted and what she wanted them to see. Watch her sing happy birthday to President Kennedy. No publicist, no adviser, no director could have done better, reached more people, or had better product placement. She was sewn into her dress, but that's what we did. We weren't there for reality. We were there for separate scenes someone stitched together in a dark editing room to make a story, like the dress sewn on her back while she waited to go out on the floor of Madison Square Garden. This was brilliant marketing for her, but also a labor of love. I don't know exactly what went on between her and the president, but something sure did.

She understood her sexuality but didn't believe it was real. She liked men but also slept with a few women. She had an open mind about a lot of things—she did, after all, convert to Judaism when she married Arthur Miller, who always said he never pushed her. She lived with her first acting coach, Natasha, for years, walking naked around the house all day. They had an affair, although Natasha said in later interviews that Marilyn didn't like sex.

I don't know—maybe she just didn't like sex with Natasha. Marilyn admitted she'd had affairs with Marlene Dietrich, Joan Crawford, and Barbara Stanwyck. Her attitude was: why not? "Sex is something you do with people you like. What could be wrong with a natural act?" she told a friend. When I asked her about her affair with Crawford, she just laughed and said, "She has bigger balls than all the guys!" Marilyn liked to conquer people. She was unsure about her intellect, but while also unsure about her body, she knew how to use it to manipulate others. It was one of the ways she sought affirmation. In the end, she could bring the greatest stars like Dietrich and Crawford to their knees before her.

In view of her need to conquer, Marilyn became insanely jealous of Grace Kelly after she married Prince Rainier. She would scowl and say,

"She got to be a real princess, and look at the rest of us! What do we get?"

Despite her box-office success, Grace was never really one of the 1950s blondes. True, we competed for roles and maybe a man or two. When she filmed *High Society*, she was widely rumored to have had an affair with Frank Sinatra, her costar. In fact, she had been rumored to have had an affair with him before the movie, when I dated him. Afterward, Frank had a certain gleam in his eye and a stupid grin whenever she came up in conversation or there was a picture of her in the press, which didn't warm me to her. Then again, she was rumored to have had affairs with half of Hollywood, which didn't warm her to the rest of us. Because of Frank's stupid affair with her, Grace and I avoided each other. We met from time to time and were polite, but I found her calculating, always seeking something more. Her "more" was to become a princess. For someone who had once had freedom to do what she wanted, her royal role became a prison, a cautionary tale of be careful what you wish for.

This was the real reason she wasn't one of us. She needed to distance herself from her past to be a royal. To play that part meant getting into character, and getting into character meant letting go of her former life. She dropped all of us even more than we dropped her.

Her career was shorter than the rest of the blondes, only ten films, eleven if you count *Fourteen Hours*, where she had two on-screen minutes. She was good, no question, snagging an Academy Award for *The Country Girl*, but she left it all behind for her biggest role, Princess of Monaco. That lasted from her marriage in 1956 until her untimely death in 1982. While I have often felt my greatest role was living as a lady, it wasn't forced on me by others. I controlled the decisions I could and made the best of those thrust upon me. Grace, on the other hand, once she made the fateful decision to say *I do*, was stuck playing the same role forever. As she told a friend, "I know where I am going to be every single day for the rest of my life."

I got out of my bad *I do's* in a way she never could. With three children who were the children of a head of state, bye-bye marriage meant bye-bye babies, too. Those shackles all of us understood. It was as close to pity as we could get.

Worse, Grace herself had to pay for this final role. She gave Rainier an $18 million dowry in today's dollars to be a princess since Monaco was impoverished. It was in no small part due to her efforts that the principality became home to the world's millionaires. Still, despite all the gossip we heard, which most of the world didn't, the rest of us wondered if we would have done the same thing given the chance.

Despite her monstrous talent, Marilyn remained completely insecure. In her continued obsession over Grace's marriage, she asked over and over if she should have gone after Rainier and become a princess. She thought it might have finally given her the respect she deserved. "With me around, Gracie never would have stood a chance," she said with a frown. She understood, however, that her sex bomb image versus Grace's ice queen one disqualified her. "I would have liked to be a real princess," she confided wistfully. "They would have to bow and not treat me like a bimbo, always waiting to see when they can get laid." While she used sex as a weapon, she did it because it was the best option she had.

I pointed out that as a princess, the reverse would be true, too. She wouldn't be able to date whom she liked either. That gave her pause.

Eventually, it must have given Grace pause, too, given her Hollywood reputation.

Sex remained central for Marilyn. She may have said it was only natural to have sex with people you liked, but she believed it was even more natural to use sex to gain power. That's how she got the Kennedys—both Jack and Bobby. Why not the president? It was the ultimate validation. Not only was he powerful, but he was also completely confident and from an important family. Everything Marilyn wasn't.

Old Joe Kennedy, the president's father, had a Hollywood stint, where he out-finagled the original Jewish studio heads whom he never liked given his antisemitic views, at one point ran three studios, and sold out just before the 1929 market crash, making a profit of $5 million, a huge fortune at the time. He had been an early backer of the talkies as well as Gloria Swanson's lover. She ended up hating him after he fleeced her production company, leaving her a million dollars in debt. The reason Roosevelt named Joe Kennedy head of the Securities and Exchange Commission after the 1929 market crash was because he could clean up Wall Street since he knew how to cook the books better than all of them.

While not exactly a pariah in Hollywood, Joe made a lot of enemies. But he had money, knew the business, and loved the girls, so he would show up from time to time. His daughter, Patricia, the president's sister, was married to the actor, Peter Lawford, whom I met through Frank Sinatra. Later, John F. Kennedy would hang out with his brother-in-law, Peter, who knew how to get hot girls. There were parties where we were invited, and others where we were not—you can imagine what went on at those. Whatever I have or haven't done, billing by the hour wasn't one of them. There were stories, none G-rated, that made the rounds. It was the fifties and sixties. Few people remember the sixties accurately because they were usually high. About drugs, sex, and the president, everyone knew, but nobody said. You could keep things out of the media in those days.

One way in which Marilyn equaled or exceeded the president was charisma. Another was fame. The charge between them was electric and felt by everyone when they were in the same room. I chatted with Marilyn about her relationship with the president, whom I stayed clear of in incriminating situations, given his well-deserved reputation. I didn't need the validation or the potential scandal. This was a major way in which Marilyn and I differed. I didn't need constant validation.

In the early sixties, Marilyn and I were having drinks at my house in the Hills, and she alluded to the president having a large cock. She saw my jaw drop, because it was unexpected to hear the commander in chief described as well-hung. For some reason, the comment struck me as funny. I laughed. She laughed. Usually, when you're laughing about a penis, it's neither funny nor a compliment. As Woody Allen responded after he was asked when he learned he was a comedian, "On my wedding night."

"At least it's big," Marilyn said and poured us more Dom Perignon, her favorite champagne. "In this town, it's usually the other way around. When I was a nobody, I had a fling with one studio head." She looked at me over the glass as she sipped. "His dick was just as small as his brain." She giggled. "We had one date. I could have managed his small dick. His mind, well, you really couldn't overlook that."

Asked once how the president was, Marilyn just smiled and

famously replied, "I think I made his back feel better."

I remembered that discussion because I would run into John, Jr., who had become a friend of my son, Anders, when he went to Yale. John would come down to New Haven from Brown to visit his cousin, Timmy Shriver. I heard a lot of the stories. The kids were famous for breaking into Yale's gym, then the largest in the world, to skinny dip at midnight. They would get caught because campus police would see the elevator lights going up and down for races at two in the morning. Anders and John became friends because when they met, they didn't recognize each other— John was in his "poodle" phase, with hair in a long Afro. Anders didn't recognize him, and they talked for a long time and became friendly. John appreciated that Anders liked him without first knowing who he was. Then, too, it became clear Anders didn't want anything and understood the press game and how to keep out of the media, to the best extent possible, when he had a mother like me and hung out with John, Jr.

Eventually they realized they had met when they were toddlers. I was invited to the White House for a dinner, where Mrs. Kennedy had started a school for her young children, including those of the staff. Since Anders and John were of similar age, I dropped him off for class on the day of the dinner. John, whose security detail allowed him the run of the White House, took Anders to the Oval Office to wait for his daddy, and the two of them spent the time jumping on the sofa and hiding under the president's desk. When President Kennedy came in, he found the two of them playing under his desk, gave them candy, and had a sweet time before the nannies arrived so he could work. I have a treasured picture of the three of them from that afternoon.

One day, Anders and John showed up at my apartment for a New York weekend. John came to talk to me privately. He had found the picture of him, Anders, and his father on my mantel. He wanted to know about his father—was I another of his conquests? I told him no, that Marilyn had been my friend. He wanted to know about her, so I told him what I knew. About a year later, John showed up at my apartment door on his own. "I can't go home," he said. "There's a big dinner I don't want to get caught up in," which I presumed meant his mother had a date, but I didn't ask. I let him into the guest room. In the middle of the night, I heard a noise in the kitchen, and there he was, stark naked, standing at the fridge drinking orange juice out of the carton, which normally drove me crazy. However, I was looking at other things. This time, it was like son like father, and I understood what Marilyn had talked about. He was completely unembarrassed about displaying his large penis. I went back to bed, and he followed. We ended up sleeping together several other times as well, and it was always sweet. I remember chatting in bed one morning, and his question about whether I had ever slept with his father popped into my mind, *I wonder what your mother would hate more—if I had slept with her husband or just have now with her son?* It was a good question, and one Jackie never got a chance to answer.

In MM's diaries, which she showed me for the last time a few months before she died, there were writings, scribbles really, that could have referred to the president, since it was about power and a white house ringed with subterfuge, whatever that meant. Those notebooks have disappeared. At least, no one has ever claimed they still exist. Alas, I don't have photographic memory, and I didn't think at the time they might be important.

Years later, the famed journalist Seymour Hersh was working on his book, *The Dark Side of Camelot,* which did much to correct the false, glowing image of Camelot, which Jackie invented. There was a scandal involving documents for sale, including a purported hush money contract between Marilyn and the President. Sy came up to my house in LA one day to ask questions as he researched his book. He reminded me of the studio execs from the early days—his energy was nonstop, and he cut you off when he had gotten enough of an answer to move things along. He wasn't rude exactly but was completely driven. No time to waste. In the end, he determined the file was faked and didn't use it, but he was accused in a media-manufactured brouhaha of almost using the documents—which made no sense, given he'd researched what would have been a journalistic gold mine and then walked away. They would have had to be forgeries. JFK was too smart and had people who were too smart to put anything that delicate in writing. As for Marilyn, she was never a gold digger and never mentioned anything to me about receiving money from any of the Kennedys.

As for the notebooks, I told Sy what I'd seen. Some of Marilyn's writings surfaced later, and it amused me to see the surprised tones from reviewers that she had a mind in there. More and more writings would trickle out in the long years after her death when someone died, leaving a surprise archive, and heirs wanted money or someone still living decided to cash out. It was the story of her life—all those others profiting from her work while it destroyed her. Some of the more intriguing notebooks— the ones I had seen about the president, ones with details—were never found.

Who knows what happened? Did someone get there first as with a lot of other things in Marilyn's life?

So, MM and the president had something going. How could it be a surprise? Each was at the top of their game. Each vanished into history much too early, gone by 1963.

Marilyn's last film was 1962's *Something's Got to Give* for Fox. A romantic comedy, it was given gravitas by George Cukor, its formidable director, and Dean Martin, Marilyn's costar. Dean was a founding member with Sinatra of the Rat Pack, the in-group of 1950s male stars who hung out together, got drunk together, and went to Vegas together, trolling for broads. Not surprisingly, the group included JFK's brother-in-law, Peter Lawford. They were known for partying and womanizing—not all of it just for media presence as is done today. Then, they mostly meant it. And they were all, except for Lawford, big enough not to worry about getting more press.

Dean was huge as a singer, actor, and comedian. Some of his greatest success stemmed from his comedies with Jerry Lewis. He had the stature to be a good romantic comedy partner with Marilyn.

Cukor was happy to make another comedy with such big stars. But he was worried about Marilyn, who was becoming more and more unstable. When she wasn't hours late, she was out sick. After thirty-two days of shooting, he had been able to get her on film for only a few minutes at huge production costs. Finally, Twentieth Century Fox fired her. She was dead within two months, and both George and I felt her firing was yet another massive jolt in her unstable life. On the other hand, as bad as the studios were, sometimes you just had to show up for work. She couldn't.

In fairness to Marilyn, she had been severely ill the past year and had had several surgeries. When filming began, she had sinusitis. Her doctors asked for a postponement, but Twentieth Century Fox refused, having already delayed and spent millions on preproduction. The studio neared bankruptcy from cost overruns on Elizabeth Taylor's *Cleopatra*. Elizabeth also missed a lot of shooting due to illness, although that didn't stop her outings with Richard Burton as they were at the beginning of their affair. Fox hoped Marilyn's film would provide the revenue to survive *Cleopatra's* cost overruns.

Marilyn was absent due to sickness much of the next six weeks. Yet with her, it was hard to know. There were press sightings and outings, which she always did to maintain her image. She had missed work for years. After she was fired, the studio publicly blamed her absences on mental instability and drug addiction. They also circulated the rumor she went AWOL to sing for President Kennedy's birthday at Madison Square Garden, but she had, in fact, been invited by the White House months before and received clearance from the producers. Watching her up there singing happy birthday to "Mr. President," where she was late as usual coming onstage and introduced as "the late Marilyn Monroe," there was no doubt about her star power. Nothing shone brighter on the screen.

This was what Cukor wanted for his film. No one expected she would have missed so many days of shooting by the time she went to New York. On the other hand, how surprised could they be? This was Marilyn Monroe. Because she felt badly that the film was so far behind, when she returned, she went nude on a cleared set for her swimming pool scene. She generated enormous publicity and hoped her swim would pull in a huge

68

audience, which sadly never happened. The nude scene was her apology gift to Cukor.

With his career on the line, and after thirty-two days of filming, Cukor asked for her firing. I was unhappy with him, but he faced ruin being millions over budget and having only seven and half usable minutes of Marilyn on film. He told me he regretted it for the rest of his life but felt he had been placed in an untenable position. In the middle, I could see everyone's viewpoints, but it didn't make any difference. I wanted Marilyn to survive and live. She had either forced herself and Cukor into a corner or been forced into one by Fox when they insisted she work when she was ill. Her reputation, however, preceded her. She had caused so many delays and cost overruns over her career that it was almost impossible to take her at her word.

I went to see her and had seldom seen her so angry. "I've made them millions, I was sick with the doctors saying we needed to postpone, and this is how they treat me? I'm crazy? I'm the drug addict? What about Elizabeth, who missed more work than I did and they're paying her a million dollars?" I didn't argue with her or tell her she had been Jekyll and Hyde, turning into an angry, belligerent monster when she was drunk. I wasn't there for those episodes but had heard about them from Frank Sinatra, who'd remained close to her after they'd had a fling years before. She was spiraling, but she had spiraled before.

Cukor couldn't take a career hit with a financial disaster. Everyone was angry, and there were legal suits against Marilyn, against her costar Dean Martin, and from Dean to the studio when they replaced Marilyn with Lee Remick, since his contract stipulated he was to play opposite

Marilyn. If Fox lost Dean, they were really in trouble, since it would be the end of the movie without either of its two stars.

Despite five nominations for best director, George Cukor sometimes had trouble, given his orientation. He found work but needed to keep his sex life secret. Red baiting and gay bashing in Hollywood had a certain ring to it since the two attitudes often came from the same people. His talent was so formidable and his skill directing women so great that he could surmount the criticism. However, he had to live with being considered one of the girls by some studio execs, which made him self-censor.

He was replaced as the director on *Gone with the Wind* because Clark Gable refused to work with a "fairy." Of course, the backstory was even more interesting. Gable had allegedly worked as a male hustler when he arrived in Hollywood, and Cukor was the client who knew too much. Despite his success, George walked a very narrow line and was scared Marilyn would cost him his career—which more than survived since he would go on to win best director Oscar for *My Fair Lady* starring Audrey Hepburn two years later.

In the end, Fox, having sunk so much money into the production, had begun negotiations to rehire Marilyn to finish the film. Instead, she killed herself. While everyone blamed her suicide on her firing and downward drug and alcohol spiral, I wondered if she wanted to be fired. She told me she was terrified—it was a lot of pressure to be Marilyn Monroe. "I've been ill, I have surgical scars, and I don't look like I used to," she worried. "It's hard to be on camera if I don't glow, and how long can I hide getting old?" she asked. "I know how I look on screen."

I always wondered if her suicide was caused not only by being fired but also because they planned to rehire her. She didn't want to be on screen if she couldn't be the Marilyn Monroe she wanted to be. She dared not refuse a part, though. If she gave in to her fear, how could her demons ever let her go back to work? A year older than I, she was terrified about getting older and how she looked. It was 1962, she was gone, and I was 35. I wasn't far behind her.

Years later, just after my father told me she was my half-sister, I watched the outtakes from *Something's Gotta Give*. Marilyn illuminated the screen as usual, but there were moments when I could see her aging despite her luminosity. You couldn't take your eyes off her—she filled the screen—but she had been right, after all, about how she looked. Her age was starting to show at thirty-six. Few people have ever looked better, but that wasn't enough.

At the end, Marilyn was very much alone although she remained close to Sinatra, who tried to protect her. He would call me when he was particularly worried about her, hoping maybe I could reach her in a way he couldn't. I had a complicated relationship with Sinatra, who was a star in the same mold as Dean Martin, except bigger. I remember that skinny kid with big ears and bigger voice—unlike the aging heavyset figure at the end of his career, after he'd been on top for fifty years. He, too, was a player, with girl after girl. We had a short fling between my marriages, but it never came to anything. He demanded too much, and I wanted to work, so I could never put him first—and he needed to be first. While he wasn't surprised I wouldn't give up my career for him, he didn't like it. I wasn't the right girl to ride those gossamer wings and have him fly me to the moon since there was no way to compete with either his colorful personal life or his professional one, which was as big as they come.

It's almost impossible today to imagine how big Sinatra was at the height of his fame. He remains one of bestselling singers in the world, selling over 150 million records, won an Academy Award for *From Here to Eternity*, starred in numerous films and television shows, including his own, *the Frank Sinatra Show*, started music label Reprise Records, and continued recording and performing until his death in 1998. He was one of the first singers mobbed by the bobby soxers, girls wearing the short white socks in style during the 1940s and 1950s. These girls would literally swoon at the sight of him and jump and scream during performances— scenes that 1950s musicals recreated since all audiences back then understood the significance. Known throughout the world as *ol' blue eyes*, he was rich, famous, successful, a true artist, and a womanizer from his twenties but had been performing since his teens. While he never fully learned to read music, he had an impeccable ear and sense of timing.

His first major break to fame happened when he toured with Tommy Dorsey's band. He recorded over forty singles the first year. Eventually, he needed to go out on his own, but he had signed a contract giving Dorsey 43 percent of his lifetime earnings. He sued and eventually got out of the contract in August 1943, but there were rumors that things were actually settled at the end of gun—with a threat by Sinatra's mob godfather, Willie Moretti, from the Genovese crime family. At the start, Dorsey and Sinatra had been close, and Sinatra learned from him the basics that made his career, but they never made up after this break, with Dorsey ever after making snide remarks like "He's the most fascinating man in the world, but don't put your hand in the cage" until Dorsey's death in 1956, when Sinatra was too big to touch.

Given his enormous stature, which permitted him to do pretty much whatever he wanted, Frank was bothered that I thought highly of Bing Crosby. Frank barely forgave me when I was asked in an interview to compare his singing to Bing's. Trying to be tactful, I said the difference was that Sinatra belted out his phrases so they stuck in our memories while Bing crooned his melodies so they flowed seamlessly. Sinatra was not happy. He felt I had publicly said Bing was better, which he was. When Frank wasn't happy—or really unhappy as he was with me—you had to take it seriously, given his friends. Or some of his friends, the ones who made it difficult for him to continue to hang out with the Kennedys once they were in the White House, like his godfather.

I had to make a peace offering. In a sense, it didn't really matter since Sinatra never completely forgave me, but afterward I didn't have to worry about sleeping, either. When my career hit the skids later in the sixties, I wondered what had happened and if anyone had done anything. When I made out my list, and checked it twice, Frank was at the top.

There were lots of stories after the JFK assassination. The links came out later, and they started making sense when you heard the names, remembering them from one party or another, and saw their connections placed into context. Judith Exner, Sam Giancana, who was at one or another party—but not with the Kennedys. John Jr. had questions about these people, but I gave an edited version of those I had met and what I knew. I'm willing to bet Jackie learned a good deal more about what happened and who was involved, but she carried those secrets to the grave.

I hoped and expected she didn't tell John, Jr. either, so as not to put him at risk. When he died in his plane crash, my first thought was to wonder if he had dug into something someone didn't want him to know. At the time, he was founder and publisher of the political magazine, *George*. He was a sweet guy and a good friend. After we stopped sleeping together, we would have lunch from time to time. I am sorry none of us got to learn what he would have become. His death was a huge loss.

I attended the funeral with Anders. We stood at the back. I never told him about John and myself—it wasn't appropriate—but he will learn of it now because of this one-woman show. Nothing says let it all hang out like telling your children you slept with their friends.

I didn't know and didn't want to, but I am not surprised. I slept with a few people that I don't what her to find about, either. But John was really a sweetheart, and it broke my heart when he died. Clearly, he was always close to my mother.

I did know Frank Sinatra, and he always gave me candy and a hundred-dollar bill whenever he saw me—and when I was young, that was a lot of money. He also made it clear that if anything happened that I didn't like, I was to tell him. The one time I did tell him, when I was 14, made my mother furious. I didn't understand then why. I had so little idea about the world when I was a kid and my mother had to teach me. She did, but when I did something she didn't like, such as talking to Uncle Frank, she could be very tough. She was right. I didn't know how badly we could all get burned. We got burned enough as it was without me being such an idiot.

Anders

MY CHILDREN

If up to now I have said little about my kids, it's because they won't like this show at all and talking about them will just make things worse. I have to say a few things from time to time, and I do, but I have always drawn the line at publicizing my children. It was bad enough they had me for a mother. Or two of me—the real me, with my human faults, and the public me, with my image in the press, which for them was far worse. I have managed my public image quite well, so I'm considered a great lady of the screen, who mostly kept her private life private except for six husbands and a couple of sensational divorces. As I said, playing a great lady has been my greatest role.

Motherhood, not so much.

Like my mother wrote, not a lot to say here. She ended up being a good mother, a good grandmother, and a great great-grandmother. Sometimes it was a rocky road.

Anders

MID-LIFE HUSBANDS

From my first divorce, I learned five things. One, don't wave a gun at your spouse if you don't want to file for divorce the next day. Two, don't expect marriage to improve problems—it just makes them worse. Three, chemistry doesn't improve over time. Four, with a small dick, size matters. And five, having the studio tell you, "It's for your own good" is always the kiss of death.

I was twenty-four and Sebastian was three when I got my first divorce. My ex and I kept most of the trash-talk out of the press, saving it for later. As a single woman, I needed companionship, not to mention a good lay every now and then, which I deserved after my first husband. I didn't cheat on him. I was young and naive, and I believed in fidelity. What a joke! It's the little woman who stays behind, keeping house, while the husband just thinks she's too dumb to know. But we know. The ones that don't, don't want to. Every time I see a woman on *Oprah* or some other show, whining that they had no idea, I just have to ask, really? No idea? He's slept with twenty women in your eight years of marriage, and you didn't have a clue? Moron!

Husband No. 1 didn't sleep with twenty women during our four-year marriage. His dick was too small for that. However, he wasn't totally faithful, either. It's Hollywood, folks, where the most important bulge in a man's pants is his wallet.

Worse than the bad sex was not being accepted, appreciated, or listened to. Sometimes, I just wanted to be heard. I didn't need advice, didn't need to be fixed, didn't need someone fight my battles. I just wanted a conversation. As Tallulah Bankhead, the great movie star daughter of the

Speaker of the House, used to say, "Darling, if you want a partner for conversation, become a lesbian." She did. I didn't.

I had to kiss Catherine Deneuve for a vampire movie. How we both agreed I still can't figure out, but we were paid. When they resort to girl-on-girl action to sell tickets, there are always pompous studio execs who think because this turns them on, others will pay for it, too. It was a nice kiss, but I felt nothing. We went to grab coffee after the take. In Paris, it was really good coffee because the French would have walked off the set if the usual American drip was served. We had one French grip on the set who took one look at the big canister of American coffee for the American crew, turned up his nose, and said in a heavy French accent, "Zhe probleme wis American coffee is zhat ten minutes after you drink hit, hit makes you shit!" and stalked off. To this day, I can't look at what is now called Café Americain without thinking of that grip.

I looked at Catherine, one of the greatest French beauties, and said, "Nice kiss, but nothing."

She laughed. "Unfortunately, a lot of guys are like that, too. You kiss them, and it's nothing."

My response? "In America, we joke about kissing a lot of frogs to find our prince. Sadly, that's no fairy tale." We smiled as the makeup people descended to redo our faces. Been there, done that.

A spark-generating kiss is a rarity. Attraction is easy, but someone who moves you, even if they're the right sex, is hard to find. This was apparent to me because I was dating. Some were real dates, and others were setups by the studio or publicists. We didn't get paid for those gigs as the kids do now. We just were working it. Eventually, I started seeing another actor. Blond, with muscles and a hairy chest, he was a stud who could more or less act. He had an action series on TV, which in those days was considered second class to film. He was smart, had a producer credit, and was financially secure, although not rich. At the time, I didn't need money, and we had a good time. Eventually, one thing led to another, and we got married.

It seemed like a good idea at the time. We were happy, but I was traveling, filming, and doing publicity junkets. You would hit a city, usually NY, LA, or London, and the press would be there. The studio would set up two cameras—one on the star, the other on the newscaster—and run both simultaneously, allowing the station to edit them as they pleased and use as much of their anchor as they wished. Local stations loved this, and we would do these things for hours—five minutes per station, so each local Podunk station could claim "An Exclusive at Six and Ten" with their anchor. There was a reason stars got paid the enormous salaries they did. Advertising a film was expensive, but this was free publicity, and the bigger the star, the more free publicity they got.

We married, had a great time in the sack in a lot of positions, and then I went on a publicity tour after six weeks. Then on location for another film. Then fittings in Paris for another film set during the war. Husband No. 2 was a hot man, and I didn't marry him because he couldn't get a date. While the cat was away, this mouse banged everything in town. His proclivities included black latex, thigh-high boots, and a whip. The deal was you couldn't leave marks where it would show if he was filming shirtless the next day. It was a thrill, but I could have a good time without latex. Or whips. Or strap-ons.

We drifted apart. It was fun while it lasted, but I couldn't see him as a father to Sebastian, and I couldn't imagine growing old with him—wheeling after him in the nursing home, still in latex boots with whip in hand. We had an amicable divorce. He was honorable and didn't ask for a thing except the Ferrari, which I was happy to give him. He deserved it for not trying to screw me in court. I continued liking him until he died suddenly of a heart attack at the young age of fifty-two. Even though I hadn't seen him in years, it saddened me more than I thought it would. He didn't leave much money, and after I was financially secure, I arranged things so I paid his kids' tuition without his widows ever finding out. He deserved it for widening our cultural scene and supporting all the S&M clubs in LA.

There was one more thing. He listened. We could talk. There wasn't much pretense in our marriage or after. He let me express myself. I can't tell you how wonderful it was to have a man actually listen. After we went our separate ways, we lived in different worlds but would talk every now and then, sometimes years apart, and could pick up where we left off. We respected each other. After latex, leather, and whips, pretense is lame, so we were always truthful. In a sense, it was a good marriage. Otherwise, I wouldn't have gotten to know him. I never regretted it, although maybe I should have. Six is a big number.

No. 3? Sadly, not much to tell. We married, and he was dead in three months. On our honeymoon, he complained about an itch on his leg. Neither of us thought much about it. We got home, and two weeks later he began coughing blood. We raced to Cedars for an exam. The news wasn't good. He had malignant melanoma, which had already spread to his lungs.

Soon after, his brain. There was nothing I could do but watch. I got round-the-clock nurses and watched him shrivel up under the sheets as the disease progressed. We kept the morphine high. I preferred he not suffer even if it meant he was out of it. It wasn't like he was going dancing otherwise. Or would have any quality of life dying at thirty-four. He knew who I was until a few days before the end, when we moved him to the hospital and he drifted away forever. I didn't know what he knew or could feel but didn't want to take a chance he was in pain. I hope the morphine shortened his life, but I doubt it—he would have built up resistance. It was gruesome, and I sent Sebastian to stay with friends in Paris who had a son the same age because I didn't want him to witness it. I didn't even want to watch.

I remember the relief I felt when the doctor said he had passed. And the guilt. For him, I was relieved since the end was coming no matter what, and I didn't want him to suffer. For myself, I was relieved because the immense pressure of watching someone you love slowly die in front of you, of waiting for it to be over and yet hoping to have more time, had ended. I didn't want him gone, I didn't want him to die, but I did want it over. I felt guilty feeling that way. I had no choice in any of this, and neither did he, but we did have to tell the doctors what we wanted. They didn't have much choice, either, since they couldn't do anything except adjust the morphine drip and refuse unnecessary treatment after I told them not to prolong his suffering.

And I had to tell them. Otherwise, they would have done all kinds of things. Feeding tube? Were they crazy? Restart his heart? Even worse. Common sense in medicine seemed almost impossible. Instead of angels looking over my shoulder, I felt lawyers instead. What they wanted was not to get sued. Above the doctors was the hospital and its board of directors whose lawyers wanted to avoid lawsuits and bad publicity. I was a risk because I generated huge media as I came and went. If I made a wrong remark to the press, it would generate days of hugely unfavorable coverage for the hospital and its board. The nurses tried very hard to reduce No. 3's suffering, but mine was less important.

I understood the hospital covering its ass, but I resented it. I wanted things to be about the preservation of health and life, but that has nothing to do with modern medicine, whose values have degenerated along with much else. I felt like I was dealing with the studio—the idea that the story remained most important was an illusion. What mattered more was money.

I knew Judy Garland a bit. Victor, my first agent, introduced us. He had made her career when he put her in *The Wizard of Oz*. However, she had so much talent, she would have risen to the top no matter what. She had a rough life and never made big money despite her talent. She was a creature of the studios who profited far more from her skills than she ever did. I learned she also had the best drugs ever. Asked if those were sugar pills for energy, her priceless reply was, "Honey, if those were sugar pills, I would have had diabetes long ago!"

I was twelve when *The Wizard of Oz* came out in 1939. Tickets cost a dime, which was a lot. I don't remember how we got the money to go— we didn't have extra—but it was a huge treat. A dime was plenty during the depression. John D. Rockefeller, the richest man in the world, was famous for handing them out. I don't think I can describe how wonderful the movie was, the first time seeing something in color let alone the dialogue, dancing, singing, acting, direction, set decor, and makeup. It remains one of the best movies ever made. Sitting there watching Glinda the Good Witch float around in her bubble or Judy dancing down the Yellow Brick Road, I never imagined I would know her, let alone call for her advice. For modern audiences, the only comparable film technology that changed how you experienced the movies might have been the first digital special effects in the first *Star Wars* in 1977 as the battle cruiser flies overhead. Not even 2009's *Avatar* in 3D rivaled that first shock of on-screen color. Despite today's new technology, The *Wizard of Oz* remains timeless—its special effects, limited as they were, not dated. Judy still causes goose bumps when you hear her sing "Over the Rainbow." Later, her daughter Liza repeated her mother's feat of dancing, singing, and acting in her own Academy-Award-winning role in *Cabaret.* Two generations and two roles of greatness, but great as *Cabaret* was, it didn't equal *The Wizard of Oz.*

There I was, depressed about Husband No. 3's sudden death, when I ran into Judy. We chatted, and then she pulled out two pills from her handbag and handed them to me. Take one now, she advised, and the other before bed. You will be fine tomorrow. The next morning, I was a bit groggy, but depressed no more. What she given me worked better than years of therapy. She had the best dispensary in Hollywood and knew what she was doing better than professionals. I used her dispensary from time to time, which was less about access than her hard-won advice, and repaid her with gifts. The one thing I couldn't do was help her help herself financially. My gifts didn't pay rent or prepare her for old age. Needless to say, she had another plan in mind, which I was very sorry about. She was one of the brightest stars in the sky and burned herself out. If you weren't married to her, directing her, or financing her, you loved her.

Of my marriages, the third was the saddest because I never found out what might have happened. After that, I was done marrying. I was twenty-nine and had already had three husbands. Enough was enough. Or so I thought.

Mother's marriages meant more to her than to us. I knew, of course, Sebastian's dad. He was around for much of our lives, but I saw him in a very different way prior to reading this book. Sadly, I will never see a diamond bracelet without thinking of him.

The other husbands, they were gone and sometimes dead before I knew they existed, which is a bit weird all by itself. Yes, I know mothers and fathers have sex, I am a father and that's how I got to be one, but still, it's something else to read about your mother's sex life.

Sebastian had it more difficult. My father was dead. His father was in the press as a cheapskate with a small dick. That's tough to live with. It was also difficult to live with my mother's unspoken anger against him. She said she forgave him, but I am not sure she really did. When she was down and out and alone, he didn't help. Not something easily forgiven.

Anders

FIRST ACADEMY AWARD

One of the greats, Katharine Hepburn was a generation before mine. We knew each other as a nodding thing through George Cukor, who had directed her in her first film, *A Bill of Divorcement,* opposite John Barrymore in 1932. I was new school and nouveau riche to her old world, Protestant ethics. That said, the great public love of her life was married to someone else and refused to get a divorce. Evidently, her life suited her, since she never disavowed the relationship or married Spencer Tracy. It certainly wasn't a question I was going to ask. There were rumors both Hepburn and Tracy went the other way and began a relationship only for studio PR convenience. While the idea was not shocking, nor the idea that a pants-wearing, golf-playing Kate might like the ladies a complete surprise, she did have a deep fondness for Spencer and nursed him through the last years of his life. Some bonds go beyond sex. Some suggested that Kate's relationships were mostly platonic while others reported she hooked up frequently. Hollywood rumors! One of Hepburn's best friends was Cukor, with whom she made ten films including her early career's best-known work: *Little Women* in 1933, *Holiday* in 1938, *The Philadelphia Story* in 1940, *Adam's Rib* in 1949 and *Pat and Mike* with Spencer Tracy in 1953. In fact, she made more pictures with Cukor than she did with Spencer. They ran in the same circles, where sexual orientations were fluid if not totally gay.

Spencer's last movie, the 1967 film *Guess Who's Coming to Dinner,* was instigated by Hepburn—who put her salary in escrow, as did director, Stanley Kramer, to make the film. Spencer was so ill that Columbia Pictures reportedly couldn't get insurance for him if he needed to be replaced. The studio had cold feet anyway about the movie—a film about the interracial relationship of the daughter's character, where Hepburn and Spencer played her liberal Californian parents. The intended was played by one of our greatest black stars, Sidney Poitier. The studio guys thought the movie would tank and was risky financially. Who cared about an interracial movie that would expose the studio to backlash given that Southern states still had laws against miscegenation? In fact, there were theaters in the South that refused to show the movie. On the other hand, Katharine Hepburn was right—the movie made money and received ten Academy Award nominations, winning Kate her second-best acting Oscar. Columbia wasn't wrong to be worried. Sadly, Spencer Tracy died a few days after shooting finished.

Spencer liked the boys. He was also a prodigious drunk. I've seen a lot of people put it away, but Spencer's drinking was legendary. He also managed to be one of the most talented actors to ever grace the screen. Watch him now and you appreciate how good he was compared to the current crop of leading men. He lived for years in Cukor's guest house, where it became an open question of who was having an affair with whom, given the all-boy parties around Cukor's pool. Hollywood was a lot more open in the '30s and '40s than later, yet all major talent had morals clauses in their contracts. What was privately known needed to remain private. It wasn't public embarrassment keeping stars worried—it was loss of income. I believe the McCarthy hearings played a role in closing things down, even in private. Hollywood was always two places—and what was in the papers was never the best part.

To be honest, I liked the image I had of Hepburn. Thinking about her sex life didn't fit with what I saw on screen. In the end, that mattered more to me since we were not intimate friends. As an actress, she holds the record for the most Academy Awards, winning four out of twelve nominations during her sixty-year career, three of her four wins in her sixties and seventies. To put the numbers in perspective, Walt Disney won twenty-two, costume designer Edith Head won eight, and an unknown Cedric Gibbons, who designed the Oscar statuette, won eleven awards for art direction out of thirty-nine nominations. Hepburn thumbed her patrician nose at Hollywood and never showed up for a single awards ceremony to accept them. She did make an appearance once—wearing gardening shoes—to give a humanitarian award to her friend, MGM producer Lawrence Weingarten. She had her critics: Dorothy Parker once wrote of a Broadway performance, "Miss Hepburn ran the whole gamut of emotions—from A to B."

I had been cast as Marie Antoinette in a serious, as opposed to silly, costume drama. Kate was cast as Maria Theresa, Queen of Austria, her mother. There was a debate at the studio about whether to hire Robert Redford, who was already a leading man, or Sean Connery, who had yet to make it big as the first James Bond, to play my husband, Louis XVI. There was a serious casting problem: Marie Antoinette didn't get pregnant for the first seven years of marriage. There were marital issues with reams of saved letters from her mother describing in detail how to be a good wife and get pregnant, which was her sole purpose in life. She was the counterpart of most of the great actresses of my day. We served to make the men around us look good. We were to know our place.

With Robert Redford or Sean Connery, it wasn't believable to an audience—or anyone on earth for that matter—that she wouldn't have been knocked up in a week. Thus, casting had a problem. They needed a leading man, but he had to be believable in our serious drama. The historical backstory was true but not discussable in those days. The real Louis XVI had a physical problem—his foreskin was so tight that if it slipped back, it strangled the head of his penis, which was terribly painful and caused him to lose an erection. He could manage things by himself, since he was a guy, but with a partner, he couldn't keep his foreskin from slipping painfully back, which was the end of the game. The only solution was surgery, which he wasn't keen on, given the state of medicine in those days, not to mention the surgery's location. Had anyone thought to ask the Jews of France, this problem would have been solved far earlier and may have prevented the French Revolution. Marie Antoinette was hated because she wasn't a Mother of France, the title of the mother of a future king. There were dozens of pamphlets printed at the time describing her as the bitch from Austria (a wordplay in the French language), so by the time she did indeed become a mother, she had been vilified throughout France.

Louis XVI had good reason to be scared of doctors. His grandfather, Louis XV, was the grandson of Louis XIV, the Sun King, who had numerous sons and grandsons and who never doubted his succession was secure. God had other plans, as he often does, and influenza swept through France, killing all of them except the king and one tiny grandson. The future Louis XV survived because his nanny hid him the attic of Versailles so the doctors couldn't bleed him as they had the rest of his relatives, weakening them enough or introducing new infections so they died, thus leaving the baby heir to the throne. In retrospect, it would have been far better for France if the nanny hadn't hidden the child and had let the doctors kill him with their barbaric treatments as they did the others. It would have changed the course of history, but he was such a bad king, it was hard to imagine worse. Until his grandson, Louis XVI.

I was to play Marie Antoinette as a party princess, growing through motherhood and political intrigue, helping her incompetent husband, the king, who was riven with pain during the revolution, providing guidance for her children, suffering the loss of a child, and ending up middle-aged, threadbare, and poor in the Bastille prison. Our producers well understood the road to an Academy Award was to make a beauty plain and unattractive, suffering from tragedy while playing violins in the background, a formula Harvey Weinstein made into an art form, winning 81 Academy Awards out of 341 nominations before he came to shame.

Like a fairy tale with endless variations, the life of a princess who goes from queen to guillotine in less than a quarter of a century has endured as pop culture. While a silent 1922 German version exists, the first Hollywood Marie Antoinette production was the 1938 MGM version starring Norma Shearer, a rare box-office success in silent films who succeeded in talkies, winning best actress Academy Award for *The Divorcee* in 1932. She married MGM's legendary head of production, Irving Thalberg, providing her with power over her competition, all of whom resented her studio access, particularly Joan Crawford. In fact, while mostly forgotten now, Joan's feud with Norma rivaled her hatred of Bette Davis. Joan, however, remained at a major disadvantage in her disagreements with Norma, who was married to the boss.

Marie Antoinette originated with William Randolph Hearst as a vehicle for his mistress, Marion Davies, but after a major disagreement with Louis B. Mayer, MGM's founder, Hearst moved his productions to Warner Bros., leaving the *Marie Antoinette* project behind. Thalberg acquired it for his wife before his early death at age thirty-seven, two years before photography began.

Despite his short career, Thalberg's 400 productions, which included *Grand Hotel, China Seas, Camille, Mutiny on the Bounty,* and *The Good Earth,* made MGM the most successful studio in Hollywood. His early importance lives on as the honorary *Irving G. Thalberg Memorial Award* given for a body of work at the Academy Awards, which has been granted to a list of Hollywood greats such as Darryl Zanuck, Walt Disney, Alfred Hitchcock, Ingmar Bergman, Steven Spielberg, Clint Eastwood, and Francis Ford Coppola. The first woman to receive it was Kathleen Kennedy in 2019. Her body of work as a producer includes various *Star Wars* films, *Indiana Jones*, *Jurassic Park*, and *E.T.* among others. She founded Amblin Entertainment with Steven Spielberg and Frank Marshall, is president of Lucasfilm, and has been nominated for eight Academy Awards.

The 1938 film rebuilt the Versailles ballroom twice its original size to provide additional grandeur. Its costumes remain the most extravagant in film history. Designer Adrian Adolf Greenberg, who was costume designer on *The Wizard of Oz* and whose screen credits read just *Adrian*, had gone shopping in Austria and France to buy antique fabrics and laces. He had period paintings examined to duplicate laces and fabrics. This cost a ton and weighed almost as much—Norma Shearer's costumes in the film weighed together 1768 pounds, with her wedding dress alone weighing 108 pounds. Unfortunately, given all these details, the film was shot in black and white because the studio needed to save money after the huge costume and set expenses. I was always disappointed not to be able to see them in the color intended by those who worked on the film.

Despite the film's great box-office success, it lost money given its enormous production cost of almost three million dollars. It received four Academy Award nominations.

Fifty years after my film, another *Marie Antoinette* debuted, and it was interesting to see what changed. For one, it had a woman director, Sophia Coppola, niece of Francis. It was a sumptuous film as had been the Norma Shearer vehicle, where Sophia got the rare permission to shoot on location at Versailles and Le Petit Trianon. The story, which contained many factual elements amid the artistic license, didn't pull me in nearly as much as the costumes, food, decor, and jewels. It was a vapid life where the modern music served to underline its triteness. While I thought Kirsten Dunst as Marie Antoinette did a wonderful job in a film that was more decorative than dramatic, I never found the story line compelling. Since everyone knew the ending before the opening credits, the story had to make the audience see things in a new way.

Some critics loved Coppola's version. Roger Ebert wrote:

"This is Sofia Coppola's third film centering on the loneliness of being female and surrounded by a world that knows how to use you but not how to value and understand you. It shows Coppola once again able to draw notes from actresses who are rarely required to sound them."

I didn't disagree with that sentiment, but Ebert loved the film more than I did. Of course, maybe I was biased.

Fifty years before Coppola, Katharine Hepburn played my mother. Sweet. We went to lunch to get acquainted before the shoot. She was twenty years older and already a grande dame. She was too upper crust to play everything. I had been a whore, a gangster's moll, a princess, and a businesswoman. I don't think anyone would have bought Kate as a whore except maybe Spencer Tracy. As David O. Selznick, producer of *Gone with the Wind*, once said when Kate wanted the role of Scarlett, "I can't see Rhett Butler chasing *you* for twelve years!"

What she did do, however, she did superbly. Despite her public skepticism about our profession, saying, "Acting is the most minor of gifts . . . After all, Shirley Temple could do it when she was four," she was as disciplined as they come.

I don't remember much about lunch except it was planned by the studio. Press were there as we went in and out—news flash, actresses eat! We made chit chat, nothing special, and laughed about one of the producer's comments that he didn't know anything about Louis XIV other than the fact he made good furniture. Few people rolled their eyes like Kate.

The important thing about the lunch was something Kate said as a throwaway line, not thinking it important at the time, but it was something that came back to me often. In discussing my role, she said, "What's interesting isn't what people become because of what's happened to them. What's interesting is what they become in spite of it."

That line told me how to play my performance. It provided the subtext along with a story told by my old French friend, the countess both by birth and marriage, about how everyone has lineage, remembered or not. She had twin sisters among her ancestors during the French revolution. One was royalist, the other a revolutionary. Robespierre, leader of the revolutionaries, picked up the wrong one to cart off to the guillotine. The royalist one stood on the sidelines, watching her twin sister wheeled to her beheading, but neither said a word. They both knew that in any confusion, the revolutionaries, not the sharpest knives in the drawer under ordinary circumstances and worse under extraordinary ones, wouldn't be able to tell them apart and would execute both of them just to be sure they got the right one, leaving no one behind to look after the children. The wrong one went gallantly to her death, holding her head high. I thought of her during my scene of my beheading, and there weren't many dry eyes in the house opening night.

They ended up casting Tony Curtis as Louis XVI. That worked. He was at the top of his career for a few more years until it fizzled out at the end of the 1960s. He was sexy enough to be a leading man but not so sexy as to be unbelievable in the part, and the chemistry between us on screen was friendly, not hot, so we could deliver the picture of a couple dedicated to each other by circumstance but not passion.

I wasn't a big fan of Tony Curtis. I found him sexist and annoying after his stint with Marilyn in *Some Like it Hot*. The movie remains one of the greatest comedies of all time, but great as Jack Lemmon and Tony were, they owed its success to Marilyn, impossible as she was to work with. If Tony had just acknowledged that fact, I might have forgiven him. Moreover, my opinion didn't improve when he married his seventeen-year-old costar from his previous film just before we started shooting. The marriage lasted five years and produced two daughters. Sometimes, I wonder what I have to complain about—I never married him.

Poor Marilyn was gone by this time, but she would appear in my dreams and give me an earful for working with him. Her appearance was a good thing. It kept reminding me to say no to the studio docs who kept prescribing if you let them. After finding out what Marilyn had been taking and what was in her medicine cabinet when she died, I got my own physician and was more careful.

Tony had been born in New York, but his family were Hungarian Jewish refugees, and he didn't speak English until he was five and went to school. His pretend accent informed his performance as king, and whenever he was in character, he spoke in a stilted accent—not French, not Hungarian, and certainly not English as we know it. It worked and gave me something to play off in my performance as his wife, who aged from a silly princess married at age fourteen to the Dauphin of France into a mature, saddened, heavyset woman two weeks shy of thirty-eight at the time of her death.

While I could play the young twenty-year-old princess and keep aging, they cast a double for my fourteen-year-old character. They decided Tony should play the fourteen-year-old Louis. I thought he looked ridiculous, but it worked better on screen than on set. It didn't matter to the studio if men were age-appropriate or not, but women had to be pretty young things until we were old enough to play mothers. As I was a princess of Hollywood who'd had to grow up and take responsibility for my own career—learning not to trust the studio's advice and control, finding ways to break free of the elaborate Hollywood rituals relating to press, appearances, what we wore, who dressed us, where we were seen, and how we walked and spoke and gestured—it wasn't such a stretch to play a queen frozen into position by elaborate French court rituals. Marie Antoinette bristled at the notion that she couldn't even wash her hands or put on her makeup without being surrounded by dozens of courtiers. The royal family couldn't eat without it being open to the public, so she withdrew as much as she could to the Petit Trianon to preserve her sanity and gain some privacy.

This was an important performance for me on many levels. I identified with the role. As an actress at the top of her career, I feared my downfall. I didn't want professional beheading, but very few escaped falling from a high perch. After all, they had fired Marilyn. Maybe Elizabeth Taylor escaped crashing down, but she was unlike anyone else. And she was a tough professional who not only wasn't afraid to use her power but also used it wisely.

Thus, this role was personal, one of the most personal in my career. My shot at an Academy Award was icing on the cake, but my drive was my realization of how the role corresponded to my professional and personal life. I was mindful of *Cleopatra* in a lot of my scenes. In my mind, riding the cart to Marie Antoinette's execution paralleled Elizabeth's entering Rome as queen of Egypt and captive of Caesar. She was resplendent and beautiful beyond mortals. I was bedraggled yet determined to hold my head high so the world could see an aging queen one last time. I played exactly the opposite of Elizabeth's performance. Elizabeth may have escaped downfall in her life, but I was never in her position. There were no escapes for me.

My clothes were beyond elegant for the first half of the film. They hired famed Edith Head as costume designer, and the first thing I did when I walked into her office was ask that I be able to move and breathe. "Make my outfits look good but be bearable to act in throughout a scene for ten hours straight," I pleaded. Edith, who didn't win eight Academy Awards for nothing, looked me over, asked me walk ten paces, turn around and come back, then sit down and stand up. She made me do it again. Again, once more. Then she told me, "I can't make you comfortable for an all-day shoot. No one could be comfortable in a ball gown that long. I can give you movement, but we need the dresses to create your character. I want you to feel like a queen in them. Let's not pretend Marie Antoinette dressed for comfort." What skill, what intelligence, and what glorious costumes.

During the shoot, Bert Stern showed up to take a series of photos for an article on the movie for *Life Magazine*. In one of them, where I wore a design for Marie Antoinette's peasant dress for the Petit Trianon, my breasts are pushed up so high and my corset so tight, I couldn't breathe. Bert kept shooting. And shooting. I hated that shoot—never was I so uncomfortable. Then there was hair and makeup, which never ended. My makeup man ran out every five minutes to adjust, powder, and reapply. This went on for hours.

I may have looked like an idiot in my Marie Antoinette milkmaid's dress with my boobs pushed up, but it became the bestselling poster that year for the boys in the military. I hadn't done as much for those in uniform since I was a young starlet on tour with Dina Merrill and Bob Hope rallying the troops after World War II. Despite the discomfort of our milkmaid shoot, in the end, I was thrilled with Bert's results and loved that the servicemen liked my poster. All those boys jerking off to me—what an honor!

My milkmaid outfit was designed by Edith as were many of my personal clothes for the publicity around the film. The best designers highlighted your assets and camouflaged your faults. I was average height at five seven but slender, so normally designers made things cling to my waist and exaggerated my bust and derriere. To suggest the more complete figure of an older Marie Antoinette for the second half of the film, I used a padded undergarment to fill me out to middle-aged thickness. It was very uncomfortable and slowed my movement because it was stiff. Edith told me to use the padding's stiffness to move with Marie Antoinette's middle age and pain from being cooped up in a damp prison. Wonderful advice! With her words in my head, she, too, was with me every moment of my performance. Clothes do make the woman on screen.

One thing custom-made clothing does when done right is allow the weight of the garment to be carried on the shoulders so it flows and holds its shape against the body. Armhole positioning and cut are key, especially for men, since women in evening gowns often don't have shoulders. Cut, shape, and draping are important. Without it, you may as well wrap a brightly colored sheet on your body just to cover your nakedness.

Edith's young assistant, Ann Roth, was on the film and worked with us a great deal. She went on to great things and would come back into my life later as designer for my one-woman show.

I wish Edith could have made all my clothes. Instead, I found a seamstress who had trained and worked under her on numerous films. I paid a fraction of what I would have for couture, and everything was cut for me, made with fabrics that suited me and colors that enhanced my complexion.

One of the assistant directors had fallen madly in love with a young girl and tried to propel her career by using her as an extra whenever he could. While gorgeous, she was also completely dyslexic and couldn't memorize a single line of dialogue. She had only one line, where she was to deliver flowers to Marie Antoinette's carriage, "Madame, welcome to France." Shooting time was running at $100,000 an hour, and after five takes that took three hours given the horses, the carriage, and resetting everyone's positions, the director glared at his AD and got someone else. Yet she kept showing up on set—a peasant here, a courtier there, here a revolutionary, there a housewife. It was like "Old MacDonald Had a Farm." It became a cast joke how many times she could play a different extra—she managed nine appearances with the entire crew pushing for her to do more for their amusement. Even the director thought it was funny although the humor failed Hepburn, who had left the set earlier than the rest of the crew because her filming was over. The gorgeous girl earned the nickname Extra and, as life in Hollywood is stranger than fiction, went on to make a career as one. She made good money all of her life never speaking a line and, with different wigs, makeup, and clothing, would appear multiple times in the same film. She got her start on *Marie Antoinette* since the production crew liked her and found using her to be a game, so they used her in later films, and those crews used her as her reputation rippled out in widening circles. She's still at it and, unknown to the world, has played more roles in Hollywood than anyone else.

The movie opened to rave reviews. Box office, however, wasn't good, which was what the studio cared about most. That year, 1963, the biggest grossing film was Elizabeth's *Cleopatra*, which, despite earning record revenues, still had an overall loss given the enormous expense of the production—just like Norma Shearer's *Marie Antoinette*. Our version of *Marie Antoinette* opened in November. Four Academy Award nominations later, including best actress/actor for me and Tony Curtis, another for cinematography, and one for costume design, which went to *Cleopatra* in the end, turned things around so the film made a profit, thank God. I wanted to keep working. It wasn't as good as a home run, but at least we didn't lose money.

Interestingly, while Coppola's *Marie Antoinette* won the Academy Award for costume design and deserved it, none of the actors garnered any Oscar nominations as both the Norma Shearer vehicle and our film did.

Our Marie Antoinette stood the test of time, not looking dated like a sixties Hollywood costume drama. Not only was I nominated, but I won, a source of annoyance to Elizabeth, who played Cleopatra and didn't win anything except public censor from the Vatican for having an affair with Richard Burton. She also got the million dollars that so angered Marilyn. We went back and forth over the years about who got a better deal. I was well-paid at $250,000 but not compared to her. Was my Academy Award worth the difference? There were times later that I would have much rather have had the money.

Yes, Elizabeth was not happy with the Academy Award going to mother. She mentioned it from time to time and, over time, because she loved my mother, began to take it less seriously. She joked that mother got the award for looking ugly. Mom would just roll her eyes. Money mattered to both of them. It wasn't just a matter of being well-off or being able to buy stuff; it was a way of keeping score. Something the Hollywood men did all the time, but when women did it, they were greedy.

I never got to know Marilyn Monroe. Mom says that she would have adored me, but she was gone before I got here. But the fight against the guys, to be taken of value, to be paid for value, was a fight that I didn't understand until I was older. Mother kept us out of it, but it was something that Bobby talked to us about.

I did meet Tony Curtis and Jack Lemmon—they were fun—but Jack was special. He had a screwball face and could always make us laugh. What joy and privilege to know him. Jack Lemmon's work is of great value. I was never close to Tony because it was clear my mother didn't like him. There was a lot about her Marie Antoinette film we didn't know. But these were some of yesterday's greatest stars, and I am sorry they have faded.

Anders

WHAT GOES UP MUST COME DOWN

By 1964, I had an Academy Award, was at the top of my game, and was turning thirty-seven, which was getting past my use-by date as far as the studio guys thought. It didn't escape me that I was now the age Marilyn had been when she thought she was losing her looks and killed herself. I had made good money by real-world standards, but I wasn't rich like Frank Sinatra, Bing Crosby, or Bob Hope. Women didn't make as much money. That hasn't completely changed. Streisand was twenty-five years too early to make the money Madonna has.

Yet here I was: a star. One day, at super-agent Sue Mengers's party, I ran into Husband No. 4. Sue had been after me to become a client. She never understood why any star wasn't. Ruthless, smart, articulate, and often vulgar, she used more four-letter words than any male studio exec, much to their shock and amusement. She played the Hollywood system like a musician, knowing what notes to hit to make all the noise turn into a hit song, payable to her. She was one of the forces that helped women in Hollywood because she showed that women were as good as the men. Except she wasn't as good—she was better. It was like Ginger Rogers— Ginger was Fred Astaire's dance partner but always got second billing even though she did everything he did except backward in high heels. It was the same for Sue Mengers.

She wasn't yet as big as she would become, although she thought she was. She was tough, smart, and resilient and threw incredible parties even at the beginning of her career. Making a name for herself, she wanted me as one of her early clients although she knew I would never sign with her because I had Bobby. She didn't like it. Or him, for that matter. She was soft and sweet with him but bad-mouthed him behind his back every chance she got. Her client list at one time or another included Streisand, Mick Jagger, Tatum and Ryan O'Neal, Gene Hackman, Julie Harris, Anthony Perkins, Michael Caine, Cher, Joan Collins, Ali MacGraw, Peter Bogdanovich, Cybil Shepherd, Elliot Gould, Candice Bergan, and even director Mike Nichols.

Her story became known to the public because of a famous interview she did on *60 Minutes*, where she played a charming, literate flirt for Mike Wallace. Later, after her death, there was a Broadway play, *I'll Eat You Last*, starring Bette Midler as Sue, showing her witty agent skills and sad decline. She was a prolific cigarette and pot smoker. For the last few years of her life, she barely made it out of bed. My old friend Ann Roth did Bette's costumes for the show, somehow seeming to bring things full circle.

There was a ruthless side to Sue I didn't like. To win at her game, she was tougher and meaner than the guys but seldom let it show. For years, she professed how much she adored Streisand, which made sense since she got 10 percent of Streisand's earnings, which was a lot for a female star even then. She was Barbra's biggest fan, told her how much she loved her, and how they were sisters forever. Yet, after some mismanagement and self-dealing regarding Streisand's professional career, things that were too much to overlook, Streisand dropped her as her agent. Sue told Barbra, "I won't be your friend if I can't be your agent," and that was the end of the "friendship." Sue cut her off totally—a blow Streisand never could forgive, particularly since it was Sue's unprofessional behavior that had caused Barbra to switch representation.

While I had my own issues with Streisand, no one deserved what Sue did to her. Yes, Barbra could be a complete diva. Yes, she could be the world's biggest pain in the ass. But she could be hurt as well. She suffered, as did the rest of us, from male arrogance and power. She was loud about it, but she was so difficult to cope with and made things always about her so that sometimes you had wonder if the studio guys were giving her a hard time because she was a smart, talented woman or getting revenge because she was a ballbuster. Streisand endured sniping about everything during her career, including her nose when she started out— why doesn't she get it fixed like everyone else? I thought she looked like Nefertiti in profile, but what I thought wasn't the point. She didn't fit the classic male ideal of female beauty held by the studio chiefs. No man with her talents would have been subjected to plastic surgery debates in or out of the media. Well, most of them, anyway. A few men had it done, but that was considered a trade secret. Given sexism in the media, no one dared to ask a leading man about what "work" they'd had done.

Finally, Streisand had a woman in her corner, a confidant and friend as well as her agent, and what does her friend do? Cut her off without a word over money. That stung. On the other hand, one had to admire Mengers's grit and determination. She made it as a top agent when Hollywood remained a man's game. There was no women's club for high-powered female execs. She gained power using her star clients as she finagled and slithered with the best (or sleaziest) studio execs. The inflation of stars' salaries was in no small part due to her. She liked her 10 percent. And no one turned down her phone calls. She wasn't only good; she was also funny and knew more dirt than anyone. You always got something from one of her calls. She dismissed Vanessa Redgrave's political pretensions, describing her as "downing glass after glass of my best Veuve Clicquot like a good socialist."

Few turned down an invitation to her parties, either, where you ran into the biggest stars, directors, and studio heads. I wasn't being unfaithful to Bobby by going—you just couldn't say no. The outsiders invited were an interesting bunch, too, which was what brought me to Husband No 4.

Dark-haired, blue-eyed, and forty-two, he was a man's man and instantly annoyed me by his presumption. He had the walk of a guy who has gotten most of the girls he has ever wanted and the stride of a guy with a big dick. It was a gait girls in Hollywood recognized instantly, the I've-got-a-big-one-don't-you-want-it stride. He came over to introduce himself. My first thought was he was just another guy trying to score a notch with an Academy Award winner so he could spend the rest of his life bragging about how good he was. I cut him dead. "I'm not going out with you. Use your caveman club to find someone who cares, because in this town, you're bound to." Ouch—even now, I wince.

He just laughed then grabbed a bottle of champagne, poured two glasses, handed me one, and said, "Someone needs a drink! Hope your night gets better," and strode off.

The next day, three dozen long-stemmed red roses arrived at my door with a note. "Sorry I offended you. I just wanted to thank you for giving me so much pleasure at watching your talent." Now I felt stupid. I had felt hit on and had lashed out because I was hit on all the time. Here he was, trying not to be a jerk, but he was undeniably hitting on me. Hence, the roses.

The problem for those of us known to the public—they know who we are, while we know nothing. They have the advantage. We are public property up to a point. On the other hand, as I have said, all of us in my position are two people, and what these people knew was the public image. I was smart enough to keep my private image private, but some of what we were inside would occasionally leak out in our performances or in our responses on talk shows. Mostly, those interviews were artificial images created by us and the studios. To someone observant, however, there were data points that could be connected. Husband No. 4 didn't bother connecting any dots. He just found me attractive. From his point of view, he would either learn what he needed to know, or he wouldn't.

A self-made man-about-town with a real estate fortune, he was also known for his racing stable. I forgot our incident until six months after meeting him. I was in London filming one of the early James Bond movies. I played the bad guy's assistant. It was less entertaining than it sounds, but my two scenes with Sean Connery made it worthwhile. I got to say, "Take one more step, and I'll shoot." I loved being a bad guy, and no one expected we were going for Shakespeare.

I had my suite at the Connaught, which has been my working home in London since I made it in film. How Husband No. 4 found me, I don't know. I got a hand-delivered note inviting me to Ascot to watch his horse race from the Royal Enclosure. It sounded intriguing. I asked Lily, who was with me to handle press, to find out about No. 4's reputation. We learned he was just as his reputation suggested: rich, successful, and prone to using his money to indulge his penchant for racehorses, yachts, and beautiful women.

I thought, let the gods decide. I called Edith Head in LA and told her I was invited into the Royal Enclosure for Ascot. If she agreed to do my dress and hat, I would go. I remember her laughing. In a week, she air-shipped a perfectly fitted, divine dress with matching hat and parasol.

I had Lily RSVP my attendance and say I'd meet him there since I would be coming from the set. The morning of Ascot, a messenger from Harry Winston accompanied by a bodyguard arrived on set and waited for Lily to fetch me so I could sign. In the package were a pair of pear-shaped diamond drop earrings, each drop totaling ten carats. Completely inappropriate for day, but no one was going to hold that against me in the Royal Enclosure. What they would hold against me was that I was an actress. Diamond earrings during the day would just prove I was as vulgar as they thought. If I didn't wear them, what was I supposed to do, return them? They were much too pretty for that. On the other hand, if I kept them, I would be expected to put out. No one purchases jewelry like that for a peck on the cheek. I decided to wear them and then return them. It was the thought that counted, right? I liked the thought much better at over ten carats an earring.

I showed up at Ascot in an outfit that would have done Cecil Beaton proud after he had won the Academy Award for costuming *My Fair Lady*. Edith Head knew how to create an entrance—my hat, dress, jacket, and parasol matched perfectly. I'd had my hair and makeup done by the studio. As I walked in, every head turned. It was a big racing day. I saw a few people I knew, but mostly, they knew me from film and newspapers. Husband No. 4 saw me, and I was pleased to see him gasp. For someone my age, I had put myself together pretty well. The earrings, I have to say, helped. I got a lot of compliments on my dress, but it was the twenty carats in diamond drops the women stared at. The guys stared at my breasts. What else was new?

He came over, kissed my hand, and offered to take me for champagne and strawberries. I smiled and thanked him for the earrings. "I will return them later," I told him. "I can't accept them, but they were too beautiful not to wear." He looked a bit conceited, so I added, "And they're so practical. Mine are too big to wear every day!"

He was rarely speechless, but that did it. I didn't mean to put him down, but I wasn't going to have this guy thinking he was God's gift one more time. It helped that a courtier came over as we were having our first glass of champagne because the Queen wanted to say hello. While it's against protocol to report a conversation with the sovereign, she was gracious and wanted to tell me how much she had enjoyed *Marie Antoinette*. I sensibly curbed my sense of humor and made no comments about a queen liking a film about another queen losing her head. The thought, however, did pop into my mind. I also noted No. 4 was impressed.

Naturally, his horse, like the Carly Simon song, *You're So Vain*, won, and he preened. The press was full of it the next day. He scored with his horse and being seen with me, but I hope not in that order. I also scored in the press—I was photographed entering the Royal Enclosure in all my Edith Head glory with the diamond earrings flashing in the sun. The caption read *Marie Antoinette Would Approve*. How sweet. Husband No. 4 was enthralled. He took me to dinner, which was lovely, and I returned the earrings, much to his shock. I didn't put out, which shocked him even more, but I did allow a goodnight kiss. It was quite a kiss, having cost him twenty carats in diamonds.

Before leaving London, I had one more memorable evening at a society dinner party. Half of those in attendance were British aristocrats, while the other half was the Hollywood elite in London. The toffs were fascinated by us, were terribly polite, and let us know they were slumming it. At the dinner was the incomparable Walther Matthau with his wife, Carole, a Hollywood personage herself. She was part of a diabolical trio consisting of Oona Chaplin, daughter of playwright Eugene O'Neill and wife of Charlie, and Gloria Vanderbilt, heiress and mother of Anderson Cooper. Those three were famous for their escapades. At dinner, Walter was seated next to an ingenue, who flirted shamelessly. When she rose to powder her nose, everyone could see that while lovely seated, she was Godzilla from the waist down. When she returned, the flirting with Walter continued until he finally asked, "How old is such a pretty young thing as yourself?" The ingenue smiled, but before she could open her mouth, Carol interrupted.

"Why don't you saw off one of her thighs, Walter, and count the rings?" she asked, causing a stunned silence as we tried not to laugh out loud. Carol demonstrated one more time why no one trifled with her. It was one way to end a flirtation with your husband.

I returned to LA a week later. My *James Bond* shoot was finished, and I needed to be home for fittings for a new film. I was not surprised the next morning when another three dozen roses arrived with an invitation to dinner. I went. Every subsequent invitation was accompanied by another three dozen roses. Eventually, I succumbed. He was smart and driven, and I was spending a lot of time saying no. He gave me back the earrings. Just when things were going well, he had the bad judgment to get down on one knee to propose with a rock even Elizabeth would approve.

"Absolutely not!" I retorted. "We have a good thing going. Why ruin it with marriage? I've already had three. You've never been married. You have no idea of the media that is going to hit you. I have no intention of letting my next husband run all over town. I am a working actress and don't need that reputation added to my list."

I still can see the look on his face. It was like the greeting card that made the rounds in the late '70s showing a pile of cocaine on a mirror with the caption, "How do you politely turn down an offer of cocaine?" You opened the card, and inside it said, "We don't know. No one ever has!" That was the look.

What can I say? He wore me down with flowers, jewels, and charm, and I trotted down the aisle in a pink dress with matching hat and shoes, designed for me by Valentino. What annoyed me was that he knew I would.

It was a perpetual honeymoon. I had a new Mercedes in two days and jewels weekly. There were yachts, champagne, caviar, and parties. And horse races. Husband No. 4 knew the Frank Sinatra crowd. I tried to keep my distance but wasn't successful. Frank was cordial but distant, and I saw no reason to push anything, believing the adage about letting sleeping dogs lie. There was also gambling, which I didn't like. I worked far too hard for my money to let it ride on chance, particularly when the odds were against you, as in the casinos. I refused to go to Las Vegas, and if Husband No. 4 went, I made my displeasure known. He would take his plane, leaving me a diamond necklace or ruby brooch as an apology. There were lots of stunning pieces.

He had a small horse farm outside of Santa Barbara. It was quiet, and I loved going to watch the horses train. By now, Sebastian was sixteen, and he took to the stables, caring for horses and learning how to ride. To my relief, he was too tall to be a jockey. I didn't want that life for him or the kind of people who went with it. But Sebastian spent a couple of summers at the farm working with the horses, and I was pleased he had the opportunity to work with non-Hollywood people, away from the temptations available to a star's son in Los Angeles. Plus, I got to spend time with him, just us two, which was pure joy despite a few adolescent rebellions.

I wasn't much of a rider. I didn't grow up that way and now seemed too late to learn. Anyway, I quickly learned that, unless you were a jockey, the idea of riding one of these horses was a travesty. The difference between a racehorse and a typical riding horse was as extreme as the difference between a middle-aged weekend jock and an Olympic competitor. A racehorse was lean, all muscle. You could see the veins under its coat, and it moved with the skill of a dancer. Racing is peculiar because all horse matings have to be witnessed, and one cannot use artificial insemination as with other animals. This protects mid-range breeders—whose stallions would become valueless if one could purchase semen from a Triple Crown winner—and also reduces inbreeding.

The poor fillies, some of whom had never raced, were retired to breed, and as former athletes, they were often not receptive to the stallions. They sounded like young actresses starting out in Hollywood. The stallions commanding enormous stud fees were worth millions, while the fillies were usually less valuable. No breeder wanted a reluctant filly kicking a stallion in the balls and ending a lucrative career, so the fillies had their legs bound in cotton wrapping and tied down to see what would happen as the breeder led in a "stunt" stallion of no value except to protect the stud. The minders were very careful to ensure the stunt stud didn't penetrate the filly, which would have meant they might lose the filly for breeding that season. Some of the stunt studs had a penis that bent to the side since it was yanked out of the way so often to keep the filly "preserved" for the stud, who could cost hundreds of thousands for a one-time deal. If the filly behaved, the stud was led in, and mating commenced. If not, she was tranqued up and then mounted. The parallels to Hollywood kept sticking in my mind. I felt sorry for the stunt stud who was permanently frustrated and for the fillies who were basically raped, but it seemed a good deal for the successful stallions who spent the rest of their lives fucking eligible fillies and getting paid for it. Clearly, this was a business dreamed up by men. I don't think a woman would ever devise a scheme like this.

I would return to Los Angeles happy after a few days away seeing Sebastian, amazed at the horse business, and lucky to live a life of such privilege. Everything was the best and most expensive, and when I flew on business or pleasure, it was on our private aircraft. He insisted. We were living in a huge Bel Aire estate with gardeners, maids, and drivers. It was like a movie, but with no director to yell, "Cut!"

When I found myself in a family way, Husband No. 4 made it clear there would be no more pictures for me until after the baby was born. It was to be his first child. He was wonderful with Sebastian, too, understanding how to deal with a teenage boy. I'm sure he indulged Sebastian, as he did me, when I wasn't looking, but he also set out what he thought were sensible rules. Husband No. 4's ideas about women were not mine, and I wasn't thrilled he might impart those to Sebastian. On the other hand, he always treated me respectfully. I had made my case about my beliefs and figured Sebastian would choose one way or another. At his age, it was out of my hands. I had either done a good job or not. Here I was—happy, satisfied, and knocked up.

I never worried about money. Husband No. 4 took over my real estate trust and doubled it. We had a prenup, but it wasn't onerous, and if anything happened to him, I would get everything in trust for me and our children, which generously included Sebastian. Our sex life didn't include whips or latex, much to my relief, and was wonderful. I gave birth to Anders, took off four months, and then went back to work. Surprisingly, Husband No. 4 didn't argue. I thought it would be a battle, but he was supportive. On the night before I was to start work on my next picture, he gave me an emerald necklace with matching earrings that would have paid for my Hollywood Hills house, which I had kept and rented out.

My next film was modern film noire. Our director was well known, established, and a prick. He started chasing me around as soon as I showed up for work. I was happily married with two children, one of whom was five months old. Our director, typical old-style Hollywood, believed in droite du seigneur. I believed he could go fuck himself. It went from bad to worse. One day, he came on to me in front of the crew, a no-no, even in Hollywood, for a married famous actress. One didn't want rumors or stories even in those days. I walked away from him, and he called me a bitch. I turned to him and said, "You know the difference between a bitch and a slut, don't you? A slut will sleep with anyone. A bitch will sleep with anyone but you. Go find yourself a slut!"

He went to slap me, but my teamster driver, the one with the gun who had been with me for years, stepped between us and warned him if he got near me again, he would knock him flat and call in a strike. The strike threat was serious. No one wanted a union fight. The studio chief called me to his office ten minutes later, where he told me to play nice. I went nuts. Rather than discipline the director, a guy who was trying to force me to have sex with him, he was asking *me* to play nice?

"Tell that sex-crazed asshole to grow up!" I shouted back. "If you want me on set, replace the fucker!" I walked off the shoot, shutting it down, with the union behind me, thanks to my driver.

It took less than an hour before my lawyers called. According to my contract, they said the studio could sue me for costs if I walked. Given studio accounting, this would also include the costs transferred from other films, too. *War and Peace* is less fiction than a film studio income statement. I would be on the hook for millions.

I countersued for harassment. It was the first major sexual harassment suit filed in the State of California and, coming from me, got huge press. The studio went nuts, saying if I won, business would come to a halt, costs would increase, and thousands of jobs would be lost. More importantly, they would lose power over the casting couch.

I went on Johnny Carson and made fun of the studio. "If my director wants a date," I said, "let him get it the old-fashioned way. Hire a hooker." The line got a great laugh. Predictably, it meant war with the studio, who felt attacked, and any sensible solution would look like caving in.

Husband No. 4 was upset with the director. Given his gamboling friends, like Frank, I told him not to interfere. Any dead bodies, and I would certainly be blamed. I was already being sued, but I didn't want to be on trial for murder, and who knew what these guys were capable of?

My husband told me not to worry. If I lost the suit, he would pay, and he told me he would transfer ten million dollars to me. Financially secure, I fought the studios. As often happens, God had other plans.

I lost to the studios, who not only billed me for legal costs and the cost of shutting down my film but also padded it for their other films that lost money as well as making me pay for "damages." I was in hock for a lot of money, but I had the ten million from Husband No. 4. I also lost the harassment suit. I was so upset after losing in court that Husband No. 4 insisted I take our plane to the South of France for a month to recover with our children. He would join me later. I remember him driving us to the plane and kissing us goodbye, not for a minute imagining it would be the last time I saw him.

He was shot and killed two days later.

We returned for the funeral, barely having touched down. In addition to my grief, the estate was in hock, the horses were in hock, the yacht gone, the plane claimed as soon as we landed in Los Angeles, and the ten million didn't exist. I discovered that the jewels left in the house were gone. All that remained were the ones I had taken to the South of France and some in my personal bank vault. I owed the studio $6 million dollars after losing my suit, equivalent to $40 million today.

Having lost Mike Todd, her third husband, in an airplane crash,

Elizabeth understood what I was going through. She raced to my house as soon as she heard we were back. She came over, gave me a huge hug and a look that told me she understood. "Hide all the jewels you can find and don't wear them so no one suspects you have anything" was the first thing she whispered in my ear after telling me how sorry she was. Then she told me to call if I needed anything, particularly if I was threatened. "You may not think you have the power to protect yourself, but I do, and I know how to use it, so you fucking call me!" she commanded. It never came to that, nor did I ever have to borrow money from her, either, which she had immediately offered since Mike had left her very well-off. Thankfully, she was there for me, quietly in the background, given all that went on. She hid things for me in her house, including jewels and a few paintings, so I would have emergency funds. She also arranged the funeral and very small church service with Lily because I was too distraught for anything more than that. I had numerous business issues that couldn't wait as things kept getting repossessed, and it seemed that lawyers were ever present. Given the scandal, the smaller the funeral, the better.

Elizabeth helped not only because she was my friend but also because it was, in part, her way of dealing with the grief she carried for Mike Todd, whose death years before had deeply affected her. Her ultimate response was to convert to Judaism to honor him after his death, something she had not done when she married him. As Elizabeth told me, she thought she would be closer to Mike as a Jew. Our friend Marilyn had converted to Judaism for marriage to Arthur Miller, and Elizabeth found kinship with her over this subject as the two of them eventually became the most famous Jews of them all, which in retrospect seems odd. I was grieving and angry but didn't think turning to religion would give me solace. I was too angry at God for too many things.

I have always wondered if Husband No. 4 knew his time was up and sent us away to protect us, which tended to mitigate my other emotions. He had never, however, taken me into his confidence, and he lied to me about our finances, both by commission and omission. The life I had led was a mirage. My rage against this enormous lie was contorted by my grief—because he had always been wonderful to me and loved me like no other. It took me a long time to be able to fit both ideas in my head at the same time and to make peace with what happened. Frankly, even today, with all that has happened since and all the years that have passed, my rage at the deception, which reverberated through my life for years, creating havoc and fear, remains underneath my grief. I blamed Husband No. 4 for a long time. I was able to channel the experience into my work, which made me a better actress, but the price of my grief and fear was so great I would have gladly never worked again just to avoid the aftermath. But who gets to make those choices? Certainly not me.

I was broke. Everything I had worked for my entire life was gone. After I settled everything and worked out a payment plan for the $6 million, I was left with my old house in the Hills, my clothes, one Mercedes, and what jewels I had managed to hide at Elizabeth's, including the twenty-carat diamond earrings. I didn't want to let them go, although the engagement ring went. They were my rainy-day fund, not to mention my children's college tuition. I kept them to support us. My real estate trust was pledged to the studio. I was at the end of my career and was going to be poor because my glory days were over. I was forty. The scandal of

Husband No. 4's murder and my suing the studio and director for sexual harassment made me a pariah.

Moreover, the kind of men with whom my husband had been in trouble were not the kind of people you wanted in your life. I spent the next several years looking over my shoulder and worrying about my children's safety. Sebastian was already in boarding school at Andover and entering college. I was glad. He was safer. I didn't want him in LA given the media and temptations. I might have been broke, but I was still a star with all that implied for my children. My problem was Anders, who was four. I packed him off to Paris with my friends, where he stayed almost two years. I visited him often, but he suffered and held it against me. However, I needed to protect him from my bad choices, and those included marrying his father. His father was shot, so he lost both of us, one after the other, which he felt was unbearable. Later, he knew intellectually it was to protect him. I still feel guilty and wish I had found another way, but the people who shot my husband were not the kind of people who took things lightly. I didn't want Anders kidnapped for ransom. Money, I could lose, but not my child. I didn't want to be owned and blackmailed. I had seen those movies, and so have you, and the possibilities were not good.

While all this was going on, Bobby discovered someone had forged a check on my business account and stolen ten thousand dollars, which was real money back then. I was essentially broke, and I owed the studio. I had counted on that money to support myself and my children. I wanted to go to the police, but Bobby held me back. He said he would investigate, but given everything, this was not a time to go to the cops. If it was "them" who had taken my money, I should let it go. If it wasn't, he would find out who did it from the bank trail and the handwriting. Bobby figured the information on who stole the money might be much more useful one day than sending someone to jail. If they did the same thing to others, let the others report it. He warned me I wasn't likely to get the money back without a huge fight and large legal fees. He promised to tell me what he had found out, but after asking a couple of times, I thought better about asking a third time and stayed quiet. I had never been so upset over ten thousand dollars.

Husband No. 4 owned an apartment on New York's Fifth Avenue. It would have to go. I flew to New York to sign papers and move out those furnishings I wanted that didn't need to be sold. James Wolfensohn and his lovely wife, Elaine, lived in the building, and I met them in the elevator. I must have looked like a wreck. Since my situation was in the press, they knew the whole story. Elaine invited me for dinner, and I was grateful to have somewhere to go without press or judgment. Jim, who made a fortune in investment banking, later became president of the World Bank and chaired both Carnegie Hall and the Kennedy Center in Washington. He has spent half of his life giving back to society and teaching his children to do the same.

He quietly advised me on my finances and never asked for anything, knowing I didn't have it. He arranged a loan to repay the studio and helped me invest the little I had left. I was able to borrow against my real estate, so I could keep a little capital as it appreciated over the years. In the end, I wouldn't be penniless in my old age although I would have to work for years to make bank payments. I was leveraged, but to the banks, whom I trusted more than the studio. After the Bel Aire house, plane, jewels, yacht, horses, and apartment went, "they" left me alone. I waited for them to contact me, but I never heard a word. I was terrified of what they would demand, but it wasn't like I could find someone to ask. Even had I wanted to, I didn't know whom to ask.

I blamed Frank Sinatra. He had been distant since I had praised Bing Crosby. I rued my comment because the costs of my running my mouth had been huge. He was cordial but distant when we would run into each other after I married No. 4. Afterward, he stayed away. If he had wanted to intervene, to stop things, he could have. He might have saved my husband or at least warned me. I resented him bitterly, but the fault was my own—my big mouth. He knew the kind of people who shot my husband. Yet not a call, not a word. Nothing. I was box-office poison, and he finally had his revenge, the heartless bastard.

I arrived back home in LA after I had settled my New York financial affairs and gotten the bank loans. By now, two years had passed since Husband No. 4 had been murdered. There was a note with my real name on it under the front door. I can't tell you the shivers that went down my spine. Someone had gotten to me at my house? With my real name? Who? How? What did they want? I was shaking as I opened the envelope. Inside was a handwritten note on personal letterhead that said simply, *Babe, everything is taken care of. Go back to work, and keep what you make for your children. Best, Frank*

Jim Wolfensohn, who read people better than anyone I ever met, had understood my situation. After I explained what I knew, he somehow got word to Sinatra. Since he also advised Jacqueline Onassis, he knew the right levers to push.

I don't know what Frank did or didn't do, but after his note, I felt badly I had blamed him. Maybe I just needed to blame someone. Did he do anything? Maybe not. I never fully understood what he did or didn't do or why he helped me. It was generosity for sure. But in the dark recesses of my mind, I wondered if it was because he felt guilty. Over what, I didn't know, but I speculated. I wondered why he'd never warned me that Husband No. 4 was on perilous ground. If Husband No. 4 was deep into the mob, how could Frank not have known and not have told me? Was he jealous all these years later, or was he still angry? I suspect he made payoffs for me, but I don't know for sure. If he did, I don't understand why, and I never asked.

Later, when I was doing well financially, all he asked was that I donate to his charities, which I was happy to do. He was happily married to Barbara, but before he died, we ran into one another and had a few minutes of private conversation. I thanked him and meant it. Those years before I got his note were my years in the Bastille, and although I escaped without losing my head, my Louis didn't. I had loved Husband No. 4 and the aftermath of his death left me not only with huge debts but recriminations and anger at the mess left to me. The risk to my children was something I couldn't forgive. It took me a long time to realize I missed him and how much I wished things might have had a different ending.

Frank was a gentleman. He said I was the one who got away, and he had been distant not because of my remark but because he had to get on with his life. I had turned him down, and it was time to move on, so he had kept his distance. Then, to my shock, he said, "As for your idea that Bing was better than me, you're wrong, but who else has the balls to tell me other than you?" He paused, smiled, and took my hand, adding, "And very pretty balls, at that!" Then he walked off.

It would have never worked between us, yet his last comment and his courtesy made me wonder. Maybe I had blown it. On the other hand, Frank was widely known for his quote, "A man doesn't know what happiness is until he's married. By then, it's too late." Since our time together, following his second marriage to Ava Gardner, he had dated Lauren Bacall, Angie Dickinson, Juliet Prowse, and Marilyn Monroe, and he was married briefly to Mia Farrow—they were the ones I knew about. My not marrying him wasn't a mistake. He wasn't ready to settle down, and I would never have been the right woman to make him settle. I thought about that conversation a lot.

This chapter was hard to read. I had been told about my father, but my mother was more delicate when she talked to me than what she wrote. There is not a lot for me to add. I was so angry for a long time for being sent away. I had no idea that it was for my protection or that my father had put us all in danger. Mother dug us out of the hole. I was a dumb kid who didn't understand the issues or real dangers involved. I don't remember the house, farm, or boat, but Sebastian does. I have no real memories of my father other than the stories and photos. In our world, all of it is based on photos and film, so for us, those don't really count. I wanted to have real memories—let alone good ones—of us as a family. I never knew we were once poor. But the diamond earrings are my mother's joy. She wears them on every major occasion of her life.

Anders

COMEBACK

I had to make a living. My picture fee jumped to a million after *Marie Antoinette*. After the studio suit, the aftermath of Husband No. 4, and my turning forty, there was not a lot of demand for my services.

I agreed to make a biopic on Madame Claude, then the most famous "madame" in the world. Bobby got me into it because he knew I had to work to keep going and needed every penny. The pay wasn't great, but it was work, and we hoped with the right touch and enough darkness, the film might be more than just fluff. Known to everyone who counted and unknown by those who didn't, Madame Claude was the most exclusive madame in the world, supplying girls to everyone from the Shah to JFK and a host of other boldface names to boot—Agnelli, Rothschild, Onassis, and even Brando. Her girls were anything but hookers. There was a widely reported story that JFK showed up and asked Madame Claude for a girl who looked like Jackie, only sexier. The girls were chic and sophisticated and often made advantageous marriages—not always to unsuspecting husbands, which is how I got to know a few.

This background seemed made for a juicy film with just enough scandal. Like a Madame Claude girl, I needed to please the guys running the studios who were paying for my services. While in my case, I didn't have to marry well to survive, I did need to have good roles. Without one, I was nothing.

Unfortunately, the movie ended up all soap opera, glitzy and over the top, filming during the period *Mission Impossible* and *Bewitched* were on television. It was a bad film that never seems to die, being the stuff that lives to be on late-night television far too often. What can I say—at the time, I thought it was a good idea, and I needed the money.

We filmed in Los Angeles, Monaco, and Paris, where I could spend time with Anders. It should have been an enjoyable shoot—and it started that way. After the first day, I became convinced a few of the actresses playing Madame Claude girls really were Madame Claude girls. She herself would have put them forward because it was good for business. These girls would be in high demand all their working lives. One of the people demanding them was our director, who spent more time in bed than on set directing. The second and third directors were competent, but this kind of film needed a delicate touch to avoid soap opera and melodrama. The light touch, however, was saved for the hot girls the director couldn't turn down.

Not a few of the Madame Claude girls had their working lives cut short when clients fell in love. There are highly placed Park Avenue, Avenue Foch, and titled wives who had been taught by Madame Claude how to walk, how to talk, how to dress, how to find a good plastic surgeon, and how to keep their clients happy. They were a sophisticated group. In her way, Madame Claude ran her own studio system, and those of her girls who made it through did very well. Some came to happy endings, and others to tragedy—a very Hollywood story. I often thought of her as if she were one of those logic questions on the tests my children took to get into college: if Madame Claude is to a studio head as an actress is to a hooker, then . . . But by no means could her girls be dismissed as mere call girls. Their style and pedigree spoke for itself, which was why Madame Claude was known by those who could pay her fees as the best madame in the world.

It became an open secret on set where our director was and what he was doing when he was missing. When the Madame Claude girls were in front of the camera, they knew how to move, turn, catch the light, and wear their costumes like professionals. Madame Claude was the ultimate director and had taught them well. Her girls appeared to be acting off screen, as well, keeping our director happy. He bragged about how good he was and how the girls said he was the best they ever had. What an idiot.

Her real name was Fernande Grudet. I never met her but saw her a few times in restaurants because those in the know always pointed her out. She was a legend, ordinary-looking but always exceedingly well-dressed. Her success at creating an image rivaled the best marketing efforts of world-class corporations. I admired that skill even if I didn't necessarily admire her work. If I was seeing a man, like an occasional date or ex-husband, who indulged while in Paris, I pretended not to know.

There were a few well-married women I met later that I suspected were former Madame Claude girls. They had a look. They were long, lanky, often blonde, self-possessed, and always perfectly put together. Models or actresses who didn't succeed in front of the camera, many Scandinavian. Naked out of the shower to a formal dinner party, they looked fabulous. If those skills didn't come naturally, Madame Claude taught them. If they couldn't learn, they were out. There were rumors Madame Claude had a testing system of men who rated the girls in bed. While there were things that could be taught, let's just say there were certain skills that had to come instinctively.

She kept the laurel of best madame in the world until French authorities busted her for tax evasion. Like Al Capone, she was undone not by her business but by the tax authorities. It was a comparison she would have appreciated, although she would have appreciated not being caught more. It was not a fair arrangement. The rich, white, middle-aged men who had made her a star went on with their lives. Her girls, whom she made into sophisticated beauties, married well or had the self-confidence to move to a new chapter. Yet she got done by French authorities and came to a bad end—old and arrogant and having to endure a stint in prison.

I made my salary from the film—not one of my better choices, but I couldn't have known when I signed how our director would spend the shoot. The lives of Madame Claude's girls and their clients were on the periphery of my world as part of the underside of Hollywood that touched a lot of things far away from California, and not only in the movies.

Then, the phone didn't ring. The silence was deadly. Bobby finally called to say they were filming a television series and, if picked up, they would pay $50,000 per episode. There were twenty-six episodes a season, and I needed the money. Good times and bum times, but I'm still here and all that. What could I say? It was quite a comedown for an Academy-Award-winning actress to do television, but I needed work. I told him I would do it, but I wanted good writers, really good writers, so we didn't do camp. I wasn't yet old enough. Besides, with that bad biopic, I had already done it.

Bobby laughed. "You know the story about the dumb blonde in Hollywood?" he asked rhetorically. "She was so dumb she fucked the writer!"

I got his point. "What do I ask for? Can we get a really good director who understands the small screen and can make something out of it? It won't be *Sunset Boulevard*, but can we skip shouting 'incoming' or doing *Dr. Kildare*?"

"Babe, I get it, but don't push too hard. The money's good. Take what comes with it."

He had a point, so I did television. I would have hung my head, but that made no sense when I was on network TV with twenty million viewers. Everyone knew I had fallen. Yet I was gratified they said I looked sensational, which I should have after a face-lift. Getting older was torture, and I looked at these young things getting good parts I could have done with my eyes closed. Faye Dunaway overacted from *Bonnie and Clyde* on. She diminished her career with *Mommy Dearest*, which redefined camp. I could have done her roles with one arm tied behind my back. I was from the fifties, but I never believed in overacting, which in television is what you get used to because the screens are so small.

We ended up with a period drama in Edwardian London just before the turn of the century. I played housekeeper to an aristocratic family with Jack the Ripper as one of the sons who ran a whorehouse. My housekeeping duties extended to the house of ill repute. I began to suspect who the son really was, and the drama turned into a game of cat and mouse where I tried to stay one step ahead of Jack the Ripper to survive. I ended up cleaning up a lot of fake blood on screen. I was also the sexiest housekeeper to have ever lived in Edwardian London, something I was pleased to see that the reviewers duly noted.

I called my old friend, Billy Wilder, who had directed me to my first Academy Award nomination to ask him for the names of superb cameramen and editors. He gave me the names of people ruined by the McCarthy blacklist who had never worked again in Hollywood. The ones he suggested were brilliant and desperate to return to the craft they loved. It would be their swan song since none were under sixty, yet they were better than anyone working in television and much better than any crew working in film that anyone in television could afford. We hired two editors and two cameramen. Bobby negotiated that they got less pay, so the network, always on the lookout to save money, agreed. Pennywise and pound foolish. In fact, we hired them for a song and a dance, but they wanted to work again, so they took it, never believing they would get more. Bobby got them syndication profits since the network thought this show would die an early death.

Our show was a smash. Why, I don't know, but I was grateful it was picked up. We had history, sex, violence, murder, and suspense. We had the best filming and editing on television, which made those guys money from their syndication points. Billy Wilder came to the rescue again, not only for me but also for the lost souls destroyed by the blacklist. Bobby's contracts paid for their retirement.

Originally, I was thrilled. I never dreamed it would be a hit, and at least it wasn't *Dark Shadows*, where I would have ended up playing a vampire. For two years and sixty-two episodes (we did five-week summer specials due to intense interest), I ended up on my feet financially, and to critical acclaim, no less. I made my bank payments and invested the rest in LA real estate with Jim Wolfensohn's blessing. When it was over, I went back into film. Our former blacklist crew was on top for the rest of their lives after such a smash, not to mention residuals and syndication profit points.

In the aftermath of my TV show success, I was able to get a good movie contract. I was scripted to play a tough female detective. It was the start of my three-part detective series. Bobby worked out that I got $1 million for the first plus points on the gross. Given studio accounting, points on profits are fiction unless you were Arnold Schwarzenegger. There are almost never profits. Bobby was smart again about my contract. It was for one picture, but he arranged that I purchase the rights to any sequels for $100,000 if I deferred my salary after expenses. They gave me the rights since no one at the studio could envision a sequel. The first film did well. I got paid on the back end. My ownership rights to both the second and third films provided me huge salaries plus points that actually paid off. Bobby had taken care of the blacklist people in our *Jack the Ripper* series, but he really took care of me for these three films.

Bobby was a master of negotiations. But the real film contract genius came along years later and was, surprise, Arnold Schwarzenegger. The bodybuilder turned out to be a magnate with a grasp of money few others in Hollywood had.

Arnold started out at Gold's when he arrived from Austria but, unlike his mentor, Joe Gold, he became a superb businessman and surrounded himself with smart people. It helped when he married Maria, whose family had invested wisely over the generations. It also helped that as a box-office star, he made $20 million a picture plus had points. I love Arnold. He is funny, smart, and completely driven. And perhaps a bit nuts. You had to be nuts to do what he did—be Republican and marry into the Kennedys.

He got good advice, invested wisely, and got points that actually paid off because he had incredible lawyers. He might thank the Kennedys for that.

For *Terminator 3: The Rise of the Machines*, Arnold earned $29 million in a pay-or-play contract that took twenty written drafts negotiated over a year and half by Hollywood super-lawyer Jacob Bloom. Arnold got paid whether or not the movie ever filmed (pay or play) plus was due an additional $1.6 million each week production ran longer than nineteen weeks. He received another $1.5 million for expenses, including a gym trailer, private jets, security, and luxury hotel suites when filming on location. The real key was Arnold also got gross points after breakeven. This wasn't unheard of for a major star, but the way Arnold and Jacob Bloom defined the points was. The contract was written so he would actually see money, when usually studio accountants made sure breakeven was defined in such a manner that it never occurred. Plus, Arnold got 20 percent of gross receipts, not just from movie theaters but also from videos, DVDs, TV, video games, comics, products, toys, and even in-flight movies. I studied that contract for days, trying to figure out how I could use its terms later to my advantage. But I was never in the position to do so.

Now, Arnold didn't get all this money just because he was worth it. He got it because he was smart, and Jacob Bloom was brilliant. They were able to demand all this because they knew the film financing, over $160 million, was contingent upon Arnold being in the film. Thus, the producers, Mario Kassar and Andrew Vajna, were over the proverbial barrel, but a barrel where the two of them would receive $10 million if they made the movie. No Arnold, no money. In the end, except for Arnold, due to the breakeven definition, the film barely made a profit after expenses.

I could never do what Arnold did. I never made $20 million a picture. My female detective trilogy was a hit but not like the *Terminator*. Bobby didn't have the same leverage with me that Jacob Bloom did with Arnold. It would take another twenty-five years before female leads could hold out for blockbuster salaries.

Nonetheless, Bobby had leverage I didn't know about to negotiate my detective series. Our studio producer, as luck would have it, was the man who had forged my signature on a check and stolen the ten thousand dollars from me, figuring no one would notice in the confusion after Husband No. 4 was shot. Bobby searched high and low to find out who had stolen from me and had identified him years ago but waited to confront him until the time was ripe. Evidently, that time was during the negotiations for my role. Bobby told him if he didn't give me the part and gross points plus the rights to the sequels, he would take the forged check to the police. The producer didn't have a lot of room to maneuver. I knew nothing about this until Bobby finally told me after the series was long finished. He said he figured if I knew, I would have an impossible time working with the producer, which was correct. I would have been beside myself. He also said it was my ticket to financial stability, and he was happy to get it. "Don't think of it as blackmail," he said. "Think of it as a return on investment for the ten thousand, which at the time was more than you could afford." It was the best ten thousand I ever invested. Bobby told the producer if anyone heard a word, it was his ass. Bobby was known as a tough negotiator who kept his word. He also kept the forged check as insurance for as long as that producer lived. It's framed now in my guest bathroom.

When Bobby finally told me the story, I wondered what kind of person could do this? How could someone steal from a widow who was losing almost everything she owned, lie about it for years, only come clean under blackmail, and then keep up a pretense with me for years while we filmed? Who was this kind of person? Only a studio exec, who was clearly a better actor than most of his employees.

After the trilogy, I was financially secure. All my life, I kept my house in the Hills. It isn't a palace, but it's big enough.

I bought an apartment in Tribeca New York City because I got a good deal on a place with a rooftop terrace, and it has a lot of light for NYC. I beat the rush to Tribeca, so I have done well with my investment.

Mother shipped me off to Paris after my father was killed and I stayed with dear friends who have been family to all of us over the years. I remember some of the TV shows, because they were so famous. I would see them when I was back in America. The detective series were the first of my mother's films I was allowed to watch. They were good and gave me some idea of who she was to everyone else. But to me, she was my mom, and, in an odd way, dependable. She pestered me about homework and brushing my teeth—and bodily cleanliness after I became a teen. When I went to boarding school, she would come up on most parent's weekends. I learned later from Bobby that she had those days put into her contracts so she could take the time off.

Then, she would walk into Andover, dressed as a major star in front of a bunch of horny teens, and embarrass the shit of me. She always took my roommates and me to the fanciest dinner within distance and talked to me privately during those visits. When I was feeling adolescent angst, there was a plane ticket waiting for me Friday morning (I got to skip one day of classes every now and then) so I could join her wherever she was filming. During this period, she called me every night before bed and made sure that Lily was always available to me, who was my crazy Chinese other mommy. When I was small, I got to know the best Chinese restaurants in New York, Los Angeles, London and Paris connected to a gamboling den, where Lily would go play cards after dinner and I would sit in the corner doing homework. I got the best food ever and, when Lily did well, she would give me part of her winnings to save for college. She did very well.

I used that money later, which grew surprisingly large, as part of the down payment for a townhouse where Lily now has the ground floor garden apartment and lives with us in her own space. My grandchildren adore her, and she takes them, too, for good Chinese and gamboling. My mother who abhorred gamboling especially after my father's death, was not happy about the Chinese dens, but this was Lily, whom she trusted with her life. And, evidently, with mine. I knew my mother didn't like it, and Lily knew my mother didn't like it, but whatever agreement they came to, and I have to assume it was discussed, I never knew. But since the rooms were filled with little old Chinese ladies and a few older men, it certainly was not Las Vegas. Moreover, I couldn't understand a word, and I am sure Lily, not to mention my mother, liked it that way. My grandchildren have learned Chinese from their Chinese nanny because Lily insisted. It will be the language of the world, she told me, and said she would pay for the nanny herself. I didn't let her, but Lily got my mother to pay for the nanny whose main job was to make sure the grandkids had a good Chinese accent. Lily is very proud of the kids. They understand the old ladies, something I couldn't do, and tell me the language is very spicy and often in slang that even they don't understand. The old ladies just laugh with their hand in front of their faces but won't tell them what they are saying.

    Anders

BETWEEN NEW YORK AND PARIS

I spent more time in New York and put Anders in Dalton, the excellent private school on the Upper East Side. It was filled with rich and celebrity children, which on the one hand was a disadvantage because it provided a lopsided view of life. On the other, however, Dalton provided cover for Anders having me for a mother. He didn't stand out, which pleased me. Expecting a normal life was unrealistic; approaching something that wasn't completely insane was the most we could hope for.

Then, too, there were a couple of Dalton parents who were fabulous. One mother was European, terribly chic, put together in a way that would have put the entire studio system to shame. I could almost smell the Chanel No. 5-drenched hand of Madame Claude wafting in from the background. Her husband was a major industrialist. She knew I suspected, and I knew she knew I knew, but we never discussed Madame Claude. There were knowing smiles when the subject was broached during a conversation, but both of us were too ladylike to bring it up. Good for her.

These parents invited Anders for weekends in the country and made themselves available so their sons and Anders could play together when I was away. The kindness of strangers brought tears to my eyes. For all the glory, press, and royal treatment accorded a well-known actress, in the end I was just a working single mother. It sucked.

One of my Tribeca building neighbors was an evening news producer. She was the one of the first women to have such a senior role. She ran a salon of sorts, and her parties were well attended by interesting people of the moment. I was often invited, since I was another "get" for her, so in addition to my extensive experiences with the media, including the depredations of Fox News, I learned more about the behind-the-scenes processing of the media. Over the years, almost all the greats made it into her well-appointed living room—Walter Cronkite, David Brinkley, Dan Rather, Tom Brokaw, Barbara Walters, and Diane Sawyer, who would bring her husband, director Mike Nichols, if he was in town and not off shooting a movie. There was a smattering of lesser mortals, too, who worked behind the scenes, and the evenings were appreciated at a New York salon where people could mingle, relax, and discuss current issues.

I got to know Mike years ago when he directed Elizabeth Taylor in *Who's Afraid of Virginia Woolf*, winning her an Academy Award as well as best supporting actress for Sandy Dennis. It was his first film directing gig, where he was completely unintimidated by either Elizabeth or Burton, obtaining their best on-screen performances together. His next film, *The Graduate*, where I failed to get the Mrs. Robinson role, was the biggest grossing film of 1967 for which he won an Oscar for best director. He was a living national treasure for film, Broadway, and comedy, and when he would show up to these soirees, we would sit in the corner trading Hollywood war stories and discussing upcoming projects. Other times, I would lead a contingent up to my rooftop terrace to continue drinks when the weather was good. Our producer host was a barracuda, constantly rushing to the phone about possible news pieces—every tragedy thrilled her. In a pre-cell phone era, she often would spend her time in my apartment tying up my phone lines, but I got used to it. Her constant, often imitated phrase—"Anyone killed?" I'm not sure she delighted in others' misery, but she delighted in her ratings and beating the competition. It brought her fame and, not incidentally, fortune. She reminded me of a male

Bobby, a comparison he hated.

One evening, I finally asked her why she never asked, "Who died?" She fixed me with this look like I should know better. "Babe, we all have to die. It's sad but inevitable and even if news, nothing major. When you die, you'll make the news—Academy-Award-winning actress dies. If you're killed, however, that will be a sensation. Even better if you and Redford die in a murder-suicide, and I get it first."

Got it. I appreciated she liked me, but not over announcing on her show Redford's and my murder-suicide. Something about such zeal for a scoop left me a little cold, although it was what made her such a highly sought-after producer. It does seem now, looking back, this attitude of news as entertainment was a harbinger of things to come, because that seems to be most of the current news. Every time I saw Redford on film or in person afterward, I smiled. He thought the story funny, too.

I had been talking on the phone a lot to a Swedish lawyer who worked in Paris about getting the rights for a Hollywood remake of an old French film. It was more complicated than usual, and we usually had a quick chat a day while we were sorting it out. I liked his voice with its mild Swedish accent and found myself sorry when we hung up. I wasn't lonely, but there was something special in our chats, which gradually moved to non-business subjects. He had a business trip to NY and was bringing papers to sign. He had just arrived, had a late business lunch at the Four Seasons on Park Avenue. I was to meet him there after his lunch. They had wine, and he was jet-lagged, and when I walked in, he was at his table with the rest of his party. I had never met him, didn't know what he looked like, but that had never been a problem for me since everyone knew what I looked like.

I walked in, took one look and somehow knew who he was, and walked over. I had no doubt. He was preoccupied with the others at his table, a bit tipsy, and so tired he didn't see me until I was standing over him, which amused me because everyone else in the room had noticed and was staring—it was always like that. Our eyes locked, and as we both described it later, it was like seeing an old best friend again. Totally odd to explain but totally right in the moment. Welcome Husband No. 5.

The attraction had started with our conversations. It wasn't so much sexual as connection, but there was something there. He told me later he had a boner with a wet spot every time we talked after our first conversation and was embarrassed if anyone else was around. Good to know. Anders adored him, too. Maybe it was the Swedish names they had in common or that Husband No. 5 was a gentle giant. He had played hockey in high school and had been a star, winning scholarships to American universities as well as being given offers for the feeder teams for the National Hockey League. He developed a huge butt and thighs playing hockey, so his brothers, all hockey nuts, called him the man with the biggest ass in Sweden. After several months together, having heard the story, I just started calling him the biggest ass in Sweden! He would look over at me so sweetly, positively glowing I had found a pet name for him.

After his hockey successes at Milton Academy in Massachusetts, he was approached by professional teams who wanted him to spend a year in the minors before joining the NHL. Then he learned he had been accepted to the Stockholm School of Economics, the Harvard of Sweden, and decided to give up hockey stardom for an education. I admired that to no end, me who had so little education.

I did *not* want to get married. We dated. Finally, I went to Anders to ask him what he thought. I wanted Husband No. 5 to live with us. I was upfront about my marriages having been disasters, but Anders's face lit up. He was old enough to need a father. Bobby loved both Sebastian and Anders and was Uncle Bobby to them, but he was not an ideal father figure. It had nothing to do with his being gay and everything to do with his being an agent who loved to party, date twenty-year-olds, and screw people on negotiations, which was his idea of a good time. Those were not values I wanted passed on. Anders was old enough at nine to understand why Uncle Bobby had so many muscular young friends, one after the other, which wasn't exactly ideal to my point of view, either. His older brother Sebastian adored Anders but was still away at school. They didn't see each other as much as I would have liked, but what could I expect with the sixteen years between them?

Yet Bobby developed a special relationship with Sebastian. Bobby was an older brother, given the two were a dozen years apart. However, Bobby started work at seventeen, which gave him added maturity. He understood the Hollywood rules and, as a guy, could discuss them with Sebastian in a way I couldn't.

I remember how I met Bobby. Victor, my first agent, was moving to the production side of the business, and I had never been entirely happy with his representation. He did a lot for me, but what I did in my career was in spite of him, not because of him. He wanted safety, but I wanted good directors and interesting characters. We both wanted money, but I didn't want a paycheck at the expense of a good part. There were times later when I felt I had made a mistake not taking more money, but that was during the bad days after I lost everything from the deceit of Husband No. 4. It was 1959 when I met Bobby, before all of that.

I went to William Morris for a meeting at Marilyn Monroe's urging since they had formerly repped her and she thought they would do well by me. In truth, it was Johnny Hyde who had been at William Morris, the one who had slept with her and got her to change her nose and chin, which made her suggestion somewhat questionable. Marilyn had switched to Music Corporation of America, which later would be run by Lew Wasserman and called MCA Universal after a series of mergers. Often handled by Lew himself, her direct agent was Mort Viner. They took good care of her—better than MCA did of me. In the end, I needed to make a change since Victor, who was at MCA, found production more profitable as did MCA, which eventually divested its talent agency after attorney general Bobby Kennedy launched an anti-trust suit.

I found Lew a cold fish. He was smart and tough, and I was smart enough not to cross him. Those who did never worked again. Lew changed Hollywood by challenging the studios and shifting power to talent and their agents. Lew's wife, Edie, was a Hollywood power herself, working tirelessly to help her husband and leverage his interests. In time, she became the major philanthropist not only of Hollywood charities but also of the Democratic Party in LA. I knew her from Betty Grable but kept my distance. I felt Edie was not a good influence on Betty, who worked for a living and suffered the fallout of some of her public scrapes from her connection to Edie, who carried on a string of affairs because she could. When Betty's career ended, I blamed Lew for not doing more to help her.

Edie was not a fan of mine, nor am I a fan of hers. Our lives seldom crossed, with her having little to say about me or my agent, Victor, who worked under her husband. But I never liked her.

I wanted to get away from MCA, so I walked into William Morris for a meeting one morning. Marilyn had made a phone call, my career was going well, and I earned enough so they would take an interest. As I entered the building, I was met by Bobby, who was all of twenty-four, having moved up from the mailroom to an assistant position. He looked me up and down, a look of appraisal, not lust, so I knew he was gay. Then he asked, "What do you want from William Morris?" as he walked me through the building to my meeting with the higher-ups. It was a gutsy question coming from a nobody, but a nobody with passion, and a pointed inquiry to someone who had yet to win an Academy Award, something I desperately wanted.

"I want to make good movies, have good roles, win an Academy Award, get paid as much as the men, and not deal with assholes," I replied, turning my head to face him as we walked down the corridor.

He burst out laughing. "So do I! But this is Hollywood, run by guys who think the rest of us are assholes." He looked at me with intensity. "I'm a nobody, which you were once. And you can get me fired for talking to you, but so be it. You have talent and should use it. I can help if you let me. But don't ask me to eat shit, because I won't do that, not even for you!"

Just like that, I fell in love. Not about sex, but about business. He got it. He got me. He had a charisma I thought would work with others, too. Finally, I didn't have to worry about someone coming on to me. I went to my meeting, told them I would switch, but wanted Bobby as my main contact. They looked at me like I really was a dumb blonde. He's a nothing, they told me.

"Then make him a somebody because 10 percent of me is a lot of money, and I want it to go to him!" They protested but were smart enough to know Bobby was a comer, and if I had recognized it, it might be time to start him as a player. I didn't so much begin his career as give William Morris a push. I didn't do it just for the money. Over the years, he didn't just take care of me for the money. Yes, he's an agent, but he's family and loyal. In Hollywood, you hold on to loyalty with both hands, unless they're crazy or criminals or sometimes both. We've been together ever since. I went with him when he joined CAA in 1975 after Mike Ovitz, Bill Haber, and Ron Meyer left William Morris to found it. It was a messy jump, but CAA did more than prosper.

Bobby pushed me to get the rights for the French movie that had started things off with Husband No. 5. Then the nosy bastard pushed me to go be with him.

"He makes you smile. You need to smile, and you've been alone for a long time. Go, and do it not just for you but for Anders." It was an argument I couldn't refute.

The question for Anders and me finally became if we moved in with Husband No. 5, did we live in NY or move to Paris, mindful I would have to travel for work. Anders, an old soul, said he loved both cities and had childhood friends in both. He didn't want to leave Dalton but was okay going back to the American School in Paris with his French buddies. We moved. At Catherine Deneuve's suggestion, I found a lovely old apartment on the sixth floor facing the fountain in Place Saint-Sulpice. It was almost in move-in condition, but I paid to have a big American refrigerator shipped over and wired for French current. I had a growing boy.

I was lucky to get an offer to do a BBC series shot in London and Paris, which was easier to manage than going back and forth to LA. Sadly, the channel tunnel wasn't yet open, but if I was lucky, I could fly door-to-door in four hours from central Paris to Pinewood, where we would shoot.

I was, in a word, shacked up. I had never done that before. I now had the opportunity to do what everyone else tried in college, except I was twenty-five years late. And I did it in full eye of the press. I wasn't going to be censored by the Vatican as had Elizabeth Taylor when she took up with Burton. On the other hand, neither Husband No. 5 nor I was married to anyone else. He did have a daughter from a prior liaison who was fifteen and lived in Stockholm. While she loved her father, they weren't close. She had been raised by her mother and stepfather happily in Stockholm with occasional weekends with her father. Sometimes he would join his ex for Christmas so his daughter wouldn't have to give up Christmas with her family and he could still see her, a very Scandinavian practicality with very little sexual jealousy, unlike the US and certainly France, where the guys practically pee on everything to mark their territory.

I felt freer to walk around Paris and went shopping for food. Just going to the fish, cheese, pastry, and butcher stores was heaven. I bought bread daily but seldom ate it, given I really had to watch my figure in my forties. It was hard work, and I had to say no to all the French delicacies my ten-year-old devoured on sight. I cooked—no one died. I got to be passable, but we had a full-time housekeeper, and what I made, I did under supervision. It was color-by-number cooking. She came to my rescue, but I learned. Slowly!

We were a happy family, Anders, Husband No. 5, and me. I saw no reason to get married. Then, to my horror, I found myself pregnant. I was getting old and had been careful. Another child at my age? But it wasn't only my age—it was my track record at the altar. I was paralyzed for days. I didn't know what to do, and the last thing I wanted to do was tell Husband No. 5, because that would rule out an abortion. Never have I to-ed and fro-ed like I did those few days.

I couldn't do it. I couldn't not tell the man I loved that I was carrying his child. I had the premonition this pregnancy was going to ruin everything. If I had an abortion and said nothing, we could go on happy as clams, but if he ever found out, well, that was the end of trust. He would be right. If I told him, he was going to want to do the honorable thing and marry me. I, too, didn't want to have a child out of wedlock. Marriage, though? No! Not if I could help it. I had learned my lesson. If we married, it would end in divorce. How, I didn't know, but I was certain.

I called Elizabeth, who was at her home in Switzerland, still married for the first time to Richard Burton but nearing the end of that run—we had discussed these issues from time to time. "Tell me what to do," I begged. "I see no light at the end of this tunnel." She wasn't much help. She didn't get married so many times because she didn't believe in the institution of marriage. "It doesn't look like our marriages have worked out so well for either of us, have they?" I asked.

"No, darling, they haven't. On the other hand, looking in the mirror these days isn't working out so well, either, but I still do that," she answered. "Look," she warned me, "do what you need to, but just ask yourself how you are going to feel in twenty years if you don't have the child and keep that secret locked away in your sagging bosom. If you think marriage is tough, try that!" She paused, then really got me by astutely adding, "Besides, what makes you think you can keep it secret? There will be doctors, nurses, cleaners, secretaries, chauffeurs, and medical records. How much do you think the tabloids will pay? What are you going to do when it comes out?" She had me. We both knew this story would run front page on every newspaper in the world, and a number of papers would pay hundreds of thousands to get this scoop.

I thanked her and hung up, thanking God for friends who understood how we lived. Neither of us could get away from the public relations equation of anything we did. Ever.

I told Husband No. 5. In a week, we had a small ceremony at the Swedish Church in Paris on the rue Mederic in the 17th arrondissement. He was delighted, but I had told him I wanted every test known to man. I was an old mother and didn't want something wrong with the baby. He agreed if the child wasn't healthy, we should abort.

First, we had the wedding. Anders was the best man. His daughter came down from Sweden to be my maid of honor. His mother, not a big fan of mine, was there. The family was old, formerly aristocratic, and clung to their crest of an upright bear claw. In Husband No. 5's family country house in the Swedish countryside, there were bear claw sculptures, bear claw paintings, and bear claw ashtrays. One night at a dinner party, with lots of people, lots of wine, and lots of food, a vapid New Yorker drove me increasingly crazier as the evening progressed with her continual whining. When she finally asked, "How come the family crest is a bear claw?" after having whined, "Why are there bear claws all over the place?" I lost it and snapped, "Because no one knew how to carve an asshole!" Everyone roared with laughter, but a snitch told Husband No. 5's mother. She never forgave me for the alleged insult to past family glory, particularly the crest, which was all that remained.

Before the wedding, we did the tests—it was my first trimester—and got the results, which showed the fetus developing normally without Down's syndrome, a risk for older mothers. Sure enough, the press found out. I don't know how or who told them, but someone must have seen me at the doctor's and phoned it in while they sent paparazzi to hide and watch.

I didn't want it known. I hadn't even made it to the end of first trimester, which is the normal waiting period before announcing. With good reason, since I miscarried two weeks later. I told Lily to send out a release because it was too much for me to have strangers, not to mention friends, congratulating me. Husband No. 5, who was now really Husband No. 5, was very supportive but downcast and disappointed. He had looked forward to being a father. It brought us closer, which was a surprise. There was a tenderness. However, I kept waiting for the other shoe to drop. Every time life had seemed really good, God or the studios willed that I step on a landmine and blow everything to smithereens.

I felt saddened by the loss of the baby. The pregnancy was hope for the future, and hope has been a rarity in my life. Jane Fonda offered surprising support, arriving one day to take me to lunch, which turned into an all-day affair with a lot of champagne. She was then married to Roger

Vadim and would be for a few more years. I was grateful for her kindness. I am the generation above her, but I admired her grit and talent. She was also into working out—and much later, when she did her workout videos, they not only toned her ass but made her a fortune that she gave away. I knew her father, Henry Fonda, who was as laconic off screen as he was on. His daughter changed Middle America forever by starting the women's fitness craze as much as Joe Gold started it for men.

We both started out as sex symbols, won Academy Awards, married more than normal—sadly, I won that race—and were in the press more than we wanted. She never totally overcame *Barbarella*, nor should she have to, although she was old enough then to know better—thirty, I think. She did it under the sway of her then husband, Roger Vadim, the old pervert, a leading French director at the height of French New Wave cinema. I give her the benefit of the doubt. Moreover, what would horny teen boys do without it? My boys loved it, although they tried to hide it, and they were certainly not alone. Jane made up for it in a series of serious pictures. Even *Nine to Five*, a supposed comedy, which was a huge 1980 hit, championed women's rights. Jane's genius produced an entertaining movie as opposed to one where you felt, "yes, I'm watching something socially relevant, aren't I special" in a film you couldn't wait to end but didn't want anyone to know. I should mention that I told Jane to use Ann Roth for the costumes for *Nine to Five*, where she did a great job, as she always does.

Our kids knew each other. Her son, Troy Garity, was so overwhelmed by both his parents that he decided as an actor not to use either of their names, neither Fonda's nor Tom Hayden's, the political activist who was married to Jane for seventeen years after she divorced Vadim. Troy and Anders became buddies. Once, commiserating on life with former sex kittens as their mothers, Garity got the winning line, exclaiming, "What do you have to complain about? Try going to grade school with Hanoi Jane as your mother!" When we heard it later, Jane and I smiled wryly with sadness, understanding the comment from front row seats.

Like Jane, I fit into almost every dress I ever wore. Yes, I have had good work. So did she. When I first did it, the science wasn't as exact. Surgeons know far more now than they did when I had my first upper eye lift, followed by a lower eye lift. The problem? Scar tissue. Every time they did something, it meant I couldn't do something else twenty years later because it would have been too much. After I did my upper eyes the first time, they were difficult to do the second time twenty years later because you have to cut out an oval of skin to get the wound to close seamlessly. That oval pulled the eye into an S-shaped curve with the outer corner up, which distorted its shape. For an actress, the eye and its shape are everything. I went ten years longer than I wanted to do my second eye lift because the first had been done in a way that might have made another obvious.

Let late-night comedians joke about Cher's pioneering efforts. Her doctors learned to improve their techniques from their mistakes on us. But I remember the long-ago confession by Marilyn that she had fixed her nose and chin. My sister went before all of us.

Both Jane and I understood that lipo, which everyone jokes about, isn't about losing weight. It's about tightening something since you can't spot diet. You have to be an idiot to use lipo for weight loss—when someone dies on the table, it's from weight-loss lipo or bad anesthesia. For spot reducing, it works, and the scar tissue there is useful because it tightens the skin, so it looks firmer and younger. After lipo, you can't wear a bikini, because although the skin is tighter, it isn't as smooth. They can take the fat and inject it into your face, which gives back youthful plumpness. Since it certainly lives forever in your ass, fat will live transplanted in your face and lips—but only about half survives. The other cells don't establish enough blood supply. As a bonus, six months after the work, the stem cells kick in, giving you another 10 percent in volume. It takes a year before you really know how you're going to look. And it hurts. The French used to say about middle-aged women that you sacrifice your waist for your neck. No longer. You can stay thin and avoid the haggard, Mick Jagger look with fat or collagen injections.

Nothing replaces youth. Hollywood runs on it. So does sexual desire. You can create an illusion after thirty-five, maintaining it up to forty-five with good work, but after that, you just look good for your age. When a young guy—because middle-aged men and women know better unless they are being catty—says, "You look really good for your age," I want to kick him in the nuts. Either I look good, or I don't. Go fuck yourself.

I am reminded of Joan Rivers's comment that her breasts were her best feature, which is why she wore open-toed shoes. We all get there in the end.

As I recovered from my miscarriage, I went for a touch-up and had my eyes done when Husband No. 5 was out of town for a week. The surgeon had worked on a number of Madame Claude's girls. I refused to look middle-aged.

When I wasn't working, I walked around in a daze. Happy, sad, surprised, and with a home alive and filled with warmth. There was a big party for the opening of *Chinatown*, so I got myself pretty with my new face, and Husband No. 5 escorted me. It was the summer of 1974. Nominated for eleven Academy Awards, *Chinatown* was considered one of the best film noire detective movies ever made. Jack Nicholson was magnificent. Roman Polanski rose to the top of his career before pleading guilty to statutory rape and beginning his Parisian exile a few years later.

I love Paris. Not always the French. I had good friends who made the others insignificant by comparison. The chestnut trees, each with peeling white bark and dark green leaves, were impressionist images in the parks, along the Seine, and on the streets. Everywhere I looked, I found new Beaux Arts buildings with limestone facades and mansard roofs. There was beauty everywhere: the streets, the stores, the fountains, the bridges, the outdoor food markets, and the clothing, which was detailed, well-made, and expensive. The cobblestone streets made a rumbling sound under the car wheels unlike any other sound on the road. It was music.

I had to worry about security: I had bodyguards for Anders and me as well as an armed driver I trusted, who often followed me in the car for protection as I walked around. I don't think I would have needed this level of protection if I had been a man. It was a period where terrorism was a threat all over Europe. I resented the added security and the lack of privacy but appreciated the blessings that had caused me to need it. I had been up and down, but up was better.

I wandered the streets of Paris for another three years until it was time for Anders to go to high school. We agreed he should follow Sebastian's footsteps at Andover. Sebastian was by then working on Wall Street and doing well. I slipped him a bit of money from time to time to give him the down payment for a classic-six apartment in a good building on Park Avenue, which turned out to be a wonderful investment for him, as well as a country house. I hoped he would get married and find a wonderful girl as a partner, but much as I liked babies, the idea of being a grandmother didn't sit well with me from a professional standpoint. I didn't want that image in the media. Since I had no choice, I shut up and resigned myself to no longer playing women with sex lives and trading my image for permanent screen motherhood. Back in 1977, there weren't films with fifty-year-old women who had sex, let alone good sex. The studio chiefs, as Viagra villains, didn't want to see that and couldn't imagine anyone else did, either. The only middle-aged people who had sex, evidently, were men who could continue to be box-office leads—but only with twenty-two-year-old female costars, because that was realistic.

I remember with great fondness those days in Paris, where I not only got to live with my mother and stepfather, but also reconnect with my French family who had taken me in years before. I loved my Swedish stepfather all of his life and appreciated that he was good to my mother. There was a sense of loss sometimes because I missed my friends in New York and missed Lily a lot. While she would come over often, it wasn't the same as seeing her several times a week.

I do remember Elizabeth coming and visiting, particularly just before my mother married my Swedish stepfather. She was just as bad as my mother, making a grand entrance everywhere she went. The two of them together were trouble and often tried to upstage each other in a joking way, however, the restaurants and stores loved the publicity.

Elizabeth was a wise old bird, not that I dared tell her that, although now I think she would have laughed. She loved me and sat me down to explain that my mother was getting married and might have a baby. She also warned me that she might not. She was practical, not preachy, and when my mother lost my baby brother, I was sad but not completely surprised. My mother was too depressed to say much but Elizabeth swept me off for a long weekend, while I guess from my reading, my mother palled around with Jane.

I miss Elizabeth a lot now. I also realized then how much I missed Sebastian, who was in the States. The great advantage of friends and family all over the world is a disadvantage, too, because they are all far away, and to see some, you have to miss others. I thought then that maybe those people who lived in a village all their lives had it made, since everyone they loved was just down the street.

Anders

FIFTY IS TREACHEROUS FOR BLONDES

I was turning fifty. Fuck that. I told myself it was fabulous fifty. So did Husband No. 5, repeatedly. His ardor was undiminished. I loved sleeping with him, and not just the sex part but the cuddling and the contact and the feeling we were in this together for keeps.

Elizabeth, five years younger than I, arranged a party for us in LA. She was by then married to Senator John Warner—not one of her wiser choices, but I kept my mouth shut. Who was I to talk? She campaigned for him. Can you imagine what it must have been like for a bunch of voters to show up to a small town in Virginia? Worse, I couldn't imagine what it was like for her, to be pulled and gawked at by people who would either be tongue-tied or intrusive.

Warner won with her help, and to give him more seniority for senate committees, his predecessor resigned one day early. At the Senate swearing-in ceremony, Liz, who was beginning her fat phase, was in full glory in the Senate visitors' box. Even for the US Senate, Elizabeth Taylor was a big deal. In a low-cut dress—I don't think she owned any with a proper Republican neckline—she leaned over the balcony to watch. From the press box, a voice was heard, evidently not sotto voce enough. "The people of Virginia have just elected the three biggest boobs in the country to the Senate."

Elizabeth, or me for that matter, never quite got away from discussions of our cleavage. It was our professional calling card. The studios—guys again—liked to play it up. Our cleavage was part of our allure. At the Academy Awards, when both Elizabeth and I were presenting, she wore the Cartier diamond that clocked in at sixty-nine

153

carats. Bob Hope, hosting the show, took one look and commented, "Ah, the little rock in the big valley." She flashed me a look of annoyance offstage after he said it. As for me, I came out wearing my twenty-carat diamond earrings, well aware that following Elizabeth, my jewels didn't count. I had the valley but no rock worth mentioning.

As for Warner, I found him boring. After a while, so did Elizabeth. Here she was, playing housewife with a man with half her experience, half her street smarts, and half her IQ. Plus, Elizabeth had worked for her money, where Warner had gotten his from marrying and divorcing a Mellon banking heiress. Yet he was overseeing the country, and she was going to committee wives' teas. Another man who thought he knew everything running things. What was wrong with that picture? Betty Ford was one answer.

Me, too, since what was I doing? I had up and moved to Paris, was now fifty, and hadn't had a hit since my detective trio. My career revolved around my Parisian home life. I had wonderful roles in several BBC dramas and smaller films that hadn't shaken up the box office or garnered any nominations. Anders had flown the coop. I hadn't yet reached for pills or the bottle, though it was coming. I needed to work. I asked Bobby what he could find. I didn't want to rock the boat until there was something worth rocking it for.

We had my fiftieth party at my house in LA. Elizabeth's birthday gift was paying for the party, with Chen and Lily arranging everything and sending out fifty invitations. Fifty on fifty. The numbers didn't work out since a lot more than fifty guests showed up, but it was a sweet idea. I got myself the hottest dress I could find, put on my most expensive jewels, including the twenty-carat diamond earrings from Husband No. 4, and let it all hang out. Elizabeth showed up with even bigger diamonds, something she duly noted with a laugh, while leaving John Warner behind, which was a relief. Husband No. 5 had a good time. My two sons came with dates, which was interesting. I felt for the girls, whom I had never previously met. I was glad I wasn't in their shoes, being introduced to the mother who was a world-famous actress dressed to the nines in Valentino and dripping with diamonds. I gave them points for just saying hello and not peeing in their pants.

Bobby came, not only with a hot new assistant, who wasn't a "date" since he had yet to come out, but also with a proposed contract as a birthday present. It was a leading role. It was a good role. It was a role I wanted. Just like that, I was back in play.

The role was a senior German lawyer in the aftermath of World War II prosecuting local city government officials for their complicity in murdering German Jews, gays, and gypsies during the war. The film was set in 1947 as Germany slowly started to recover. It was to be shot by Nestor Almendros, one of the greatest cinematographers, whose lush scenery and use of light belied the darkness of the storyline. Among other films, he had shot Eric Rohmer's *Claire's Knee*, a brilliant film that had done exceptionally well, and Truffaut's *The Man Who Loved Women*, which I loved, and he was currently editing *Days of Heaven*, directed by Terence Malick, which would go on to fame in no small part due to the cinematography for which Nestor won the Academy Award.

In the course of the case, the prosecutor finds evidence that her aging father, who was in the Nazi government during the war, was directly involved in killing local citizens and lying about it. Up until this point, she had believed her father was an honorable man, suffering to survive and protect his family during the war. The knowledge that what he had done including the suffering of their family during the war had been based on a lie profoundly changed her as she realized the suffering was needless, wasn't based on honorable resistance to evil, and might have been avoided except for the vanity of her father. It changed her relationship with her father and with men forever, since she now saw them as vain creatures completely driven by power, glory, and ego.

But not sex. In the script, the forty-something prosecutor is married but sexless, typical of a Hollywood script, even one as good as this one, that neutered aging females, while even her aged father had sex with a younger second wife. Really?

I got the part but at a reduced fee of $500,000 with profit points, not as good as gross points, but Bobby told me I wasn't in a position to bargain. Before signing, I asked for a script meeting. I needed to know who the director would be. It had been offered to François Truffaut, and would be his first major Hollywood production, but his native language was French, which scared the studio. I pushed for him, as I had adored him since coming to know him from my Paris days. It didn't hurt that he was funny, ironic, charming, and very attractive.

Bobby didn't want me to go to meetings. Sign first and then say whatever you want, he said. This was a great script, but if I made too many demands, "They will find someone more pliable. They always do." I asked for the meeting, knowing after I signed, I had no leverage whatsoever and they could do what they wanted. Bobby conceded the point and arranged the meeting, warning me they could do what they wanted anyway since they had final cut. That and the fact the studio often lied. We got our meeting, and Bobby, Lily, and I showed up with the writer, producer, and studio people.

We met on the lot, and it's us, the studio execs, and Truffaut, who had flown in from Paris. He hadn't yet signed—whether it was because of his own doubts or those of the studios was unclear.

We finished the introductions, and the food cart was there with the coffee, fruit plate, deli sandwiches, smoked salmon, and pastries. Truffaut was there with his translator, Annette Insdorf. She taught film at Yale, including my kids, and then later at Columbia University in New York, and over time had become friends with Truffaut. Although he understood English well, he worried about his heavy accent. He also wanted to make points with greater subtlety, for which he needed his native French translated.

He said, "What I like about this story is the twist. How this woman is going along in her life, trying to be honest and God-fearing amid the suffering of the Germans after the war, and she finds out everything she has believed is a lie, that her life was convoluted for lies, and that her neighbors were murdered because some of the townspeople, including her father, curried favor from Nazi officials. How do you go on after that? How do you make peace with not just your life but the relationships with those you love?"

It was why Truffaut was a genius. He took a hundred-page script and condensed it into a paragraph. I looked up. "I have two issues. One, a German upset at what her country did to Jews during World War II is not

157

a novel storyline. Isn't there a way we can make this more applicable to a modern audience? Second, more generally, the lead character is sexless. Everyone in Hollywood thinks women over forty should shrivel up and die. Can't we have a mature woman who has sex, like the men?"

The studio execs freaked—the usual adolescent studio mentality. Truffaut, who really loved women, all women, understood the sex part easily. He addressed it simply. "You are quite right," he said with a heavy accent. "We don't want a neutered lead. We can provide her with a sex life like any male lead."

I thought the studio execs would wet themselves. No one wants to see that, they wanted to scream, but felt cowed because there were seated with a huge French director who made brilliant art films they didn't understand. They feared he had what they didn't, whatever it was, because they focused on money, while Truffaut focused on stories.

The next issue was more daunting. Truffaut looked puzzled. "This is a profound existential story about betrayal occurring out of immense social suffering from the war. How do you provide that danger, that pressure from reality except from the after-war German experience?"

It was a good point. You should have seen the studio execs' faces. They were lost. Going from Nazis to existentialism in five minutes was too much for them.

Then something popped into Truffaut's mind. "What about the boat?"

"What boat?" asked Bobby. "You mean the one where they turned back the Jews?"

"Exactly," he said. "The Roosevelt administration turned back a boat filled with Jewish refugees because they didn't like Jews, so it went back to Europe, and they ended up in the camps. They did that. Why?"

Truffaut got more intrigued as he thought. "That might work. A survivor sues the US government for the death of his wife in the camps which would have been avoided if they could have gotten off the boat. We could do the same story. Woman investigating, her father in the war office who turns back the boat because he knew the administration didn't like Jews."

It was a better storyline. Nazis allowing Jews to die for their social advancement in Germany wasn't novel. Americans allowing Jews to die for their own political advancement was. Plus, I got to be a real woman with sex.

The studio gents didn't understand what had just happened. What they understood was they had a famous intellectual French director, which made them nervous, a famous Academy-Award-winning actress who wanted to have sex, which would be revolting but maybe kinky enough to work and, if too offensive, they would just cut the rushes and leave them on the floor, plus a brilliant cinematographer on the cusp of an Academy Award and a relatively small budget. This was an art film with no plane, car, or boat explosions, no significant special effects, and no aliens landing.

If it didn't make money, it might generate awards and good press. They could always write off any losses against a blockbuster and screw those actors out of their profit points. It would be okay.

The thing about Hollywood, which made it such a treacherous place to work, was no one would say no, yet no one wanted to sign a check.

Neophytes would arrive in Hollywood and go to meetings where everyone would tell them this is a great idea, we want to be involved, let us read the script, let's do casting for a dry run, it's so novel, so new, so exciting! Young and naive to the Hollywood runaround, these kids would then either move to Hollywood or, if they were already there, quit their jobs to work full time on their projects, now that they'd been given assurances it was a great idea and sure to be a hit.

Then they tried to collect on these promises or, worse, tried to get money. Suddenly, no calls were returned, no meetings were arranged, and if they managed to stalk the people who had told them how much they loved the idea in a parking lot, they were brushed off politely with more vague promises.

The rewrite took a month. While the location changed, most of the other changes were relatively minor and the psychological issues remained the same. The prosecutor, who loses the suit in the end, because winning in that scenario wasn't possible, raises important issues with the audience. It would have to be enough. The lead, a middle-aged woman, which was a rarity in itself, would have a love interest, also a rarity. Where it got dicey was her sense of betrayal and her obsession with the men who had controlled her destiny behind the scenes—here, not only her father, but also the anti-Semites of the Roosevelt administration. I was scripted to play her as a prim, straitlaced lawyer, unsexy in her career and her life, except in private.

I had gone back to Paris with Husband No. 5. He supported my doing the film, but it would be shot in LA, where I could live at my house in the Hills, and on location in DC. He didn't want to come for three months because he needed to work. I didn't want to be away that long, but I needed to work, too. This was a great opportunity, so I went, and he stayed. Big mistake.

The shoot was arduous but rewarding. Nestor filmed us in color, but there were lots of dark colors—grays, browns, and maroons with shadow—as befitted the story line. Just as important, he shot me softly, carefully lighting me. Middle age never looked so good. With diffusion lenses—Vaseline on the lens was also an old trick in those pre-digital days—I was hot again for my few love scenes. I was shot seminude from the back, which was fine since I had kept my figure through diet and exercise, and there was one full-on shot of my breasts as I rolled over. Since I was on my back, they stayed put and didn't descend as fifty-year-old breasts usually do. From the rushes, they looked great. My sadness in the film was palpable.

As in *Marie Antoinette,* this became a personal story for me: betrayal by men for no good reason other than ego. They made decisions, and others suffered from their mistakes, with nothing to be done after the fact except the hard-earned wisdom that this might have been avoided. I channeled all my emotions from the aftereffects of Husband No. 4's murder and financial betrayal, which got stirred up by the storyline. This was the story of my life and of other women's, too. Men may be victims of their position in society as well, driven by testosterone, but as the ones who hold power, they are in a position to make changes. Women have other drives that can offset men's, as in a good marriage. I finally understood how that worked with Husband No. 5—or thought I did.

He was supposed to come visit every month. He came the first month, which was great. He was happy to see me, literally and figuratively in a Mae West kind of way. He kept putting off the second trip. It was such a long flight for a few days, he said, and he had a lot of work.

A week later, I was on set, having just finished a harrowing scene with the actor who plays my father in the film, and Lily was there, looking particularly ill at ease. "I don't know how to tell you this," she started, which is never a good beginning. "You need to see these," she said, handing me the newspapers. On the gossip page were pictures of Husband No. 5 exiting a French café accompanied by a very pretty young woman who had reached over to touch his arm. The photo credit was from a French paper, so it was all over Paris, too.

I was away. Mice played. He was a man, this was Paris, and I wanted to work, so this was the cost of my working. I didn't say anything. I didn't want to have the discussion. I thought I finally had what I'd dreamed of. I was hurt, and I used my grief and betrayal for my performance. I had to channel it somewhere.

We hit the second-month mark and were working on final scenes, final reaction shots, and exterior shots on set before the DC shots, which would be fairly easy, since they were to establish the film and set it in the late 1940s, but almost all of the drama had been indoors and already filmed.

We went to DC for a week. These were long days, but not emotionally draining. Back to LA. Final shots. I had been gone almost three months. The studio booked me a first-class ticket back to Paris, where I was to have a few weeks off and then back to LA for looping dialogue, which was always necessary. I flew home.

Husband No. 5 greeted me warmly. I had suppressed my feelings from the press photos, a lot more in Paris than LA. I didn't know what people thought as I walked through the airport and in the streets, but I was used to having people gawk at me, trying to figure out what I was doing, making assumptions about my life because I was in the press so often, they felt they knew me. It was nice to be home, but at dinner the bomb hit.

"We need to talk." Okay, this wasn't going to be good. A lot of hemming and hawing. Okay, really bad. Sinking feeling in the stomach. This marriage is over. Or he has cancer, but he looks pretty healthy. Maybe he stole all my money, but I would know that by now. After my prior experiences, I had it locked up tighter than the vault at Tiffany's.

And then it came out. She was knocked up. The one in the pictures. This was Catholic France, so no abortions.

"I'm sorry." The famous words of every philanderer. What a surprise—his dick works, and babies happen. Good to know. No protection. What was he thinking? I have to say, along with my sadness and betrayal, which I had already felt after seeing those pictures, it did flash through my mind that this was going to be his money and not mine, since I didn't depend on him for support. Certainly, no court would compel me to pay child support for his out-of-wedlock child. I haven't written about Husband No. 5's money because it didn't matter. He earned a nice upper-middle-class salary as a partner in an international law firm, but I made more per movie than he made in a year. I didn't care—I had already lived the life with the weekly jewels on my breakfast tray and was happier now. Or had been.

I had failed to give him a child. One I hadn't wanted, but one I would have loved dearly had it survived. He wanted a kid. You don't bang a hot girl without protection unless in the back of your mind you want that result. He needed a chance to be a father—not like the father he was with his daughter whom he barely saw, but a real one with a kid who would run into his arms every night when he got home.

I knew what was going to happen without his telling me. This was a movie where you knew the ending even before they run the opening credits. He was going to leave me to be with her, marry her, and be a daddy. Biology is destiny.

Life in Paris had come to an end. He walked around with so much guilt on his face I couldn't look at him. I wasn't bitchy; I just packed up and flew back to New York by the end of the week.

The worst was the effect on Anders, who was losing another father. I wanted Husband No. 5 to remain in Anders's life, and he did in his fashion, but I had seen what had happened with his daughter and understood he would fade out of Anders's life. Either we cut the knot now or left it to fray slowly, keeping Anders in pain. I wanted to rip off the Band-Aid.

With the facts, a divorce was easy. I loved that apartment on the Place Saint-Sulpice. Catherine Denueve and I had been neighbors, and we'd see each other every other month or so. I went over before I left. She was understanding. Kind. Sad for me. We both understood we lived in a world run by men and had to live within their rules. I was reminded of Gloria Steinem's line about Jackie Kennedy—she played the game with the rules written by the enemy and won.

I lost.

Nestor, François, and the editors spent more time editing and on visual effects than usual. François wanted to dazzle with his first Hollywood production. I was prepared for reshoots, but the nice thing about a French director used to working on a limited budget was he got what he needed first time around, since a reshoot was a luxury French films didn't usually permit.

They finished their rough cut, which except for music and final tweaks that would come as the premiere drew close was mostly complete. There was a bit of contretemps over my bare breasts. If they showed them, they would get an R rating, which concerned the studio, who feared it would cut ticket sales. We had another meeting. All of us, the usual bunch plus François.

The head of distribution—known throughout Hollywood as Lurch, not that this nickname should color your thinking—attended. Calling him Lurch didn't do him justice in the same way calling the Eiffel Tower an interesting building didn't do it justice, either. He moved like a monster, he looked like one, and his thinking was so slow and turgid you wished you could put him on fast forward. He was without doubt the most unimaginative exec I have ever met in a town where the bar was set particularly low.

The studio execs, including Lurch, launched into their concern about lost ticket sales, and Bobby rose to the occasion. He coolly pointed out a drama about war criminals and anti-Semitism was not going have a lot of under-sixteen viewers. This was not a kiddie date movie. Moreover, he added, "Think about the free publicity with Babe topless. No serious actress in America has done this, and every reviewer and paper will talk about it. You'll get guys coming in just for that."

Cha-ching, this was all the execs needed. Even Lurch understood the sound of a cash register. R rating, here we go.

America was so primitive. The film opened in a limited run with great reviews. As Bobby had predicted, every endless article talked about my breasts. You would think from the press America had never seen one before. Certainly not aged USDA grade A prime as mine were. There was as much discussion of my bare breasts as there was about the subject matter of the film, which depressed me to no end. The issues were real and serious, and I had put much of my life's frustration into my performance. I don't think I was the only woman to feel let down by our male-dominated society or to have found that what I had thought I had experienced turned out later to be something else.

Truffaut, whom I adored, didn't understand the fuss. In France, bare breasts were on TV and advertisements, and no one thought about it. While they admired them, caressed them, and inspected them, they were just a part of normal life. In Paris, when you went bra shopping, there was a middle-aged lady who stood behind you, cupped your breasts with her hands to get an idea of size, heft, and weight, and then told you which bras you should wear. They were always right.

Anders called from Andover to voice support and tell me how much he liked my performance. He surprised me when he said, "You were right to show your breasts. For you, this was about equality." While I was pleased he understood, I was shocked at how embarrassed I was to have my son discuss my breasts. I was used to being public property, but I didn't want my children to know. Most people can compartmentalize their lives.

They build fences. They don't talk about their sex lives with their parents and children. If they cheat, they don't talk about that, either. In my case, I couldn't cross the street to buy lipstick without its color being discussed on Page Six.

I was more prude than I realized. Talking to my children about the birds and bees after they reached adolescence was difficult. I had this image of myself as liberal, open, able to discuss anything with anyone, but that image went out the window when I tried to discuss sex with my children. I don't think they ever knew how hard it was for me. Inside, I was really more conservative than I had ever contemplated, which was difficult to acknowledge. I did talk to them, since it was necessary to warn them about disease, being used, and girls who could get pregnant. As I pointed out, paraphrasing Marilyn's famous line as Lorelei Lee from *Gentlemen Prefer Blondes*, those girls wouldn't be after my sons' money—they were after mine.

I have been on Johnny Carson a dozen times. As an old star, I was well known in his monologues. My marriages, my divorces, and now my tits. After a while, it got old. I walked on one night to promote our movie. They had the right clip lined up. I wore a tight black sleeveless cocktail dress with a low neckline covered with black gauze to my neck with black Manolo high heels and my twenty-carat diamond earrings.

I walked out, did the air kiss thing, because otherwise these guys smudge your makeup, which took two hours for a makeup artist to apply, and took my seat. First thing out of the box, a crack about my breasts. "Didn't know you knew how to wear a dress!" Titters from the audience, whose collective IQ left something to be desired.

I smiled sweetly because I really wanted people to see my movie. It was worth seeing and dealt with serious issues, like the asshole sitting next to me who got paid $20 million a year and was focusing on my boobs because it was an easy joke. If I was too aggressive, it would turn off viewers. Given his usual guests, I wanted to respond that he certainly would know a boob when he saw one, but I took the high ground.

"Johnny, I have been completely overwhelmed by the attention one twenty-second scene has received compared to the issues of anti-Semitism, Nazis, and guys making decisions women have to live with but don't get to make."

He was completely uncomfortable. Motherhood, apple pie, and pro-Jew is a Hollywood mantra. He laughed and came back with, "Your performance humanized the story. You were just tremendous."

Applause. I had to play nice but didn't want to. "That's so sweet," I answered. Then less sweet, I asked, "What did you like about it?" wondering if he had seen the movie, which was not his kind of thing, or had just read *Cliffs Notes* from his staff, who sat through these screenings.

His answer surprised me. "Because you showed how it feels when the world you think you know isn't the world you live in." Maybe he had seen it after all.

"Exactly. Thank you. I was hoping to convey that. Working with Truffaut was a dream come true."

A Carson lob back, "Why did you bare your breasts? You're an Academy-Award-winning actress and didn't need to, although it was tasteful. And tasty?" Big wink to the audience here. "So, why?"

The answer was easy and short. "I was fed up that the only women you see in film having sex are twenty-somethings while male stars go on past sixty. Women my age have sex. We are equals to men. We don't need a Hollywood double standard just because things are run by fat, middle-aged white guys."

Huge applause. Catcalls even. I was surprised but not as surprised as Johnny. I just answered what I thought, but the response was immediate. The coverage was overwhelming, and my answer finally booted my breasts off the pages of the papers. The studio, needless to say, was infuriated, because nothing annoys fat, middle-aged white guys like calling them fat middle-aged white guys on television.

From there, I went on the morning talk shows. Barbara Walters treated me like a goddess, and I think I struck a blow for many women who felt marginalized after a certain age.

Elizabeth called to complain I should have waited for her so we could have gone on Johnny together. She pointed out, "Darling, you better marry really well next time, since if you piss off the studio, they won't let you work." The articles about my latest divorce inevitably compared my track record to hers with the unkinder articles making bets on which of us would go on to have more. It was pulling wings off a fly. I wasn't happy about my last divorce, either, and Husband No. 5 got a bouncing baby boy for his infidelity. If we had never married, this might have been avoided. Once he had an expectation of fatherhood, that drive took over.

Elizabeth was glad, however, to duck the sniping coming from Joan Rivers, who had a field day about my breasts, my divorce, and my being a poster child for women's lib. What wit, aimed at everyone, including herself. Although it was difficult to stay mad at a middle-aged comedienne who used to say about herself that it was a good day when she didn't step on her breasts, I managed to do just that for several months after she pulled me apart on stage. I loved Joan. Loved her. Except when she was talking about me. Some of those comments were hard to forget.

She was brilliant, funny, and hardworking. Joan did everything Johnny Carson did, except backward in high heels, and then she got blackballed. He was a pig with her. He made her career, it's true, put her on as guest host, promoted her and adored her—as long as she knew her place as a pet rabbit. When she got the opportunity to do her own talk show on another network, she took it. Why not? What did her long-standing friend do? He blackballed her from NBC for twenty years. Johnny, despite his many wives, ran around like crazy, and the girls always got a gold Rolex to show for it. A dickhead who could get away with it.

While he was decent with me when I was on his show promoting my films, that didn't make what he and NBC did to Joan less reprehensible. For years, Joan got lots of press herself, and when it wasn't about her plastic surgery, it was for jokes that offended someone. Her attitude? Get a life. It's comedy. Someone has to make the joke, and if it offends someone, maybe that's good—it reminds us there remain lines that shouldn't be crossed, things that make us wince. Comedy makes us think. The reason court jesters weren't beheaded for taking a political fact and twisting it into humor was they made people laugh about the unlaughable.

Joan was a pioneer. She took sex and innuendo and used it. Johnny was certainly not above making breast jokes at my expense. Joan just became the first woman to make penis and vagina jokes. Where would Kathy Griffin or Margaret Cho be without her? She paved the way, took the hits, and didn't work for a long time because of it. If she was tasteless, have you listened to male comics on late-night?

Guys use sex to sell tickets, but a girl who does the same thing? She's a ho when she goes on late-night and calls it like a man. Hollywood perfected the double standard.

Joan changed the red carpet forever with her witty and vulgar comments about fashion, shoots, and beauty. I miss her. I just didn't like her ammunition aimed at me.

My divorce went through with Joan's monologues keeping a running score. There was even sympathy for me in the press. On the whole, compared to my other divorces, there was less bad publicity. Five was a big number, which is what the press focused on. I decided to sell the Place Saint-Sulpice apartment. Too many memories of a former life. I owned it outright and, according to French law, since I had brought it into our marriage, it was mine free and clear. Husband No. 5 wanted it. It was a wonderful apartment in one of the chicest areas of Paris, and its value had doubled. He could barely afford half of it. I owed him nothing. I dithered. I'm old-school. Jewels and real estate gifts don't have to be returned or shared. Elizabeth roared with laughter when I told her I was dithering. "Tell the bum to take a hike. You got the publicity. He got the twenty-year-old, and he wants a bargain on an apartment you bought with your money? Fuck him!"

She had a point. On the other hand, for reasons I didn't understand, I still liked him. He was a father and had lived in that apartment for five years. What I found incomprehensible was that while I couldn't bear to be reminded of my time with him, he wanted to live in our home with a new wife and son. That made no sense. Men! My lawyers worked out a deal. I got half in a lump sum, and at his death or on sale of the apartment, I would get the other half at today's value plus 4 percent a year appreciation. It was a good deal for him, but it meant his widow would have to move for certain, so we put in certain clauses and got her signature, too, just to make things official. Done and done.

My life seemed to change after my comments on Carson. I had become the beautiful but aging face for women's lib. Suddenly, no one was talking about my breasts but about how I wanted to be taken as an equal to a man. Or about how men kept us down. Surprise! My popularity scores skyrocketed, and my film did well for such a serious topic, surprising us. We were nominated in four categories, including best actress and best cinematography. More talk shows, more promotion until Oscar night. Valentino again, bright red this time with matching shoes and my twenty-carat earrings. I was fifty-one and delighted not to be up against Meryl Streep! I won. I hoped it was for my performance, not my breasts or the academy feeling sorry for me, given my fifth divorce and Husband No. 5's subsequent marriage and fatherhood all over the press.

Bobby, along with his latest boy toy, was beside himself with joy. He felt he was responsible for this because he had championed me. He was right—I owed him. I bought him a Mercedes convertible. He still has it. The car is now ancient, but he tells me it remains in perfect condition and turns over faster than a Vegas showboy.

I started searching for another role. Two Oscars and a sexy serious role at fifty—what could be better? And famous now not just for being pretty or an Academy Award winner, but with my fellow women who were just as fed up as I was with the way decisions as a society were made. There were a lot of women who felt what they wanted counted for far less than the desires of men. They even printed T-shirts with the slogan *Not a fat, middle-aged white man!* When I saw a young, dumb white kid wearing one, I wanted to walk over and say, you will be!

With the awards out, I had junkets promoting the film around the world. François would often join me. We ended up in Hong Kong for a few days, which I loved. It was a Chinese London, up and down on the hills with left-hand drive and crazy Chinese drivers who didn't understand a word of what you told them. We had a fling. In another life, I might have considered what it would be like to be with him. He was completely French and with his own baggage from a troubled childhood. He loved, absolutely loved women, something described in his film, *The Man Who Loved Women*. It was great when you were with him but a little less great when you realized if he wasn't with you, he was probably with someone else. I enjoyed our junket and experience together, but when it was over, I was grown-up enough to go back to New York to figure out what I was going to do next.

This was very difficult. I was very sad to lose my stepfather who assured me that he would always be in my life. In a way he was, but he mostly was not. At Andover, the other kids were impressed that I was my mother's son. My classmates' discussions of her breasts were enormously embarrassing. But when she became known for women's lib, I got popular with the girls, who thought with a mother like that, I had to be cool. Haha! The fiftieth birthday party was legendary. I got drunk and laid.

Anders

173

STUDIO 54 LIFE

At this point, nightlife in New York revolved around Studio 54, which had just opened and was the best nightclub ever. Other clubs have tried but failed to replicate its glamour. No cell phone cameras, no tape recorders, no videos, and no red velvet ropes separating the celebrities. You either got in or, most likely, you didn't. The doorman, Marc, became a celebrity in his own right and got used to having people he refused entry start complaining when they saw him on the street. He had a photographic memory, not only remembering who you were but who you were with. Anders started going when he was down from Yale, introduced by Nan Kempner's son. Nan was a New York socialite married to an investment banker and known for having the best collection of Yves Saint Laurent in the world. The collection was so extensive that when she died, the Costume Exhibit at the Metropolitan Museum of Art ran a three-month show titled, *Nan Kempner: American Chic*. Nan's son took a lot of jokes about his mother's obsessive fashion collection and would give tours of the family apartment to Yale classmates, showing each closet with the tagline, "Here, too, are my mother's clothes."

Anders went one night, and Marc the doorman clicked on the connection to Nan, not knowing Anders was my son—realizing it later when Anders took me to Studio so I could see what the fuss was about. Nan and I shared a table while the kids ran around having fun. Liquor licenses seemingly came and went in the club, as did the police, until Ian Shrager and Steve Rubell went to prison for tax evasion when the police discovered garbage bags stuffed with cash in the basement, which brought the party to a screeching halt.

Studio 54 was entertaining because we knew we could blow off steam and not worry everyone was taking pictures to sell on their way home. Now, there have to be VIP areas, just so celebrities don't get their drinking, making out or bad behavior ending up not only on the internet but also on the evening news. Thinking about cell phones, I have to say I didn't think it possible for New Yorkers to be more self-involved, but cell phones proved me wrong. There are a lot of smart phones being used by a lot of not smart people, who step off the escalator and stop to check their phone, completely oblivious to the fact there are ten people behind them that can't stop even if they want to, and they usually don't. There are a lot of us who want privacy when going to the grocery store or walking to the corner without makeup, and that's exactly when an asshole with a cell phone snaps a shot and sells it to *TMZ* or *People*. If cell phones had existed at Studio, they would have recorded a lot of evidence, because when the liquor license was gone (and sometimes while it was there), record company execs would bring attaché cases and pop them open. On one side was a mirror and on the other a pile of cocaine and quaaludes. People helped themselves.

The main stage was the dance floor, and every now and then the sets would change while people were dancing—one fabulous set would go up, another down, and you would go from Venice to the circus or Mars to the Moulin Rouge. The theater seats around the stage were removed on the main floor where the bars were located with tables and booths. Upstairs on the balconies, the seating remained—people went to chat, watch the dance floor below, make out, have sex, or do drugs. The drag queens used the ladies' room—everyone used the ladies' room. And they treated me like an old friend, even if we had never met. It was celebrity heaven—Liza, Halston, Calvin Klein, Andy Warhol, Elizabeth Taylor, Nan, me, and pretty much everyone else who went out at night and could get in, including Jaqueline Onassis. There were the singers, from Donna Summer to Frank Sinatra, Barbra Streisand, Diana Ross, and Michael Jackson, and then you sat with them to have a drink.

The wait staff were dancers, singers, and models and were just as hot as the guests and much younger. Anyone who wanted to got picked up, and a lot did. A certain celebrity was famous for taking a different young blond boy home every night she was there—and she was there a lot. Given the drugs and alcohol, inhibitions were inhibited. Steve Rubell, who was an entertaining host when he was high, which was often, would run around with a vodka-filled squirt gun aimed into the mouths of friends or hot boys. It was as if Sodom and Gomorrah had been imagined by a Hollywood set designer and filled with beautiful people. Everyone wanted to be there, while most were turned away by Marc the doorman. It was a club with the only membership card needed was the fact you were inside. Entering Studio 54's doors, I was sorry the real studios weren't more like it—exciting, special, imaginative, open to ideas, and brilliant at public relations, given my often-contested relationship with them.

I missed the big night when Bianca Jagger had her birthday party and rode in on a white horse. After that, pretty much anything went. My second night there, Elizabeth Taylor showed up, having flown in from London where she was filming the Agatha Christie mystery, *The Mirror Cracked*, with Angela Lansbury, Rock Hudson, and my old *Marie Antoinette* costar, Tony Curtis. I didn't know she was in town but knew she was playing the part of a bitter old actress fighting with a rival on a production of *Mary, Queen of the Scots*. In imitation of her role and having a bit of fun, shocking her guests, I walked over and said haughtily with a wink, "Avoiding me?"

"I've been avoiding you for years, darling, and after your last Academy Award, which I can't understand, I'll continue!" she replied in her *The Mirror Cracked* character, pouring another drink with a scowl. Given the press after my first Oscar while she wasn't even nominated for *Cleopatra*, this remark provided fish bait for the press.

The next day, sure enough, the papers were full of our feud, to our great amusement. We played this out for a few more days—she was in town before she had to return to filming. Seeing each other at lunch, we snarled, "I'm not sitting anywhere near *you*," and called each other later to laugh and plan our next "fight." We got reams of press, which helped her movie, and we enjoyed ourselves because we were playing with the press when it was usually the other way around.

In the end, we went back to Studio 54, sat at the same table with a bottle of champagne, and laughed. The next day, the press reported we had "kissed and made up." Of course, there were the usual obnoxious headlines. "Comparing Divorce Notes" was particularly touching.

Just about the only big name I never saw at Studio was Spielberg, who did what he wanted, which didn't include Studio 54. I had reconnected with him through Truffaut, who had starred in his *Close Encounters of the Third Kind*, a success that saved Columbia Pictures from bankruptcy. I had originally met Steven on Martha's Vineyard, where I eventually had a house, when he was directing *Jaws*. Richard Dreyfuss didn't think much of *Jaws* during filming because it used a mechanical shark. Spielberg, too, was concerned the shark would not be scary enough. In the pre-digital era, the only way to accomplish those special effects was with mechanics, and Spielberg was a huge tinkerer. Given the tide, waves, effects of salt water, and the film's lighting and focus requirements, a mechanical shark was more than a challenge but one that worked given the success of the film. Dreyfuss's whining had an effect on Spielberg, who needed encouragement, not sniping. It was the old Hollywood rule— you never know who's going to make it, so be careful. Dreyfuss wasn't. But Steven didn't hold it against him since he put him into *Close Encounters* later.

One afternoon, Spielberg brought over a protégé for lunch. Bob Zemeckis was a budding director who had just directed a critically acclaimed flop, *I Wanna Hold Your Hand*. Zemeckis would say forever after that the flop taught him a lesson—doing well in previews didn't foreshadow doing well. Bob had come to Steven's attention when his student film won an award and he barged into Steven's office, to his secretary's everlasting horror, to show him the movie. Steven loved it and believed in Bob, who had a slow Hollywood beginning. His first two films, both exec-produced by Spielberg, were bombs, so Bob asked Spielberg to direct *1941*, which Bob and his longtime writing partner, Bob Gale, had written, which also did miserably at the box office. He became known as a good writer whose movies flopped, which meant he couldn't get a job. Finally, Michael Douglas hired him to direct *Romancing the Stone*, but after viewing the rough cut, everyone involved thought it was another clunker and fired Zemeckis. What saved him was that it went on to be a hit, which made his career and allowed him to make the 1980's *Back to the Future* series and thus his fortune. Proving once again that no one knew anything, except maybe Spielberg, who recognized Bob's talent. On the other hand, Steven directed *1941*, which was a lemon.

Bob started inserting historical footage and figures in his first film, *I Wanna Hold Your Hand*, which was a tale of several girls going to a Beatles concert. The mixed media productions, if I can call them that, finally achieved genius in *Forrest Gump*, for which he won the Academy Award for Best Director. I met him just after his first flop and enjoyed talking to a man who adored film as much as Steven did, was just as fascinated by gadgets, and knew so much about the movies that he could cite scenes from the Billy Wilder film that had jumpstarted my career with my first nomination. As a gangster's moll, I had a line—"I'm not bad. I'm just drawn that way."—that Bob loved. We talked during lunch, and other times, about the idea of fictional characters dropped into the real world.

I loved bouncing ideas off Bob, both because I was producing my own films and wanted his opinion and because I had long wanted to perform a fictional personage in the real world or take a historic figure and bring her back to life 200 years later, like putting Marie Antoinette in present day. Zemeckis liked the concept and we talked for hours. Years later, he based the cartoon character Jessica Rabbit from *Who Framed Roger Rabbit* on me, making her a redhead while giving her my signature line from my old gangster's girlfriend role, "I'm not bad. I'm just drawn that way." I was amused and grateful. Even better, he never talked about it. I took the compliment, but after so many marriages, I didn't need the notoriety of a cartoon character who was light on her marital vows. She, too, had my breasts, as Zemeckis readily admitted when Spielberg asked him. When I finally told my kids Jessica was based on me, they smiled and said, yes, they got that.

"How?" I asked.

"Uncle Steven told us not to tell you he told us," was their reply. They knew before I did, and I thought I was clever. Evidently not!

The idea of taking a fictional character and dropping him into reality achieved fruition in Zemeckis's Academy Award-winning film, *Forrest Gump*, which won for best picture, best director, and best actor. His skill with technical effects was brilliant, and Spielberg had met a kindred spirit who not only loved stories but also the technology used to create them. The two of them with supercomputers changed the movies.

Forrest Gump barely made it to the screen. It had been kicking around for nine years in the hands of Wendy Finerman, who at the time was married to Marc Canton, head of Columbia Pictures. While Wendy championed the script, she optioned it for less artistic motives. Jaqueline Onassis was at Doubleday, author Winston Groom's publisher, so Wendy got her hands on it because she wanted to finally meet Jackie, which she did dressed to kill. Jackie showed up late with her notes in a brown paper bag for a working lunch at the Stanhope Hotel, allowing precisely one hour. Social pinnacle achieved—Wendy set into motion a great film. She would go on to produce another great hit, *The Devil Wears Prada*.

The initial story was loved by Michelle Manning, then Paramount's Senior VP of Production, one of the most astute people in the business, who worked on *Sixteen Candles, Dances with Wolves,* and *Silence of the Lambs*. She felt that *Forrest Gump* would be another strong story and pushed it from inside Paramount. There were problems with the script after years of various people tinkering with it. People were attached and unattached, including Penny Marshall at one point as director. In the end, it was Bob Zemeckis at the helm with Tom Hanks as his star.

Script genius, Eric Roth, who ultimately won the Academy Award for his script, wrote several versions from script conferences with different producers, directors, and studio execs during the life of the movie. It took his wife, Mary Ellen Trainor, to complain that the script lacked heart, at which point Eric Roth made the love story between Forrest and Jenny the spine of the film. In a sobering addendum, after all his success, Eric lost his money in the Bernie Madoff affair. When that happens, it paints your Academy Award a whole new color, as I learned when it happened to me.

After years of effort, the script was finally put into production at Paramount with Eric's great friend, Tom Hanks, attached. As happens so often in our industry, then everything blew up: Sumner Redstone purchased Paramount. Sherry Lansing was head of the studio and under pressure to improve results after Sumner's acquisition. She tried to kill the picture, thinking it had a choppy storyline, was about someone semi-retarded, was going to be too expensive, require too many untested special effects, and was never going to make its investment back.

I got a sad call from Bob, whom I loved after his patterning Jessica Rabbit on me. "Sherry's gonna kill it," he told me. I had found the script special. So had Spielberg.

"Steven has a lot of clout. Tell him to call Sherry and push it," I responded. I was sad I didn't have power or anything more to help.

"Could you call?" he asked. "Maybe a woman's touch is what we need."

What could I do? I called Spielberg and told him to tell the first woman head of a major studio that if she killed the next film starring the man who had just finished a performance in *Philadelphia* so outstanding he was a contender for the Academy Award just from the rushes (which Tom Hanks would win), it would be embarrassing.

This was not an easy time for Zemeckis or Tom Hanks, whom I also adored. In the end, fate was fate, the movie was made, and it was a great success winning best picture, proving the old Hollywood adage that no one knows anything. Just like *Casablanca*, it was impossible to know that one held a winning script, one that brought Hanks back-to-back Oscars for best actor, equaling Spencer Tracy, who won back-to-back in 1937 and 1938 for *Captains Courageous* and *Boys Town*. I had never thought to connect Tom with Spencer, but knowing both, I think they would appreciate the connection. While Spencer drank a good deal more than Tom, both were alike in many ways, appreciating brevity, intelligence, and good scripts. If you reversed the two in history, I imagined either would fill roles easily for the other. The difference, as I saw it, was that I knew Tom as a young man. I never could think of Spencer as a cub. He was always fully formed to me since I came of age when he was already in his prime. As the only two men to win best actor consecutively, they were in a league of their own.

As for the film, *Forrest Gump* was at the time the third largest grossing movie of all time—paying over $30 million to both Zemeckis and Hanks. Its author, Winston Groom, however, who was supposed to get 3 percent of the profits, found that Paramount had declared the film lost money, even though at the time it had earned $660 million, and he didn't see his profit participation until he sued. And sued. One judge even told him he deserved to be screwed since he was dumb enough to sign a contract for an accounting profit when everyone knew Hollywood defined it so that it never happened. The judge dismissed that case in fifteen minutes. It took years, but Winston finally got his money.

One person I saw at Studio 54 who mattered more than the rest except Elizabeth was Frank Sinatra. No longer young, but a great presence, when he entered, it had the effect of Moses parting the Red Sea. He was *ol' blue eyes,* and everyone knew it. When he saw me, those blue eyes lit up. I was touched. We couldn't talk or sit together—I didn't trust the press and didn't need the notoriety since he was married to Barbara. Yet we still had a connection. He came over to say hello. "Congrats, Babe, for the award, the performance, and your tits, which brought back happy memories!" he whispered as he kissed my cheek. This was all the conversation we could manage before he went back to his circle. I would have liked to talk more, but there was no place we could—in private would have been too intimate and suggest other things, while in public, we had no privacy and had both been burned in the press too many times. Publicity and my many marriages stopped me from seeing an old friend to whom I owed a great debt. While to the public, people like us get to do what we want, the reality is that we are circumscribed far more than most people realize. We are public property, and those who thought they could escape the public part quickly came to ruin. I wanted one more time to sit and talk to Frank, but it never happened.

At this time, I attended a benefit for the American School of Ballet.

There was a premiere performance, and then the dancers mingled with us during the after-performance dinner. The first person I saw was Jacqueline Onassis, a longtime board member of ABT who was one of the evening's hosts. We smiled the polite smile of celebrities saying hello. Her look was veiled as she appraised me—another Hollywood star her husband had slept with?

I hadn't, but it wasn't the kind of thing one could say, so I smiled, shook her hand, thanked her for her good civic works, and got the hell away. Except a photographer got a picture of us shaking hands. It ran with the caption, *Jackie Greets Marilyn's Successor*. Ooh, was I pissed. First, for the implication. Second, because Marilyn was my friend and my sister, and finally, because Jackie was really going to hate me. I sent her a note to apologize.

I never heard back. Not a word; but I didn't like being ignored. I ran into her a few more times—we smiled and pretended. I thought I deserved better. I hadn't screwed her fucking husband, the one who screwed everyone else. Of course, I had slept with her son, which would have probably bothered her a lot more, but I hadn't done it for revenge, but because John, Jr. was a sexy sweetheart. Still, the thought occurred. Choke on that, Jackie!

There had been one other occasion when we met. I never told a soul but a mutual friend because I was worried about her. We were at Elaine's, a restaurant on Second Avenue and 88th Street on the Upper East Side—separate tables, separate parties, just by chance the same night, sometime in 1964 after she moved from Washington, DC to New York City. Elaine's was as special in its own way as Studio 54 for writers and intellectual celebrities. The list of patrons included everyone from Jackie and me to Norman Mailer, Joseph Heller, Gay Talese, George Plimpton, Mario Puzo, Woody Allen, Tom Wolfe, and Sally Quinn, as well as Leonard Bernstein, Michael Caine, Kirk Douglas, Clint Eastwood, Mick Jagger, Willie Nelson, Pavarotti, and even Elaine Stritch, who worked there as a bartender one summer when she didn't want to go on tour. Jackie was friendly with Elaine Kaufman, our proprietress, who once threw garbage can lids at Ron Galella, the notorious photographer who chased Jackie so much that she finally got a restraining order. Everyone pretty much ignored the famous as just fixtures—Elaine famously told a new customer looking for the men's room, "Take a right at Michael Caine," with the quote appearing in her obituary in the *New York Times*.

In time, the place became so famous it was featured in movies such as Woody Allen's *Manhattan* and *Big Business,* starring Lily Tomlin and Bette Midler, while Billy Joel sang about it in his song, *Big Shot—"They were all impressed with your Halston dress and the people that you knew at Elaine's."* In 1963, Elaine started to establish it as a landmark watering hole by attracting its signature clientele.

During a dinner, I went to the ladies' room and found Jackie inside, smoking away, clutching a glass of vodka, clearly distressed. She appeared dazed. She saw me and locked the door—we were the only two in there.

"You understand," she said, taking a gulp of vodka, "there is no escape."

Not sure what she was talking about, I responded, "I can get you out the back if you want." My studio training made me locate basement exits in case I needed to avoid the press and make a getaway.

"Not the press. I can't even go to a stupid dinner without someone talking about him. How sorry they are, how I should still be in the White House. They mean well, but I can't live like this. Every stupid comment puts me back in that car with his brains on my lap." She drained her glass. "We lost our happy ending."

Got it. While the grieving widow in the press and our minds, for her it was agony being thrown back into the horror of the assassination by the well-meaning comments. If not yet suicidal, she was close.

She went on. "I need an island where even staff know not to talk. Maybe then I can have one whole day without being back in that fucking car."

She was more than a little drunk. I wasn't sure what to do but reached into my purse and handed her my two emergency pills, the same kind I had once gotten from Judy Garland.

"Take one before bed and the other tomorrow when you wake up," I told her. "You have two children to protect who will be fed to the lions without you. Don't drink another drop if you want to wake up."

She put down her glass, took the pills, and put them into her purse. "What is it?"

"Something I got from Judy Garland. They worked for me when I was at the bottom. It seems you are there now."

At the mention of Judy Garland, Jacqueline smiled. She instantly understood, as did everyone in the know. We parted, not to meet again until the ABT premiere. I never knew how or if she excised her demons. She did, however, get her island when she married Onassis, for which she was vilified in the American press. For her, the marriage made sense, even if no one would discuss publicly while she was alive how close to the edge she had come after those bullets. I doubt she remembered our encounter in the ladies' room. She was drunk and, even without taking any pills, her memory would have been impaired from vodka and distress.

I was sufficiently shaken that I immediately went to find a phone and call a mutual friend to warn her how precarious she was. She told me her family knew, her lawyers knew, her household help knew as well as her Secret Service detail. She survived, had her comeback, and achieved peace and happiness in her third act. But getting there could not have been easy. Still, I was annoyed years later when she never answered my apology note while I was enraged once again at the press.

Elizabeth Taylor and I discussed Jackie's adroitness with the media. Elizabeth was then married to Burton, who sang the famous *Camelot* title song. While all of us were public property, even Elizabeth understood that Jackie lived in a fishbowl different from the rest of us. She carried a burden we didn't. Until Princess Diana, there hasn't been a woman in public life who maneuvered the press as successfully.

Jackie formed the history of her husband from associations to images rather than words. Even as one of the most photographed women in the world, her personal history was one of silence. From reading history, Jackie understood how it was shaped by those who reported it. Thus, she used the caisson that had carried Lincoln's body to carry that of the fallen JFK. And she tied *Camelot,* the musical of King Arthur's court, to the Kennedy administration in her only published interview while alive. It was her genius to connect JFK forever to the once and future king.

Don't let it be forgot

That once there was a spot,

For one brief, shining moment

That was known as Camelot.

Something struck both Elizabeth Taylor and me, odd as it may seem. Just as Jackie connected Camelot to JFK, the bloodied copy of the Chanel suit Jackie wore during the assassination connected Jackie to Marilyn, since it was almost the color pink that Marilyn wore singing "Diamonds Are a Girl's Best Friend." Jackie's two most memorable outfits were the pink suit of the assassination and the veiled black one as she walked behind her husband's body as it was drawn on Lincoln's caisson. Marilyn's two were the pink dress in the *Diamond's* number and her white one pushed up by the subway. Elizabeth commented to me that she thought the symbolism of the pink and black of Jackie versus the pink and white of Marilyn was appropriate.

"Jacqueline was a darker creature and better suited fighting for what she wanted," Elizabeth said sadly. "Poor Marilyn deserved the white, since she was so often the lamb served up to the slaughter. She had none of Jacqueline's toughness." Elizabeth's word choice, *suited*, struck me as an intended double entendre. When I asked her to explain further, her response stayed with me ever after. "Jacqueline wore clothes as armor. Marilyn wore them as an invitation." Truer words were never spoken.

Elizabeth always referred to Jackie as Jacqueline, given how particular she was about being called Elizabeth. Liz was reserved for outsiders and the press. If you got to know her, you only made that mistake once.

Jackie's distaste for Marilyn carried over to me. The photo caption about the president and me just made it worse. At the time of that awful headline, the *New York Post* was owned by Rupert Murdoch. Through News Corp and ownership of Twentieth Century Fox, he changed American journalism and politics. You have to go back to William Randolph Hearst to see another press magnate managing events, politicians, and elections with the same power. There was good reason Orson Welles's greatest work, *Citizen Kane*, detailed Hearst's excesses. With twenty-six newspapers, sixteen magazines, and eleven radio stations, Hearst did everything he could to quash the movie and make it fade away. Yet, brilliance has a life of its own, and the movie consistently made most best film lists. Hearst's power of the press had its effect in stifling Orson Welles's career despite his genius. Things got really bad for Welles, including his being warned by the police not to go back to his hotel room because Hearst's people had hidden a fourteen-year-old girl in the closet with photographers waiting to frame him.

Whatever Murdoch and his people did, he used his political might and cash for his own gain, including ownership of a major studio, Twentieth Century Fox. What can you say about Fox News becoming a Republican shill and lying repeatedly? Rupie has been at the base of all of it, although what does he care—a man who gifted each of his children $150 million just as part of his estate planning, which was only a small part of his assets.

Disagree with me, fight with me, but don't lie about me. Greed and power for their own sakes seem petty and small, but we return again to studio guys. Testosterone is an evil drug.

The photo of Jackie and me with the evil caption had not a shred of proof but was used to sell papers around the world. Meryl Streep as Miranda Priestly says in *The Devil Wears Prada*, "Rupert Murdoch should cut me a check for all the papers I sell for him." What about me?

We loved Studio 54. I couldn't go often but would come down from Yale when I could take the time. I think my mother liked it more than I did. It was her world reimagined. We went together a few times, but I think when we were there, we inhibited each other—even my mother was reserved about some things in front of her children despite being in the press so often.

I remember that Jessica Rabbit was based on her, although I think we only found this out later when we were older. We thought it really funny and appreciated that it honored my mother's work. But I think it's difficult to discuss the boundaries that our family had in place for our private lives. Sex, drugs, and rock and roll were off limits. I didn't want to know about hers, and I certainly didn't want her to know about mine. Ditto for my brothers. Bobby, in fact, ran as intermediary. Nothing shocked or surprised him, and he could be surprisingly direct. Lily, I had such a soft spot for her—she was like another mother to me, so I didn't want to talk to her about this stuff either unless I absolutely had to because I had become involved in the media. It wasn't about trust. It was about separation and privacy. I learned about that when my kids became teenagers. They didn't want us to know anything about their sex lives. Quite frankly, we didn't want to know either, unless we had to protect them from disease or pregnancy.

We were all far more private than we thought. But we all have more illusions about ourselves than we think. My mother would tell us that, and she was right. I think that my mother's not having many illusions about anything, except on rare occasion herself, was also difficult. She was so direct that when we messed up, there wasn't any room to hide. And she didn't want us to hide. She felt it was far too dangerous for Hollywood children to get away with anything, including too much privacy. She was very tough. I didn't appreciate her toughness as a mother until I had teens of my own. Neither did Sebastian. Oddly, we went to her when we didn't know how to handle our children, and she always found a way to put them in their place. She was so direct and so fierce that the teens backed down.

It was also true that our teens looked at us wimps when we got grandma to fight our battles. But it worked, so we learned to live with the rolling eyes of our teen children.

Anders

FIGHTING AIDS WITH ELIZABETH

The next few years were not gratifying. Roles were offered, but I took few because they were bad. When I worked, it was mostly because I optioned something and produced it myself. I made three films in five years. Producing wasn't easy because I needed a studio to finance and distribute. I was bankable, but barely, and it helped if I got bankable costars. These were not the major films I had made previously, but I'm proud of them, and I played roles that were complete women, not mothers who show up to serve dinner or listen to their daughters talk about men or fag hags in a musical production.

On one of those productions, my makeup guy suddenly got ill. He became thinner and weaker. When he couldn't work, we made sure we took him food, but he couldn't eat. He was dead before the film finished editing. He was the first. Others, too. All gay men. The AIDS plague had struck, terrifying everyone, because no one knew how it was caught, how it was transmitted, or if they could find a cure. All we knew was it was a death sentence. Hospitals refused to take gay patients, mortuaries refused bodies, and prejudice was everywhere.

Elizabeth called and said we have to do something. She was one of the first. She didn't care about anything except helping these men and took on everyone from President Reagan on down. She started raising money right away. In our industry, the closets faced the outside. Inside, we knew who liked what, but nobody cared. Stars like Rock Hudson played straight in the media, but everyone in our business knew. What mattered was who we were in the press and our box-office pull. Like the 1950s communist hearings, people started segregating themselves and censoring contacts.

There were those who were scared by physical risk, like hospital and mortuary workers, but the real cowards were scared of guilt by association. The studios were particularly bad—they wanted nothing to do with any of this, and the ones getting sick were their people. Of the hairdressers, designers, costume designers, hair and makeup people, set designers, florists, directors, actors, stagehands, assistants, executives, and performers, you want to guess how many were gay?

Reagan was in the White House. He finally uttered the word AIDS because Elizabeth pushed him, but he and Nancy distanced themselves from the issue, as did most of his administration. There was his political support from the religious right such as Rev. Jerry Falwell, who infamously claimed AIDS was God's punishment for homosexuality. Then, too, Pat Buchanan, Reagan's Communication Director, said it was "nature's revenge on gay men."

Those of us who knew the Reagans suspected their son was gay, as did his Yale classmates, including Anders, who was there when Ron Junior dropped out after one semester to become a ballet dancer prior to the AIDS crisis hitting the headlines. Ron Junior was reportedly a very good dancer. He had a sense of humor about all the rumors, stating in an interview years later, "Ron Reagan—rich gay man unaccountably married to the same woman for thirty years." He only got upset at insinuations his marriage was a sham because it insulted his wife.

I believe AIDS was an issue the senior Reagans wanted to avoid because it was political—while they may have been protecting their son's privacy, that is a charitable assumption given their ambition. Their silence allowed a disease to progress and kill millions. I knew them, but they were not friends. I liked that you knew where Reagan stood. Compared to the Republicans we have now, I miss him. I can't forgive him and Nancy, however, for their silence on HIV and what it did to our community. When he died after years of Alzheimer's, a fate worse than death, I was struck that it was an evil poetic justice of sorts, given so many AIDS patients also died out of their minds, hallucinating, not knowing their loved ones. God laughing at us again?

Had his administration stepped in earlier, much suffering might have been averted. Nancy Reagan turned the other way when Rock Hudson was dying in Paris and needed her help getting into a hospital. She claimed she couldn't pick and choose favorites since she couldn't help everyone. So, she chose to help no one, something I never forgot, and something Elizabeth didn't, either.

Ronald and Nancy Reagan were products of Hollywood. They were looked after by the same people who looked after the rest of us, and a lot of them were gay. They couldn't possibly have been in our business so long and be anti-gay personally. They couldn't have had their careers if they had. They socialized with William Haines, who gave up his acting career so he could live openly with his lover, Jimmy Shields. Haines became the decorator for the rich and famous and befriended Nancy as she worked her way up the social ladder. In fact, after Reagan won the California governorship in 1967, they held the victory party at Haines and Shields's house. A California political gay scandal later that year and, ever after, both Reagans disavowed homosexuals publicly. I was vexed at their opportunistic stance for political positioning. On the other side of that equation, people were dying. At great cost to others, the Reagans did not do what they should have.

The first AIDS Project Los Angeles dinner was instigated by Elizabeth and held in 1985, the year Rock Hudson died. We were devastated by his death but proud he had gone public, which was a turning point in starting public acceptance. He also left $250,000 to amfAR to help bankroll the organization. Elizabeth added to his grant by working the phones, raising donations like a mobster calling in protection money. She feared gay men were going to be treated as lepers with right-wing commentators encouraging it.

Elizabeth started her fight against AIDS because of her friends, but what cemented her devotion was personal—her daughter-in-law Aileen. Trusting her famous mother-in-law wouldn't turn her away, she came to Elizabeth for help when she found she had contracted HIV from a fling. Elizabeth took Aileen to her famous bosom and fought an amazing battle, not only for her daughter-in-law, who was a Getty Oil heiress, but also for those much less fortunate. I only say any of this because Aileen herself has gone public, so I am revealing nothing not already known.

What opened my eyes was not Elizabeth, who pushed everyone she knew—it was watching so many people I loved sicken and die. By the end of the dying, when they started using the drug cocktail, half the gay men I had known in the '80s were gone. I particularly remember a man in his late thirties in Palm Springs. We met only once and talked for two hours, but it was a formative experience. I had gone to a hotel spa for a massage and manicure, and on my way out past the outdoor pool, there was a handsome muscular man on a lounge in the shade. As I walked by, he shivered, which I thought odd, because it was ninety degrees in the shade.

I turned to bring him some heavy beach towels for warmth and asked what was wrong.

He told me he was sick. He had come of age as a gay man in the late '60s, worked in porn and as an escort, got sick, and had turned his life around in the past two years, getting off recreational drugs to spend his remaining time lecturing and counseling at community centers about the risks of HIV. At this point, I can't remember when we learned about safe sex, not sharing needles, and the risks of blood-to-blood contact as well as the danger of transfusions.

He was frank that he was dying and using the rest of his life to help others who had his fate as well as prevent other young men from getting sick. He had arranged to use the last of his money before he died. He wouldn't need it anymore, he told me, and he had no one to leave it to, since everyone he knew was gone.

He was a hero, and I have never forgotten him. He knew who I was and gave me his hand to shake when introducing himself, but the focus was on him—what he was doing, how he was doing it, and how little he wanted for himself. He asked for nothing and didn't ask questions, which was rare for a stranger talking to me: he just wanted someone to listen.

I sat there for two hours, holding his hand. The temperature drops quickly in the desert and when the sun went down, he was shivering again. I helped him up and walked him to the lobby, where we parted as he went to his room. I drove off, preoccupied. I have thought of that conversation often and of that man's courage. He had an epiphany and answered its call. I was in awe of him. He is the only saint I have ever met.

For years, I would see the gay pride parties in LA and NY that ended with fireworks, thinking each spark in the sky was the soul of someone who died of AIDS. There were that many. I told this to Elizabeth, who took my hand, and we just sat there grieving. There was so much death in the eighties and nineties. My gay friends over fifty lived through a plague with almost half of their generation gone. When I hear people complaining about young gays and their lack of values, I remind them an entire generation of leaders was wiped out—role models, parents, friends, senior pillars of the community. Simple devastation.

There were so many dead. Bobby still can't talk about it. We asked him if he wanted to add anything to mother's words, but he couldn't. There was too much loss. We had friends who just disappeared as Mom described. Before email or cell phones, we just lost people and had no way to reach their families to ask. Of the Studio 54 crowd, many of them are long gone. And, by now, they have no one to remember them.

I did get involved with helping because Elizabeth had me addressing and stuffing envelopes for her fundraisers. While she was enormously generous, for this she wouldn't pay: it had to be a gift to those who couldn't help themselves. But she would order very expensive platters of sushi or Chinese takeout for everyone helping. And she would have me drive her to the houses of gay men who were alone and needed care packages. Or a just a visit from fame so that they felt important and not forgotten before they died. Mother did this too. The two Hollywood ladies delivering soup and sandwiches. It was a family effort. And the memory still makes me cry.

Anders

THE LAST DIVORCE

Despite AIDS, show business needed to go on. We were casting for one of my productions in LA for an actor to play a young colleague of my husband's character with whom my character has a fling in the crazy days leading to their divorce. It was a tragicomedy about life in the suburbs. We found an actor, handsome yet with a look of intelligence. Finding a hot man for a ten-minute role was easy. Finding one that looked intelligent in LA was more difficult. Sadly, in retrospect, I wish he had been less smart.

Welcome, Husband No. 6. I was twenty-two years older, famous to his anonymity, and no longer had to worry about money. I didn't think anything about our scenes together—we kissed in one of them, and he took his shirt off in another. I think we had one day's shoot for a four-line walk-on role. At least one of those lines should have been "I am going to try to take you for every cent you've got" and another "I am going to embarrass you for as long as possible," but we didn't have the foresight to write such realistic dialogue.

Weeks later, at his audition for another role on the studio lot, his car wouldn't start as I was leaving. I saw him looking under his hood, offered him a ride, and dropped him off at his apartment on my way up to the Hills. The next day, he came over to our set to invite me to dinner as a thank you. I thanked him for the kind offer but politely declined and explained I wasn't going out in public on anything the press might perceive as a date. He countered he could make dinner at his apartment or my house, because he needed to thank me and was a good cook. He appeared to be too good to be true, which should have been a warning. I don't know what was wrong with me, but I agreed. I went to his apartment because I didn't want a stranger in my house. He made it there in the end, anyway.

I liked him, didn't want to be alone, and he was sweet. Plus, I have a thing for hot bodies. Why I married him, I don't know. The sex was mind-blowing, yes, but I didn't need to marry him. I guess it was something about aging. I was just like a guy who cheats to show he still has it. That realization hurt most of all.

After we were outed in the press, tipped off by someone at the studio who saw us and called it in for a finder's fee, not being seen in public no longer mattered. Because I had become a face for women's lib after my remarks on Johnny Carson and my fight with the studio, the press took great liberties with this relationship. It was a May-December or vice versa, whatever applied. I was a hero to some and an embarrassment to others, particularly my children.

My lawyers got the media clippings before I did. This was a major livelihood in Hollywood—protecting clients' money in divorces. They called to ensure my money was protected and said I needed a prenup in case I was crazy enough to marry him. He sued later anyway.

He was smart enough but hadn't made it, and at thirty-eight, he was too old as an actor to have a shot. Studios wanted younger stars who had a longer shelf life. Thanks to our marriage and its media attention, he got offered more parts and took them. I was happy he was working and making his own money, since it gave him independence and dignity.

I was less charitable about his many flings. I liked younger. He liked younger. I didn't want to be with an old guy who didn't take care of himself—in other words, fat and middle-aged. Who is turned on by a guy with an expanding waistline who hasn't seen his dick in years and gropes around in the morning to find it? No thank you. Then Viagra came out. It was one thing for someone who needed a bit of help or had been drinking too much, but a guy who couldn't make it up the stairs without wheezing wasn't going to be on my dance card. All these old ladies whose lives have been ruined by Viagra. They're expected to put out, still, to the old guy? Wanda Sykes says anyone getting a prescription for Viagra should be required to provide affidavits from three people who want to fuck them. Yup.

I am grateful Viagra didn't exist at the height of the AIDS epidemic. Then, when someone was high or drunk, physical limitations were reached and performance not possible. Now, kids use Viagra as a party drug. They get drunk or high, pop a pill, and are off to the races. The fact that they can't remember who they're with, what they're doing, or what they might have caught or passed on is incidental. At least now we have the cocktail if no cure. Back then, given what went on in the gay community, no one would have survived if they had used Viagra with the rest of their drugs.

What did everything in with Husband No. 6 was a spectacular divorce—no, not ours, but one between a studio chieftain of my age (duly noted in the press) and his much younger wife (also duly noted). My husband was named co-respondent. There were photos taken by the studio chieftain's detectives that were introduced into the trial. The studio head was fighting for his life, because the dumbass didn't get a prenup. Husband No. 6 flashed across the pages of every tabloid with his private parts blocked out.

My divorce was quiet only in the sense that its terms and negotiations were not initially in court. Then he sued for money, and the circus started. His lawyers knew to ask questions that had nothing to do with money but everything to do with embarrassing me on the stand. I had more press coverage than the White House. There were endless obnoxious headlines. Late-night comic jokes. I was back in favor with Joan Rivers again. And there was one really annoying headline, "Elizabeth and Babe's Dozen Divorces Sunny Side Up," which for some reason kept Elizabeth laughing. By then I was enraged. I paid to end the suit. It was more than the fucker deserved. I had an ironclad prenup, and he couldn't have won at trial. His lawyers were looking for a payoff and got more than he did. He couldn't work again in Hollywood at anything decent because my friends refused to hire him. He was left with third-rate offers, of which he accepted far too many, which further put his career down the toilet.

My fault. I had said (again), *I do*. Then I said, *I don't think so*. After the marriage ended, in addition to having to listen to my kids asking, "What were you thinking?" ex-Husband No. 6 decided to pose for *Playgirl* so everyone could see what I was now missing. I did get compliments—at least people understood I wasn't completely nuts. He went on talk shows and wouldn't shut up. I was tempted to call Frank Sinatra to have some goons have a chat with him, but I stopped myself because what I really wanted would have put me behind bars for life. I wasn't sorry I was divorced; I was sorry I wasn't a widow. I shut up, hid as much as I could, and prayed Joan Rivers would find new victims for her monologues.

Things were so bad that even Husband No. 5 called because he was worried about me. He joked that with all he had done, at least he hadn't posed for *Playgirl*. I wasn't mean enough to point out he wasn't hot enough. Somehow, his call made me saddest of all. I had once wanted life with him to work out. Was Husband No. 6 residue from the aftermath of No. 5, now living in my apartment in Paris on my money?

I needed a great role. That had worked before to take everyone's minds off my half a dozen divorces, but I had been younger then as Elizabeth pointed out. I responded she wasn't far behind, which almost shut her up. Meanwhile, I was squirming under the microscope, at which she took just a hint more pleasure than was dignified because, again, it was someone else. Eventually, I forgave her. She'd had her enormous share of bad press, too, and there wasn't anybody else who understood what our lives were like who had been with me as long. I got more grief for a younger man than she did for all her visits to Betty Ford. By the time she married her No. 7, Fortensky, I had already paved the way, and she got off relatively unscathed. Well, compared to what it could have been.

It was then that Bobby walked into my life with this one-woman show offer. As I said earlier, he really wanted me to do it. I had never been on Broadway, and the idea scared me. I didn't know if I could do it. My work has been scenes sutured together in editing rooms from miles of film, take after take—turn a little more to the left next time, smile wider, cry harder, kiss more passionately (he'd better have breath mints!), show more cleavage, show less cleavage, angrier, sadder, happier, drunker, hit your mark one foot closer to the camera, and so on. Often, there was no way to know if the film was going to be good or not before I saw a rough cut because there was so much wiggle room in editing. We understood you could take a mediocre performance and make it better with a skilled editor. What you couldn't do was make a great performance, but sometimes good was good enough. Sometimes you got lucky. On stage, however, night after night, they would know a fraud when they saw it. I wasn't that good. I wasn't Vanessa Redgrave or Helen Hayes, but then, I had much better breasts—or at least I used to.

I wasn't rich then. I was well-off, but nothing like later. By the time I made real money, I didn't need it. Yes, more jewels would have been nice, but it's one thing to have Ali Baba's cave when you are thirty and hot. It's another thing to have it at seventy, hoping people won't notice you're no longer desirable.

My moneymen told me to do it. Lily told me to run away as fast as I could. If the producers had brought me a script, that might have been one thing, but what they wanted was for me to agree first. That meant after I signed, I would be at their mercy. If I refused to go on, they could sue, and I had been down that road once before and had almost lost everything I owned.

In the end, once burned, twice shy. Husband No. 6 had ensured I didn't want any more press, good, bad, or indifferent. I didn't do my own grocery shopping, but just going out into the street or to a store meant I saw the looks on people's faces as they stared at me, knowing they had stared at him in *Playgirl* and were either wondering, "What did he see in her?" or, if they were a certain age, "I would have paid for that, too," which almost seemed worse. I wasn't paying for it.

Who am I kidding? I paid for almost everything I ever had, even when I didn't think I was. I was so public that everyone who could, tried to take advantage of my fame one way or another. Even when they didn't think they were, like Husband No. 5. He didn't want anything except a divorce and my financing his apartment. Where did he think the money came from? No one gave me money because they were being nice. I got things the old-fashioned way—I worked. And not on my back like Husband No. 6, not that I'm bitter.

We hated this marriage. We hated him, the press, and how miserable mother was, and we hated when the magazine came out after we had thought all that was behind us. For all our mistakes, we never did something this stupid. Mother didn't want to get old, didn't want to stop her career, and didn't want to be irrelevant. She wanted to continue to be sexy as she always had been, something difficult after 60 both for men and women. I miss those days too, but I know they are over for me, as well.

Anders

THERE IS LIFE AFTER SIXTY

Bobby came to my rescue as usual. He optioned a script for me about a sixty-something woman who finds her terminal diagnosis was a mistake and, after saying her goodbyes and making peace with life, she's not dying after all. She undergoes a major reassessment about how she interacts with her husband and children and colleagues. There are wonderful scenes where she turns things around on her children, asserting herself as a person, not just a mother, and with her husband, when she says she won't go back to the way things were before and if he doesn't like it, he can leave. What surprises her is he doesn't want to leave. He wants to do what she wants, but he was never certain what she wanted before, because she never told him. His reaffirmation shocks and moves her. She realizes that by not living as her authentic self for so long, not only had she forgotten who she was but also so had everyone else. Through a brush with death, she regains her sense of self with enough time to use it before she does die.

For me, with my now feminist credentials, this was a huge find. The studios, to give those guys their due, recognized I would be perfect in the role. They lost a little street cred when they asked Bobby if I would show my breasts again. Really, after all this? I was so happy to get financing and a starring role that I shut up.

The shoot was hard work. It was emotional—bleak and then uplifting and then sad facing these emotions, which were mine as well as those of many other women. I relished the opportunity to be a representative of my generation who had once learned to be seen and not heard. Yet, we were not children.

During the shoot, Anders came to tell me he had found a girl—the one—and he planned to propose. I looked at him and asked, "You sure this is the one? You've only been out of Yale a few years."

"Mom," he said and looked at me sadly, "I hope so. Looking at you, how can I know?"

I didn't know what to say. I had set an enormously bad example. "Darling, your life doesn't have to be my life," was what I came up with.

"Mom"—a bit of wail here—"our lives have been in the press, and I don't have any sense of how normal people live." Good point. Nothing of importance we ever did wasn't picked up or commented on by someone. He continued, "And Father, I don't know much about him, since you always protected me. I barely remember him. That's what's so difficult. I don't have actual memories. He died when I was so little that I have nothing to hang on to."

How could I explain to him what had happened when I wasn't sure myself? I understood the gist of Husband No. 4's business arrangements, but what could I tell his son? I was upfront with him that I didn't know everything, and it was better I didn't. Did I need to tell him about Frank Sinatra's intervention and why he intervened? Would that be necessary, or would it make me just more of what I was already, unstable with men? My image with my children—private this time, not public—wasn't good. How could I reconcile what had happened and everything I had done with the idea of normal motherhood? I was never going to fit into the apple pie motherhood mold. Usually, I didn't want to, because it was a mold made by men, but this time, it would have made things easier.

For my child, I grieved because what he wanted was normalcy—to be like everyone else. What he didn't know, and I hoped he would learn one day, is that sometimes being different is a gift. You get to be outside the box, you have a perspective everyone else doesn't, and you have a voice inside your head saying something different. I wanted him to learn this, but I didn't have a way to explain it. You just have to wait for people to learn their own lessons.

I told Anders his father had loved him and had been proud of him. I told him his father did very well and then had business reverses, when he borrowed money from people who were very dangerous and killed him when they thought he couldn't pay it back. I told him that his father was honorable, didn't want to worry me, loved me, but didn't confide in me, because he was a guy. I said, "As a man, he needed to be tough. He died because I couldn't help him because I had no idea what was going on."

Absolute silence. Then, Anders took my hand. "Mom, I had no idea. You had nobody."

Now I was silent. This was my baby, my love, who I had been forced to send away for his protection, a sin I thought he would never forgive. He understood. It had taken twenty years, but he understood I had done what I had to do as a mother. Tears welled up in my eyes.

"Mom, can I be a good husband? Will this last? Am I going to be married six times?"

What wonderful questions, and how they burned. "Darling, none of us can see the future. You can learn from my mistakes, but as a man, you face different issues. I was a woman at the mercy of men. I was a sex symbol with a brain who wanted to be a serious actress. That's not you." I paused. "You and Sebastian have been my rocks, because what mattered most was that you never looked at me with disappointment. The hardest thing I have ever done was disciplining you two, knowing you would resent me, but my job wasn't to be your friend. It was to be your mother— and, sadly, your father, too. It's hard. You will learn this as a dad."

Anders digested this. "What about Dad? Was he a good man? He lied to you."

"Sweetheart, it was a different world. His idea of being a man was to give me jewels and fly me on private jets. He didn't know I was tough and just needed the people I loved. No matter what, you were his hero. He was prouder of you than anything. What he would want most would be for you to have a hero of your own."

Now, Anders eyes were moist. I had lived with the guilt of sending him away every day of my life.

"The media?" He looked so serious. "Mom, Sally has no idea what's coming. I tried to explain, but people who haven't lived our lives don't understand what the press is capable of. Can you help her?"

How do you boil down forty years' experience for a young girl used to doing what she wants and not having others interpret it in the cruelest possible way to sell newspapers? Living under a microscope is hard. I had been taught how to do this since MGM charm school. Those who didn't learn the necessary lessons came to grief. Even those of us who did, like me, had a difficult time just living our lives with every mistake publicly thrown in our faces.

I tried. Sally was a good girl and loved my son. I gave her the one-page tutorial. First, you are peripheral to the news. You function as a way for the press to get to me, write about me, or build me up or down. I am the story, which is your protection, since if what you do doesn't affect me, they can't use it. They can use a scandal or a possible scandal, whether or not it involves me. They will invent the connection. That said, never speak in public without thinking someone has a tape recorder. Never touch a man, even put your hand on his arm, who is not your husband. If the press gets a shot, you will be accused of having an affair. If you get drunk at a party, someone will take a picture. If your hair and makeup isn't flawless, someone will comment. If you cheat, do a line of coke, or gain five pounds, someone will write a story. Most difficult of all, if someone new comes into your life not vouched for by someone you have known and trusted for a long time, treat them like a stick of dynamite. They may be a friend, but they may want something or be press, so be sure you know what you are dealing with before it explodes in your face.

I got a call from Anders five minutes later. "Mom, I said help her, not scare the shit out of her!"

"Darling, I did what you asked. The problem is the truth is scary."

It took a long time to sort this out. Meantime, I had other decisions to make, not the least of which was preparing for my new role. Anders needed a ring. I took my twenty-carat diamond earrings to my jeweler and asked him to take out the big stones to make engagement rings for my sons. Anders was touched because it came from his father. He was more touched when I told him it was the first thing his father gave me. He also gave me a look that told me he understood that as much as I had loved those earrings, I loved my children more. I had done what I had to do so we could have a good life. I was vain, proud, and had an ego, but I was a working mother despite my fame and trappings. Sebastian, when I told him, refused the ring and tried to make a joke, but I shushed him. I can help you, I paid my dues, let me. Those two's thank yous meant the world.

I replaced the stones in the earrings with tanzanite. Not the same, but nothing was the same. I didn't mind the change, but from time to time, I missed the diamonds. I had held on to the earrings, which pleased me, since there was a time when I didn't get to keep much.

We held the wedding in LA at my house with the tent out back. Sebastian showed up with his pregnant girlfriend. I was marrying off my youngest and expecting to be a grandmother from my eldest. I didn't want to be old but had to acknowledge I had finally reached a point where even I thought I looked good for my age. That was a comedown from just looking good. Nearing sixty-four, what more could I expect? I gave Anders the down payment for a house as a wedding present and a PR consultant on speed dial for emergencies because Lily was getting tired. My whole world was growing old.

My new film opened with publicity tours, junkets, and premieres. It got good reviews, and the critics were kind although they kept referring to my comeback, which I didn't completely understand. As far as I was concerned, I had never been away. I was always still here. There just hadn't been decent roles.

There was one good sex scene with the husband. I had insisted we get a middle-aged guy with a good body. Funny, no one commented on my breasts. They talked about the hot, passionate scene of an older couple, but the discussion was more about people our age having sex and less about an actress showing her breasts. I was pleased so much had changed in the few years since I had done it the first time. I went back on Johnny

Carson again, and he was deferential, something that surprised me. Maybe he had mellowed—it was near the end of his run, and he would retire from television the following year. I still looked good, but at almost sixty-four, I couldn't make it as the hot thing any longer. I admire Helen Mirren so much because she has maintained her ageless sexiness. I have tried to do that, but I'm not sure anyone notices.

I got an Academy Award nomination, which was a surprise. This was an art film, not a mainstream Cineplex movie, but I still had enough clout to ensure it got good coverage and reviews. I was thrilled to be nominated but not surprised I didn't win. It was a great role in a small movie—best actress is usually reserved for great roles in big movies. I was just happy to not yet be a has-been.

Then, something I never imagined happened. Even a bad movie wouldn't have had this plot. Husband No. 5, in New York for a week with his new wife and now ten-year-old son, called. "I shouldn't ask, but my wife is in the hospital deadly ill, and there is no one to take care of my son. Can you arrange for someone to care for him over the next few days? I don't want him to see his mother so sick."

What could I do? Little Frederic showed up on my doorstep. Le petit Français spoke little English, and that with an atrocious accent, so it was a struggle. He tried to be a little man—how French of him, I thought—and was completely unnerved at being served scrambled eggs for breakfast, which was so un-French as to unsettle him completely. Husband No. 5 showed up after the second day, completely disheveled and distraught.

The wife was now in Sloan Kettering, the best cancer hospital in the world. That it took two days for her to get there was a bad sign. Ex-

Husband No. 5 didn't know what to say, so I took him to the guest room, next to Ander's room where I had put Frederic, and told him to go to sleep and we would talk in the morning. It felt surreal. Part of me felt that extreme circumstances mean extreme accommodation. At the same time, I was screaming inside, *You fucking asshole. You dumped me for this bitch, and now you're back for me to take care of her child as she's dying?* Clearly, it was a little late to belabor the point. They were both already in my home—easily in but not easily out said the lobster into the lobster pot. I kept hoping I wasn't the lobster.

The wife went from bad to worse. After a week, they were able to stabilize her for the flight back home—Paris at the Institute Pasteur had its own magnificent clinics, but she was leaving Sloan Kettering to go home to die. Frederic's English improved during that week, and we bonded. Yell at me for being a sap, but he was a child, alone in a strange city with a strange language with his mother dying. He knew. And he knew, too, who I was. I don't know if he had made the connection his father was once married to me until he arrived on my doorstep. He knew who I was even if he was too young to have seen my movies.

Later, we would have talks about language differences as he learned to use English. I never could keep up with him in French, which he didn't hold against me. Language is fascinating. I miss William Safire's Sunday column in the *NY Times* a lot, because he would make us think about language and its (mostly correct) uses. For me, who had never been to college, this was my favorite part of the paper.

Frederic didn't know until he entered Yale that we used the word "drumstick" for chicken legs. He had done just fine with "dark meat" or "leg." It must have escaped him when others used the term. He commented how odd it was to think of playing the drums when eating a chicken leg. Except I never thought about it, just as he never thinks about apple of the earth when he says potato. I started thinking about these things in script conferences, where the studio and the writers would do battle over each word. In time, I understood the discussion. Not at the beginning. I didn't think about what the abstractions mean—because words are mostly abstractions, except not in the case of drumstick or pomme de terre, which are metaphors. When I was trying to learn French, I used to think pomme de terre seemed such a wonderful expression. Not for the French, where it wasn't an expression, it was just a word. My meaning wasn't their meaning. After all this time, alas, I mostly just think potato now, too. Thinking about Mr. Safire's column, which I miss, and the others who have contributed to my life who are now gone, whom I also miss, I find words mean different things than they used to. For Frederic, we bonded over these discussions, which he thought were very strange when he first came to live with me.

The night before ex-Husband No. 5 left to return to Paris, he found me in my kitchen and sat down to talk. "I have nothing but profound gratitude," he said. I started to brush it away, but he waved his hand so I would stop. "I can barely talk. I was unspeakable to you. I left, and you gave me the apartment so my son would have a good place to live. I always knew how big your heart was. I don't know how to say thank you."

How often does the scorned woman hope to hear this, to have the ex crawl back completely crushed. It's not a believable script, since this only seems to take place in bad movies. I can tell you, when it happens, it doesn't go the way you imagine. Revenge is not so sweet. What I wanted was not to be hurt in the first place, not to see someone beaten down so thoroughly by life. A young woman was dying, and a child was going to be left alone. I loved ex-Husband No. 5, but his track record with children on his own wasn't good. I was worried about Frederic. Given how I was as a mother, that you should tell you something.

They went back to Paris, but there wasn't a lot to be done, and the poor woman was gone in six months. Ex-Husband No. 5 sold the apartment and paid what he owed me under our contract. I couldn't stay in it without him, and he couldn't stay in it without her. Funny how life works out. He asked if he could send Frederic for the summer. For the second time, how could I say no? And then could he enroll Frederic at the Lycée Français in NY for fall. On one condition, I told him, he can stay with me—you need to move to NY. He needs his father and doesn't need to be further abandoned. Which is how, at sixty-five, I had an eleven-year-old motherless boy living in my house. I knew I wasn't a great mother, but I was able to be there in a way Husband No. 5 couldn't be. The irony of my being the one turned to in this situation did not escape me. Chosen by default.

In time, the sadness in Frederic's eyes lifted. In time, ex-Husband No. 5 could come around and act normal. I wondered if we might ever make it again as a couple, because he was a good man at heart, but somehow, I preferred being friends. I didn't want to go back down that road. It wasn't pride or rational thought, and I wasn't protecting myself. I just couldn't, so I didn't.

By now, thanks to Sebastian, I had become a grandmother. Then

Anders and Sally had a son. I was now a two-time Academy-Award-winning actress, former sex symbol, and grandma. Ha! I loved the babies and was in a good place in life, except for work, of which there was less and less. I kept wondering where time had gone. I kept thinking I was in my early forties—grown but not old. Burping wee ones suggested otherwise.

One incident that reverberated in our lives concerned a pitcher of plant fertilizer for my orchids on the terrace. I was working PR for a new film, and Anders and Sally were at my house in LA. Sally found the pitcher of fertilizer the housekeeper had mixed for the orchids and put it in the refrigerator. Anders came home from a run, overheated, poured a chilled glass, drank half of it before he could taste it wasn't lemonade, and yelled out, "What is this shit?" Trip to ER. They administered an emetic. Nothing happened. Second dose, still nothing. They pumped his stomach. He was fine but a bit groggy when the head of the ER came in to ask about family history. "We gave two doses of a powerful emetic that makes everyone sick. Is there anything in your history to explain why it didn't work? Are you taking other medications?"

Anders without thinking, replied, "After a couple of years of my wife's cooking, I thought it was dessert!" The headlines ranged from *Babe's Daughter-in-Law Poisons Husband* to *Poison is Better than Hollywood Wife's Cooking*. It was a funny enough comment to be repeated, which was Anders' undoing. Those kinds of public remarks are not for people in our position. My downstairs neighbor news producer ("Anyone killed?"), who lived for her ratings, surprised me with a call. She refused to run the story, telling me it was a tacky attack. I was touched.

None of this was enough, however. Sally went catatonic. She couldn't live with the pressure. She loved my son but not her life with him. I felt somehow responsible in the aftermath. If I hadn't been the mother-in-law, who would have cared? As it was, Anders was sadder, wiser, and now alone. Am I petty? I bought the ring back from Sally. I told Anders he could have it again, but he said it was cursed.

"Darling, I don't believe jewels are cursed—only their owners."

History had repeated itself. I wanted to give sage advice, but there wasn't a lot to say that might make anything better, and probably any comment from me would have made things worse. My sins had been visited upon my children.

We thought it very odd at first when Frederic moved in. After all, Mom was no longer young. And her divorce from my stepfather was not pleasant—we had trusted him, and he betrayed both of us. But Frederic is part of our family, and I can't imagine life without him. He became our baby brother. My stepfather, after all the commotion, came back into our lives, and I am glad he did. It wasn't the same, but nothing is the same years later.

As for Sally, that was really difficult. I feared I was going to be like my mother with six marriages. Thankfully, only two. That catastrophe was a wake-up call that our lives were not what they seemed. Managing in the public eye isn't easy or for everyone. I have remained friends with Sally, but the fertilizer pitcher affair was terrible. Being human was sometimes a liability, and I couldn't help being human. So, I became the liability. And that wasn't easy for me to cope with or Sally to stay married to.

I admire Sebastian so much. He has been a role model for me because he found a way to live his life on his terms. He never married, but he never strayed. They have been a stronger couple together than any I know. Because of the age gap, and because Sebastian loves him, Frederic had another set of parents—ones who set normal rules with normal regularity and normal give and take. He could live for a time without the trappings of my mother's life, the limitations of my stepfather's and the confusion of his own. What he didn't become was a regular guy, which he thought he might. He's had his own American Express card since he was 12 and thought nothing of charging a business class ticket to wherever, whenever. He did get into trouble when he tried that once when he was 16 to impress a date, enraging my mother. "You don't have my American Express card to get laid" was a phrase that has lived on in our family lore. My mother was later secretly amused.

I told Sally to sell the ring back to my mother. The diamond meant a lot to her, and the money would mean more to Sally. The earrings are our connection to my father and my mother's connection to a lifestyle that she almost lost. I never cared for jewelry because I was privileged enough to have a life where people wore it all around me. I understand that it can have great meaning. Those earrings are almost my mother's other children. Do I dare say that diamonds are a girl's best friend? And I have to say, they are beautiful.

Anders

BABE'S BEAUTY BUSINESS

I had been a workout freak since my film with Betty Grable. I found a good gym, David Barton in its original incarnation. Its slogan appealed to me: *Look better naked*. Too bad its management never ran it properly so it might have grown into what it should have. It was semi-underground in a 6th Avenue apartment building in those days, not well known except to the gay guys of Chelsea and a few celebrities who liked it because they were left alone and treated like one of the gang. Susan Sarandon was there, puffing away on the treadmill. I ran into Calvin Klein with his trainer several times a week and became friendly, talking between sets, including about his daughter's wedding—he was so proud. He also had a collection of very hot, very young Latin trainers. Because of my experience with Bobby, I didn't have questions. I complained to him one afternoon that I didn't need his initials on my underwear. What I needed was a T-shirt that made me look ten years younger.

"You? What about me?" he responded.

"Oh, in your case, Calvin, twenty years!" Did I get a dirty look for that!

There was a live DJ on the floor from time to time. David was often on the floor working out with the rest of us, his fireplug body more and more muscled. His wife, Suzanne Bartsch, was the nightlife impresario, and her Halloween costume party at the gym was famous. I loved the gym. It wasn't well run, which was not a big secret given that gyms have opened and closed with great regularity with a few bankruptcies thrown in.

David's gift was also as impresario, but his business sense, like his attention span, left a lot to be desired. It seemed more than a few of the employees had been in twelve-step programs, and an "it's all good" attitude pervaded the gym. That attitude might have worked for recovery, but in business, not so much.

There was a parade of downtown hipsters, models, and druggies. Cameron Douglas, son of Michael, was there often, working out, and was buddies with the trainers. He went to prison for dealing, a huge tragedy for someone so smart with the world open to him, as did a trainer or two. What had originally appeared as hip began to appear sad. I loved it while it lasted. It was gay but pretended publicly not to be, which was a good strategy, offering protection to the members. Either you knew, or you didn't.

One person I loved there was the writer, Michael Cunningham, who won the Pulitzer Prize for writing *The Hours*. As they made the book into a film, I remember our chats about editing, casting, and how he felt being on set. Lively and intelligent, he wanted my opinion because this was his first big film. I was flattered but didn't have a lot to say about a script I hadn't seen, a director I hadn't met, or a cast working as an ensemble whom I had not seen acting together. I was pleased for him—writers have given me so much. It was good to see a writer celebrated. Often, it's the rest of us who get the glory while they are ignored yet provide not only the story but also the exact words we say to win our awards. This time, for once, life had been fair. He deserved it.

One thing I never figured out—with all their muscles, these gym boys couldn't figure out how to re-rack the weights. When they did put them back, it was inevitably in the wrong places, which meant I wasted a lot of time looking for the weights I needed. Since these guys could calculate their discounts at Prada to eight decimal places, I never understood why they couldn't figure out how to place the tens back where they belonged. I wondered if we had put the signs in Braille, would it have worked better, given they wouldn't buy a shirt or a sweater without turning it upside down and inside out.

There was the old story about Barbra Streisand going to buy a chicken. She asks the butcher to take it out, she pokes it, she smells it, she pulls its wings, she shakes it, turns it upside down, tugs its legs apart to look inside, and then hands it back. "I don't like it," she tells the butcher. He replies, "Excuse me, ma'am, but could you pass a test like that?" Indeed. It was the ultimate touch test, which these guys could have managed. Yet they couldn't re-rack a simple weight.

I kept thinking about the gym business and how it worked. I had learned a lot watching Joe Gold in Venice in the early years. I had fond memories of how Betty Grable had warned me to keep my ass in shape. In my industry, everyone worked out unless they were satisfied playing the fat next-door neighbor who pines for sex but never gets laid. In Hollywood, sex was easy, because hotness was a commodity as much as soybeans or pork bellies. If you let yourself go, you were selling short your most precious commodity—your image. I realized getting older was one thing I could do nothing about, but staying in shape and going for discreet touchups at my plastic surgeon were just part of maintenance. It was harder to find appropriate dates. I had options, but they were fewer than when I was thirty. Every woman and gay man knows this. I don't know what straight men know. Power is its own aphrodisiac, which explained why, at industry functions, even the guys who stayed married showed up with wives of similar age who looked twenty years younger. The women worked at looking good, and the guys got old and looked it. Does it mean women didn't care about hot bodies, or was it they had no choice unless they wanted a divorce? Again, it was the fellas making the rules. Why should we have to be eye candy—couldn't middle-aged men get off their fat asses to please us? It seemed only fair.

With the gym business, serious gym bunnies were buying workout clothes, toiletries, including shampoo, body washes, conditioners, and moisturizers, as well as supplements, food bars, and vitamins. I wanted to capitalize on this at the same time the industry was looking for celebrity brand names. Elizabeth was making a fortune from Passion, her first fragrance, and urged me to do the same. Bobby found a major consumer product company launching a skin care line with toiletries, sunscreens, and lip balms. Elizabeth's example and her nagging pushed me to sign. I became the face of the brand at my age, and since I looked good, women wanted our products. We were in department stores, but at $15 to $25 a shampoo or sunscreen, we were a sensibly priced luxury.

I got pretty good at looking over numbers and the SKUs (each product had its own Stock Keeping Unit number: each bottle, size, and fragrance were individually tagged so stores could track sales and order more, while shippers and producers would know if it was eight ounces or twelve, and which fragrance, color, and line). I needed to learn marketing, positioning and pricing. Every quarter, we would have a board meeting with the consumer product company execs on the Babe beauty brand. It would take a week of preparation just for me to know what questions to ask. In the beginning, it was guys from the consumer product company running everything, but they had to consult with us and get our approval for products, scents, and marketing. We finally hired a couple of capable women who knew reams of data on consumers and products to help us make these decisions when we were consulted. These women gave me courage to learn the business side and use my film marketing experience. I understood how my movies did and how they were marketed to different consumer groups around the world. I always paid attention to my participations and residual accounting statements, and I developed a grasp of how things worked. Slowly, we, as opposed to the big company, made more decisions and became more involved.

I quickly learned I needed help. I opened a small office to take care of my business affairs. Lily, who had finally moved to New York, in part because she was getting too old to drive the Los Angeles freeways, was based there, and Bobby used the office, too, when he was in New York. I went in several times a week when I wasn't on location. In the beginning, I wanted to pull out my hair because of the vapidity of the assistants. We started with four people, but one assistant totally confused me. She could calculate her salary to the penny—and woe if a penny was missing—but when thousands of dollars of my money was at stake, she didn't notice. We had another assistant who was perky—big mistake—but they said she was really smart. She treated me like I was already in a home with the slow, patronizing, perky voice they use when you call the cable company. She liked to comment on my clothes and accessories, as if I cared what she thought. For someone working in the beauty business, her personal taste left a lot to be desired. I finally had her fired after she kept saying how good I looked for my age in her perky voice. My lawyers told me I risked getting sued, and I told them to find me a lady judge over sixty and tell her the bitch said I looked good for my age. Bang. Dismissed. Next. We never heard a word from her. So much for the lawyers.

The brand grew from a few exclusive department stores to 1500 outlets around the world. The Japanese adored the products, and from there, the rest of Asia, including China, followed. My small office kept expanding and now has over twenty-five people in a large office suite. As of this writing, the brand is doing $250 million a year worldwide. I get a 6 percent royalty. Lest you think I'm rich, the sales figure is retail total sales, I am paid royalties on the wholesale number, which is the price the stores pay when they make their orders—and it's much less. However, my annual earnings from the BBB line are millions, and more than I ever made from film. I became a businesswoman, to everyone's shock, but not Bobby's. I didn't only owe Elizabeth—I also owed Bobby for this windfall as with many other things.

He told me he was convinced I would be good in business from watching me fight with studio accountants over how much they owed. He said, "After the first time they squashed you with details you didn't understand, you made sure it never happened again." It was true. Nothing humiliated me more than being told I didn't know what I was talking about. There was one more thing Bobby said—"I watched when you lost almost everything. You had to figure out how to pay off the studio. You had to borrow, beg, and cope. But you didn't disintegrate. You figured out how to do it and how to get help. You were good then, and you will be good now."

Since he gets 15 percent of everything, agent fees having moved up from 10 percent, he is living pretty well, too. His judgment is colored by self-interest, so I take his compliments with a grain of salt. If someone tries to cheat me, however, watch out, because he is a fiercely loyal bulldog.

As the business continued growing, I kept asking Anders, who had been working as an executive, to run it. He finally agreed and has done a wonderful job. I get to work with him, although I have slowly backed out of day-to-day. I still do skincare ads, which are enjoyable, but I let him do the heavy lifting. What pleased me most was that Anders valued my opinion and liked talking to me. We don't always agree, which is not surprising, but he asks and listens—to me, his mother. This is a hard-won victory, and I treasure it.

While I posed for many of the ads, we had male models for our men's line, which we marketed differently to reach that difficult-to-get consumer, as well as female athletes for the action sequences. Guys are a difficult advertising reach. On TV, they watch sports. In films, they watch explosions. In music, the louder the better. And an overlay of tits and ass always helps—no one watched *Baywatch* for the scripts. The jokes I had heard over the years about troubled Hollywood productions came true in a smaller, more limited way on our advertising photo shoots or commercials, when we finally got big enough to do television advertising. The joke that the only thing worse than having your director run off with your leading lady is having him run off with your leading man—it happened. The one about the expensive female model who shows up for a beach bikini sunscreen ad with unshaven underarms? We had that, too.

Then there was the time we did a shoot, and the camera was broken so the footage came back out of focus, and the time the entire crew got food poisoning the night before the shoot and spent the next three days throwing up in their hotel rooms at our expense.

We had a girl sports model we shot first skiing and then running on the beach for our different sunscreens and moisturizers with a month gap between shoots because of other commitments. The model, who as a jock had a small bust, came back for the beach bikini sequence with large implants. She saw my director staring and said simply, "God gave me lemons, and I decided to make them into cantaloupes." Sadly, her comment couldn't make up for continuity problems with already shot footage, so we had to tape down her new implants—ouch—and shoot to cover them up so it didn't look like we were suggesting our products increased your breast size, which would have gotten us into trouble with the FDA.

There was the "perfect girl" we signed to do a photo campaign who went off her diet in a big way and showed up with an ass the size of a living room sofa after we had signed the contract. I never made that mistake again. There is now a material change clause—if a model gains or loses weight or has surgery, we have the right to cancel and not pay. It may seem mean, but this is a business.

We've had wrong packaging, typos screened onto our bottles, and a batch of "juice" (what the industry calls the product that fills the bottles) for Mother's Day specials mistakenly loaded on a freighter bound for Milan when our bottler was in New Jersey.

I quickly learned the actual cost of producing what we sell, including packaging, came to 6 percent to 10 percent of the retail price. A $20 dollar bottle of moisturizer cost at most two dollars to make, including the bottle, cap, box if any, and pump. The rest went for overhead, marketing, testing, shipping, and development. You would think the profits were huge, but they weren't.

A luxury fragrance, like Elizabeth's Passion, only cost $8 to $10 dollars to make while it retailed for one hundred and, as a luxury product, had much better profits. Its exclusivity cut down on sales—Elizabeth didn't come cheap, and her marketing didn't, either. A luxury brand has higher profit margins, but think of the ads you see in the magazines and newspapers and on television. Maintaining that image costs a lot while carrying large risks. No one wants to come out with a celebrity brand, spend the money designing, producing, shipping, marketing, and buying media placement, and have your celebrity go to rehab or, worse, die of an overdose. Amy Winehouse eau de cologne would not have been a good investment. The nightmare of every studio exec as well as luxury product manufacturer was product guilt by association, where sales fell faster than a dive off the Golden Gate Bridge.

By 2000, I was more than financially secure. I had enough money for me and in trusts for my children and grandchildren, including Frederic, who was mine, too. Sebastian was fifty-two, which was a shock. I couldn't believe I had a son that old. His two children were a delight, and he had been with the same woman all these years but never married. I didn't push this and didn't discuss it. *If it ain't broken, don't fix it* continued to be my motto for many things. I assumed his not marrying was fallout from my misadventures down so many aisles. When Sebastian's father had his own spectacular divorce, with his then wife claiming he had the dick the size of a ten-year-old, Sebastian crawled into my house, went to the guest room clutching a bottle of Scotch, and said, "I am pulling the covers over my head until this is over." I made him get up the next morning because otherwise he would have been in bed for a month, and one bottle of Scotch wasn't going to cut it.

Much as part of me enjoyed that blip of revenge for his father leaving us without a dime of support, even when I was down and out and Husband No. 1 knew it and had money, I wouldn't have wished this humiliation on Sebastian. At least they weren't talking about his penis in the press, which was much, much larger, I pointed out, which elicited a loud groan and a shocked, "*Mom!*"

I told him we could escape if he wanted. I would rent a house somewhere off the grid on the Adriatic or in Thailand or in Bahia in Brazil. We could all go for a year. The kids could come with a tutor or else stay in boarding school. He was grateful for the offer but decided to continue working on Wall Street. I was glad he went on with his life but will always be sorry we didn't have that year. It would have been wonderful to have them around. Holding that thought, I bought a country house where we could escape for long weekends and the month of August. I wanted South of France, which was elegant and sophisticated, and I spoke some French, but with my kids working, it was impossible to take four weeks off in America, unlike Europe, so I needed somewhere they could get to on weekends. JFK to Nice, even with the best planning, is ten hours each way commercial and eight private. With weather and other delays during high season, it could be worse, so it wouldn't work for a family spot.

We ended up on Martha's Vineyard. I knew it from Sebastian and Anders's boarding school days when I would rent a house when they worked during the summers. Then, all the kids worked; the rich kids didn't get internships while the scholarship kids waited tables like today. Those summers and later ones, too, when the kids were at Yale, the Rockefeller kids waitressed on Nantucket while Sebastian and later Anders and his buddies worked in Edgartown. It was a dream summer job. I don't remember what they made, but it was their pocket money, and my kids were very proud of it. Most of all, the kids understood how hard it was to earn a dollar and that the plane ticket for a ski trip took three weeks of hard work and a used car wasn't possible even working all summer without a day off. While these are rich people problems, these kids from good schools were going to be running things one day. Understanding the value of a dollar was important. I don't know how the kids of the rich today, with ever widening gaps between rich and middle class, are going to understand the pressure of a working-class life if they've never lived it, never seen it, and have no idea a lost iPhone isn't replaced with just a call home (from their roommate's iPhone).

Those summer jobs had other perks, too, because you never knew who you might meet. As a kid, Anders worked Christmas break at Sherry Lehman, the high-end Manhattan wine merchant, which taught him about wine and vintages. Michael Aaron, who inherited it from his father, would have tasting classes for the young staff so they would know what they were selling and could answer questions semi-intelligently. One day, there was a delivery of a case of white wine to Gloria Swanson's Park Avenue maisonette—a maisonette was defined as having a separate entrance.

Anders thought it was cool and volunteered, wheeling the case on a trolley up Park Avenue.

I remember her so very well. We had met, not surprisingly, through Billy Wilder, who had directed us both—she in her greatest role as Norma Desmond in *Sunset Boulevard* in 1950, and me several years earlier to my first nomination. She was several generations above me—even for stars in the fifties, she was the resurrection, a dinosaur from silent film who crossed over to the talkies. Gloria was so old Hollywood she had been nominated for the first-ever best actress Academy Award. In her early career, she worked with Cecil B. DeMille, Charlie Chaplin, the Keystone Cops, and Rudolph Valentino. She got a second nomination in the twenties and then came back from the dead with her third nomination for *Sunset Boulevard* twenty years later. After that, she was finished in Hollywood but remained a legend. During World War II, she spent her considerable energies rescuing Jewish scientists and inventors who otherwise would have ended up in concentration camps. She also had her own clothing label using her very well-known reputation as a fashion icon.

Whenever I saw her, she was always stunning and mercurial. After my divorces, she was practical rather than judgmental, having been married six times herself. Her view of men fit her image—they were useful as toys but to expect more was asking too much. After talking to her a while, you began to wonder how much of Norma Desmond was really Gloria as there were a lot of parallels. Billy knew this. When she wrote her memoir, *Swanson on Swanson*, at age eighty-one, Janet Maslin of the *New York Times* commented, "Whatever else she may have been, Miss Swanson was never confused."

Anders, my strapping young Yalie, showed up at the maisonette door with the case of white wine on the trolley. The maid answered, took one look at the heavy box, and asked if Anders could possibly carry it into the kitchen, which he was happy to do. On the way out, he paused in front of a full-length portrait of Gloria Swanson at the height of her career. She wasn't tall, maybe four foot eleven, but it gave a sense of the size of the foyer that the painting fit comfortably over the fireplace. Then, as Anders stared at the painting, out from the shadows stepped Gloria Swanson herself, dressed in a pale-yellow pantsuit with matching turban (naturally, I asked). She looked at Anders and said, "I used to be beautiful, wasn't I?"

Again, how very *Sunset Boulevard*, and how I identified with her sentiment. Anders told me he introduced himself and stayed twenty minutes chatting before he needed to get back to work. Gloria was a recluse by then—it was the last months of her life—and she was thrilled to have a cute young man as company.

Anders told me what surprised him was her sexiness, even at eighty-three. I must have raised my eyebrows at him. "Mom, be serious, you're my mother! You're not sexy to me! It's bad enough you are showing your breasts every other film!" Okay, point taken. I backed off.

Whatever she had, she still had it, her charisma astounding someone like Anders who had been around a lot of it all of his life. You could see why old Joe Kennedy fell for her, Anders told me. It didn't seem possible to resist her. I didn't bother to correct Anders that as sexy as Gloria had been and still was, Joe Kennedy used her to leverage his business interests in Hollywood and discarded her when he was finished, leaving her in debt. Another predatory guy using women.

The kids' summer jobs made for a tight crowd with lifelong friendships created between those with privilege and those with less. One waitress friend of the kids ended up staying with us for a couple of summers at the Vineyard house. She was so smart that I pushed her to go to medical school. I helped her out a little with some extra cash from time to time but mostly provided moral support. She is now my internist.

Finally, I bought an old-fashioned white clapboard house with dormer windows and a barn in West Tisbury off the marshes, which was more or less in the center of the Vineyard. There were six bedrooms and four bathrooms, but we fit more on sofa beds in the barn. I remember well the shock of that first summer when the island population jumped from the off season's fifteen thousand to a hundred thousand. Cars were limited because you needed a ferry reservation. I kept a jeep and an old station wagon there and would fly back and forth—mostly commercial, but sometimes I splurged and hired a jet. For the kids, I picked up the airfare and told them not to worry. The teen grandchildren would come with friends (I paid for them, too, so it was coveted to be invited). Frederic, who was about to enter Yale, worked following Anders's and Sebastian's example. He lived in the house all summer and was indeed its custodian. He took a lot of initiative and, armed with my charge cards, decided one summer to redo the barn kitchen, which had been four burners over an old electric oven and a rusting refrigerator. I saw a few bills, but he told me the refrigerator had died and we needed rewiring, so I didn't think a lot about it. I finally arrived a few weeks later, and it was all done and done well—updated and modern, fitting into the barn loft space perfectly, with brown woods, granite counters, and double dishwashers, which were a miracle after everyone was used to carting dishes to the main house or doing them by hand after a party.

I loved the Vineyard, with its New England morning chill and hot afternoons. We bought supplies at Alley's General Store in West Tisbury. You ran into everyone there, including Spielberg, Doris Kearns Goodwin, who wrote so movingly about Lincoln and LBJ, Bill Styron, author of *Sophie's Choice*, and even Sy Hersh, who had interviewed me about Marilyn's diaries. This was before President Clinton decided it was chic. Jackie Onassis had already bought her estate there in one of the best real estate deals on the island. Needless to say, we didn't hang out.

I drove around and, like the rest of the island, picked up hitchhiking kids, who would often recognize me and ask pretty good questions. From my grandkids and their friends, I learned it provided bragging rights if you got picked up by Carly Simon, James Taylor, or me! I felt honored to be in the same class as those two, even if it was only for picking up hitchhikers. I could do my own thing because there were so many other more important people by then, and everyone pretty much left them alone, too. The low-slung 200-year-old stone walls, the grassy fields, the birds, not to mention daily cocktail parties kept things going at a lovely, livable pace.

Frederic's father spent time with us, too. I was pleased Frederic spent time with his father, and we became extended family. Ex-Husband No. 5 also made a rapprochement with Anders. While they weren't as close as before, there was something tender there. I was getting too old to care anymore, at least with ex-Husband No. 5. There were a few others that made me long for sweet revenge, as you may guess.

One island resident who had a lovely estate in Chilmark was the computer executive who had told me so many years ago to do things only on my terms. While he was referring to my one-woman show the first time around, years ago, when I was dithering, that advice worked very well applied to lots of other things. Sam would come for dinner now and again or invite me to his estate for his gatherings. He had made several fortunes in computers and software, had become a partner in a Silicon Valley venture firm, and spent much of his time on freedom and democracy issues around the world, where he put his fortune to good use. I met the computer generation heavies at his house. Larry Ellison, with his fixation on winning the America's Cup, Bill and Melinda Gates before their divorce, who were turning their focus to Africa and vaccines, Steve Jobs, who was too obsessive about everything to be truly enjoyable but was so fascinating you were willing to overlook it for a time. Spending every day with him, I thought, might have been too much.

I found Sam overbearing. He was used to getting things his own way—with several billion dollars, not a lot of people told him no. We argued every time we saw each other. I thought he was a rich man playing savior by trying to spread democracy around the world to places that didn't know what it was. He thought I was a spoiled Hollywood star who had no idea what hard work was. Maybe we were both right in some of our judgments, but the way we were right was probably less important than the way we were wrong. He told me that without my makeup man and jewels, I would fling myself under a train. I told him that without his fortune, he would just be an overbearing pain in the ass. He pointed out I was drinking his champagne. I responded I could afford my own and didn't lack dinner invitations. I remember the looks both of us would get from the other guests. My children just asked that if we were going to start throwing things to warn them to get out of the way.

Sam had his charms, however, one of which was his Gulfstream. He would give me rides to and from the Vineyard when he was going to New York or LA and I was going the same way. It got to be so we would call each other when we knew our schedules. We both had people but respected each other enough to make these arrangements ourselves. Then, we fought from the moment we got on the plane until we landed. The crew was beside themselves. Yet we kept doing it. I was pleased I got him involved in women's issues in the third world. I told him if he wanted democracy, there needed to be education, and if he wanted education, he needed to start with the women, who would in turn educate their children. "Men's egos are too big to change," I said, looking at him. Sam glared at me but said nothing. A few weeks later, I read in the paper he had hired an expert in women's education in the third world for his foundation. I decided to not rock the boat, so said nothing.

I was twelve years older. We certainly were not dating—the idea sent chills down my spine—but I found I liked arguing with him until he infuriated me too much. Then I was happy not to see him for a couple of weeks unless I needed a ride. He had a couple of kids in their thirties, a younger daughter from a second marriage, and three grandchildren. His older sons and my three started to like each other. Anders told me I should date him.

"Hush your mouth, sweetheart!" I told him. I was entitled to have friends. I didn't need a man. Bobby just rolled his eyes.

"Don't roll your eyes," I protested. "It's not like I've had your track record!" This got Bobby laughing.

There was another reason I was determined not to date Sam—his young daughter. She came one weekend to see her father on the Vineyard, and they ended up at my house with my kids plus other friends for drinks and dinner. The kid, who was all of seventeen, decided to call this dubious guy she liked, who wasn't turning down an invitation to my house to see a billionaire's daughter. He was twenty-two, a bit old for her, but that was not what really bothered me. What bothered me was that he was just as spoiled as she was. The two stole drinks behind our backs all evening and then got high on pills. They disappeared for a while, and then Frederic pulled me aside and said she was outside crying, her arm bleeding.

Her face was puffy from tears, her too-tight dress for her overweight figure was torn, and she was in shock. Evidently, the boy, fucked up as he was, took a moped in our garage out for a late-night ride. He flipped it over, and the girl walked back a couple of miles in the dark to the house and didn't know how he was. I was worried about him lying in a ditch bleeding to death but mindful, too, of how this would play out in the press and the fallout.

I was about to call the local police because if he was injured, I didn't want to wait until daylight to find him. I just had to hope they would keep this quiet. Then, while we were all scared of what we might find, we heard the hum of the moped, and the dumb kid drove back into the driveway, a bit wobbly, but at least upright.

Huge sigh. "You okay?" were the first words out of my mouth.

When he said he was, all the anxiety about what might have

happened started to hit me, and I snapped.

"Are you out of your fucking mind? Drinking and doing drugs with a seventeen-year-old and stealing a moped for a midnight joyride? If you had hit a vehicle or a person instead of flipping it over, there would have been police and jail for driving under the influence."

The dumb kid just shrugged and said it wasn't a big deal—he had borrowed the moped, not stolen it, no one got hurt, it was "just a little fun." Since his eyes were glazed, and now I knew he was unhurt, I asked Frederic to drive him home and told him I never wanted to see him again. If I did, I would press charges and let him take his chances on a judge ruling about his giving alcohol and drugs to a minor plus theft.

The daughter, hearing my anger, went sobbing to her father, complaining I had been rude to her "boyfriend" and she wanted to go home immediately because I was such a bitch.

Sam gave me this look of apology at the word but didn't correct her. So, I did.

"You truly are a spoiled brat. You think I'm a bitch? Me? You drink and do drugs with this idiot who could have been arrested for driving under the influence and giving drugs and alcohol to a minor. *You* knew he was fucked up and went anyway. *You* didn't know better? What were you thinking? No helmets—you both could have been killed. You want to be dragged into the press as the dumb chick riding with this kid if he had killed himself on the way home and have to live with that following you around the rest of your life?

"I did you a favor by throwing him out, and now you're whining to your father? You're worse than that dumb kid because you egged him on and knew better. And what were your hands doing on the moped ride to distract him?"

Sam's eyes bugged out at this. My insinuation of sexual shenanigans startled him, but what did he think the two kids were going to get up to drunk and high? The fat, spoiled daughter had clearly never been spoken to like this and immediately whined she wanted to call her mother to fly her home. "I'm not having a good time, Daddy," was her winning line, a badly written one at that since it was her father who owned the plane. I didn't understand her logic, but then logic was apparently not her strong suit.

I usually like kids, but not her. Despite her privilege, she didn't take any responsibility. True, she was a mess from alcohol and drugs, but my experience with substances and bad judgment, not an unusual Hollywood predicament, was that an almost tragedy could work to sober people up. Not this time. Plus, this was someone who had been fucked up many times before and knew how to hide it. At seventeen, this was not a good sign.

Later, Sam got really mad at me for my remarks. He complained it took hours to calm her down after I had provoked her. I just asked, "What were you thinking? This boy was a good idea? You didn't tell her to shut the fuck up and go to bed? Or tell her she was whiney, spoiled, and stupid?" I left off adding fat although I was thinking it—at seventeen, already overweight, something was clearly out of kilter. I never let myself go. Why had she?

He responded that she was having a really difficult time and needed his support. To me this was blah, blah, blah. He had invited his daughter because he had hoped to spend time with her. Her response was to push the boundaries by drinking, doing drugs, and asking over a twenty-two-year-old boy she barely knew.

I'm sure I rolled my eyes. "She needs a good kick in the rear, not sympathy," I told him. I knew that song and dance, but Sam couldn't see it. He didn't understand how he had missed putting his foot down and setting clear limits when she was a child, and now it appeared to be too late. He couldn't take responsibility, either, just like his daughter. He assumed his kid would be like him—hardworking, driven, and honest. He couldn't acknowledge how far from that reality she really was. I had no idea if she could change, but she remained completely self-involved when she or the boy could have been killed and couldn't acknowledge any of it. You almost die with a drugged-up moped driver flipping the bike over, and your main complaint is you're not having a good time? I hate whiners. As for Sam giving tough love, it didn't take a genius to see that in this scenario, even if read his kid the riot act, his ex-wife would have undermined him.

Sam and I didn't see each other for a while. When we did, we didn't discuss his daughter. How could I tell him I couldn't respect her and didn't respect his parenting, either? I feared what would happen to her with the huge amount of money at stake—and knew it would destroy Sam if something did. Sam would never forgive himself and he would never forgive me, either, since he would remember this episode every time his kid did something else that brought her to the brink. I would be blamed no matter what, either for interfering and upsetting her or for not making him understand the risks she faced. I wasn't sure I could pick up the pieces if he lost his daughter. I hadn't the strength. There was no winning here for anyone, and I just wanted the situation to go away. I had seen how young people reacted to privilege and unlimited money. This story was in the papers all too frequently with Hollywood stars.

As the fallout from Sam's daughter's sad visit to the Vineyard continued, I also needed to worry about my sagging career. Film is a visual medium, and we are its subjects. People watch my movies and see me as I was, which becomes a shock when they see me now, the older woman before them. The look on their faces makes that distinction quite clear. The surprise, like the look that Anders must have had on his face when he met Gloria Swanson in her foyer, is not pleasant.

I don't find it easy seeing the looks I get from people appraising what I used to look like compared to what they see now. As this product line has been in production for seventy years, it should not be so surprising that there have been design changes.

The past years, all I have done are small roles or an occasional supporting role for projects I believe in, where I can help a production that is less commercial or a new director. I work scale, since it's the minimum they can pay, but it costs me more to show up and pay for my hotel and driver than I ever earn. For this, I get to go to the premieres, dressed up and wearing my twenty-carat diamond earrings again, since Sebastian never married, and I bought Anders's stone back at his divorce. (He did remarry, and so far, it seems like it is going well, but let me bite my tongue, as you will well understand.)

While my career has languished, my interest in fashion has not. Current styles, however, confuse me. I look at the old movies and see the clothes with perfect fit, colors selected to enhance the actress, and designs to give emphasis to the role, whether it's hooker or princess. I go to the big New York evening event, the Costume Exhibit at the Met, run by Anna Wintour of *Vogue*, who more or less invented modern fashion and sponsored most of the current designers by promoting those she liked in her magazine.

A recent opening evening was enjoyable for a society circus but not for elegance. At MGM, we were taught to enhance your assets and detract from your flaws, so if you had chunky fingers, you didn't wear bright nail polish or huge rings; you wore gloves. I have never worn open-toed shoes because I don't have lovely toes. Thus, I don't call attention to them. I don't paint my toenails, either. It's not a big deal—I work with what I have. Dresses with fluff or bows at the rear make your ass look huge, bare skin should be suggestive but not like a hooker on her day off, and architecture is for buildings. Clearly, that's all out the design window now. Fashion as a statement seems wrong. It's about the human body and its beauty and limitations. It's about setting an image, playing a role, and living a life, which we do whether we think we are or not. When I see a kid walking down the street in khakis and Top-Siders, it's one image. The same kid with baggy pants falling down around his ankles, a backward baseball cap, and a T-shirt that says *fuck your mother* is another.

At the costume exhibit, there were, in effect, a lot of very expensive "T-shirts" saying fuck your mother, too. Why? Where were the stylists and designers? Give me back Edith Head or Pat Fields from *Sex and the City*, or even *Gossip Girl*, whose actresses would never have been allowed to look as bad on the show as they did at the museum that night. I guess ugly is in. At my age, ugly doesn't need attention. I have my face for that.

The costume exhibit is New York's Oscar night—high risk socially and fashion-wise, with winners and losers and rankings closely held within an in-the-know group. An old friend told me about an heiress who had inherited her grandmother's magnificent jewels while beginning a wild affair with her trainer. They carried on for several months until the trainer either tired of her or got a better offer and left early one morning with the jewels, which were not insured. Once the police were involved, this story made it all over town in ten minutes. The night after the robbery was the costume exhibit opening, so the heiress in question bought a new necklace and earrings, which were nice but nothing like what she had lost. Everyone noticed, but nobody said anything until the heiress went up to the bar for a drink. Then, one of the other Upper East Side ladies, and I use the term lady loosely, came over, looked at the new jewelry, and asked, "What is this, a starter set?" and walked off. Bam! They were not my kind of people, but I laughed, too.

At the costume exhibit opening night, I didn't have a date, which was fine with me. I was used to going out on my own or with a friend. Sam called. He had paid for a table and asked me to join him. I was pleased to do so. Then he called again and asked if we could go together since his date canceled because she had to be in Paris. I wondered if she was a supermodel. I also wondered what he wanted with me. I was a bit startled. We had, after all, been friends now for ten years. "This isn't a date?" I asked. "You know, I'm getting old."

He laughed. I'm not sure if it was at me or with me. He said, "You must think I'm really slow if it has taken me this long to ask you out. I just thought we could go as old friends. And my foundation people are with us, so you can argue and drive them crazy, too."

"I don't think I can remember such a charming invitation, ever," I said sarcastically. "Okay, but I warn you—the press may have a field day with you being my new boy toy."

"I'm a little old to be a boy toy," he responded.

When I said, "No kidding!" he got hurt and bothered, just like a guy.

We went together, but something had changed. He wouldn't argue, was trying to be attentive, and had a stupid grin on his face all evening. *Oh shit*, I thought, *he likes me*. Another friendship down the drain. The idea of reconnecting with his daughter was also something that put a damper on any thought of dating him. She had apparently not improved with age. We had a lovely evening, and then Sam and I avoided each other for several months. I didn't want a guy, and he was embarrassed, something I had never seen in him before. When he finally called, he made a lame excuse about traveling, saying he had been out of the country, something I had done with him occasionally to help promote his education programs, since I could garner press attention.

A few months later and far too suddenly, it seemed, I was turning eighty. My boys, no spring chickens themselves, wanted to throw a party. I didn't want one. It's one thing to be eighty; it's another to announce it to the world. I had been blessed with health, could stand straight, looked good for my age (ugh!), and had most of my faculties intact. A big party, however, was not what I wanted.

I had been at a dinner around the time Rose Kennedy turned one hundred. I was seated next to one of her grandchildren, whom I had known for years, and asked him how she was doing. He said she was in and out of it, but a week ago, he had been talking to her—and being ignored—when he finally asked her how she felt to be one hundred. She raised her head, summoning her once considerable presence, and retorted, "I'd rather be sixteen!" Exactly!

We settled on a lovely dinner at my house in the Hills with the usual suspects, including Bobby and Lily. Frederic was there with his significant other. His father, too, as well as Sebastian's father. Two out of six was better than expected. The only other still living, No. 6, could rot in hell although I was curious how he'd held up now that he was approaching fifty-eight. I wasn't curious enough to find out. Elizabeth came wearing her best jewels, including her thirty-three-carat diamond ring, and escorted by her security, given the bling. She wore it to honor me and show off that even in a wheelchair, she could outshine me. Her health had been bad for years, and it pained me to see her deteriorate.

Chen was gone by now. She had kept her illness secret and had died at Elizabeth's house, cared for and loved by Elizabeth and her staff. Lily went over daily and was completely crushed, as was Elizabeth. The service was heartbreaking. Afterward, Lily told me she was not leaving me but would spend time transitioning Elizabeth. She set Elizabeth up for life without Chen. Part of it, maybe the most important, was to allow the two of them to commiserate together over their loss. Both Lily and Elizabeth remained close for the rest of ET's life.

Sam came, too. Bobby invited him, thinking it was a good idea. Why, I didn't know. We had just started talking again after our evening at the Costume Institute. He came bearing a gift, a lovely still life of flowers in a vase by Balthasar van der Ast, a Dutch painter from the seventeenth century. Of course, I didn't know who the artist was, but the painting was magnificent—a generous gift from a billionaire.

I cornered him to thank him. And to tell him to stop being weird. Or, as I tactfully said, weirder than usual. We were friends. Stop mooning around.

"I miss you," he said simply. Then, like a teenage boy, he added, "And I feel stupid."

I just looked him in the eye and said, "Get over it. I'm now eighty. How long do you think I've got? Waste your own time, but don't waste mine because I don't have a lot!"

He had more to say but hemmed and hawed like a teenager, something at odds with his usual arrogance. Finally, he managed to get out, "I'm sorry."

Yes, I thought, *how nice. The arrogant one has finally apologized.* But what about? He stammered on a bit and it slowly emerged that his daughter was in rehab. The shrink had told both him and the ex the kid needed tough love and a job to support herself. I had been right, and he was sorry he hadn't had the balls to yell at her for calling me a bitch.

I could imagine how bad things must have gotten for him and his ex-wife to join together to force the daughter into rehab. There was no pleasure in being right when all I wanted was to be wrong. I was, however, relieved she was getting help—this might not become the tragedy I feared. I kept my big mouth shut and just told Sam how sorry I was. In front of me stood a humbled, formerly arrogant Sam. One who wanted to make his apology, judging by the expensive present. After our talk, it seemed we would be able to go back to arguing as usual, but not that night.

Just before the party, ET had been honored at the Macy's Passport Event for her AIDS efforts. At the event, *Access Hollywood* interviewed her like the little old lady from Pasadena, with puffball questions, including one about how she would advise young actresses getting too much paparazzi attention, a veiled comment about either Paris Hilton or Lindsay Lohan.

She laughed about it with me later. "Darling, I smiled sweetly instead of saying if you don't want to be taken as sluts, keep your legs closed. Certainly, don't fuck the press. That's their job—to fuck us! If you don't want to be photographed falling down drunk, drink less. What assholes!" We howled.

"We had our moments," I pointed out. "How many marriages did we have between us, thirteen?"

"Oh please, darling, only twelve! I am not double counting Richard. And neither of us made a sex tape and released it on the Internet—really bad taste. We were public only because we couldn't help it and never had a minute to ourselves. But we never asked for it!"

I shook my head, "Ex No. 6 and his *Playgirl* spread made the Hilton girl look virginal."

"Ha!" came the retort. "Those pictures made everyone understand it was worth it. No one imagined you married him for his mind, and now we have proof! None of my husbands posed for *Playgirl*."

How kind of her to be concerned, I thought, and responded, "The game isn't over yet. Just wait!" and we descended into merriment, imagining what her husbands might have looked like posing. Richard in Mark Antony's toga was a particular source of glee, me with a drink, she

248

with a painkiller. We were not particularly complimentary about our various husbands. Sadly, she was in bad shape. While we had a good night together and laughed a lot, she left after dinner, tired out. There would be fewer and fewer outings for her. She had aged far faster than I and suffered serious illness all of her life. Genetics are such a wild card—such overwhelming beauty amid such physical frailty. Was God really up there laughing at us?

Before she left, Elizabeth noted Sam's gift and knew the artist, given her own extensive collection. "He does like you. Maybe our number is going up!" she joked.

"Bite your tongue," I told her. "I'm done with marrying."

"Well, sweetie pie, no one who doesn't like you buys a six-figure painting."

"It's not like I'm putting out," I retorted.

Her counter—"That's my point, pumpkin"—left me with nothing to say.

She faded slowly for the next couple of years until she died. I felt Elizabeth's loss keenly. I was honored she wanted to see me at the end, and we could sit on her bed, visiting without pretense, except for her jewels, which she knew were much better than mine. Before she died, she gave me a bracelet. I should have let it be sold at her auction for AIDS but couldn't bear to part with this memento. I gave a donation instead and wear the bracelet. At times of strife, it's comforting to have her around. Those days, I wear it. I will wear it on opening night.

The most touching parts of the evening were quiet moments with each guest, my three sons, their wives and significant others, my three grandsons, my exes, and Bobby, Lily, and ET. Sam, too. They were my world, or what was left of it. I was lucky. There were many regrets, too. So many things I had hoped would have worked out better. Then there were my dead, the ones I wanted to talk to, the ones to whom I had much to say. Elizabeth used to tell me I could talk to them, and the good news was they couldn't answer back. I was tired of one-sided conversations. It would have been like talking to the studio—I talked, and no one listened.

Anders gave me a letter on the occasion. It read:

Dear Mom,

It's hard to imagine you're eighty. It took me a long time to grow up and understand you were protecting me when you sent me to Paris. I think I'm still mad at Dad for what he did to us. The one thing Sebastian and I wanted when we were young was to be normal. What you gave us was extraordinary. The people we met, the places we went, our education, and our family. We have been blessed. All that rested on your work and the life you created for us. They never gave you an award for that, but you deserve one. Happy birthday.

Love, Anders

I read that letter over and over. It was affirmation, but not one I expected. My life and everyone in it revolved around me. It wasn't that I took that for granted or was the center because of ego. It was just the way things worked. I was a business. I was glad my sons saw another facet, because they could easily have found me selfish. I didn't mean to be. Like a shark, I continuously swam forward.

I keep the letter in my vault, next to my twenty-carat earrings. If I could carry one thing with me, however, it would be the letter. I will be buried with it.

We love Sam. We pushed Bobby to push Sam and Mom to be together. I never thought of my mother as old even at 80. Now, it's different. She really is old. But she put it off for a long time. And she's still with Sam. He's used to getting his way, she's used to getting her way, and the combination is both explosive and tender. They pull back for each other at the last minute. And Sam is nuts—he didn't know what to get us for Christmas one year and bought everyone Mercedes—children, grandchildren, his, Mom's and who knows who else's. He bought over a dozen and laughed when Mom got angry. We were delighted.

The beauty business has been my baby for a long time. It's fun to work with my mother, who is as opinionated as ever, can't keep her mouth shut, and yet listens to advice. She won't do something I don't want; on the other hand, she does nag. But she's not wrong often, which is something she points out. We've made a lot of money from the company, and it's made my career. I love what I do, and I get to go to sports events whenever I want since we sponsor so many.

Anders

BACK FROM THE DEAD

Twenty-five years after they suggested the one-woman show, the phone rang. It was Bobby, now retired but still repping me, since I, too, was retired except for a few things they figured I could do during the shoot before dying. I am still insurable and considered a better risk than some of the current young stars. The only reason I won't show up on set is I am dead. They have much more variety in their excuses. I was in my New York apartment reading the Sunday *Times,* or the parts I could wrestle out of Sam's hands since he had come over for brunch, when the phone rang.

"They have come back from the dead," Bobby said. No introduction, no hello or how are you. It's been this way for years and, as an agent, niceties weren't really expected.

"Who this time?" I wanted to know.

"Well, remember I said the offer to do your one-woman show would never come again?" he asked. I had a sinking feeling about this now. I wanted friends back from the dead, not deals.

"Sadly, yes. And have a very heavy heart at the thought," I responded.

"They're offering more money. They want to get you on stage while you can walk."

I paused a moment for dramatic effect and said, "If we wait for me to do it in a wheelchair, will I get more?" which got a laugh.

"They figure the Broadway blue-haired ladies will kill to see you while they can. It's a toss-up of who kicks first." Nice. Even for him. "Take the money. I know you don't need it. I don't need it. But it's your career. Make a comeback, have fun, tell everyone to fuck themselves while you're on stage. They can't stop you, and you can settle old scores. Do it while you can, and let them pay you to insult them."

He knew how to get me. His logic was impeccable. I had been thinking about this since the last go-around. I was now eighty-seven. I wasn't going to get another chance in twenty-five years. The idea was nice, but given how I felt when I got up in the morning and how long it took to put on my face, I wasn't sure I wanted another twenty-five years. On the other hand, I didn't like the alternative, but doddering wasn't for me. In any case, it wasn't like I had a choice. For a long time, I had told people I wanted to live as long as I could walk, talk, and poop on my own, but now that I had gotten there, it was no longer true. I wanted to be desired, to be beautiful, and have natural breasts that pointed up, not got in the way. Those days were gone.

I was in my eighties, even my grandkids were grown, and I still had a big mouth. My grandchildren had learned I spoke my mind. My little great-granddaughter, four, who was adorable, referred to me as Grandma Monster after I yelled at her for writing on the wall with red lipstick. Not being an idiot, she denied it and lied, until I roared, "Who wrote on my walls in red lipstick?"

The response, a sulky, "It wasn't red. It was dark pink!" made it difficult not to laugh. I thought, *maybe she'll be a lawyer—but probably not at Harvard.* A little Windex, a little bleach, a call to the painter, and all was well. It warmed my heart to see how embarrassed my grandson was about his little daughter's misadventure with my wall.

I had to keep up appearances after such a sweet remark, since I certainly didn't want any more lipstick, dark pink or not, on my walls.

Thus, the sobriquet of Grandma Monster. I loved it. It got into the press—what else was new? The little one was meeting me for dinner at a fancy restaurant, since I was babysitting so the kids could have a date. Her nanny brought her to meet me, and the little one walked up and asked the maître'd, "Have you seen Grandma Monster?" and Page Six had its headline. Of my physical assets, my mouth has remained. The others have descended.

The wee one came over often, which belied her calling me monster. One day she was hungry, and my housekeeper was out. I took her into the kitchen and made her a peanut butter and jelly banana sandwich. She looked up at me earnestly and asked, "Grandma Monster, am I going to die?" Such a serious question for such a sweet child.

"No, darling," I responded. "You are going to live a long, useful life and be a Grandma Monster yourself!" Big smile. "Why do you ask?"

Looking questioningly at her sandwich, she said, "Daddy says if I want to live, not to let you cook!" From philosophical to practical in ten seconds. If you thought my grandson was embarrassed about the lipstick on the wall, you should have seen his face after this! I let him squirm a bit before I let him off the hook. It's true—I have never cooked much except in Paris, and then only under instruction. Left to my own devices, you wouldn't want to come for dinner. Other than eggs, I make one dish, a roast chicken—drizzle with olive oil, sprinkle with garlic powder, rosemary, and black pepper, squeeze a lemon over it, and bake for an hour to an hour and a half at 400 degrees. Once, during the period when I was counting my pennies after Anders's father was killed, I put the squeezed lemon in the cavity to provide extra moisture while it cooked. Anders, who was four, went racing out of the kitchen to summon help, finding Bobby in the living room. "Mom just shoved a lemon up the chicken's butt!" he exclaimed. We have called it lemon butt chicken ever since.

My last leading role was two years ago. It had been well-received but small. It won small mentions, but the studio, where surprisingly it ended up being produced, didn't want to pay for marketing for any major bigger awards. I wouldn't have won anyway that year, since the Oscar went to Meryl Streep, who can seemingly do almost anything, the bitch! I was up for the Margaret Thatcher role and wouldn't have needed nearly as much makeup, but they felt she would be better than an aging blonde sex symbol. I also had a lot of reservations about the script, which focused on the former prime minister's decline from dementia and her, mostly, imaginary discussions with her departed husband, Dennis.

I had asked for a rewrite, because again the studio guys took a towering woman, the first world leader of a western power, and what did they focus on? Her years as prime minister, her interactions with Ronald Reagan and George Bush—"don't go wobbly, George"—her relationship with the Queen? No, those are brushed over, and we are left with a doddering old woman—charming, touching, but decaying. I was incensed. As for Meryl, it was a forceful performance, written to show off her range, but we already knew she could act. A story about a decaying woman, I understand, but to do this hatchet job to Thatcher and her position as a role model for women who could be the next generation of world leaders was wrong. One script discussion, and I was out. Streep was magnificent, winning another Oscar for the role. I was sorry because it could have been me. But I couldn't keep my mouth shut.

My non-nominated role had started out with me playing a woman coming to terms with her child's autism as she realizes she is dying, and her sixty-year-old son will be left alone. There is no one to take care of him, and every institution is worse than the last. She makes a lovely last dinner for the two of them, mixes in poison, and commits a murder-suicide. The story was so depressing I didn't want to do it, but the writer begged me to call attention to the lack of long-term care.

Then the studio got their hands on the project, buying it in turnaround, and suddenly I was working for them again. They wanted a love interest, as usual, and asked if I would consider baring my breasts one more time. I looked at them with disgust and pointed out, "You realize this is a story about autism and a mother's sacrifice, not sex. You want my eighty-year-old breasts for that story?"

They said it would break barriers.

"You guys are morons," I replied. "No one who has ever seen eighty-year-old breasts wants to. We want to sell tickets, not scare the audience." As the kids say now, WTF. When one went to argue, I responded finally, "Tell you what, I will show you now, and you decide!" Not surprisingly, they declined.

One more time with fat, middle-aged assholes. Bobby, who was there, was beside himself laughing. He told me later he was hoping I would do it so he could see the expression on their faces. I asked him the last time he actually saw a real breast. He paused and said, "The '60s, but I'm not sure. I don't really remember the '60s, as you know."

Sam heard the story and laughed so hard he started wheezing. I was starting to get worried about the old coot. He was no longer young, either.

We would have dinner several times a week when we were both in the same city, often out, but there were quiet evenings at our apartments just hanging out or screening new movies, which they sent to me since I am a voting member for the Oscars.

We had moved on with our lives together. I had decided he wasn't so bad all the time. His daughter had gotten better after rehab and had been working steadily, although with a few bumps. I had started to respect her, which made life with Sam easier. I helped her get a job. She couldn't work for Sam or any of the companies he invested in and be evaluated fairly or honestly. I told my friends to give her a chance, but if she didn't work hard or messed up, to fire her.

The press more or less left Sam and me alone as well as the daughter after the initial story about her going to rehab. I told the kid the media might not be so terrible in the long run—she could be a role model for others, later, when ready, which seemed to offer her and Sam comfort. It's hard to ride things out in life while being in the media.

While there were stories linking Sam with me as the older woman, neither of us cared. We were just glad to be walking. He wanted more. I wanted less. We remained in stalemate yet enjoyed each other's company, arguing about politics and the third world. How the media thought we were dating, given our arguments, was unimaginable.

Sam had a big row with me about the murder-suicide movie. "Your character is murdering her child," he warned. "You will be vilified."

I explained that this was a way to call attention to a difficult issue that I felt passionately about. And I wasn't getting a lot of good roles. We agreed to disagree.

He told me, "Well, it's your career," trying to get the last word.

I snarled, "That's big of you!" He ignored me, asking what I wanted for dessert, and just like that, the argument faded. A relationship, as they say, is two people asking each other what they want to eat until one dies.

We started the shoot, but the director was incompetent and going for camp—not the way to go for this story. After two weeks of shooting, already over budget, I went to the studio. "Get rid of him," I told them. "Otherwise, I'm out." The studio execs told me he was doing his best, which made me burn. I stole from Sean Connery's character in *The Rock* when I said, "Losers whine they did their best. Winners go home and fuck the prom queen. This prom queen is going home until she gets a winning director."

They protested that I couldn't. Oh yes, I could. Read my contract. Bobby had added clauses after I lost my suit with the studio (and all my money) that if the script changed materially from what was agreed upon at signing, I had the right to renegotiate. This clause meant I was out. Otherwise, I could demand $5 million, and for that amount, I was willing to do camp. The studio blinked and whined—then who would direct? Before I could say anything, Bobby said, "She could" and pointed to me. I could have killed him. The idiots agreed. I directed. Myself. And the others. It was a simple, sad story, and it worked. We won a few festival awards and got praise in the press as well as notoriety and picketing. In the end, the story line was too sad for most people to spend an hour and twenty minutes of their free time.

After that, decent scripts were gone. Guest appearances, offers to do camp, but nothing meaty. Sam had the bad grace to tell me he told me so.

You can imagine my response.

I wouldn't let myself be used for shock value. I have always detested cheap cinematic tricks. It's easy to scare someone if you jump out from behind a door and yell, "boo." I was the equivalent, used for my former image and the shock value of *look at her now*. No way was I going to do that. I stayed home or worked with Anders on the Babe beauty business. I wasn't getting old—I was old. After eighty, who was I kidding? Not even me, which was saddest of all. I liked fooling myself. I didn't really have to know, did I? I wanted an injection to provide science fiction rejuvenation—tight skin, youth, fifty more years, my boobs back where they used to be, men drooling. This was the science fiction I wanted.

That was a tough film to watch. Mom was brave but shouldn't have done it. On the other hand, she didn't have a lot of roles coming. I got used to her plastic surgery—she would come back a week later looking fifteen years younger, which was bizarre. On the other hand, why not? She never descended into caricature as did some of her colleagues. So, as her movie career died down, she worked with me more and made a real contribution. After my years being sent away, now we got to be together in the office. We had arguments, but they are very different 40 years later. She also babysat a lot, which was both beautiful and weird. She was a terrific grandma. When I asked her why she couldn't have been as good a mother to us as she was to her grandkids, she told me to fuck off. She wouldn't take shit or self-pity from anyone. Good for her. And I knew that she would say that the moment I made my comment. We've been together a long time!

Anders

MATURE RELATIONSHIPS

I was miserable. I had lost my career. Sam tried to cheer me up. I was at his house one night for dinner. The maid kept refilling my glass, so I didn't know how much I had drunk. I ended up spending the night. With him. I was old but looked good for an old bag. Better than Sam, at least, who played tennis, golf, and sailed, but time isn't kind for a guy, either. Afterward, in bed, we talked.

"I don't want romance. We can sleep together. I'm only doing it because you're really rich. You're only doing it because I'm more famous than you. Let's leave it at that."

"What's wrong with a little romance?" he wanted to know.

"We're too old. It's not fun. Everyone is going to look at us like I'm playing Jane Fonda to your Ted Turner."

"I have more money than Ted Turner," he said with a sigh.

"That's good, since I'm after your money."

"You have enough of your own." He paused. "So, no romance, but we have dinner several times a week?"

"I can live with that."

"And I don't want you sleeping with anyone else," I added.

"I can live with that."

We reached an accommodation. I was too old to fool around. Being in love was my first six marriages. Who needs butterflies, worry, and angst, not to mention divorce lawyers and prenups?

A few days later, after our second night together, Sam gave me a box with a lovely Harry Winston diamond bracelet. "It's not that I think you're a hooker," he said with a wink, "but you did say you were only sleeping with me for my money."

"Actually," I responded, channeling again Marilyn's Lorelei Lee, "given your estate planning, I'm sleeping with you for your children's money."

He smiled and went to sleep. Thus, things changed. I wondered—was this a relationship? Or worse, my last relationship? I wasn't sure. I don't know who will outlive whom, something I never contemplated with any of the others, except Husband No. 3, who died after three months. I don't want to lose Sam, but don't tell him I said so. The truth, as Bobby had known all along, was that we had been in a relationship for years—I just hadn't let Sam have sex. I still liked it, I wasn't too old for it, but the physical need had changed over the years, and I just didn't want what came with it.

Romance is too all-consuming. On the other hand, over the years, I've started telling the cooks to make more fish and less beef—Sam's not a young guy, and I don't want his arteries clogging up. I also insisted he use a trainer every other day. I've started to worry. I just don't want to pay anymore—and as Queen Elizabeth said after 9/11, grief is the price we pay for love.

In my eighties, after ten years and along with a one-woman show, I started sleeping with Sam. I wonder if my biographers are going to focus on how I kept going. But as Woody Allen said, I didn't want to achieve immortality through my work. I wanted to achieve it by not dying. Not a lot of luck there.

The one-woman show percolated along. We didn't have a script or director and hadn't signed a producer. The guys who had re-broached it got points, but we lost them when they wanted me to take a physical with their doctor. I needed a physical for insurance but had no intention of going to a stranger I didn't know or trusting a new office that could leak things to the press. I had been burned too many times. I was perfectly happy with my own doctor, my lady who had worked a couple of summers on the Vineyard with the kids long ago.

This producer was relentless, and I got to the point where I couldn't stand him. One day at the drug store, picking up normal things, including a couple of lipsticks I liked, I happened to see a box of Preparation H. With a flash of genius, I bought it, along with a box of Grecian Formula hair dye for men, and I sent the two items with a note to the producer. The note read as follows:

Dear Producer, try to remember which end is which. Best, Babe

We never heard from him again.

I went to talk to Elizabeth Williams, whom I had sat next to at a dinner and had been charmed. She started out in art history and archaeology and ended up a Broadway producer. What I didn't know when I first met her was she had produced *Les Mis* and *Phantom,* bringing them to Broadway, and had a string of hits over the past fifteen years, winning twelve Tonys. What I loved most, in addition to her eye, was that she wasn't one of the guys. She was a success, made money, and wasn't on drugs like the last female producer I had admired and wanted to work with.

Julia Phillips had been one of the smartest people in Hollywood. She produced *The Sting,* for which she won the first best picture Oscar given to a woman producer, followed by *Taxi Driver* and, finally, Spielberg's *Close Encounters of the Third Kind,* from which she got fired in post-production. Her cocaine problem caused her descent. When she wrote her memoirs, *You'll Never Eat Lunch in This Town Again*, she made a comeback that pulled her out of the poorhouse until she died from a brain tumor a few years later.

She always maintained that had she been a man, they would have rallied around her. Instead, she railed against the white-guy establishment, pointing out that current execs had lowered Hollywood's already low standards. Her book—funny, profane, poignant, and well-written—sniped at Spielberg and the other pillars of the Hollywood establishment, saving its choice attacks for David Geffen, which did not go over well. She didn't so much burn her bridges as dynamite them. One Hollywood producer referred to the five-hundred-page book as "the longest suicide note in history."

She did, however, have a way with words. Mean but funny. She dispatched summary judgment in a sentence, describing Aaron Spelling, the immensely rich television producer of *Beverly Hills 90210, Dynasty, The Love Boat,* and *Charlie's Angels,* as "obsequious to the point of becoming one giant can of Crisco, he was so oily."

Her view of the dropping standards in Hollywood being a man's game had a point: being a smart female producer meant that no matter what she did, she was outside the guy club. Her copious cocaine use flushed her career down the toilet. I always wondered if the pressure of being a woman meant having to constantly measure up, what might have happened if she hadn't had to dance backward in high heels? Who knows?

In the end, she didn't care. Her book was a smash success, remaining number one on the *New York Times* Nonfiction Best Seller List for thirteen weeks. As she said, "I wasn't a pariah because I was a drug-addicted, alcoholic, rotten person and not a good mother. I was a pariah because I hit them with a harsh fluorescent light and rendered them as contemptible as they truly are."

In an odd moment of fate, Elizabeth Taylor presented her with her best picture Oscar on stage when she won, the first woman to win. Years later, as soon as her book came out, everyone raced to get a copy—some to laugh, some to see if they could sue, and the rest of us to see what she said about us. Elizabeth and I didn't find her book all that funny. It was depressing, and we suspected it was true.

Truffaut told me when he directed our film that Julia was one of the brightest women he ever met, but he blamed her for production overruns and other problems on *Close Encounters of the Third Kind* (dah dee du da dum). I had so rooted for her, wanted to work with her, but she flamed out before I got the chance. Now, thirty years later, I was hoping to work with another brilliant woman, Elizabeth Williams, who had beaten the men on Broadway at their own game—fundraising, syndication, producing and winning a long series of Tonys. I wasn't hoping to win a Tony. I just wanted to live long enough to finish my run.

I didn't want to be on stage for two hours by myself. It was okay for Julie Harris playing Emily Dickinson in *The Belle of Amherst* or Vanessa Redgrave doing the *Year of Magical Thinking*, but I didn't think I would be interesting for that long talking by myself. I would bore myself, let alone an audience. Even a member of Congress wouldn't talk for two hours straight if he wanted reelection.

I finally had my meeting with Elizabeth Williams. I was sorry my old friend Elizabeth Taylor wasn't alive. She would have howled with laughter at this and wanted to join in, as she did when we first talked about it so long ago. It was a get-acquainted-and-toss-around-ideas meeting. Bobby, Lily, and me, just like the old days. We were all getting on. How would we open? Nothing grabbed any of us. Finally, Bobby offered up, "You could start with a wedding."

"No! I am not starting with my weddings!" I protested. "You know me better than that!"

"I wasn't talking about *your* wedding. I was talking about mine," Bobby said, grinning.

"What?" This was from Lily who tended to be reserved in these meetings unless it was about media coverage, and we were a long way from there. "You found someone stupid enough to marry you?"

"Think so," Bobby said, surprisingly shy. "He said yes anyway."

I wanted to ask how they met but wasn't sure I wanted the answer. They were high at a sex club or in the gym sauna. Maybe his last flight attendant. Bobby had done them all. Opening my show with his wedding— it was a novel idea, but nothing would have been gayer other than opening with Liza Minnelli, which I was happy to do, too, if I could get her. But they had done that already with one of the *Sex in the City* movies.

That tantalizing news was tossed out at the end of our meeting. We jumped up and hugged Bobby, both Lily and I surprised he could spring something like this without us having a clue. We didn't know he was dating someone special, but he could be surprisingly private when he wanted to, which this news made clear. As for our meeting, Williams said she would think on our project and look through my bio and press clippings.

Unable to resist, Bobby had said, "You have the *Playgirl* clippings, too?" at which point I hit him over the head with my notepad.

Elizabeth Williams laughed. "I think you can use the tawdry to your advantage. What the media reported is not how you lived. Play off the differences." Good point. I was liking her more and more.

"If I agree to do this show, how do I keep things private when those things are what everyone wants to know and what I don't want to tell?" I really wasn't sure I could do this.

She smiled. "You survived, prospered, did amazing work, and came back to make a fortune in skincare. I am less interested in sex and marriages than who you became because of it. Then, if you talk about sex or divorce, there is a contextual element rooted in the storyline, not the tabloids."

I wish I could be that smart. We agreed to think about it and meet in a few weeks.

Meanwhile, I had a wedding to plan. I told Bobby I would be throwing it—no questions asked. It was my wedding gift. It wasn't that I owed him, which I did, but he was family. The question was where—Bobby wanted it at my home in the Hills. I didn't spend much time there now, but I couldn't part with it. I had held on to it through thick and thin, and if I lost everything, I would live there and grow vegetables and raise chickens. Actually, I'm not sure I'm zoned for chickens. God knows I would have them showing up for Bobby's wedding (chicken being slang for young gay boys).

Bobby's intended was thirty-four, a lawyer, smart, earned his own money, and made Bobby happy. When we had time to chat properly, the first thing I said was that California was a community property state, but Bobby cut me off. "I have a signed prenup. I used your lawyers, since they had enough experience with you," he said, smiling. "When I go, I leave a lot to amfAR, but he gets the house and a trust if we're still married. If we don't work out, I give him $100k for every year we're together. I bought him a car as an engagement present." Fair enough. His agent's share of my skin business alone was enough to keep him going.

Sebastian was best man. I was touched. I had stayed out of their relationship and was pleased they remained close after Sebastian grew up. I knew Sebastian usually stayed with Bobby when he was in LA on business despite access to my house, which mostly was empty. He just wanted to hang with Bobby, who had taken care of him, fed him, and watched over him as he grew up and I traveled all over and married and divorced. Best man, wow!

Bobby told me the story of how Sebastian had lost his virginity. I was away filming, and Sebastian was on his own in LA for a week at age sixteen. Bobby took him to dinner one night at a fancy restaurant to chat. Sebastian kept stealing his beers since he was underage. They had a good dinner, and when Bobby finally asked him how he had spent his Fourth of July, Sebastian's reply was, "Not too bad. I had a six pack, a joint, and got laid, but don't tell Mom!" Bobby was good about not telling me, waiting years, but the line was too good to forget. It was telling that the person Sebastian had confided in was Bobby. He saw a maturity few others did. Bobby provided wise counsel to a growing young man. I always thought

Bobby got to be a father because of his relationship with Sebastian, which ran deep as evidenced by Sebastian being best man. The odd thing was that the age difference between the two of them wasn't that large. Paternity (or semi-paternity) was attributed to love, not age. I was proud of both of them.

In addition to everything else, Bobby's mother was coming. She was a couple of years younger than I, but not an easy woman. She resented my fame and influence on her son's life and resented her son because he refused to let her contact me and be part of my life, God forbid. I would see her rarely at his family events but found her loud and grasping. Her envy made her snipe at me for my success, much to Bobby's embarrassment. She also didn't like that he was gay and kept trying to marry him off, initiating discussions about girls he should date before he came out even though these conversations clearly made him want to die.

I tolerated her because of him, and he tolerated her because she was his mother, but she was an unpleasant creature he tried to escape. He supported her financially, but what she wanted was to move in and run his life. Funny how that didn't appeal to him. He begged me to find a solution. He had to invite her, he wanted to see her, but he didn't want her monopolizing things or, worse, trying to convince him that he wasn't gay and needed to find a nice Jewish girl.

He had made a good life for himself, but he was being pulled back into the abyss because, as a decent human being, he wouldn't cut his mother loose and let her go. He was stuck by his past, as we all were, but for most of us, our pasts didn't include his mother.

I was stymied. I didn't want to be rude and didn't want to talk to her because I knew she resented me and anything I said would be held against me. I wasn't sure whether she would leak to the press. Lily came to his rescue, because his mother knew her and her role in our lives. She called and said, 1) we want you here, 2) that said, you break any of the following suggestions, security will show you out, 3) no discussions with anyone on gay issues or marrying nice Jewish girls, 4) no discussion of money of any sort, 5) don't ask anyone what something cost or how much they earn, 6) don't ask for autographs or photos, 7) don't yell at Babe and tell her that she makes Bobby work too hard, 8) do not talk to any press before, during, or after the wedding, 9) try to smile, 10) be nice to Bobby's husband at all times, and do not ask him if he is really gay, and 11) when you are tired, ask someone to take you back to your hotel.

I would have not thought to be so direct. Given this list, Lily was right to be specific. Bobby was as shocked as I was at Lily's boldness and thrilled not to be involved. Few people tried to intimidate his mother. As the saying goes, good fences make good neighbors. His mother came and went without major incident—I also slipped her a couple of thousand cash for her expenses, not that she paid for a thing, which helped soften up the old battle-axe.

I had one other memorable experience with Bobby's mother. Years ago, when she made one of her rare visits to LA, Bobby and I took her to see Clint Eastwood's *Unforgiven*. Every time someone was killed, which was often, she cried out, "Oy vey." She was, after all, a Jewish mother. By the end of the movie, thirty bodies later, the entire theater was shouting "oy vey" every time someone bit the dust. Bobby found it so embarrassing and never got over it, but it was a memorable movie night.

Lily's mother was also invited. The contrast between the two mothers couldn't have been starker. She was funny and had worked hard her entire life to educate her children. Now that Lily could help out financially, she had learned to relax a bit in her nineties. When she wanted to go dancing one night, I loaned her clothes and good earrings. She dressed, came downstairs, and announced in her Chinese accent, "I want to go dancing at a gay club and be a fag hag."

Lily looked up quizzically. "Mom, who says the boys want you as their fag hag?"

"I am in Harry Winston and Chanel. What's not to like?"

I wanted a wedding to beat all gay weddings. We had a tent in the back, flower and fresh fruit arrangements everywhere, a rabbi and a reverend to account for a Californian mixed marriage, hot air balloon rides for the guests, circus acts—flame thrower, gymnasts, and caged tigers, for which I had to get extra liability coverage in case a drunken guest lost a hand by sticking it in a cage when no one was looking. I insisted the tigers be well fed before they showed up, but that made them sleepy. I was okay with that—I didn't want some idiot losing an arm. Given some of the guests, it was a possibility: we had to invite the studio guys.

I had *Along Came Mary* cater. I had known Mary for years, and I thought it appropriate, given she was out and had been for a long time. She also had the skill and the staff to manage the high-profile guest list, having catered everything from the opening of the movie *Titanic* to Barbra Streisand's wedding. She knew how to deal with the crazies, and more importantly, how to kick out press posing as waiters.

Several of Bobby's exes were invited and asked if they could contribute. We told them to write checks to amfAR in memory of how Elizabeth Taylor had gotten Bobby to write his first check. "You know, every time I see the Statue of Liberty, I think of Elizabeth's remark and smile," I confessed.

Bobby grinned. "Me, too. And it cost me a hundred grand." Poor Lady Liberty, virginal, representing hope for those who came ashore, a gift showing France's friendship to America, and all we could think about when we saw her was everyone who had seen Bobby's junk.

There was one touch Bobby asked for. I hesitated initially, thinking about what the press would do. Then I thought, fuck them. He wanted drag waiters for the evening. I was curious as to why, and his explanation touched me. "I lived my early life pretending. I want those who need to pretend to do it openly and be who they really are. I want the drag queens to be able to make a living." This was not the explanation I expected.

There was more. We talked about the professional guest list, the studio execs, the lawyers, other agents, business managers, insurance people, and union guys, who worked on the backside of the industry and made it tick. Most were the fat, middle-aged white guys.

Bobby was vehement about excluding several. It was a long list, and we sat and laughed over each major transgressor until one of us called "next." Strangely, it wasn't the studio execs we hated most. It was those we suspected of tipping off the press.

Then what he said was surprisingly tender. "We've looked after one another a long time now. I don't want any guys who fucked you over. They fucked me over, too. I know you have your anger at the guy club and what they did, but they also did a lot to gay men. No one in this town cares who you fuck, so gay or straight doesn't matter as long as it's not in the papers. There were a few straight guys who liked to put us down, keep us from being fairly paid, and make us look like second-class citizens. Then, there were the gay execs who used their power to have sex and take advantage of people who couldn't say no. Those assholes are not coming."

I knew some of this but not how it directly affected him. He added, "I know everyone laughs at me because of the twenty-somethings, but I never took advantage. I never forced anyone or held a job or money over their head, unless they were a hooker."

"Hookers, really?" I asked, half teasing but not surprised.

"It's not the same in the gay world. It's not exploitation of one sex by another. Hookers are not discriminated against in the gay world the way women are in the straight one."

"I'm not shocked," I told him. "Guys think about sex differently. Maybe it would have been better if I had thought that way about men."

"Didn't you with Husband No. 6?" he asked, for once not joking. I had to think about that.

After we decided on drag waiters, my concern was how we would be able to tell the waiters from the guests, given the amount of makeup. We resolved the problem by giving the waiters rhinestone tiaras and telling guests that anyone who showed up in a real one might be taking drink orders. This alerted everyone, and expectations were running high before a single guest arrived. My great-granddaughter wanted one, so she was the only other person besides the waiters to wear a tiara at the wedding. I half expected some guests to ask her for a drink.

It went down as a great LA wedding. My great-granddaughter was a flower girl and insisted on wearing her tiara down the aisle to Bobby's and his intended's considerable amusement—and she called me Grandma Monster all night. I was wearing a vintage Edith Head ball gown from one of our films. The little one took one look, called out "pretty," and said she wanted one, too.

Our family was together, which for me was the best part of all. When someone, who shall remain nameless, got drunk enough, grabbed the mic, and launched into "I'm Still Here," I just groaned and got another glass of champagne.

It struck me that maybe Bobby was right. I could open from here. I could just come out on stage from the wedding to freshen up. Talk to my guests before I have to go back out. We could even have "I'm Still Here" playing offstage at the wedding as I walk on to huge applause. Why not?

And again, Sam was there. Bobby invited him. Bobby had evidently done a lot of inviting Sam, unbeknownst to me, or more accurately, without my permission. Sam and I had had a big fight a few weeks previously, and I'd walked out. Bobby didn't want me to have a big party without Sam there. I accosted Bobby when I saw Sam's name on the guest list. "I love you, and it's your wedding, but you're interfering."

"Damn right," he retorted. "You finally find a good guy who likes you not just because of your ass but because he admires your tenderness and toughness. He likes who you really are. You're an idiot to walk away. All the other guys looked first at your tits, and you complained for years about guys running things. Now you're complaining about him when you got what you always wanted."

I didn't know how to respond, so I merely said, "No one runs after eighty-year-old ass." He gave me a dirty look, and I shut up.

Our fight had been as follows. Elizabeth Williams needed to put together an investment syndicate to pay for the show, which is how Broadway gets funded. Bobby, without asking me, called Sam, who called Elizabeth to say he would invest. Sam had one condition: no one could tell me. They kept that secret for almost two months. It slipped out in an argument. Sam couldn't keep his mouth shut. He never said he had invested, but he knew more about the syndicate details than he should have. I read between the lines.

"Working for you? I don't think so!" I thundered, really angry, but he refused to back out. What could I do? I wanted to do the show for my great-granddaughter. "I refuse to be a trophy wife."

"Aren't you getting a little old for that?" he responded.

"Clearly, too old for you," I said and walked out. He called, but I told him I was done. I didn't want to be owned. Why hadn't he asked me?

"Because you would have said no," he said.

"You did an end run on something you knew I wouldn't like. You didn't ask. I don't need your fucking money. I can pay for this, but it doesn't count if you pay for a show about yourself by yourself. It only matters if it gets financed, because then others believe in it and it's real. You're not a writer because you write. You're a writer when people buy your book!"

"But it's an investment syndicate with outside investors."

"You're not an outside investor if you're sleeping with the star! If a reporter wants to fuck elephants, that's cool, but don't cover the circus!" Sam recognized the famous quote from *Washington Post's* Ben Bradlee, who used it firing a reporter who started an affair with a candidate while covering an election. He gave me an embarrassed smile.

He kept calling, but I refused to talk. Mid-eighties and a breakup, really? But I was enraged. This scenario was just not my movie.

For Broadway, I decided on a simple spotlight as I walked out onto the stage at my open. I walk out, pour myself a Scotch, talk to the audience. Retell the tales I have just told you. The spot increases the lighting until you see the entire stage bathed in light with three separate areas. I am center stage, in my dressing room, talking to the audience. Stage left and right are above me on large balconies. Each left and right set lights up separately to show scenes from the past and then moves to center stage so the audience can see it better. I resume talking to the audience as the historical scene fades to black and moves back to the balcony as the memory dims, whether it's sitting on Elizabeth's bed drinking bourbon out of teacups, or getting Marilyn out of my dressing room, or sleeping with John Kennedy, Jr., which should get the blue-haired ladies' attention. If I got a well-hung actor on stage, we'd have the old ladies lined up down the block, but that was tawdrier than I wanted. Thus, the story can return to me, center stage, after each vignette. I don't have to have everything balanced on my eighty-seven-year-old back. I get to be in the center ring of the circus, where art imitates life, since my entire life has been lived on the high wire.

There will be three of me. The young twenty-something beauty. The middle-aged tragedienne. Then, the real one in the middle, because I'm still here, my dear.

While this sounds simple, it took a lot of time to figure out. The moving set would also be expensive to design, build, and operate. We would need a bigger running crew, and Broadway hourly rates at union prices are expensive. We were, however, moving ahead. We needed a final script, a director, music, marketing, and set design. I wasn't worried about costumes because Ann Roth was doing them. Normally she did film, but for me, she would do Broadway. We pulled old Edith Head designs to use for the actresses playing my younger selves.

Bobby, Lily, and I met again with Elizabeth Williams. Now we needed to find two actresses to play me as well as a few supporting roles. We didn't need many. The idea was for me to talk, nursing my Scotch. I gave in to it being caffeine-free tea—if I nursed a Scotch and kept repouring for two hours, I would be falling down drunk by the end of every evening and certainly would have trouble remembering my lines. On the other hand, what I might actually say might make for a much more interesting evening. No one could buy that kind of media coverage! I thought better of it, to Lily's relief.

I was thrilled to be working with a woman producer who understood my point of view. My era was based on the decisions and desires of men who not only figured that they knew best but also thought everyone else agreed they knew best, too.

We were resigned to the coming circus. Everything that we wanted forgotten was going to be discussed. The husbands, the children, the breasts, my marriage problems, the business problems, my father's murder. Mom writes that at first she wondered if Bobby had met his husband on the trapeze at a sex club—this might end up being worse. And, because it was my mother, the press would be watching from front row seats to call in their copy for the next day—and we knew that they would almost prefer a flop to a hit because flops were more fun to snipe about.

Bobby and Lily calmed us down. They told us that our mother would never have a flop, had the balls to pull it off (Bobby's comment), and knew her fans better than the rest of us. She had taken risks all of her career and she was still standing on top. So, we just shut up and groaned a little bit that the past was about to come back to bite us. I teased Sebastian about his father's small dick, and he teased me about my mobster father. We survived.

Anders

RETURN OF THE FRENCH TRAMP

Anatomy matters, which was the first thing that popped into my mind when I received a panicked phone call from Frederic. His father was in the hospital. Ex-husband No. 5 was dying of pulmonary edema at eighty-five. They could keep him more or less comfortable but not reverse the process. I was horrified—he would eventually drown in his own fluids as his heart could not keep up with his lungs.

It wasn't a good way to go, but most weren't. Ex-Husband No. 5 meant well his entire life but was easily distracted. A good heart unable to follow through somehow made the good seem less relevant. Certainly, to me, on the receiving end. Little things like flowers or bringing a bottle of wine he did with wonderful European flair, but being there when Frederic, Anders, or I needed him didn't happen. Frederic had me and his older brothers for that.

Ex-Husband No. 5 was in Yale New Haven Hospital. He had gone to Connecticut to attend meetings for a theater program to which I had given money after my kids had graduated. I also funded a scholarship for outstanding talent from the Babe beauty business. Me, who had no formal education, went to Yale every semester to lecture and take questions on student productions. They always wanted me in them—but no thank you! Sadly, the hospital called to say they were doing what they could, but options were limited.

I went to New Haven to see ex-Husband No. 5 and support Frederic, who was now thirty-one with a longtime girlfriend. Tall with Gallic dark hair and eyes despite his Swedish father, Frederic needed support to help manage decisions. One of the senior doctors asked me to meet him privately in his office. He had a pile of patient files on his desk, including those of my ex-husband and Frederic. He started off asking if Frederic was, in fact, my son. No, I said, he was from my ex and his late wife. The doctor gave me a long look. Evidently, there was a stem cell procedure for heart valves that sometimes worked, and they had looked for compatible donors. Frederic and his father were not a match—apparently not a match anywhere. Frederic was not his son genetically. Ex-Husband No. 5 had been lied to by the deceased wife. I had had my life upturned by a liar who wanted my husband as her child's father.

Again, something about a good heart but not good follow-through. The irony being the good heart was now not so good. Was this God laughing at us again? I was startled when the doctor told me about the genetics, but when I thought about it, not shocked. I should have known. Frederic had brown eyes—both my ex and his late wife had blue, while brown is dominant. You can have two parents with brown eyes who have a blue-eyed child, but never the other way around. This knowledge had been staring us in the face all these years. But who knew?

I love Frederic. Yet I was cuckolded along with his father. The word cuckold always fascinated me—the cuckoo lays its egg in another bird's nest, and the other bird raises it and brings it worms, thinking it's her own, while the cuckoo outgrows the other chicks and takes nurture from the genetic offspring.

I didn't regret Frederic, but I regretted what had happened. Such odd feelings all at once. Telling ex-Husband No. 5 was not an option. He was dying, his heart already under stress. What would be the point? I didn't want him back and hadn't for a long time, and any desire for revenge had vanished long ago. I didn't know whether to tell Frederic or not—protect him and lie or wound him with the truth. True, it was a lie by omission, but it was a pretty big omission. This lying by omission brought back memories of my to-ing and fro-ing when I found myself pregnant by Husband No. 5 in Paris so long ago. Elizabeth Taylor was right—secrets have a way of coming out, particularly for people like us.

Poor Frederic was already upset. Did I want to confuse his grief at his father's passing with these other feelings right now? Eventually, I would have to tell him. It would be an extraordinarily painful discussion. The life he thought he had wasn't the life he really had—the storyline of my second Academy Award. I told him later he wasn't alone in this, but it was a particularly pernicious way to learn this terrible truth.

I was depressed. Sad at the loss of an old friend, unhappy at the loss of a dream so many years before, blue I never had a lifelong partner, sorry the child I had loved and nurtured would have to undergo pain for no good reason other than he needed to know the truth and I couldn't lie to him. Was it better in the long run to know who you really were? Who was he? Who had been his genetic father? The problem was there was no way to find out with his mother dead twenty years.

Ex-Husband No. 5 died. There was a quiet funeral. I had arranged for his Swedish daughter and her children to fly over to say goodbye. They spent several days visiting and then returned a few weeks later for the funeral. Life went on, but my world kept getting smaller. Of my husbands, I was down now to ex No. 1, the small-dicked wonder in the press as well as ex-husband No. 6, known for opposite reasons. It was, as I suggested earlier, as if God was up there laughing at us.

What kept me going was my one-woman show. I hadn't signed yet with Elizabeth Williams. I wasn't talking to Sam, who had the nerve to send an email calling me a chicken and asking what I was waiting for. It was a final, annoying push, and I signed later that week. Elizabeth offered more or less the same deal as before adjusted for inflation: $100,000 at signing and $20,000 a week with 10 percent of the profits. I knew her syndicate to fund the production was mostly Sam's money, but she also invested her own—as well as her reputation—so she was really on the hook. She didn't want to limit the run to ten weeks, which was too great a risk given our production costs, even with HBO filming. Brave girl, I thought, risking so much on me at my age. For Sam, this was pocket change, and unless his accountants told him, he wouldn't even know if he made a profit or lost all of this so-called investment.

I was overwhelmed by what I had to tell Frederic. I went up to the Vineyard for a few days of quiet and to gather courage. Bobby, again without asking or telling, called Sam, who flew up and met me there. I told him to go away, but he walked into my kitchen, opened a bottle of my best red wine, poured a couple of glasses, and told me to shut up.

"I'm not leaving you alone, and if you want me out of here, you need to call the police—and good luck with that since the chief of police came to dinner at my house last month," he said, arrogant as always. It was easier to let him stay. We walked on the beach for hours before going back to my house for dinner. I didn't really need someone to lean on, but it was better he was there. I was touched he was worried about me. He wasn't perfect, and I wasn't going to marry him, but I decided to take the good with the annoying—sometimes really annoying. He shouldn't have gone behind my back to finance my show, but if I waited for the perfect man, I was going to be alone. Six husbands had taught me that. He stayed because he said he was worried I was too emotional to leave me by myself. What he didn't say, and I had the good grace not to either, was that he had found a way back in and took advantage of it, while pretending he was doing it only for me. How like a guy. While he was being kind and taking care of me, he was also trying to get me back. It's true I was vulnerable, but not that vulnerable. Although evidently vulnerable enough to let him back in my life. I didn't know why I mattered so much to him. After all, I wasn't a supermodel. But I decided life was better with him than without him. He could drive me crazy sometimes, but we didn't have to live together. He didn't have to be perfect. We didn't argue the entire time on the Vineyard.

Bobby had played matchmaker with a vengeance. He looked after me the best he could, which he always did. He didn't want me to be alone, so he fixed it so I wouldn't be—and not very subtly, either.

I dreaded telling Frederic. That was why I was pacing on the Vineyard beach. I loved him, and there was no way to do this without exposing him to enormous pain. We talked when I returned. Frederic was shocked and sad. He was losing his father all over again. He was also worried he would lose me, the only parent he had left. He asked if I regretted taking him in. He seemed so alone, and despite being six feet tall, he looked quite small again.

I remembered that scared little boy who had showed up at my apartment, barely speaking English and horrified we wanted to make him eggs for breakfast. I remember the sulky teen who would look at me with a cartoon bubble coming out of his head with the caption, "So sad. She used to be smart. What happened?"—an adolescent phase that lasted years. I have heard those imaginary comments in my mind with the slightest of French accents ever since. I remember the initiative he used on our Vineyard house to redo the barn's kitchen and how his skill led to a career in architecture. Here he was before me, pleading he needed what was left of his family.

My answer? "Absolutely not. I am blessed to have you. You are my child, and that will never change." He seemed somewhat reassured but was processing a lot. While it was true, he was my child, it was also true I was enraged against his lying tramp of a mother who did this to us. Would I change anything if it meant not having Frederic in my life? No, I am sure of that. Did I want revenge on the bitch? You bet. Would I have liked to have stayed with Frederic's father? No, I don't think so. I did at the time, but I didn't like the pain he put me through. I was sorry how things worked out, but what I was most sorry to lose was the idea of a lifelong partner, not the man. Frederic's father was a good man, if imperfect, and a fool where women were concerned. But weren't they all?

Frederic's father, my stepfather, left us for a lie. I was so angry when my mother told me. After his father's death, Frederic came to my brother and me not knowing what to do or what to say. He was worried that we might reject him in the same way he was worried he might lose our mother. That's just it: our mother—our baby brother. We'd known him as part of the family since he came to New York at 11. Initially we thought he was part of Mom's entourage, but he ended up our baby brother.

In a way, his experience mirrors mine when I learned my father wasn't who I thought he was. At least he was my father. And that's what we told Frederic. His father was his father, genetics or not, and he loved him, being there in his own way as much as he could be.

Processing this took time for all of us. For my mother, she was also adjusting to accepting Sam into her life as a permanent arrangement. Sam was overjoyed, although he wouldn't admit it. He finally won—his prize being my mother. He was completely ridiculous in his way. He had so much money and there was nothing he wouldn't do for Mom, including making her coffee in the morning and taking it upstairs. My mother didn't need anything; she had enough jewelry, but she still loved getting presents—chocolate or diamonds: she was happy to be center of attention. Anders

BROADWAY COMES TOGETHER

During the repercussions of Husband No. 5's death, Elizabeth Williams found a writer I liked. Michael wasn't well known but had done off-Broadway work that had been well-received and was known as a script doctor because of his skill with dialogue. Crisp dialogue mattered since I would be talking much of the evening. What finally sold me was not reading his prior work or seeing a tape of his play—it was he said about music.

In our meeting, when we talked about the needed moving parts, Michael said music would be critically important. I had been aware of how background music colored my roles. How I looked, what I said, how I was shot and edited made the performance, but what set the tone, even if the audience was unaware, was the scoring. Music cued you into emotion. It's why aerobics classes use high-energy music—try working out to Mahler one day.

I had thought about music a lot after seeing my old friend Michael Cunningham's *The Hours*, with Philip Glass's score being heavy. Harvey Weinstein, of all people, got me to think about the importance of music because he complained publicly about the music in *The Hours* during filming.

I haven't talked about Harvey, who produced *The Hours,* because I never worked with him. I was too old for him to run after. A power in film for twenty-five years, he has strong opinions and fought with a lot of people who are quick to complain about his bullying—as anyone who picks up a paper knows. He is a throwback to an earlier era of studio bosses who used their ability to make or break careers on the casting couch. As I have reflected, I suffered from this attempted abuse as did pretty much every other female actor and some of the guys, too. While I've called the studio exec abusers "fat, middle-aged white guys," Bill Cosby proved that race isn't a qualifier, only power—the power of money, signing contracts, using lawyers to bully, abuse and write nondisclosure agreements, payoffs, blocked media inquiries, tickets to red carpet events, film star interviews, additional advertising buys, hiring reporters with fat writing contracts, bribing editors and media owners with Hollywood access, and the sheer power of knowing that they could remain one step ahead with their army of staff, lawyers, and publicists and their access to studio coffers.

Just when these guys think it will go on forever, they stumble, have a bad year, or finally get caught in a public scandal where they can't buy their way out, and then boom, it's all we hear about for days. How many movies have been filmed with the storyline of the aging arrogant mob boss, bully, or lead politician who is brought down when he weakens, and then all his enemies come forward to feed on the carcass? As Dorothy Parker responded when someone oohed over all the people coming to pay their respects at Louis B. Mayer's funeral, "They're not here to pay their respects. They're here to make sure he's dead."

It would be hard to imagine anything more Byzantine than the weakened old lion pulled down past his prime by the young ones. It's a familiar story.

When they filmed *The Hours*, there was gossip about infighting between director, producer, and studio, respectively Stephen Daldry, Scott

Rubin, and Harvey Weinstein. My old friend, Ann Roth, did the costumes, so I heard about the backstage tension. Harvey understood that to build a great cinema experience, music mattered. One of his battles on *The Hours* was he felt you don't need heavy scoring when you're watching actresses as good as Meryl Streep, Julianne Moore, and Nicole Kidman, who won a best actress Oscar for her work. Yes, Philip Glass was a genius, but the film wasn't a showcase for his music, which should have been a storyline motif, not something overshadowing the actors. When I watched the movie, I saw that Harvey was absolutely right. Regardless of creative differences or power grabs covered over as creative differences, subtler music would have been better. In the end, however, it was a great film based on a Pulitzer Prize-winning book.

Harvey wanted to work with me once on an art project, but I turned him down. I didn't care about the pay; I just don't like being screamed at, and I really don't like being threatened. I waved a gun at Husband No. 1 because of that, which I pointed out to Harvey. "You promise not to scream at me or my people," I told him, smiling sweetly, "and I promise not to wave a gun in your face." Clearly, he didn't like that arrangement since we've never worked together.

When Michael, our proposed writer, met us during that first meeting and talked about the importance of the musical score, I was sold. He said, "Theater is based on words, but your words can't explain everything. In film and theater, what is unsaid is often more important than what is said, which makes it really difficult for the writers." And not just the writers, because it falls on performers' shoulders to show what cannot be said. The audience needs to feel and think for themselves. They need to anticipate, and music can set the mood. I didn't have to keep talking—what wonderful words. Michael added that he didn't want the music to be overpowering, thank goodness, but it was going to be important.

I was grateful to have someone understand how music should add to but not overwhelm a performance. When music is not subliminal, it's jarring and kitsch as in 1940s melodramas. I wouldn't have to explain everything. I could act like the audience was intelligent, and our score would cue them. I started believing this show might not be a flop after all.

We had a writer. Now we needed a director. I wanted Mike Nichols, whom I knew and trusted. He'd make us a success. He was polite but having had more than his share of Broadway hits, he understood how tough it was. He wanted a script before making a decision. I couldn't blame him—I wouldn't accept a role without one, either.

I tried to guilt him into it by complaining he owed it to me after not giving me the role of Mrs. Robinson in *The Graduate*. I had wanted the part and was a bigger star than Anne Bancroft but couldn't get out of my contract at the time since I was promised to another film. And Mike wouldn't have given it to me, anyway, as he kept reminding me. While that was the big one that got away, no one would have done a better job than Anne Bancroft. She was perfect. But she wasn't the original first choice. This was Hollywood, after all, and Ava Gardner was the biggest star of them all in the '40s and '50s.

Mike went to see her about the role. Ava, mid-forties at the time, received him, diva style, in her hotel room and played the grand star. In the end, Mike decided she was too much of a diva to work with—said the man who directed Elizabeth to an Academy Award—and the part went to

Anne.

To show Mike's ability as a director to drill down into the heart of a character, when casting *The Graduate*, Mike chose Dustin Hoffman for his first major film role. Robert Redford, already a star after *Barefoot in the Park,* went to Mike and asked to be switched in for Dustin, something established stars often did—and I had tried to do, too.

Nichols looked over his glasses and asked, "Bob, what did you do the last time a girl turned you down?" Bob, clearly puzzled, stood there and asked, "What do you mean?" Nichols shook his head and said, "My point. You don't know the answer because no girl turns you down. How in hell do you think you can play this role?" Since there wasn't a good response, Dustin kept the part.

Mike understood not just casting but also how his cast would react before they did. His death was a shock—and proof of a smaller and smaller world. A genius with a sense of humor and brilliant timing, his passing provided impetus to get on stage while I could.

Thus, while looking for a director, we moved to the music. Bobby found someone successful who seemed promising, experienced, not insane, and worked well with others. In theater as in film, working well with others is prized but seldom guaranteed. Crazy works if they make money. On the other hand, everyone else suffered, particularly cast and crew who hadn't any of the upside going to investors and producers.

We were set to meet the composer, the usual gang plus our producer, Elizabeth. Bobby and I spent a lot of time together these days on the show and the beauty business. He'd gotten an apartment in New York since his lawyer husband Billy worked between New York and LA, and Billy came into my life when we needed a contract lawyer.

My great-granddaughter was with me a lot these days, too. I worked but had more time than my kids and grandkids. Major roles had disappeared. After male children and grandchildren, she was a pleasure, someone to sit and read with and take shopping, someone who seriously observed every move I made putting on my makeup, and someone who liked to go through my jewelry boxes as if given the key to heaven.

There was no more writing on the walls, lipstick or otherwise, but the rule for my jewelry was inflexible. She couldn't leave her chair in front of the jewelry box unless she put everything back. She couldn't go to the bathroom. She couldn't stand up. She couldn't have anything in her hands. That worked until the day we were to meet the first Broadway composer for our show, when she walked into the kitchen wearing an $80,000 Bulgari emerald clip on her dress. "What are we wearing?" I asked.

"Nothing," was the reply.

"So, are we naked?" I asked.

Giggle. "No."

We went back and forth, and then I made her look down. "Oops," she said, more or less surprised. "I forgot." I think I believed her but wasn't sure. She was awfully fond of that clip and wanted to take it home.

I had to leave for our meeting with our proposed composer, and the nanny was late. Really late. I took the little one with me. A little reality wouldn't kill her. I called the nanny to pick her up at Elizabeth Williams's office.

We rolled up to the office, and the music guy was there. I brought the little one with me with crayons and paper minus the emerald clip, over which she had cried. I had visions of how that discussion would go with my insurance people.

The music guy came in, and the first thing he said, in a gay accent, was, "I've seen all of your pictures and love you!" Too old for Bobby, who is married now, so no scandal. Okay, this might work. Then, with a big smile, he said, "I have been humming *I'm Still Here* all the way here." Bobby saw the look on my face as I glanced at the large letter opener on Elizabeth's office table and quickly said, "We'll call you," and hustled him out.

The wee one looked up and said, "Grandma Monster is angry!" and Bobby just cracked up. I have never seen him laugh like that. Pretty soon, he had us all laughing. The little one thought we were nuts. She asked if Grandma Monster was angry, why was I laughing? I didn't think it appropriate to explain to a four-year-old that sometimes when you can't kill a horse's ass, all you can do is laugh. It did cross my mind, however, that maybe I should. I wasn't going to live long enough to teach her that lesson when she would be old enough to understand it.

The little one wanted to know what we were talking about and loved the idea of my going on stage. She had seen my movie where I played a princess, which was one of the few appropriate for her. She didn't believe it was me. "Grandma Monster is too old to be her" was what she told her mother. I agree.

She liked the idea of a play with me in it. She knew about plays, having gone to several children's productions at the Danny Kaye Theatre in Manhattan. "Can I do it, too?" she asked. I told her no, but if she was good and didn't take any more jewels, she could come on stage at the opening and give me flowers. That was acceptable to her. "Can I wear the em'ald?" she asked, and like a fool, I said yes.

The realization that I had so little time left kept pushing me to get out on stage. It also applied to Sam. If I wanted time with him, now was what we had. I had been traveling with him to the third world for the opening of schools, which he funded. When we were lucky, various media outlets beamed information into those countries that sometimes evaded their censors. These were the places Sam wasn't welcome. I helped generate additional media coverage, which helped protect us both.

So, I traveled often with him. He never asked me to go to treacherous places, but he was happy I went. Rich as he was, I generated more publicity. Hollywood always does. As a guy used to running things, Sam didn't actually say thank you—guys and their egos, which wasn't a surprise—but he became increasingly tender, so I took what I could get without regretting what I didn't. He liked spending time with me, and that was thank you enough. I just didn't want romance to ruin things. I was an old broad by now. He could have anyone, but I wouldn't have liked it if he started dating someone else.

For a long time, I had a walk-in closet and bathroom off the master suite in his country house in North Salem, New York, down the road from Mike Bloomberg. When we weren't on the Vineyard for weekends, we were often there. So were our kids, grandkids, and my great-granddaughter, who found a way into Sam's heart. Or he found a way into hers. Somehow, they had sized each other up and decided the other was worthy. She came downstairs one day wearing a Mickey Mouse headband. Sam smiled and said, "Hello, Mickey."

She corrected him. "No, Minnie." Sure enough, there was a tiny red bow between the mouse ears, too small for Sam to see.

He asked, "How do you know?"

She looked at him with disdain and said, "Because I don't have a penis," and walked away. Hard to argue with that. Later, when she told him she wanted a pony after learning there was a barn on the estate, he got not one but two. He told her it was so the ponies could keep each other company. When I complained he was spoiling her, he called me a hypocrite. I backed off, and she got to keep the ponies. What also endeared little Babe and Sam to each other was her relationship with his grandson, who was little Babe's age and also named Sam. The two wee ones started playing together and became friends, although little Babe didn't want to admit it. She kept complaining that boys are icky. Sam asked her why.

"Because," she responded, "all they talk about are boogers and farts." Again, there was no good comeback. On the other hand, she kept asking for playdates with his grandson. With the two ponies, they learned how to ride together, something Sam had counted on when he got the ponies. He hired a riding instructor for the weekends.

One weekend, Sam's daughter drove up. She was there from time to time to see her father. She had the jittery attention span of someone who had abused drugs—her life was never going to be easy. I was in the house when I saw her and told her Sam was on the tennis court. She surprised me by saying she actually came to talk to me, because she never had warmed to me or I to her. We were polite but distant. I sat down and waited to hear what she had to say.

She started to talk. Slowly, carefully, words cautiously placed. The boy from the moped ride on the Vineyard was dead. Killed in a car accident that paralyzed the girl riding with him. The daughter didn't want to cry in front of me but was close. She was scared. She now understood this kid had been bad news. Now, she knew how lucky she was not to be in that car with him, which she might have been if she'd continued down the same path she was on at the time of the moped ride. Death and paralysis had sobered her up in a way it hadn't years ago. Much had changed, thank God.

I talked to Sam later that evening. He understood that if things had gone differently with his daughter, I wouldn't be with him. I couldn't. I had so many strong feelings about being a good parent that I couldn't manage it when I saw it badly handled. I hadn't been a great parent, but I feared what Hollywood would do to my kids and tried to limit the fallout.

I wanted to be a better parent than mine. In fact, I created myself in my own imaginary image. Most people talk about their parents and siblings from time to time, but not me. I talked to Sam that night for the first time about my past. In public and to the press, I never discussed my early family. There were studio bios of course, but those were written by publicists and completely imaginary. I finally talked to Sam the day his daughter managed to put the pieces together. I was proud of her and direct with him. I had been determined to be a better mother than mine was—to give to my children and not take from them. One of my greatest joys from my success was what I could give others. I had more than enough for me.

I told Sam about my father telling me Marilyn was my sister. "Who'd believe me, anyway? It will generate a firestorm. People will see my show without it."

He understood but told me, "Just because people may not believe you isn't a good reason not to tell the truth. Do what you want, which I always tell you, except sometimes regarding me. Who cares what strangers think?"

I had no answer but must have had a premonition that my past would come up soon with the writer of my one-woman show. I had never talked directly about my parents. I had walled off the past and didn't intend to take any walks down memory lane.

This came up the day we interviewed the first composer, whom Bobby hustled out the door. Our writer, Michael, who had researched my life and spent hours with Bobby and Lily and me reminiscing, was at the meeting. He had talked to friends, studio people, read clippings—Lily had every one saved, filed, and indexed—and had spoken to my kids. He, like everyone else, was entranced by my great-granddaughter as she ran in and out with great regularity, all the while calling me Grandma Monster.

Our writer looked up. "I've almost finished a first draft. I heard nothing about your parents other than your mother remarried briefly after you were already at MGM."

Thanks to my recent discussions with Sam, I was less surprised than I might have been. Bobby, Lily, and I exchanged glances. Elizabeth looked at us, our cabal, then at her writer. She had a questioning expression but didn't say anything. She just waited—smart lady.

I took a deep breath and was thankful the really-late-without-explanation nanny had finally arrived to take the wee one home. I waited to make sure she was out of earshot.

"You will find nothing about my mother because Lily erased her.

You couldn't do that now with the Internet, but you could in the fifties. It's not cool to say you don't like your mother. It's not polite to say she was a conniving, self-centered, aggressive woman who used other people. I don't want to be quoted that way. So, we erased her. Does she add to our story? Does our audience have a different sense of me with that knowledge of her? I think her absence says something better left unsaid."

While we didn't like Bobby's mother, we loathed mine. When I entered MGM charm school, I was underage. The studio paid me, and she took it all. I needed clothes, makeup, and carfare, but what mattered to my mother was only herself. I was an only child and her meal ticket since her second marriage didn't last. Thankfully, I didn't have to protect a younger sibling from her predations. She was beautiful but not as beautiful, for which she never forgave me. It was difficult to know how intelligent she was—she didn't work and never cared about being smart, since for her, all that mattered was money. She took my money until I was eighteen, when legally it was mine and I could start socking it away for my old age. I gave her a large allowance, but she always wanted more. If I didn't give it to her, she threatened to sell stories about me to the press.

My image in the media was as a lady—what well-bred lady hauls their mother into court for blackmail? She had me. She had me for a long time. I kept her from my children, allowing carefully orchestrated visits, but I knew what I was dealing with and wasn't going to allow her to do to my children what she did to me.

She was the definition of ball and chain and didn't care. Cutting, insulting, arrogant, and a fishwife when she didn't get things exactly her way, she could make me feel small easily and took it as her right to do so.

I cut her out of my life. I gave her money on the condition she never spoke to the press. I didn't see her, I didn't invite her to my weddings, but I had her to my children's christenings because I couldn't avoid that. My exit from her control was after they shot Husband No. 4. She was terrified. Not for me, of course, but for herself. My subsequent loss of almost everything terrified her even more—what would happen to her?

Bobby dealt with her in the aftermath of Husband No. 4's murder. He went to her in a cold-blooded way and scared her. He said they were coming for me, and if they think you have money, they will come for you. She will give you only what she can afford until she gets back on her feet. For a year, she had her allowance cut in half. I resumed it until her death. Bobby told her to stay away, stay silent, don't talk to the press, and don't make noise if you don't want them coming after you.

Finally, I had something over her. She stayed away. I saw her a few times before her death. Bobby had found a way for me to escape her clutches. I never told anyone. Neither did he or Lily. A great lady appreciates her mother, is taught by her mother, and receives her entrée into society from her mother. I didn't want to say that mine was cruel, grasping, and self-centered and I didn't respect her. Thus, Bobby and Lily helped omit her from my life.

I finished speaking, and Michael and Elizabeth sat there digesting while Bobby, Lily, and I looked on. "Use what you want," I said, "but remember, I am who I am, and she was who she was. I don't miss her. I miss what might have been. If you can work that into the story, great. If not, let Lily's erasing her from my life continue. You have no idea how much she did to achieve this and how much I love her for it."

I waited for the obvious next question. It never came. Maybe I had shocked them. Maybe they were too polite. I asked, "My father? No questions?" Again, silence. I told them I knew who he was, but he left when I was two and I have no actual memories of him from my early life. My parents both made bad choices, but who am I to condemn them? He was too blue collar to make my mother happy. She was too much of an ogre to live with. He popped into my life, later, after I had made it. He didn't want anything, only to meet me to say he was sorry for leaving me to grow up on my own with my mother. He had another family but never told them about me, and we never had contact. I saw my father maybe four times before he died. He appreciated me from a distance, and when we visited for a quiet dinner, I didn't know what to say. He just told me he loved me and was sorry, and I believed him. Yet there was a pain from not having had a father, even if he wouldn't have been the father of my dreams. He was a decent man who wanted to escape my mother, even at the cost of leaving me behind. I had a hard time being abandoned and left in my mother's clutches without a referee. I can't say he abandoned Marilyn— he was never there to begin with. It was just a one-nighter with her mother, Gladys, but after her birth, given her mother's instability, he might have done something. However, I don't know when he learned that he was Marilyn's father. Even though he was my legal father and deserted us, Marilyn was left in far worse condition, in and out of foster homes or left alone with her mother's mental illness.

My father never asked for a thing. I told him if his new kids went to college, I would pay. They never did. We never met. He didn't want them to know of his failures as a father—his abandoning Marilyn and me. He was ashamed, which was why he kept apologizing. I have a half brother and sister who don't know we are related. Except, in my will, I have left something to my nieces and nephews, who will be surprised when they get a small bequest. I have had my lawyers draft it in such a way as they won't know where the money came from, respecting my father's wishes.

I don't think I will ever understand why my father waited until his deathbed to tell me about Marilyn. Did he think I wouldn't believe him? Maybe he thought he might be wrong? There weren't paternity tests in those days, and Marilyn's mother, Gladys, was crazy and spent most of her life in institutions. Why tell me at all if he had waited so long? I was sorry we didn't have time to discuss it. When I thought about it, it felt true we were sisters. Some of our similarities were peculiar but striking to both of us at the time, which is partly why we became friends. Genetics frequently outs.

There were more differences, however, than similarities. I had a toughness she never did. Maybe I had more of my father in me, a man who was hard enough or selfish enough to walk away from me. Marilyn had more of her mother, who spent her life in and out of mental institutions, in her. We didn't share those genetics. I think of her like the candle that burned itself out from both ends, what Elton John called a brilliant flash of light that disappeared in his song "Candle in the Wind." I burned slowly, which is why I am still here.

I came to the conclusion that my father wanted me to know where I came from and to whom I was related so I might understand who I was when the camera was off. For him, while he appreciated who Marilyn and I became, he was just our father and that's all that mattered to him. He didn't want to use us or take money—something few others in his position would have had the decency to do. To him, we were his daughters and he had failed us. He felt guilty. He felt guiltier about Marilyn, since he believed she had taken her own life. In fact, I thought so, too, but there was enough doubt and the world was a strange enough place, that I wondered. They managed to kill JFK, and we still don't really know what happened. If they could do that, they—whoever they were—could certainly have gotten to Marilyn.

My father was grateful I had been her friend. He left a lot of damage when he turned away from his earlier life. When he finally got away and settled down, he didn't want to be dragged back. Marilyn's mother and mine were so bad that neither was worth returning for. His daughters were collateral damage. My father understood and acknowledged that we paid the price. Given his reasons for leaving and his life choice, I understood his decision. I just regretted my early life. If he had been part of Marilyn's life, maybe she might be alive.

On the other hand, no one I have ever met was less equipped to grow old than she was. Marilyn died just a few months past her thirty-sixth birthday and had complained for years how she hated her body changing. "They're a little lower now," she commented, referring to her breasts when sharing a bottle of champagne after she turned thirty-five. She had said this every birthday after she turned thirty. "On the other hand, no one is complaining, so I guess I can live with it." She didn't giggle as she normally did after making one of her trademark observations, which suggested she didn't believe it. She hated aging. I believed that was why she couldn't show up for work for her last movie with Cukor.

Her adult life had been a frequent battle between Marilyn Monroe's persona and Norma Jeane. Norma Jeane was truly Gladys's daughter with all the insecurity, instability, and paranoia. Marilyn was the brightest star who ever lived. In the little time she showed up on set, Cukor was able to catch Marilyn. The rest of the time, she was Norma Jeane. It was becoming impossible for her to maintain the star's persona. Somehow, as her body aged and her breasts began to descend, Norma Jeane took over. Marilyn was perfection itself, but weakened by illness, surgery, and aging, Marilyn wasn't strong enough to remain in control. Or else enough reality intruded and forced Norma Jeane to realize if Marilyn was not perfect, she wasn't real.

Marilyn remained terrified all of her life that she had inherited her mother's mental instability and Norma Jeane would win out one day. Given her increased instability toward the end of her life, I wonder if she was right—did Norma Jeane assert control and begin to cross over to madness, never to return? Marilyn didn't want to be a prisoner of mental illness like her mother and end up permanently institutionalized as Norma Jeane for the rest of her life. Did Marilyn assert control one last time to avoid becoming Norma Jeane forever? There are things worse than death.

Thus, whatever extra self-confidence Norma Jeane might have garnered from having our father in her life might have helped her survive. While I had more security than she did, it would have changed my life to have had a father who had my back. Children who have that have everything. Norma Jeane had nothing.

If my father knew he was Marilyn's father, could her mother, Gladys, have known? Maybe not. Marilyn never knew, and Gladys never said. If she had, Marilyn would have told me. We talked about her mother many times while she wondered quite often who her father might have been. She had no idea, and that fact alone tortured her.

I wondered about a man who fathered two Hollywood legends and never wanted anyone to know. It was a contradiction of everything Hollywood stood for. All he wanted was peace, and I hope he found it. Clearly, he had a way of getting involved with the wrong people. Marilyn's mother was a one-night stand. Gladys was crazy enough to send anyone running. My mother was extraordinarily difficult, too. It occurred to me to wonder if part of my problem with bad choices was passed on genetically from my father. Maybe that applied to Marilyn, too.

I thought about the differences between the two of us. Maybe the three of us—Norma Jeane, Marilyn, and me. And that was the difference. I didn't have two different parts. I remained me, myself. My views, my mistakes, my loves, and my hates were all just me. The price for Marilyn's brightness was a descent into a multiple personality. I wonder if Norma Jeane and Marilyn understood this.

I had something that mattered above all to me—my children. They put my life in perspective in a way nothing else could. I was scared more for them than for me. Marilyn never had a child. On the other hand, sometimes they don't help. Gladys had Marilyn, but she was too far gone to be pulled back from the abyss. I am not convinced Marilyn and Norma Jeane could have been, either, in the end.

I never told a soul about Marilyn except Elizabeth Taylor. We pretty much told each other everything. I went over there, shaken at my father's death, and she greeted me with a big glass of bourbon at the door. I half expected her to laugh about the absurdity of Marilyn and me being sisters. Instead, she took me in her arms, saying, "Darling, I'm so sorry. Learning you have family when it's too late really salts the wound." This remained part of a longer conversation. She understood the battle between Norma Jeane and Marilyn, too, although she hadn't been as close to her as I was.

Did my troubles with my husbands come from an absent father who had saved himself at my expense when he deserted his former life? Maybe. Maybe not. It seems much too easy an explanation—something a shrink might say. And not a good one.

Sam told me we all make our own lives, and escape is as much a part of that as taking control. I think he was referring to my erasing the past, but he might also have been referring to my father. Of course, escaping is a lot easier with money, which both Sam and I have. I'm not dependent on anyone. Those times I was, it didn't work out so well— witness the six walks to the altar. Yet, I have started to count on Sam. I can walk away but don't want to. This is new.

When I had walked away from Sam that time, it put him on notice that I needed to be consulted about decisions affecting my life, and he couldn't treat me like his businesses where he made the tough calls on his own. He didn't want to lose me and didn't do it again. I was embarrassed about dropping him—it was an immature moment—but either Sam was too scared or too decent to bring it up.

At the meeting with the writer, I said nothing whatsoever about Marilyn. When we walked out of the meeting, Bobby, who was not physically demonstrative, hugged me in the hall. "My mother is a bitch, but yours was a monster." I felt badly I hadn't told him and Lily about

Marilyn. I wasn't ready. I didn't know what to do.

My little great-granddaughter was ever present in my mind. She had given me courage. It was the only time I had discussed my mother with strangers. The wee one has had such a different experience, and I didn't want her to know this part of my life. It reminded me of my French countess friend in Paris who said all families have lineage, but when there's rape by Cossacks, you don't pass that on to the grandkids. She was right. I didn't want my little one to know where I came from because, really, it is also where she came from, although she had no idea and would be too young to understand anyway. Let sleeping dogs lie. But did she need to know Marilyn was part of my genetics, and thus part of hers? The greatest star of all hadn't vanished from the earth. Her blood ran in our veins. And the veins of nieces and nephews I had never met as well as her other half-sister on Gladys's side.

Little Babe's life voyage will be very different from mine. I don't know where my little great-granddaughter is headed or how, but she has the brains to do whatever she wants, which I hope won't be show business but fear might be. We who have made it in this theatrical world have a side made for public consumption. So does the wee one. That she was given my name, too, seems a cosmic tip-off. She is only six. I will be eighty-eight. I won't live to see her in high school. Certainly not to attend her wedding, which makes a lump in my throat. How I would love to hear, "Grandma Monster, adjust my veil" or "Can I wear the em'ald clip on my wedding dress?"

The one-woman show changed for me. It started out as revenge but ended up with my wanting to counsel little Babe. She will have money, position, parents and grandparents who love her. God bless the child who has her own. But she won't have her Grandma Monster.

We didn't have an open. I talked it over with Elizabeth, our producer. I talked it over with Sam, too—after all, it was his money. He just looked at me and said he would never dream of interfering. This was too much. Was he really playing the impartial card now after he invested behind my back?

"What about your objecting to my film where I played the mother of an autistic?"

He snorted. "That wasn't about your world. It was how you might look playing such a controversial role. You can't hold that against me, particularly since I was right." He had me. It had stalled my career. On the other hand, all of us blondes aged out of roles. It was how the system worked. While I fought to be taken as an equal, I wasn't getting the roles that Clint Eastwood and Robert Redford did.

Truth be told, I didn't ask Sam's opinion just because of his investment. I valued his judgment. Now, that was new.

We held a family dinner—Bobby bringing Billy, Sebastian and his longtime partner of thirty years, Anders and his new wife, Frederic with his girlfriend, Lily of course, and Sam, since I had to conclude he was part of the family. My housekeeper knew everyone's likes and dietary restrictions, and she chose a menu like a ski racer slaloming down the slope trying not to miss any of the gates to reach the finish line. She wouldn't bore me with this information, and I wouldn't dream of interfering. For me, I eat simply since I watch my figure, but we always have good champagne and a decent bottle or two of red wine.

Before dinner, I took Sebastian's partner upstairs. In my bedroom, I handed her a box. "I want you to have these," I said as I passed over a Van Cleef and Arpels diamond and ruby necklace with matching earrings.

"You do so much already," she said, admiring the gems but trying to hand them back. I didn't let her.

"You've been there for Sebastian all these years. You've raised my two grandchildren and are now a grandmother yourself. Maybe you two never married because Sebastian saw my mistakes, but you're family and it would please me for you to have these."

She looked at me and shook her head. "You know my medical practice runs at a loss?" I nodded.

She continued. "It runs at a loss because I do things for people who can't pay, and we never had to worry about our kids' tuition. I got to do what I loved, helping other people, so it seems odd to get rewarded with rubies when you subsidized my practice by paying for my kids' educations."

I thought out loud. "I liked watching you help others. In my industry, that doesn't happen. I can't do much for people in a meaningful way—I'm just an actress. The people who depend on you get care they couldn't otherwise. But these jewels aren't a reward. They are because I am an old lady who will pass them on one day or another, and I want to see them on you before that day comes. Not as a gold star, but to tell you while I can that you are family and I love you."

We sat there for a while without talking. "Shall we try them on?" I asked.

"Only the earrings, I think. The necklace will be too much for dinner."

I had been revising my will earlier that day with Sam's help. I finalized a few trusts, but the issue was income from my skincare line. The royalties belong to my estate. I wanted them fairly distributed. I left my great-granddaughter my twenty-carat diamond earrings plus my house in Hollywood Hills. I wanted her to have a bolt-hole the rest of her life, no matter what happened. It had been my bolt-hole, which I thought might work for her since I wouldn't be there to pick up the pieces. I was sure she would end up in Hollywood for a while, at least, testing the waters. God bless the child that's got her own.

It was a lovely dinner, and Sebastian was touched when he learned of my gift and our chat. He had done well, but it takes more than that for Van Cleef and Arpels. Bobby, on his way out saying good night, commented, "Elizabeth Williams isn't worried about the open."

"Why the hell not?" I demanded.

"She knows you're old-school and won't disappoint an audience." Somehow that was a double-edged compliment. It seemed to put the weight on my shoulders to find a solution. Because Elizabeth, as producer, had money riding on this. Just to break even, I had to fill every seat in the Belasco Theatre for six weeks. We were guaranteed for ten. I needed people to buy tickets—no pressure there! A Tony nomination or two wouldn't hurt, either.

I didn't want anything predicable. Yes, I wanted a financial success, but not by doing what they did with the play, *Kinky Boots,* which is a work of financial genius. The blue-haired ladies love it, the masses get to see singing and high-energy dancing, and there's an uplifting, predictable, happy-ending storyline that feels so cool and modern it's easy to forget that one is watching a play about a transvestite. I only wish Harvey Fierstein, who co-wrote it with Cyndi Lauper, was the leading lady. Every seat is filled, every cash register rings, and it gets a standing ovation almost every night as the audience proves to themselves they have spent their money wisely. I wanted something better. I'm glad *Kinky Boots* is a success. However, plays like that risk making Broadway a cliché. That wasn't for me.

I became engrossed about what I needed to include. I wanted to discuss the roles I never got. The audience would want to know how I begged George Lucas to let me play a female Yoda, a strong Jedi knight who is sad but still beautiful. Alas, he turned me down, explaining the scripts were written. I pointed out that's what rewrites are for. I got my makeup artist to make me bald with prosthesis, made up into a Jedi knight warrior Yoda princess and did my own screen test. I still didn't get the part. George was sweet about it—he took me to lunch and said he loved my character but couldn't use it. I give him credit because he could have used assistants to wall himself off, but he respected the craft and understood my effort, which was worth honoring by taking me to lunch. He got a big kiss for it—on the cheek. I could almost be his mother. He promised me a role in the next trilogy, but sadly, he is no longer connected to the series after having sold Lucasfilm to Disney.

I wanted to show power, strength, and ability like Sigourney Weaver displayed in *Alien*. Now, actresses were starting to do those leads at last—tougher, smarter, stronger, and wiser than the guys, yet beautiful and sexy. I hoped I had paved the way for this, that my sacrifices for independence and equal pay made a difference.

The lack of an opening haunted me. There were so many choices. With modern technology, I could show footage of my role in *Marie Antoinette* or receiving my first Academy Award to open and then have the spotlight focus tight on me, contrasting my past success and beauty.

Or was it better to show me as the beautiful princess dancing in my Edith Head ball gowns or my serious role as Marie Antoinette in my middle-aged corset, riding the cart to execution? I was a good actress when they let me be. I wanted my audience to see that. An Academy Award means a lot, but there were great roles unacknowledged, too, and what mattered was that I had them. A movie star is media coverage, but an actress makes people think. I wanted to talk about that.

Or should I start with my baring my breasts for my second Academy Award and my comments on feminism on *Johnny Carson*? We could open with how my life evolved and changed things—I wasn't who I was because of what had happened but in spite of it, as Katharine Hepburn had advised long ago.

I wonder what my life might have been if I had started fifty years later? I had it easier compared to many, but that doesn't always make me less angry. What about the nights I sat on the bathroom floor with my arms wrapped around my knees, crying, because things were unfair? Or the days I wished I was dead? Not enough to jump out the window but enough to know just being alive wasn't enough. I didn't want to be fucked over by the guys one more time. I wanted to show what I could do, and instead I had to use so much energy fighting back. Fighting not to be taken as just a dumb blonde, fighting not to be taken advantage of, fighting not to be paid less or ignored, fighting not to be forced to sleep with a creep, fighting to be understood, and fighting to have my voice heard.

If I had truly found my voice, I needed to tell Bobby and Lily about Marilyn. I didn't know how to tell the two people who had been with me most of my life that I had lied by omission for thirty years. How could they not feel upset I hadn't trusted them, even if trust had nothing to do with it? I didn't want to upend my life and Marilyn's memory, all based on the word of my father. He had no reason to lie, I'm sure, but could he have been wrong? From knowing Marilyn as well as I did, I felt we were indeed related. But it's one thing to feel something in one's heart and another to see it on the front page of every newspaper in the world. Nothing in my life ended up being secret.

Until I talked to Sam, I had only told Elizabeth Taylor. I was scared of letting Bobby and Lily down. Bobby had gotten me doing Broadway as a way to say thank you to the many who gave me the strength to prove them wrong, which was a nicer way of saying, go fuck yourself. He had stressed those fuck-yous when he pitched the idea the first time around. And the second. Now, in my old age, having rewritten my will and gotten Botox and collagen to look good, if I said anything about Marilyn, it would not only upstage whatever else I said in the show but also risk hurting two of my family. Then, too, I had to face telling my children and grandchildren.

My life didn't turn out to be what I expected, or what I believed it should have been, or even what I imagined. I finally had to accept who I was. There was relief in letting go but also sadness. Giving up any dream is always difficult. Even imaginary ones. I had huge gifts during my life but paid heavy prices. While I don't have much to complain about, that never stopped me from doing so. Bobby and Lily had been with me for most of those years, and I was about to tell them I had kept the biggest secret of all from them. I didn't want to acknowledge the truth about my relationship with Marilyn because I had let it go for so long. The longer it went, the harder it became.

I told Bobby and Lily one afternoon. Then, they shocked me almost as much as my father had when he first told me about Marilyn as he lay dying. They already knew. "How could you?" I stammered.

Lily looked over at Bobby, who looked away. I sat there waiting. Finally, he looked at me. "You behaved so oddly, watching all of Marilyn's old movies after your father died. You even asked me to get footage from her last film with Cukor. No one knew who her father was, and I wondered if you knew something. I didn't at first realize it was your father. Then I suspected, so I bought a hairbrush from the crazies who collected her things and had the hair follicles tested against yours. It was a genetic match. The lab never knew who the samples were from, clearly."

I digested this. She really was my sister. My father wasn't mistaken. Marilyn's mother—was she lucid for once when she told him? And truthful? It's possible she might not have remembered or known what she said two days later. Or maybe she herself really didn't know. Gladys was most likely either too drugged or too crazy off or on her meds to remember. If Marilyn's father remembered the date of conception and put it together with her birthdate after Marilyn became famous, he himself wouldn't have known until Marilyn was grown. How could I blame him for abandoning a child he didn't know he had until twenty years later? By telling me on his deathbed, he managed to do to me what life had done to him—neither of us knew of the relationship with her until it was too late.

"Why didn't you tell me?" I asked Bobby and Lily.

"I told him not to," Lily said. "You spent your entire life creating your past. I figured when you wanted to talk about it, you would, and then we'd tell you. If you didn't, we would keep your secret."

"But what if I didn't know?" I asked.

Lily looked serious. "We were sure you did. You were so shell-shocked after you talked to your father when he died. More shocked than seemed possible just by his death. It seemed logical."

As Elizabeth Taylor had observed many times, it's impossible for people like us to keep secrets. I had gone thirty years thinking I was the only person on earth who knew Marilyn was my sister and had been wrong. Was there anything I could keep secret? Yet Bobby and Lily knew and had kept my secret from everyone, including me. They preserved all my secrets. A safe secret—there was a conundrum buried in there somewhere.

Thinking about Elizabeth Taylor, it slowly occurred to me how they must have figured out to run the tests. I looked at Lily, who had been close to Elizabeth at the end of her life. "You *knew*. You asked Bobby to get proof, but you knew. You talked to Elizabeth!"

Lily was completely relaxed. "Well," she said, "Bobby told me his suspicions. I waited until Elizabeth was softened up with a painkiller and some bourbon and asked if she thought you and Marilyn were related. She gave me an odd look. Very odd look, but she held your secret. All she said was that stranger things have happened. And then she walked away." Lily gave me a long look. "You know as well as I do that pushing Elizabeth was a big mistake."

"You weren't worried I might be mad?" I asked them. "I was scared to tell you because I thought you would think I was dishonest."

Lily began laughing, "For all your marriages, you didn't manage to learn there's a huge difference between truth and full disclosure? We were protecting you. If you were angry, it wouldn't be the first time." Bobby nodded.

I was silent. There were secrets we could keep. Not that no one knew, but at least my old friend Elizabeth kept my secret as had these two. I was touched at Elizabeth's faithfulness but not surprised. She was my friend. We trusted each other. I wanted her back. This show might have been the two of us, titled *A Dozen Marriages Sunnyside Up* since she wouldn't count Burton twice.

I could put Marilyn in the show now. I told Sam, and he smiled. "How lucky you are," he said. "I'm so glad they were with you before I got the chance to take care of you." It was a wonderfully sweet thing to say. Then, we discussed what to have for dinner.

I know what's in the show now. I know how we close. I knew that long ago. Sam will be there in the audience with our kids and grandkids. Bobby and Lily will be there, maybe just a little worried. Little Babe will bring me flowers for curtain call, finally wearing the Bulgari em'ald clips. My world. Or what's still alive from my world. It's their story, too.

We finally end my one-woman show after debating whether or not I should do it with me on stage turning my back on the real audience. I walk away from them toward a curtain at the back of the stage and then turn back again to face the actual audience and say, "Tell me to break a leg," and then again turn away, walking toward the back of the stage as klieg lights go up, blinding me and audience. The backstage curtain begins to rise on my pretend audience. As the back curtain rises, cue the music. The real front curtain begins descending behind me as I continue walking away from the actual audience into the lights to greet my pretend audience. Hopefully the real audience's applause supplies the expected applause from the pretend audience that I am walking toward. As the real curtain comes down, more applause. Hopefully, thunderous applause. I have the closing of my one-woman show. Finally. As for the open, I tell them about Marilyn. Start with the biggest shock of all. Except the biggest shock is I am still here.

At least I was there. And I'm still here, my dear!

The End

Mom gets the last word. Well, apart from the fact that we love her and her show was a smash. Unbelievably good, except since it was my mother, not so unbelievable at all. As Lily and Bobby told us, she knows what she was doing. She always has. All of us were there. Cheering, laughing and groaning. We got into the press all over again. My mother complained but loved every minute. And made another small fortune; Sam got his money back with interest, something that my mother has gloated about ever since.

Little Babe wore the emerald clips and got to keep them, locked up in a safe where she can't get to them. That's my mother.

Anders

316

www.ingramcontent.com/pod-product-compliance
Lightning Source LLC
Chambersburg PA
CBHW031334020726
47499CB00005B/1257